Because of Winter

Nikki Brochetti

While some elements in this story are inspired by real events, this work remains a piece of fiction. Names, characters, and incidents are either products of the author's imagination or are used fictitiously.

ISBN: 979-8-9918328-0-9

For my daughters

Map of Annapolis

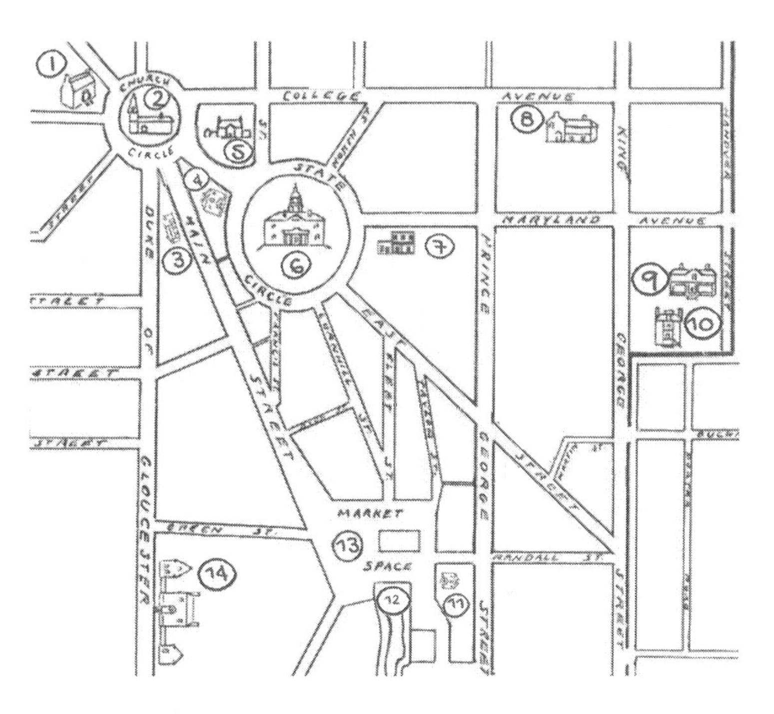

1 - Reynolds Tavern
2 - St. Anne's Church
3 - Maryland Inn
4 - Brooks Inn
5 - Governor's Mansion
6 - State House
7 - Galway Bay
8 - Ogle Hall
9 - Collins - Brooks House
10 - Peggy Stewart House
11 - Old Jail/Dock St. B&G
12 - City Dock
13 - Market Space
14 - Ridout House

Map Credit: Somerset County Library

The Howe Brothers' Route Up the Chesapeake Bay, 1777

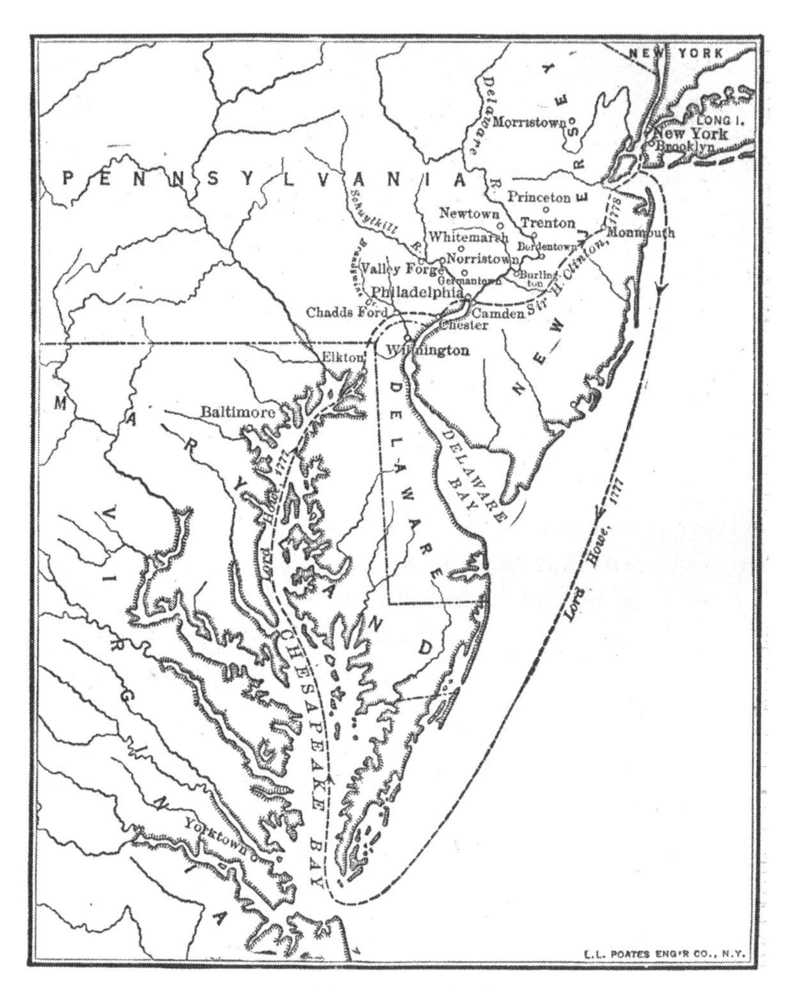

Howe's Route to Philadelphia, 1777

Robert Hall, Harriet Smither, and Clarence Ousley, A History of the United States (Dallas, TX: The Southern Publishing Company, 1920)

Prologue

Wilmington, North Carolina
April 1781

ALL EYES WERE ON HER, drawn to the striking pendant clinging to her collarbone—giant rubies and plump pearls set in a triangular pattern around a pointed blue diamond. Dangling beneath the intricate arrangement was a solitary pear-shaped pearl.

She basked in what they knew not.

How that very necklace had unknowingly changed the course of their lives forever the moment it was stolen.

How their leaders were now tracking it down like bungling hounds pursuing a fox.

And how remarkably satisfying it felt to dangle it under their contemptuous gazes.

Chapter 1

Annapolis, Maryland
December 19, 1990

In the dark hours before daybreak, fluorescent lights buzzed above a deserted hospital hallway.

The sound of an infant's tiny wail pierced the air in a nearby room.

A night nurse, well into her shift, hurried toward a labor and delivery suite, her focus fixed on her clipboard until she was stopped in her tracks. The skittish teenage girl standing before her had wide-set, brown eyes that were shadowed and darting. The nurse's gaze then shifted to the girl's trembling hands, struggling to hold a sleeping newborn swaddled loosely in a blanket. A pink hat laid askew on the baby's head.

"What's wrong, darlin'?" The nurse's heart quickened as she dropped her clipboard and instinctively took the infant.

"I have to go," and the way the teenager said it, with such a panicked need for escape, made it seem as if the most chilling demon were pursuing her.

She recognized the look of desperation on the new mother's face—hollowed eyes and sunken cheeks that spoke of needles and pills. "Please stay. We can help you."

But before she could say another word, the girl fled past her toward the exit and disappeared into the snow-speckled night.

The nurse looked down at the newborn, whose eyes sprung open, almost as if she suspected her world had suddenly been catapulted into a distinctly divergent existence.

Chapter 2

Annapolis

December 19, 2012

Twenty-two years later

An old Maryland inn sat nestled near the bay, its tired bricks bearing a weathered coat of salted wind and rain. Darkness surrounded it and lingered within its walls.

In an upstairs guest room, a young woman curled herself into bed, the giant feathered duvet engulfing her instantly. A fireplace popped nearby as midnight's chill beckoned.

A clock ticked away somewhere in the shadows.

Rest mercilessly eluded her.

Minutes turned into an hour.

Finally, her pillow settled and gently cradled her weary mind. As she drifted to sleep, light replaced the blackness. Her husband stood before her at a distance. As he moved closer, her stomach clenched. Exhilaration blended with comfort as he came into view.

She yelled out to make sure he saw her, but as she stepped forward, the edge of a cliff jutted out at her feet. Her eyes shot down, then back up at him. He wasn't far from her now, but the pitch-black, endless chasm that loomed before each of them wouldn't allow them to meet.

Their gazes gripped one another.

He clasped something in his hands. What was it? She squinted slightly.

As he stepped closer, a book came into view. He was lifting it up for her to see, peeling the pages back to reveal a fire blazing from within.

She saw his lips moving but couldn't hear a word.

A fog fixed itself between them.

She pleaded for him to stay, as if her frantic cries could somehow mend the gaping hole cut between them.

But it was no use. When the fog lifted, he was gone.

Two wet eyelids snapped open. She was back in bed, clammy and unsettled. An inky haze still clung to the windows, but she knew sleep wouldn't be greeting her again soon.

After prodding at a nearby lamp, the clock on the wall finally came into view—half past the hour. The shorthand goaded her as it inched away from the lonely one.

The woman forced her feet to the floor, squeezed into her favorite pair of jeans and an oversized sweater, then grabbed the key to the inn, slipping it into her purse. A stand-up mirror, trimmed in tarnished brass, languished alone in the corner. Her reflection startled her slightly as she passed it on her way to the door.

What a mess, she thought.

She fingered through knotted hair and rubbed both pinkies against the shaded skin under her eyes, willing the shadows to fade. Taking a step back and still unimpressed, she sighed, shut the door behind her, descended a set of steep stairs, crossed a ghostly foyer, and tugged the front door open.

Outside beneath the soft glow of streetlamps, she could breathe easier.

But only for a moment.

Frosted winds suddenly stung her lungs, and a shiver shot through her body.

Should have grabbed a coat, she almost said aloud while trying to ignore her own skepticism for being outside at all at that hour. While a few people lingered, mostly the night's revelries were a thing of the past, so with closing time looming, she trudged on.

Galway Bay, a nearby Irish pub, still glowed from within. She squeezed her arms around herself and jogged the last few steps to a heavy wooden door that creaked familiarly until safely tucking her inside.

Three round, radiating Guinness Beer signs and a few moody pendants peered down from the walls, but the tiny booth she'd always sat in with him remained hidden alone in the shadows.

She had to look away, so her eyes traveled upward to the large vintage farm tools tied only with string to beams on the ceiling. A subtle smile tightened across her lips as she remembered stopping by the bar with her father as a child. They used to frequent all the bars around town so he could grab "a shot and a beer, just one of each." But at Galway Bay, when she'd seen the giant, sharp-bladed sickle looming overhead, she'd sprinted immediately outside and told her father he'd have to get his drinks without her.

"What can I get you?" the bartender asked.

His voice was deep and soothing but somehow managed to bring a piercing throb inside her chest. She mechanically made her way onto a red stool and stared at the endless liquor bottles lined up at attention behind him.

"Double Jack with a splash of Coke," she said.

As he moved closer to grab a tumbler, the clean, lingering trail of his cologne replaced the sharp scent of spilled whiskey.

She kept her gaze on the liquor bottles behind him as she silently counted *1, 2...12, 13...22:* the age she'd turned just a few hours earlier.

"Here you go, sweetheart." The glass of brown liquid slid toward her. While the supposedly endearing name made her slightly cringe, she directed her attention to the drink. Four ice cubes, an even number. Perfect. She tipped it back, and the whiskey's burn made everything else almost disappear.

She closed her eyes as it coated her throat, faithfully softening her edges. Sucking down several gulps, she noticed a gradual loosening where her back curved sharply toward her neck, those unceasingly sore trapezius muscles she recognized from nursing school.

She exhaled slowly. Maybe there was hope she'd get some sleep tonight after all.

The sharp clang of a cash register door snapping open reminded her she wasn't alone.

"Do you live here in town?" the bartender casually asked. He stood at the opposite end of the bar, packing coins into a bag for safekeeping. Part of her wished she could instantly wrap herself in a quiet, snug place for the night, but deep down, she knew that even being alone in her bed no longer gave her peace.

She looked back at her drink, now just two lone ice cubes bobbed in a sea of murky brown.

He's tall, dark, and handsome...and he knows it, she mused, trying not to smile.

"I grew up in Annapolis, close to the Bay Bridge," she finally answered, plunging into her glass one last time. Releasing it onto the gleaming counter, she realized he was directly in front of her, the bar and a few feet of air all that separated them.

He reached out to take her glass. "I hear that's a nice area over there. I don't know about much past downtown. You want another drink?"

He looked older than her but couldn't have been more than thirty. She felt tempted to stay and have just one more. His eyes were piercing, a light gray-green, and he didn't shy away from hers.

She dug through her worn, caramel-colored, leather clutch, removing the large inn key and setting it on the bar so she could get to her cash. "I would...but it's late."

Drying a glass with his tattered dishrag, he eyed the brass key. "Staying at the Brooks Inn, I see. I know old man Brooks."

"Arthur's a good guy," she returned.

"He's...interesting. How do you know him?"

A sudden heaviness overcame her. "I'm connected...to his family."

"Connected?"

"I really need to get going."

"Will you be back?" His tone was casual, but she sensed something deeper as he looked away with a sheepish grin, setting a glass behind the bar. She noticed he smiled with his eyes.

"I'm actually leaving town soon."

"The cops on your tail?"

"I'd say, but I'd have to get rid of you."

The grin remained. "Don't think I wanna know that badly."

Getting up from the stool, she hesitated before speaking, "I've got unfinished business down south."

His eyebrows arched slightly.

"College," she finally admitted.

"I'm sorry to hear that." He crossed his arms over his chest.

"Listen, thanks for the drink." She tossed down a ten-dollar bill beside a "Kiss me, I'm Irish" coaster.

"Don't worry about it. It's on me." He pushed the bill back toward her.

Without retrieving it, she turned to leave. "I've got it, but thanks."

After a few slow strides, she reached the door, pressing her shoulder into it just before a wintry breeze spun itself through her hair.

"Wait!" he yelled. "You left your purse." He held it up, forcing her to abandon the crisp air calling her name on Maryland Avenue.

She retraced her steps. "Can I blame it on Jack?" Reaching back across the bar, she pinched the clutch between her fingertips and immediately spun back around.

"Jack?"

"Daniels," she said over her shoulder.

He let out a crooked grin. "You wouldn't be the first. Can Jack tell me your name?" His words stopped her halfway to the door.

She carefully turned. "I'm Lorna."

"Nice to meet you, Lorna. I'm Conor. Hopefully, next time you'll let me pay?"

"Next time?"

"Surely you're not moving just yet?"

"Right after the holidays."

"That's plenty of time to get to know someone a little better over a drink, isn't it?"She pushed past the lump in her throat. "In my opinion, the holidays aren't exactly a great time to get to know someone. People are either happier than normal or super depressed. I'll be the latter this year, so I'm going to kindly save you the trouble."

For once, he was speechless.

"Goodbye, Conor."

And with that, she was back out into the night.

Chapter 3
Annapolis
July 2008

Four years earlier

Lorna stared down at the yellow-tinted milk that once contained her dinner, a sweet and salty bowl of Cap'n Crunch. Cereal was her dad's go-to, unless it was the night before one of her lacrosse games, in which case he'd strike up the stovetop and make spaghetti instead.

"All As on your report card again?" Lorna's father, Kevin, was returning to the table as he shook his palm across the top of her head, ruffling her *mousy brown* hair, as her mother sometimes called it. He held his second course in the other hand: a box of Rice Krispies.

"We'll see. Would you think any less of me if I got Bs?"

Kevin set the bright-blue box on the table and picked up a cigarette from an ashtray perched beside his cereal bowl, sucking in a deep drag from his nub of a Winston. "No, but I'd be shocked," he said, tucking his legs under him as he sat across from h
wooden kitchen table. The distinct clinking sound of hu
grains of Rice Krispies spattered into his bowl.

The tightly strung muscles along the ridge of her neck stiffened further.

An ancient metal fan clanged away in the corner as her dad rested his cigarette on the edge of the overflowing ashtray and finished pouring his mountainous heap of cereal. "You're a smart kid with far better grades than I ever had," he said, looking up at her.

Lorna forced a smile. "Thanks, Dad." *If only he knew I stole half the answers.*

She'd been doing it since second grade, the same year she found out she wasn't technically "theirs."

Kevin took in a huge spoonful of puffed rice and thankfully, but not so thankfully, changed the subject. "I hear your mom finally bought her dream home in Bay Ridge."

"That's what I hear too."

"I see her face everywhere now on For Sales signs around town. Guess she finally found her calling in real estate."

"Yeah, guess so."

"Do you get along with her new boyfriend? I hear he's some chump from the yacht club."

Lorna looked toward the lone kitchen window. Tall grasses swayed and gleamed in the evening light, just as a fly squeezed itself through a hole in the screen and made its way into the house.

The moment always came back to her, stealing the breath from her lungs. That time she had to tell her dad the truth about what her mom had done. Kevin's late nights drinking with his buddies had slowly turned into her mom coming home later and later. Lorna, barely out of middle school, found herself babysitting Kate more often than not. It was Emma who first saw their mom in the car with "him" late one night. He was one of her real estate clients, but the man never seemed especially interested in finding a house, and Lorna suspected something was off long before they caught her. She specifically remembered avoiding her dad's eyes when she finally delivered the news.

"He's old." She snuck a glance at him. "And boring."

Kevin stopped eating and set his spoon down, a slight smile breaking forth.

Nothing but the sound of the fan remained. What more was there to say? And a person can only stare at a bowl of yellow milk for so long.

Finally, he spoke. "So, now's the point where you ask me to borrow my truck tonight, right?"

She forced a slight grin.

Finally, Lorna reached out and grabbed what she wanted to say. "You and I both know mom will never find what she's looking for out there. She can raid the yacht club till she's picked through every white-headed rich guy, but she's not gonna find it."

"What *is* she looking for? After all these years, I still don't think I know." He took one last hit from his cigarette.

"I don't think she knows either." Lorna set down her spoon.

She wanted to ask him. She'd always wanted to ask him. Why he'd gone after one of them—a girl with money? Her mom had grown up perched high atop a sixty-two-foot motor yacht with a small rectangular piece of plastic in her pocket that never seemed to run dry. Hadn't he realized it would be impossible to live up to expectations like that on a blue-collar salary?

But she said nothing.

Kevin checked his watch. "So, are you going out tonight?"

"That depends."

"On whether you can take my truck?"

"Pretty much. And it's okay if you say no."

"Right, because it's actually Emma who's asking if the two of you can take it."

"Pretty much. How'd you guess?"

"Because I know you'd be happier hanging here with a bag of Doritos and a decent movie or curled up with some book." He pulled the keys out from his back pocket and dropped them on the table. "Go have fun, for God's sake—celebrate being young. Besides, if you don't, Emma will find her way over here and talk your ear off until you can't take it anymore."

"True."

"Remember, though..."

"Of course, I will not drive drunk, and yes, I will return before your hunk of junk turns into a pumpkin at midnight," she confirmed.

"Off to your ball, Lorna Mae. And no racing down Whitehall Road," her father added.

"I will keep my rusted-out carriage at a suitable speed."

A high-pitched voice resonated off a nearby hallway wall, "Can I come?"

Lorna and her dad pushed back in unison, "No!"

A skinny twelve-year-old, who was all kneecaps and braces, joined them in the kitchen with her perfected pout.

"Kate, your time will come," Kevin insisted. "Sooner than I wish."

Lorna made a beeline for the door, waving goodbye just before the screen door slammed. Then, after climbing up inside Kevin's blue 1995 Ford pickup truck with its single bench seat, she hit the gas, spraying gravel back toward the house as she spun the wheel onto Whitehall Road.

A few minutes later, she pulled into the driveway at Emma's house along St. Margaret's Road, a small stone cottage with the lawn always meticulously groomed—Emma's father's touch, of course. Her parents were so put together, so painfully put together.

The yellow front door squeezed open—slowly at first then suddenly flinging backward just before Emma's tiny body slipped through the threshold. She didn't go far. She was stuck in place even as her legs tried to run and her arms flailed like a half-drowned hornet. Finally realizing her folly, Emma reached back to unlatch her oversized JanSport backpack from the doorknob, then she plunged into the yard, a mile-wide grin spread across her face.

When she finally crawled up into the truck, Lorna hit the gas. "That's what you get for trying to sneak a bottle of vodka out of the house that weighs more than you do."

Emma dug hastily inside her backpack, untwirling her burgundy Broadneck High School hooded sweatshirt to make sure the half-full bottle of Crown Russe remained intact. "My sister says this is the last one she's getting me for a while," Emma complained, her lower lip flipping downward.

"I have a feeling you'll drive her insane until she changes her mind." Lorna kept her eyes glued to the twists and turns of St. Margaret's Road.

"A girl's gotta do what a girl's gotta do. And especially since we're finally seniors and need to live it up!" Emma screamed over the piercing wind pouring through her window as they reached Greenbury Point Road.

Lorna grinned but said nothing, so Emma continued, "Which means eventual freedom for you, my darling butterfly. I know you've been ready to soar away and ditch this town for years."

"It feels like decades." Swiftly shifting the dial on the radio, Lorna hoped desperately for something upbeat. She could already feel her energy draining as she envisioned the crowds of kids who were hiding away in the woods—their destination too. A weary sun drifted toward the horizon as Emma gazed across the rolling greens of the Naval Academy Golf Course.

"I'm happy for you, Lor. You'll get into any school you want. I, on the other hand, will be content to grace Anne Arundel Community College with my presence," Emma laughed.

"You'll be saving money on a great school. I know your parents want you to stay, but are you sure it's what you want?"

"I will rock the townie role."

Lorna glanced at her closest companion since childhood, who snapped her eyes shut to avoid the copious amount of wavy red hair whipping across her face. "I don't doubt you will. I'm sure you'll keep me well informed on all the happenings."

"More than you'll ever need to know," Emma added.

Lorna swung her truck into the Greenbury Point Nature Center parking lot and hopped out. As they started down the narrow, wooded trail, her eyes skimmed across button-sized mushrooms scattered underfoot and ivy clinging tightly to towering trees that sheltered them from the last rays of the day.

They were nearing their destination when a flying human came into view. His body, visible through the tree line, shot up into the sapphire sky, soaring like an osprey, his tanned back glowing in the twilight. His legs, refusing to submit to gravity, rose above his torso, so that just as he let go of the swinging rope, he spiraled backward, flipping wildly through the air. As he disappeared from view, Lorna envisioned him crashing into a canvas of dark gray ripples below.

Lorna's face pinched together. "Who's the show-off on the rope swing?"

Emma jogged ahead to a sharp drop-off that descended toward the water. "I think that was Will Brooks. You know who he is, right?"

Lorna shook her head. *I'm gonna guess another of your crushes.*

"Oh, he's this super cute Saint Mary's football player. I think he played baseball against Jack too. They've become good friends."

Lorna turned her attention to a group of high school kids gathered on lower ground just down the bank. Hoping to remain unnoticed, she stepped behind a broad oak and watched as Emma's face lit up beside her.

"There he is. Hey, Jack!" Emma yelled, jogging his way.

Lorna stepped out slowly just as Jack came striding up a steep, trampled path.

"Emmy! You made it!" A wide grin grew across his face.

"We did!" Emma hugged him tightly.

"Where's Lorna?" he asked just as she crept out from behind the tree and wrapped her arms around him as well.

"You smell like booze and the bay," Lorna joked. "And I don't see one other Broadneck kid down there, so would you mind grabbing me a beer?"

"Never did like meeting new people, did you?" Jack grinned devilishly.

Lorna stuck her tongue out indignantly as he patted her shoulder.

"Emma, do you want one too? Or would you prefer your poor man's vodka that I imagine you've got strapped to your back?"

"Classier than cheap beer," she retaliated, pulling off her pack and digging inside.

When Jack returned with a lukewarm can of beer, the three of them sat down against the dirt-covered ground that also served as the rope swing's jumping-off point. Slices of glistening water shone between tree trunks.

"Cheers!" Emma lifted her glass bottle of vodka, clinking it against their aluminum beer cans.

They threw back their drinks, liquid courage pouring inside as a gust of wind glided across the water and through the swaying branches, cooling Lorna's skin.

A voice abruptly echoed from behind her, "I won't make you move if you let me catapult off your shoulders."

Lorna turned to see the "show-off" they'd recently seen somersaulting through the sky, now coming toward them with rope in hand, his eyes fixed on Jack. Dirty-blonde hair and bronzed skin was still wet from his previous plunge.

"Will! What's up, dude?" Jack stood, stumbling a little as he rose but catching himself on his friend's arm.

"You okay, buddy?" Will put his hand on Jack's shoulder, grinning at his clearly inebriated companion.

"Oh, yeah, havin' a blast," Jack continued. "Have you ever met Lorna and Emma?"

"We've sort of met. Hi, Will," Emma beamed.

Will smiled. "Hey, how's it going?"

Jack chimed back in, "Lorna, have you guys ever hooked up? I mean, not 'hooked up,' but you know what I mean," he stammered then broke into a snicker.

"No, Jack, we haven't met." Lorna felt herself grinning awkwardly. "It's nice to meet you, Will."

Will wiped his brow, taking everything in stride. "You too, Lorna."

It was peculiar when he said her name. Something inside her clenched, catching her off guard, so she pressed the aluminum can to her lips and slowly took in a gulp of the bitter beer.

And that's when it happened.

Jack, his veins pulsing with enough alcohol to serve a pub full of people, grabbed the rope swing from Will and, before anyone could react, was over the edge of the bluff. But Jack's journey was the opposite of Will's earlier plunge. Instead of possessing strength and finesse, it was clear from the start that Jack could barely hang on, his legs dangling clumsily as they flailed around, making him look like a fish out of water.

Emma gasped. "He really should not be doing that. He can barely walk, let alone swim!"

Lorna's mouth sprung open when Jack didn't let go of the rope, over the deepest part of the water, at the crest of his glide, like he should have. Her heart squeezed and tightened inside her chest as his body came hurling back toward them. "Jack, don't let goooo!" She screamed just before he released his grip.

Lorna ran to the edge of the drop-off, terrified to look below. *Damn it, Jack.* She finally took a deep breath and shot her gaze downward.

Chapter 4

Shadowed water rippled near the shoreline, a reassuring sign that Jack had just missed hitting land. But when his head didn't come to the surface, the panic inside Lorna emerged yet again.

She watched as Will retrieved the rope and flung himself into the water. Opting to stay on land as long as possible, Lorna rushed down the steep path that led down to the bay, dashing past a collection of drunk and oblivious teenagers until she was ankle-deep in sloppy, cumbersome mud along the water's edge. The muck eventually grew deeper, hindering her forward movement.

But as Lorna ventured into deeper waters, she managed to lean forward, slipping beneath the choppy current. With her legs now free, she hastily kicked, propelling herself to the area where Jack had fallen, though he was nowhere to be seen. Trying to open her eyes beneath the surface, all she could see was cloudy brown sediment, accompanied by a burning sensation that stung beneath her lids. Shutting them tightly, Lorna swept her arms out desperately in front of her, anxious to locate her friend. Without any success and gasping for breath, Lorna rose to the surface, noticing Will swimming in her direction, just as frantic to find Jack.

Then something appeared out of the corner of her eye.

Even closer to the shore, under a canopy of low-lying trees and shrubs, she glimpsed just the top of Jack's face floating above the surface. Lorna was panting as she neared the shallower water, gaining her balance on slippery stones until she finally reached Jack's body.

"I can't feel my fingers. Or my toes," Jack said, forcing out the words through a clenched jaw. His eyelids remained shut as if he couldn't bear to look at his body.

I'm scared to touch him, Lorna thought, but eventually reached gently under his back, "Shhh, don't move. It'll be okay, I've got you." Then, despite the searing heat in her lungs, she called out loudly, "He's over here!"

Several seconds later, Will was by her side. His eyes met hers, a gaze that seemed to scream, *What should we do?*

"We need to get him out of the water," Lorna whispered, hoping Jack couldn't hear the fear in her voice, "but it has to be carefully."

Will reacted immediately. He scooped their friend gently into his long arms, waded through the knee-deep water, and laid Jack down as gently as he could on a flat spot along the bank.

Lorna and Will fell to their knees and curled their bodies over him.

"I can't feel my legs." Jack's tone was panicked but fading, as if he was about to lose consciousness.

"Hang with us, buddy. We're gonna get you help," Will gasped for air himself.

Lorna and Will exchanged another terrified look. They stood in one motion and gathered a few feet from Jack, so he couldn't hear. Lorna spoke first: "I hate to move him, but we need to get him to the hospital."

"Absolutely. A friend brought me, but he's drinking now. Did you drive?" Will asked.

"I did, but we'll have to put him in the bed of my dad's truck. There's just the one bench seat." Lorna looked back at her friend, appearing lifeless on the bank. She choked back tears. "What about an ambulance?"

"My cell doesn't have service out here. Does yours?"

She didn't even have to look; there was never any service here. "Crap, no. Okay, let's go. I can carry him with you," Lorna said.

"The trails narrow. It'll be easier if I do it myself."

Lorna nodded.

Will returned to Jack and crouched down beside him, wrapping his palm around his friend's limp shoulder. "Listen, Jack, we need to get you to a doctor, so I'm gonna carry you back to Lorna's truck."

"I'm scared, Will."

"You just hold tight, and we'll get you help. If it hurts too much at any point, just tell me so we can stop and take a rest, okay?"

Jack's eyes remained closed, a tear slipping free as he nodded ever so slightly, grimacing in pain as Will swept his seemingly lifeless body back into his arms and carried him up the steep bank toward the wooded trail.

The crowd of kids from St. Mary's stood motionless, eyes like saucers as Will passed them holding Jack.

Emma was crying hysterically as she sprinted to Lorna. "What's going on, is he gonna be all right?"

Lorna turned. "I don't know. We've gotta get him to a hospital, though. We're putting him in the back of my dad's truck. Do you wanna come with us?"

Emma bit her lip. "My parents would absolutely kill me if they found out we've been drinking in the woods."

Lorna nodded, half expecting her response. "Can you find a ride?"

"Kelly Perkins says she can drive me home."

Before Emma could finish her sentence, Lorna was gone, sprinting down the trail ahead of Will, beads of sweat scorching her eyes. *I hope it was the right call to move him. No going back now.*

When Lorna got to the truck, she threw a tattered blanket on the rusted-out bed. Will and Jack arrived just behind her, and she quickly helped him get settled.

"I'll ride back here with him." Will sat beside Jack.

Lorna nodded, flew into the driver's seat, and eased on the gas pedal, trying not to jerk the truck too much.

Two hours later, Will and Lorna sat across from each other in the cramped waiting area of the Anne Arundel Medical Center Emergency Room. Nurses and doctors bustled in and out of Jack's hospital room, while his parents anxiously paced nearby. Lorna was numb, her gaze fixed on the window, where she watched the headlights racing along the highway below. Will, with his head bowed and hands clasped, seemed lost in thought.

After a moment, Lorna turned to him and asked, "Are you all right?"

Will looked up, fear etched across his face. "I'm praying he's not paralyzed."

Lorna suddenly remembered the countless prayers she'd uttered in her life, from begging for her parents to stay together to pleading for her injured dog's recovery. She'd even prayed for years that her birth parents would show an interest in meeting her, but all was in vain. Disappointment had become a routine companion.

Suddenly, Jack's parents, Ed and Melissa Easton, appeared beside them.

Mrs. Easton, her voice filled with emotion, spoke first. "The doctor says he'll likely walk again."

Mr. Easton added, "It's going to be a long road to recovery, but he's already moving his fingers and toes, which the doctor says is a significant sign."

Lorna stopped biting her nails long enough to sigh in relief, and Will buried his face in his hands.

Mrs. Easton took a step closer. "We can't thank you two enough for getting him here. The nurse explained how you both..." She had to pause before continuing, "How you both dove into the water after him—he's lucky to have friends like you."

"And *we're* lucky he has friends like you," Mr. Easton added before sitting down beside Will. "Listen, guys, they had to pump Jack's stomach too. I realize kids drink, but it looks like there was a lot of alcohol at Greenbury Point. Which one of you is driving home?"

"I am," Lorna said.

"Have you been drinking?" Jack's father looked her in the eyes, his gaze penetrating.

"I had two sips of beer several hours ago, so...no, I really haven't. I had just gotten there when everything happened."

Mr. Easton nodded. Lorna noticed Jack's mother's hands shaking as she wrapped them around her sides. "Jack is sleeping. I know you've been here a long time. Please go home to your parents and get some rest. We'll keep you updated on his recovery."

"Where do you live?" Lorna turned the key in the ignition and the engine gave a raspy, booming purr.

"Murray Hill. Do you know that side of town?" Will asked.

"Nope."

"Oh. It's the neighborhood right next to the courthouse and Church Circle, close to downtown. How long have you lived here?" Will turned his head toward Lorna, but she kept her eyes glued to the road.

"All my life. I go downtown all the time, but I've never been in that neighborhood."

"I got ya. Just jump on West Street, and it'll lead you there."

As her beat-up, blue truck in all its rusted glory rolled through Will's neighborhood, Lorna suddenly imagined a filthy pig prancing through a fancy parlor. Giant porches adorned the impeccably cared for turn-of-the-century homes that lined the streets. And each perfectly placed streetlamp seemed to shoot a spotlight on her bruised and battered pickup.

"We're close. Want to find a place to park so you can come hang on my porch for a few minutes?"

Lorna's stomach rolled itself into a tight ball. "I really don't see any parking spaces."

"There's one right up there. Can you parallel park?"

The brakes let out a peevish squeal, but Lorna skillfully maneuvered into the parking space.

"Well done. I'm a little surprised."

"Why?" Lorna asked while switching off the ignition.

"Didn't you say you live on Whitehall Road? No parallel parking needed out there."

"My dad taught me."

After strolling down the sidewalk together, Will stopped in front of a charming, two-story, red-brick home, grabbed the gate of a waist-high, wrought-iron fence, and swung it open for Lorna. They proceeded through a small front yard and onto a wide porch adorned with the largest welcome mat Lorna had ever seen. Will walked over and sat down on an oversized swing. Lorna joined him.

"Are your parents here?"

"Nope, they have a gala event."

"I went one time to one of those *galas* with my mom," Lorna said.

Will snickered at her touch of mockery. "Yeah? Which one? This town has about a million of them."

"It was called the CASAblanca Gala. Way too fancy for me but I know it raises money for a great non-profit."

"Which one?"

"CASA. My mom's a volunteer," Lorna explained.

"What's CASA?"

"She says it stands for Court Appointed Special Advocate. She supports kids in the foster care system."

"Cool. Like how does she help them, though?"

"Well, she talks to their parents, teachers, grandparents and foster parents and tells the magistrate who she thinks should keep the child."

"So sad to think little kids have to go through that." Will's eyes skimmed the ground. "That's great your mom tries to help them, though. She sounds like a nice lady."

"Well, I mean, she does have a really kind side to her."

Will squeezed his knuckles as Lorna changed the subject. "How about your parents? Are you close with them?"

"My parents are...well, they're super supportive. Overprotective at times but not too bad. I have two older brothers, so I think they're a bit worn out."

"Wow, I don't blame them. Three boys? They sound like the type of parents who've never missed a game."

Will's lips pressed together, and a shy softness set into his eyes. "None that I can think of. They're awesome."

"Are you gonna tell them about tonight?"

"I almost called. But I'm afraid it'll ruin their evening. I'll tell them tomorrow."

"Aren't you afraid they'll be mad?"

"You mean the drinking part?"

"Yeah."

"They're pretty cool about that type of stuff. As long as there's a DD. And in this case, I have you." Will grinned slightly. "How about your parents?"

"My mom's out of town. Haven't decided what to do about my dad."

"You should tell your Daddy," a voice echoed from somewhere out of sight.

Lorna looked at Will, who sighed. "That would be Dalton."

They simultaneously stood. Staggering along the sidewalk was a tall, high school-aged kid with a chiseled jawline and haughty gaze.

He looked up at Will. "Just passing by and realized you were up there with a lady friend. Couldn't resist."

Dalton gripped the railing as he pulled himself up onto the porch steps.

Will looked slightly annoyed, but he remained cordial. "Lorna, this is Dalton. Dalton, Lorna. He's our quarterback—and my neighbor."

Leaning back against the nearest porch column, Dalton's eyes narrowed. "Did you know your honey boy here likes to draw little pictures?"

Lorna's stomach knotted but she refused to show it. "You're an artist, Will? That's awesome."

"I wouldn't call myself that. I draw sketches sometimes."

Dalton took a sudden, awkward step toward Lorna, "Oh, honey boy here is being *much* too modest. He got his pretty artwork in the paper for winning his super special art contest."

The unease was clear in Will's eyes, but Lorna pressed on, pleased to hear about his unexpected talent and hoping to make him feel more comfortable. "I'd love to see your sketches, Will."

Dalton took another step closer to Lorna, speaking abruptly. "Where do you go to school?" The sharp smell of alcohol invaded her nostrils.

"Broadneck." She curled her arms around her midsection.

"Uh...I know a chick that goes there. Emma...Sullivan, I think her last name is. Do you know her?"

Lorna began to tightly twist the hair behind her ear. "Yeah. She's...my best friend."

"Really? Ha! I've got a few buddies who know her well too. And I mean *really* well."

Dalton's cackle rang in Lorna's ear. Her eyes drifted toward the neighboring porch's overhang, where a robin's nest perched precariously on the edge.

Will stepped toward Dalton. "Dude, really? Get out of here, man. Take your drunk ass home where it belongs."

"Hey, hey, relax. I only say what I've been told."

Lorna felt a heavy weight press down on her chest, stifling her breath. Gathering all her courage, she finally met Dalton's gaze but immediately regretted it. The mocking grin he wore as he appraised her from head to toe pierced through her, leaving a lingering bitterness in its wake.

"I mean it. Get out of here before I help you leave," Will pushed further.

Dalton roared at Will's threat as he struggled down the steps, shooting straight into the street.

A black BMW hit its brakes and honked, just missing the teen.

"Sadly, he would have deserved that. I'm not saying I want him dead. Just a few deep bruises." Will was still standing, his arms crossed tightly as he watched Dalton slink away toward home.

Lorna started for the porch steps.

"You're leaving?" Will said.

"I have to get back."

Will's mouth opened, but he didn't speak.

As Lorna reached the sidewalk, he finally called out, "Let me walk you to your truck."

"I'm good."

Will charged down the steps anyway. "Lorna, wait up." He reached her at the corner. "I'm so sorry that he was such a..."

"You don't need to apologize." Lorna looked both ways and started across the street, her heart hammering away.

"But why are you taking off so quickly?"

"It's just been a long night."

"Right."

She reached her truck and crawled up inside it. Will shut the door for her. The window was still open as she glanced back at him, his expression muddled.

"I'll see you around," she said, unable to make eye contact.

Will nodded uncomfortably. "Bye, Lorna."

Chapter 5
Annapolis
March 2009

Nine months later

The wind still hadn't surrendered its chill. Winter wasn't giving itself up so easily. Lacrosse fans sitting in the stands at Broadneck High School's Knight Stadium pulled their coats in tighter, some flung blankets over their shoulders, as a blast of crisp air shot across the field, shaking itself through thin burgundy uniforms and over red, chaffed skin before continuing on.

It was the first game of the season.

Broadneck was down by one with less than a minute to go in the game. Lorna stood poised on the 8-meter line, about to shoot a penalty shot, the ball all alone atop her stick.

Her focus was razor sharp on the goal, but in the very back of her mind she knew her dad was standing just behind it. He always did.

The other players, her teammates and opponents alike, spread out to her left and right, their sticks poised—like her, waiting for the whistle.

The world around her grew suddenly silent. It seemed as if

hundreds of people were holding their breath. She knew every eye rested on her.

A single voice reached her ear. "You know the spot, Lorna. Hit it!" Her dad, of course.

The whistle blew.

Lorna's start was fast, her first few steps longer and quicker than the rest. Her aim: the bottom left corner of the net. The head of her stick soared back like a catapult, eventually flinging forward, the ball releasing just feet from the goalie.

Right on target.

Except for half an inch.

It ricocheted off the thin metal post and went flying out of bounds.

I missed! came pounding through her brain.

A heaviness settled inside her, and while she tried desperately to get the ball back from the other team, it was too late. She'd lost her chance.

"Those are the shots You. Have. To. Make," was the first thing out of her father's mouth when she walked off the field.

No kidding.

Lorna's insides were on fire, her throat dry as ash.

"Did you hear me?" Kevin pushed.

Still, she said nothing. What could she say? In her mind, she'd failed everyone.

"You choked kid," he said under his breath, but she heard.

A punch in the face would have felt better.

"All right, well, we'll get back out here tomorrow and shoot a hundred shots at that very spot," her dad pushed.

Lorna nodded.

"I'm gonna head out," he said, turning to walk away, dragging his right leg ever so slightly. He never told Lorna how it had happened in Vietnam. Her mother mentioned something about an attack on a mountainside where his radio relay site was located. She'd said he was only nineteen. Her dad never talked about that period of his life. Ever. One time Lorna saw a letter he'd accidentally left on the kitchen table. It was from a father who'd lost his son in the war. Apparently, Kevin had been there when his son had died. The father's words were kind. He had questions, though. Lorna always wondered if Kevin had ever written back.

She looked down at her cold, shaking hands then tucked them into her hoodie so no one could see. Lorna grabbed her bag and stick, needing to get out of there, but she didn't want to go home either.

"Lorna!" came a voice from behind.

She stiffened, in no way wanting to talk to anyone. So, she pretended not to hear it and started for the parking lot.

Again, it came. "Lorna, wait up!" She recognized it this time: *Jack.*

She turned to face the inevitable. Jack wouldn't give up. But he wasn't alone.

Standing there beside him was Will Brooks.

Anxiety bubbled within her. She hadn't seen or talked to Will since that crazy summer day nine months earlier. He had on jeans and a dark winter coat pulled up around his neck. She would always remember the look on his face: gentle and warm. .

Still, though, Lorna felt mortified that he'd seen her lose the game.

"Hi," she mumbled.

Jack began rambling about it being a tough loss, but that she had so many "killer goals."

"Except for when it counted," she heard herself saying awkwardly.

No one responded. Then, finally, Will spoke up. "I dropped a ball in the end zone last fall. It cost us the game. My grandpa always said, 'We're imperfectly human' and that 'it's easy to mess up when you're out there daring greatly.'"

Lorna had trouble making eye contact, but she smiled slightly. "The Man in the Arena."

"The what?" Jack chimed in.

"The phrase 'daring greatly' comes from a Teddy Roosevelt speech," Lorna said softly.

"Did you know that, Will?" Jack turned to him.

"Do you think I read enough books to know that?"

Jack laughed. Even a little spilled from Lorna.

"Come get ice cream with us," Jack said, grabbing Lorna's gym bag off her shoulder and taking off.

"Jack..."

He turned, still jogging. "I'll take your bag hostage if you don't."

Lorna and Will watched him zigzag his way through fans, nearly knocking into several. Finally, Will spoke up, "You could chase him down, beat him up, and steal it back, but that would require a fair amount of energy."

"Which I'm sort of lacking at this point."

"Guess it's settled, then. Ice cream it is." Will said.

Several minutes later, the three of them had cones in hand as they filled a wide bench.

"Hey, there's Jordan and Matt. I'll be back." Jack jumped up and headed toward two friends stepping out of a Honda Civic.

"Can I ask you something?" Will began immediately, as if he'd been pondering the question for some time.

"Sure."

"Did I say something that offended you last summer when you left my porch so quickly?"

Lorna didn't speak.

Will finally filled in the silence, "Because if I did..."

"It wasn't you," she broke in.

"Was it what Dalton said?"

"No."

"Then?"

"It was what I didn't say," Lorna finally answered.

Will stopped speaking, hoping she'd continue.

She went on, "Dalton was saying obnoxious things about my best friend, and I didn't speak up."

"But he was the one..."

"No. There's no excuse."

Lorna could hear the buzz of cars down on the highway and the voices of other high school kids nearby, but she and Will ate their ice cream without speaking.

Eventually, his voice cut through the silence. "So do it differently next time."

"That's the hope. But not necessarily my track record."

"The thing is, that doesn't matter. You get the choice the next time around."

Lorna studied him. "Sure." She shrugged. "I'm just tired of making the wrong one..."

Will scratched the back of his neck. "Do you know how often I say the wrong thing?"

She waited.

"Every seven seconds," he added.

Lorna let go a little and grinned as she bit her lower lip.

Jack was back. "Are you guys ready to head out?"

"Sure," Lorna agreed.

Will hesitated, nervously adding, "Only if Lorna will let me take her out one night soon."

Jack's eyes lit up. "Ohhhhh, what do you say, Lorna?"

Lorna grabbed for the hair behind her ear, forgetting it was still in a tight ponytail. She quickly crossed her arms instead. "Why not?"

Chapter 6

April 2009

Two weeks later

The afternoon sun cast shadows across the water's surface as Lorna and Will crossed the bridge over Spa Creek into Eastport, an inviting laidback neighborhood in Annapolis where boats gently swayed, and a diverse array of local shops and restaurants created a welcoming, relaxed vibe—a refreshing change from the bustle of downtown.

They parked in front of a quaint, single-story home with a weathered yet inviting façade that echoed Eastport's rich, storied past. Slipping around back to a private dock, they launched two paddleboards that had been waiting for them by the water's edge. Several days prior, it had taken Lorna fifteen minutes of staring at her phone to finally call and ask Janet, her mother's best friend and Lorna's godmother, if they could use her paddleboards.

"He's just a friend," Lorna had assured her.

"I'll believe it when I see it," Janet said, chuckling.

"Aunt J, please don't embarrass me."

"Would you consider letting me watch from the window with binoculars at least?"

This is probably a terrible idea, Lorna had thought to herself.

But still she'd proceeded.

Just before calling Janet, she confided in Emma, "I want to do something where I don't have to talk to him the entire time."

Will had never gone paddleboarding before and immediately fell in twice. Seeing as it was their first date, Lorna tried to contain herself but failed miserably.

"I see why you brought me out here—pure entertainment." Will joked, pulling himself back up on the board, his t-shirt soaked, water dripping from hair and limbs. It took her back to the day they'd met that previous summer at Greenbury Point, when he was perpetually drenched from his swinging plunges.

Lorna finally settled her snickers and clenched her teeth. "I'm sorry it's so cold. Maybe early spring isn't the best time to do this."

"Have you ever done the polar plunge? I'm having flashbacks."

"Let's head back."

"Not a chance. I'll get it."

Lorna wanted to help. "Maybe try not to be quite as stiff. Loosen your knees a little."

"Aye aye, Captain."

She grinned, her focus on the horizon before them. Lorna loved being out on the water, watching the sprawling white sails drifting by, feeling the cool breeze shift across her skin. After navigating through choppy water near the mouth of the bay, they retreated beneath the Spa Creek Drawbridge, past the sweeping red-brick facade of St. Mary's Parish and School, and meandered through the quiet inlets along the creek, where herons soared aimlessly, and fish leapt from the still, smooth surface.

As they glided side by side, Lorna suddenly felt Will's eyes on her. She looked his way, and he didn't shy away, meeting her gaze and beaming as if his board wasn't soaked and his underwear weren't dripping wet.

Lorna looked down at her paddle as she spoke. "What are you grinning about over there?"

"You know. Just sort of, well...thinking I like this."

"You're enjoying paddleboarding?"

"Not really. I feel like I'm gonna fall back in at any second. But I like being with you."

Lorna could feel her face flushing. "Um, thanks." *What do I even say back?* "It's really nice out today." *Not that.* "And I'm having fun too." *Okay, maybe a little better? Why am I so awkward with guys?*

When they made it back to the dock, Will changed into dry clothes inside Janet's boathouse. Then it was his turn to plan the second half of their date. "Want to walk downtown?"

"Sure. Let me run inside the house first for a sec."

When Lorna nudged open the back door, Janet was sitting at her kitchen table.

"Did you use your binoculars?" Lorna asked.

Janet stood from her seat. "It was tempting. Especially with a cutie like that."

Lorna hugged her. "Thanks for letting us paddle."

"Anytime. Are you two still just friends?"

"Um, yeah, of course."

Janet gave her a mischievous smirk. "You've always been a pretty bad liar."

Lorna and Will strolled through the quiet streets of Eastport, crossing the same drawbridge they'd driven over and paddled under, as traffic surged by and dinghies drifted to and fro in the waves below. Lorna vaguely noticed any of it, though. Her focus, instead, was on him.

The bridge's sidewalk was narrow, and Will's fingers would occasionally brush into hers, sending a warm, shooting sensation straight up her arm. On the other side of the bridge, bustling Annapolis welcomed them with its rattle of cars and shuffling of visitors.

Little girls tossed bread toward eager ducks bobbing along a narrow strip of water that for centuries had rambled its way into the heart of downtown. Will went right up to one of the youngest ones who couldn't have made it to his waist and bent down, so they could speak face to face. "Is there any way I can have a small piece of your bread? I've never fed a duck before."

Lorna stood back, grinning.

"Sure." The little girl handed him an entire slice.

"Oh no. You don't need to give the whole thing to me."

"Yes, I do!" the girl insisted, with hands on both hips and her bag of bread dragging along the ground. "You should feed the slice *correctly* to the duck. It's no fun just throwing it at them."

Lorna was sure her tiny, raspy voice was one of the cutest things she'd ever heard.

"Oh. I'm supposed to give it *right to the duck?*" Will looked apprehensive.

"Yes. They like it better that way."

Will looked over at Lorna as he nibbled his lower lip.

"She's the pro, Will. Do as you're told."

Just then, a brown female duck came waddling over. Will dropped to his knees and tentatively stuck out the bread toward her. The duck seemed to notice he wasn't tossing it out to her and stopped to give him the side-eye.

"Don't get scared and drop it," the girl pushed.

Lorna covered her mouth as she watched the dual unfolding.

The duck started walking toward Will again. "What if she bites me? She's gonna bite me," his voice went up an octave, and Lorna couldn't help but burst out laughing.

"No! Stay still!" the little girl hissed at him.

A few inches were all that separated the duck and Will's piece of bread. She started snapping her beak. "Gentle duckie," Will reminded her just as another female duck made a B-29 bomber-dive straight at his bread, nabbing it from both man and fellow bird, and forcing Will to fall backward, yelling and flailing.

The girl pulled out another piece of bread and casually handed it to the duck who'd just lost out. She then turned to Will. "Duck feeding isn't for everyone," she said before strolling away.

Lorna walked over and helped Will to his feet. They snickered the entire way to a nearby bench by the water.

When was the last time I laughed this much?

Will shook his head. "Boy, I did not see that airborne lady coming."

"My dad always says, no matter where you are, keep your head on a swivel. Guess that also applies to duck-feeding."

"I guess so." Will slowly blew out his breath. "My three-foot-tall, duck-whispering sensei forgot to mention that part."

Lorna smiled and took out a one-dollar bill. Will watched as she quickly folded it in a million different directions.

"Wow, you're like the balloon guy at the fair whose hands move at the speed of light."

She held up a small, folded, dollar-bill duck in the center of her palm. "Your consolation prize for at least *trying* to feed them."

Will grinned and pinched the paper duck between two fingers as he studied it. "Seriously, how'd you do that?"

"I've been doing origami since I was little."

"What got you into that?"

"I found it in a book at the library, and I was hooked. I still do it occasionally, like if I'm watching a movie or something. It kind of calms me somehow."

"Will you teach me?"

"Sure."

Lorna looked down at their hands, both resting on the wooden bench next to one another. Her eyes shot up as she peered out at the water. It took her a few moments to gather enough courage to inch her pinky a smidge closer to his. Will was still holding his consolation prize with his left hand, but he must have sensed her drawing near as he too slid the fingers on his right hand ever so slightly in her direction.

Their skin finally touched, and the world went still.

Chapter 7

June 2010

One year later

"I can't believe tomorrow's the day. You'll be *Lorna Brooks*. So... strange. You still have time to run, you know?" The voice drifted down from high up in an immense willow tree.

"The real question is, what will you do without Will around to get mad at?" Lorna said, smirking, the skirt of her muted-green rehearsal dress splayed out across the grass, her head propped against the willow's broad trunk. She looked up at her fourteen-year-old sister, who was lying flat on her back several limbs up. Long, dark, wispy strands of hair swayed back and forth, mimicking the tree's languid branches.

"I can still be mad at him from afar." Kate kept her eyes on the skinny green leaves above her, each one intricately painted on a backdrop of celestial pastels—evening's final glow.

Lorna made it to her feet, patting away touches of dirt, before sliding her finger along the curved hills and valleys of an indented "W+L" that had been carefully sliced into the thick bark. "You still don't forgive us for carving our initials into Grandma Tree, do you?"

"Can't say I have." She sighed. "But you know I'm happy for you, Lorny." She met her older sister's gaze. "And even though he stole you away, I suppose he's not the absolute worst."

Lorna's face broke into a subtle grin, one Kate always knew how to evoke.

Her sister sat up on the limb as it creaked and groaned. Immediately, Lorna felt twelve years old again, remembering herself watching in horror as another tree branch split beneath a much younger Kate, sending her plunging to the ground. Thankfully, her nimble sister landed mostly on her feet, like a cat, but she still managed to scrape her hands on the maples's gnarly roots as she tumbled forward. Blood pooled in her palms, which sent Kate through the roof. Lorna swept her up in her arms and carried her home, grabbing a cool, wet dishrag—its fibers faithfully absorbing the deep-red flow. While the sight of blood always terrified others, Lorna never minded it much. After what felt like an endless rush of tears, Kate finally sighed and whispered, "Thank you." Something about the way her lip stopped trembling—or maybe it was her chest's sudden stillness—had a lasting effect on Lorna. A penetrating purpose rose up inside her that she'd never quite felt before. Not long after that, she discovered *The Elephant Man* at the Broadneck Library and marveled at Dr. Treves's tender care for a man with severe deformities who'd been shunned by the rest of Victorian society. She loved to imagine being a nurse or doctor herself one day but dismissed the idea after receiving a D on her middle school biology exam—a grade she neglected to share with her parents. The medical field was for smart, capable people.

As she brought herself back to the moment and watched her sister descend from the willow tree, Lorna felt a wave of calm wash over her, thankful there wouldn't be another tree limb incident.

"I'm just a quick call away, Kate."

Kate looked away. "Sure, there's always the phone. It's just..."

"It's just what?" Lorna pushed.

"Well, you know, I understand why you left, but I'll miss getting to see you in College Park all the time."

"I know. I'll miss seeing you too. I'm sorry."

"You don't need to apologize."

Lorna dropped her head. "I've just gotten used to apologizing, I guess. We both know Mom and Dad will never forgive me for dropping out of UMD and losing my scholarship."

Kate shook her finger and sharpened her voice into a mocking tone. "Lorna, I spent all those years taking you to lacrosse practice."

"Not bad. Almost as good at mimicking Mom as I am."

Kate smiled. "Definitely gaining on you. And when, by the way, did Mom *actually* take you to practice?"

"Seriously. It was *always* Dad."

"I bet he misses watching you play."

"Does he, though? Lacrosse always seemed to bring out Crazy Kevin."

"Yikes, so true. Either way, you're done with sticks and off to get hitched. Geez, I hate to say it, but marriage seems like even more blood, sweat, and tears."

Lorna sighed. "You do realize every marriage isn't like Mom and Dad's, right?"

"Maybe not that bad, but I've rarely seen a good one."

Chewing her lip, Lorna walked over to the chairs she and Kate had set up for the next day's ceremony. She adjusted them, creating a slightly straighter aisle. Her sister drew closer, but neither spoke until Kate finally broke back in with, "I admit...if anyone has a shot at happiness though, it's you and Will."

The following evening, Lorna slipped into the beaded vintage wedding gown she'd found at a West Street thrift shop. Emma and

Kate gazed up at her from their position on her bed, and Maggie stood speechless in the corner.

"You look stunning." Emma dabbed at her eyes with a wadded-up tissue. "Why did I even try to wear mascara?"

Maggie handed her daughter a black box, containing a thin, ornate, gold ring with tiny diamonds embedded in the band. "Something *old...*"

Lorna slipped it on her right ring finger. "Oh, Mom, it's stunning. And Grandma Jo's, right?"

"Yes. I was saving it for this day."

"Thank you. I remember her wearing it. I still miss her. This means so much."

Maggie nodded, a smile forming on her lips, her eyes blank as if a thought had just taken root in her mind. Lorna's mom wasn't especially close with her own mother—they were far too different where it mattered and only similar where it didn't. And yet, in her later years, when the edges of Grandma Jo finally began to soften, allowing for an unexpected connection with Lorna and Kate, she still couldn't quite reach her daughter. "The damage has already been done," Maggie had once shared.

As her gaze came back into focus, Maggie reached for another small box, this one containing Lorna's favorite perfume, Marc Jacobs Daisy. "And something *new*," she said to Lorna. "I noticed your bottle was low."

Emma had insisted Lorna buy the popular scent a few years earlier during one of their mall outings. Lorna balked. She'd never used perfume before...and wouldn't that clearly be trying too hard? But Emma swore it was worth it—the perfect mix of wild strawberries, violet leaves, and jasmine; and naturally, she said it would attract all the guys. "I can live without that," Lorna assured her. "You're the guy magnet so I'll leave that to you." But Emma grabbed her wrist anyway, aimed the nozzle, and fired—a cloud of mist stinging Lorna's eyes before it ever reached her nose. She had run away, hacking, but the scent lingered on her skin, and every time Emma dragged her back to the mall, she couldn't help but notice that bottle—the 3D daisies perched atop the lid, as if blooming directly from it. "Aw, fine," Lorna finally said one day, handing the box of perfume to a woman at the beauty counter, along with her hard-earned babysitting money. "I'll probably never use it, but just in case."

Lorna noticed Emma grinning from the corner of her eye as she opened up the new bottle and gave herself another spritz. "Thanks, Mom. I could use a bit more. It's hot out there, so best to be safe."

Maggie agreed. "Yes, always have backup—especially on your wedding day. Goodness, I cannot believe you're getting married. Now, do I wish it was in a few more years down the line when college was over..."

Here we go. "Please, Mom, not now."

"Okay, okay. I'm glad at least you found yourself a good one," Maggie continued just as Emma stepped in beside her with a steel-blue handkerchief.

"Please take this fast before I have to use it," Emma said. "My mom made it with special direction by yours truly. Something *blue*, of course."

Lorna examined the delicate piece of linen, tracing her fingers over the finely stitched border and eventually across the initials at the bottom: the broad, flowing curves of the cursive L, the simple but significant +, and the rhythmic peaks and valleys of the W.

Emma continued, "I remember the night you and Will carved your initials in Grandma Tree. You called me to say the two of you had finally said the L word. I love that you're now getting married under 'her.'"

Lorna bit her lip, grinning.

Kate spoke up. "Remember that time, Emmy, we were playing tag in the dark and you ran into Grandma Tree?"

"Yesssss, Kate, I recall. How does your weird little brain even remember that? Weren't you, like, four?"

"Little sisters never forget. It's our secret weapon," Kate returned.

"You're only weapon." Emma turned back to Lorna. "Anyways, since you can't take a giant willow tree with you down south, you'll at least have this handkerchief to remember the moment you fell in love and the moment you said, 'I do.'"

"I love it, Emmy. I'm so grateful you also remember it all. All the details. All the little moments."

They hugged as Kate stepped forward with something hidden inside her closed fist. "Thanks, Emma," Kate said. "So, how exactly am I supposed to beat that?" Lorna laughed as Kate went on, "They gave me the 'something *borrowed*' thing since I have no money." She held up her hand, unclenching her fingers to reveal a small, smooth, red piece of glass that resembled a flat marble with tiny black dots painted on top.

She passed it to Lorna. "Kate, your lucky ladybug! I still can't believe you haven't lost this thing. You made it in what, first grade?"

"Yep. I never have a bad day when I'm carrying it. I hope it makes your wedding day extra awesome. Oh, and don't lose it."

"I will not. Thank you, Kate. I'll tuck it in the bottom of my bouquet. Mom, promise me you'll put my bouquet and borrowed bug somewhere safe when the ceremony is over?"

"I'm on it, honey."

Moments later, Kevin wove his arm through Lorna's as they stepped away from their home and across Whitehall Road toward the ceremony.

"You look quite dapper, Dad. I don't think I've ever seen you in a suit."

"And you likely won't for a very long time, so please enjoy it."

"Oh, I am."

Kevin grinned. "How ya feelin', kid?"

"Well, my heart's about to burst through my chest, but other than that..."

"And that, I imagine, is exactly how you're supposed to feel when you're about to walk down the aisle. As long as it's a good nervous and not a *what the hell am I doing?* nervous."

"I'm happy, Dad. Genuinely happy." Lorna noticed Kevin's eyes seemed tired, but with her words, his dimples grew deeper.

"I'm glad, because running away from your own wedding is a whole lot easier when you haven't invited everyone over to your house. Either way, I'd have your back."

"I know you would, Dad."

Kevin and Lorna reached their neighbor's barn, knowing all their guests were seated, waiting just around the corner. Will's five-year-old niece was on "look-out flower-girl duty." She squealed when she saw them coming and sprinted back toward everyone, yelling, "Shhhh! They're here!"

As the chatter faded, Lorna heard the solitary strains of a violin drifting in on the breeze. Her body temperature rose with anticipation, making her grateful she'd opted for a low bun over wearing her hair down.

What she never could have foreseen came next.

As she and Kevin emerged before the crowd, Lorna stopped and gasped.

It wasn't the people who caught her attention, but Grandma Tree, adorned exquisitely for the occasion. Hundreds of white origami birds hung from her weeping branches, swaying peacefully. She was breathtaking.

Will beamed from under the willow as he watched his soon-to-be wife take in its beauty. He'd spent endless hours folding the birds and, the previous night, had secretly tied them to the countless tree branches.

A tear slipped from Lorna's eye as she proceeded down the aisle.

Will soon forgot about Lorna's surprise and simply stood in

awe of her, his eyes glistening, two older brothers at his side. All three of them looked tall and debonair in their pale gray suits.

"Best surprise ever," Lorna whispered to Will when she finally reached him.

"You've got plenty of surprises ahead, just wait," he said.

She took his hand and looked up, the paper birds soaring through swaying leaves, peppering every speck of green with white. A serene but elated feeling settled deep inside her.

After the ceremony, guests gathered under a nearby tent that Maggie had worked diligently to acquire. She'd also spearheaded its setup with help from Will and several of his football friends. It had been Maggie, too, along with Will's mom, who strung the countless fairy lights across the tent's rafters. The same lights that illuminated the tent and set Lorna's beaded dress aglow as she and Will shared their first dance. Lorna didn't miss her shoes as she glided across the grass with Will.

His oldest brother, Caleb, had agreed to do a toast before dinner. He cleared his throat and began. "Will, you grew up the fastest among us—literally and figuratively. Fitting, I guess, that you fell hard for this kick-ass lacrosse player who can likely run a forty faster than all of us." Laughter filled the space as Lorna flushed, and Will nodded in agreement. "It's crazy—one minute, you were this wiry kid; the next, a star football player and Marine, marrying the woman of your dreams. If I'm being honest, though, I can't say I'm surprised. You always had a way of focusing in on what mattered most to you in life and sprinting a hundred miles an hour toward it. The night you met Lorna, you whispered a secret to Mom." He paused and looked around, grinning devilishly. "Come on, what fun is a secret if someone doesn't get to tell it, right?"

A resounding snicker went up among the guests.

"You told her you'd met the girl you were going to marry. She slipped your confession to Mick, who passed it along to me. We both howled and said you were a victim of puppy love, but damn it if you didn't follow through. Please raise your glasses for a toast to Lorna and Will. May you brave the world together and know how much we love you both."

After dinner, Will's mom, Morgan, a petite, energetic blonde with a magnetism about her that few people could resist, took a break from the guests so she could find her son's new wife. She drifted toward Lorna, eventually grasping her hands. "Welcome to the family, beautiful bride. I couldn't ask for a better daughter."

Lorna wrapped her arms around Morgan. "I'm the lucky one."

Chapter 8

December 2012

Two and a half years later

—

Three days after Lorna met Conor

"I'm leaving, Emmy." Lorna's eyes narrowed.

Through a nearby window, an icy tide rushed in, only to break against the jagged rocks guarding the Severn Inn, a restaurant perched just across from the Naval Academy, offering a million-dollar view of the bay.

"What? Where are you going?" Emma leaned in.

"I want to become a nurse so I'm finishing my LPN degree at Cape Fear Community College in Wilmington, and Will's Uncle Rob says the house on Topsail Island, where we used to live, is available this spring. He's letting me stay without paying rent like he did for Will and me.

Emma stuck her fork into a wobbling cluster of scrambled eggs. "Why can't you finish at a school around here? Why would you go all the way back to North Carolina?"

"Lorna, isn't it?" a deep voice interrupted.

Both ladies turned at once toward a tall presence peering down at them.

"Do you remember me from Galway Bay? You stopped in for a drink a few nights ago." He wore a teal, collared shirt and a crooked but endearing grin.

Emma's brows rose sharply.

Lorna's mouth dropped for a split second before she clenched it shut. "Yeah. Hi. This is my friend Emma."

"Hi, Emma, nice to meet you."

Emma grinned but didn't say a word, likely too busy studying Conor's dimples.

"Can I buy you ladies a drink?"

"That won't be..." Lorna began.

"Of course," Emma intervened. "Mimosas sound good, right?"

Lorna stared at her.

Conor waited a moment, but when Lorna didn't speak, he did. "Two mimosas coming right up." He drifted coolly toward the bar as Emma watched him go.

"If you weren't my best friend since kindergarten, I'd disown you right about now. How did you not mention meeting Mr. Holy Moly?" Emma scolded.

"I'm the one who should be doing the disowning. As for him —it's a long story."

"I'll begin. Once upon a time, there was a tall, handsome man with stunning eyes and a fine behind..."

Lorna drew closer, whispering, "Stop, he can hear you."

"He cannot. When were you at Galway Bay? You never go out to bars without me. And by the way—"

Lorna, frustrated with the volume of Emma's voice, cut her off. "The other day when you took me out for my birthday dinner downtown...well, I didn't mention it, but I got a room at the Brooks Inn that night."

Emma's shoulders dropped, and she rested her fork on the table.

Lorna shot a look at the bar to make sure Conor was still there before she stared down at her untouched omelet. "I hadn't been there since our wedding night and I...well, it was strange. I saw Will in my dream, and I felt like he was trying to tell me something, but I'm not sure what."

"He was probably trying to say, 'Please don't go to places that torture you with my memory.'"

Lorna shot her a look and Emma retreated. "Whatever you need, Lor."

Conor was back, two drinks dancing dangerously close to the rims cradled in each hand.

"Pull up a chair," Emma insisted.

"I'd love to, but I can't. I was just heading out. I'm meeting a friend in a few minutes, but I'd love a raincheck. Lorna, any chance I could get your number?"

"I would, but remember...I'm moving."

"Then how about we meet up tomorrow night?" He was clearly unwilling to give up. Did she like his confidence or find it annoying? Maybe both.

Lorna looked over at one of the walls. Was it actually closing in on her?

"Come on. You could use a fun night out." Emma's eyes pleaded back at her.

Lorna barely contained a sigh as she reluctantly told him her number. Hastily stabbing the digits onto his phone, Conor then fled victoriously out the door.

Something undeniably uncomfortable settled into Lorna's abdomen.

"It's time," Emma said softly, leaning in toward her. "It's been almost two years. Listen, I don't mean to push you. I just really think you need to feel happiness again. And maybe this Conor guy is one more sign you should stay here. Besides, Will's uncle's house —don't you think living in the home you and Will used to share could make moving on so much harder?"

"It's one of the few options I have."

"It's not. Can I be honest?"

"When have you ever not been?" Lorna took a swig of her drink, awaiting whatever verbal lashing was coming her way.

"You're trying to run again."

"Emma," Lorna's voice grew stern, "I cannot live at home anymore. You know I love my dad, but seeing him languish back at the house, still not over my mom, is too much. And I don't have the money to rent a place."

"What about Will's life insurance money?"

"It's almost gone."

"What do you mean?"

"Most of it went to my dad's cancer treatments."

"What?"

"He doesn't have medical insurance."

"Oh, Lorna. Why didn't you ever mention that?"

"There's nothing to say, really. I had the money, so of course I gave it to him."

"Well, sure, but..."

"I'm just glad he's doing better."

"Absolutely."

"So, it's time to move on," Lorna reiterated.

Emma now plunged into her mimosa as Lorna continued, "I may have dropped out of both U of M *and* Cape Fear, but I learned one thing."

"What's that?"

"I don't have to cheat on tests to get decent grades. Who knew?"

"I knew. I've tried to tell you that since middle school. You never gave yourself enough credit. Whereas I had all the confidence in the world and would bomb the thing."

They both laughed. "Come on, that's not true," Lorna said.

Emma ignored her, nibbling the tip of her nail.

"Are you sure you'll be all right moving back down there?"

"It'll be tough at first. But no harder than living here. Everyone I run into knows what happened, and their faces instantly fill with pity. I hate it. I need a break. Topsail's transient. Every three years, military families head to a new base, so it won't be the same people there. Then, once I get my degree, I'll probably come back, get a nursing job, and we can resume our weekly brunch ritual." Lorna raised her glass.

Emma blew the air from her lungs and clinked her glass against Lorna's. "If that's what you need, then fly, my little bird. But while you're still caged here in town, will you please at least go out with Mr. Galway Bay tomorrow night?"

Chapter 9

The following evening

Tiny gleams of beaded light stretched out above Maryland Avenue, one of Lorna's favorite spots in town, a tucked-away street just blocks from bustling Main Street. Treasure-seeking shoppers sprung in and out of shops, searching for the perfect gift on the eve of Christmas Eve.

Lorna, wrapped snuggly in her winter coat and scarf, stopped outside the window of a children's clothing boutique on the corner of Maryland and Prince George's Street where Santa was visiting. Inside, a little girl gasped as she looked up at jolly St. Nick. Her parents' eyes glistened to see their daughter filled with such joy. Lorna appreciated their merriment, even as a pang of sorrow swelled within her chest.

She turned and pressed onward, her gaze glued to the sidewalk so no one could witness the salty sadness welling in her eyes. Her inattentiveness made for an effortless collision with a man looking down at a small but lovely bouquet of white tulips.

"I'm so sorry," he gasped.

Lorna looked up to discover Conor standing bewildered by her side.

"Oh, I didn't realize you were in such a rush to get your flowers." His bewitching smile rushed forth.

Still flustered, Lorna had nothing clever to return. "Naturally," was all she could muster while wondering if he noticed her disguised grief.

Conor masked it well if he did, handing her the flowers. "For you."

"They're beautiful. Thank you."

"I think tulips represent spring, but you know, I thought maybe you could use a little sign that new beginnings are possible."

She felt the warmth rush to her cheeks. *Can he see me blushing?* She shot her gaze down at the flowers. What was there to even say? Begin again? What if starting over wasn't one of her options? What if staying in the dark felt safer? What if some wounds just refused to heal, no matter the ointment?

Thankfully, he moved on. "Want to head up to Reynolds Tavern a few minutes early? We could grab a drink at the little pub underneath the restaurant."

"Why not?" *Despite the awkwardness, at least we'd be out of the cold and away from blissful shoppers.*

As they walked toward State Circle, the narrow road curving tightly around Maryland's 240-year-old State House, Lorna glanced up at the towering structure. Its white spire pierced the heavy, low-hanging gray sky. A symbol of Annapolis, one of America's earliest cities, it gleamed with colonial charm. But for Lorna, it was also a reminder of her own past—a building she'd stared up at since she could barely walk. Somehow, it looked different now, looming over her like a forsaken ghost.

Lorna and Conor increased their pace as they reached State Circle, anxious for warmth. When Annapolis was first designed, planners placed the State House at the center of what looked like a wheel, with its spokes being the many narrow streets that drew out from it. Lorna and Conor turned onto one of those side roads: School Street.

The day prior, when Lorna had finally agreed to grab dinner, it was Ryan, Conor's friend and a bartender at the 1747 Pub underneath Reynolds Tavern, who got them the last minute 6 o'clock reservation.

"Have you ever been there?" Conor asked her.

"I actually used to work at Reynolds in high school," she'd told him.

"Oh really? Yep, Ryan's been there a while. I have friends everywhere: Reynolds, Harry Browne's, Lewnes' Steakhouse, you name it, I can get us in. And I know you like the Brooks Inn, but if you want to try another hotel, my best friend works at the Maryland Inn and can set you up nicely. I love that place. I walk there to get espresso every morning."

They finally reached Church Circle, which was set up just like State Circle except instead of the State House sitting regally at its center, St. Anne's Episcopal Church had taken up residency ever since the seventeenth century. Nestled across from St. Anne's and on the corner of one of the many streets radiating out from the church was Reynolds Tavern, a red-brick colonial with a steeply pitched roof and a small front porch jutting out to welcome visitors.

Conor led them around to the side of the building and down a flight of steps to the 1747 Pub. Lorna could barely feel her nose as Conor tugged open the hefty door. One compact basement room, equipped with a bar, led them to another—this one complete with a huge, blazing fire warmly crackling against an adjacent wall.

She found a two-top beside the massive walk-in fireplace while Conor greeted Ryan at the bar and grabbed two Irish coffees. As Lorna studied the familiar bumpy, brick floors and rippled, stone walls, the nearby flames slowly began to thaw her frigid limbs.

Conor's voice came from behind her. "Rumor has it young George Washington had a thing for this tavern owner's wife." He set a foamy cup of heaven in front of her and sat down at the table.

"Guess his name was William Reynolds. Anyway, he chased Washington right out into the street and said he was no longer welcome here."

She sipped the liquid warmth: freshly brewed coffee complete with a generous splash of whiskey. "I'll have to tell your friend Ryan that he makes a fabulous Irish coffee. And I heard it was Reynolds's second wife, Mary, who chased Washington out."

Conored shed his coat. "Is that so?"

Lorna wasn't ready to remove hers and continued, "Apparently, he took off after she publicly scolded him for not supporting Maryland troops during the Revolutionary War. It was his third wife, also named Mary, who I've heard the most about, though."

"What was her deal?"

"She began as Reynolds's housekeeper and created a scandal around town when she married him after the death of his second wife. While she wasn't considered 'well born,' she was incredibly hardworking and kept their hat shop and tavern running smoothly. I can tell you, she runs a tight ship."

"You mean 'ran' a tight ship?"

"*Runs*. Haven't you heard about her ghost?"

"Ryan told me occasionally he gets freaked out down here, like something feels off, but that's about it."

"The stories I could tell you from when I waitressed here." Lorna held out her hands toward the fire. "You did not mess up the place settings or Mary would leave all the silverware in the middle of the table for you to redo."

"You're joking?"

Lorna couldn't help but enjoy the bewildered look in his eyes. "Never happened to me, but a girl I work with swore by it. Mary even locks people who get too drunk in the bathrooms."

"You're messing with me." Conor scanned the room before landing back on Lorna. "I feel like she's gonna come strolling in here any second." He laughed, but moments later, the door creaked eerily open.

Conor seemed to notice someone out of his periphery and

visibly squared his shoulders toward the fire so his back was facing the entrance.

Lorna felt the air shift in the room. Had she really freaked him out? "Listen, I didn't mean to..."

But he awkwardly interrupted, "Oh, yeah, so anyway...about Mary."

Lorna watched him press his palms together tightly.

"Hi, Conor." A slender woman with sharp features and an outpouring of auburn hair suddenly appeared at his side. "I know you said you've been *so* busy with *work*. Well, looks like you found some time to get away."

"Nice to see you, Tara." Conor would barely look at her.

Lorna drew in a breath as she watched the storm unfold. She was waiting for Tara's eyes to shoot a lightning bolt straight through Conor's head.

"I saw a pic of your son on Facebook the other day. He's so adorable. It's sad his dad can't just call me about breaking up instead of ignoring me like a coward."

Conor shifted in his chair. "You know, I really don't think this is the time."

"The only thing there isn't time for is your pathetic excuses." Tara turned toward Lorna. "Good luck with this one."

"We're not..." Lorna began, as Tara spun away, perfectly curled locks flowing furiously through the air and two sharp heels clicking across the bricks.

Lorna pressed her lips inward.

"It's not what it looks like. She's crazy," Conor finally said after Tara walked upstairs to the restaurant above.

"Look, Conor, as I said, I'm leaving town soon. Let's just have a good night. I'm not looking for anything serious, so there's no need to explain yourself."

Conor pressed his glass to his lips and took a significant swig before speaking. "Right. I hear you. So, I'm curious... Can I ask *why* you're leaving, beyond the school part?"

Her eyes met the stairway that led up to the restaurant. It

would be easier to feign a sudden need for the restroom than it would be to detail her past.

"It's a long story, but it's just best for me to head back to North Carolina for a while."

"What took you down south in the first place?"

Lorna winced slightly before gathering herself and forcing the words from her mouth. "My husband and I moved there together."

"Your husband? You have a husband?"

Chapter 10

June 2010

Two and a half years earlier

—

A few days after Lorna and Will's wedding

A "Just Married" banner fluttered in the wind.

Emma and Kate had haphazardly strung the sign across the back of Kevin's beloved truck. The rusted, blue beauty was now all Lorna and Will's.

"Keep an eye on the fuel. You know bad things happen when she gets below a quarter tank," Kevin warned as he handed Lorna the keys. "And promise me you'll use her to go back to school. You're too damn smart to wait tables forever, you understand?"

I don't know about that. "I promise, Dad."

The highway that drew them south was dusty and steaming as it begrudgingly bore the southern summer's ubiquitous heat. Lorna's vibrant purple toenails hung from the passenger seat's open window. Her cheek leaned against Will's shoulder while his hands hugged the bottom of the steering wheel.

"I can't believe we're finally doing this," Will broke in. "All those days we dreamed about getting away together. It's finally happening."

Lorna's eyes were closed, exhausted from the delirium of their wedding, packing, and saying goodbye, but a grin grew across her lips. "We're finally free." She kissed Will's shoulder, the heat making his natural smell pleasantly intense, as the midday sunlight shot through a cluster of billowing clouds above.

Bustling Virginia turned a touch more tranquil in North Carolina, where endless fields stretched as flat as parchment across a baking plain of grains. The sun melted itself against tiny, tin-roofed shacks, scattered like cornbread fritters in an iron skillet—every hundred acres or so. Vast farmland eventually faded as four lanes turned into two, revealing the faces of small-town locals emerging from two pump gas stations perched beside the road. Lorna's truck panted like a worn-out pup as it pulled into a Texaco.

"What did your grandma mean at the wedding when she told your Uncle Arthur you were righting a family wrong by serving our country?"

Will shook his head. "Oh—Nana. I guess Arthur's daughter, Allison..."

"The author?"

"Yes. She wrote her first book about one of our relatives. Arthur helped her with a lot of the research, I guess, and he told Nana about our one ancestor, who was apparently a British spy during the Revolution."

Lorna smirked. "How very un-American."

"I guess old people have more time to think about the past." Will unlatched his seatbelt and gave a brawny push to the rusted-out driver's-side door.

Lorna shot back, "Okay, now hold up. Old people aren't the only ones who care..."

"Oh, that's right, when I was sleeping through history class, you were across town, on the edge of your seat, soaking it all in."

"Very funny. Listen, I get it. When your forefathers are traitors, naturally you'd rather bury the past."

Will slammed the door behind him as he began to pump gas.

Lorna sat for a minute staring forward. *Too far, maybe?* Noticing a patch of dandelions in the distance, she couldn't help herself from counting—1, 2...14, 15. She stopped, got out of the car and walked around to Will's side.

Only the gas nozzle separated them. "You know I'm teasing, hun," she said.

He narrowed his eyes but smiled ever so slightly. "Fortunately, we get to choose our own path, regardless of what's been done before us."

"I can definitely get behind that." Lorna peered up at the powder blue sky, its wispy clouds unable to contain the sunlight.

"You're right, though," Will admitted. "I should have paid more attention in history—and especially to my own family's past. Now that my grandpa's gone, it's just that he loved to tell family stories, and I feel like such a jerk. I was barely listening most of the time."

"I'm so sorry he's gone, Will. I realize it's not the same, but I'm sure your Uncle Arthur would love to share those stories with you. I know it was awkward for you to talk to him when your grandpa was alive because of their—"

"Bitter feud," Will finished.

"Yeah. So sad for two brothers to never speak like that. How did it start anyway?"

"You know, I have no idea," Will confessed. "No one ever talked about it."

"You should give Arthur a call. He seems so nice. I saw you two talking at our wedding. It's such a shame he lived in Annapolis all your life, but your parents never took you to the Brooks Inn to see him."

"Pop made it tough. He asked my parents to stay away from Arthur." Will snapped the gas nozzle back into its holder and turned to Lorna. "Maybe I will, though. He's never done anything to me. Thanks for keeping me on track, Lorna Brooks."

The sound of her name, matched with his, felt strange and natural all at once, and when he looked at her that way, really looked at her, the counting stopped, useless thoughts seized, and all she knew was that moment—a quiet pause amidst the chaos.

By the time they reached the North Topsail Island Bridge, Lorna had taken over at the wheel. Swells of evening light glowed against the cobalt water that shifted and swayed below.

"Make a right up here. My Uncle Rob's shack is about a mile down the island."

The refreshing fragrance of ocean air flooded through open windows as they neared the end of the bridge and the sound of crushed oyster shells crackling further greeted them as they eventually pulled into the driveway. Lorna's eyes widened. Chipped, deep-peach-colored board and batten wrapped the exterior of the quaint, one-story home.

"This isn't a shack; it's a cottage."

"Whatever you say," Will laughed.

"It's perfect."

Wind whipped across the Atlantic and met them head on as they opened the truck doors.

The house sat a street back from the ocean, but thanks to an opening between two massive beach front properties, their pocket-sized bungalow had its own million-dollar view of endless blue.

"You've gotta be kidding me." Lorna's eyes melted into the sight before her. "Why didn't you tell me we have a view of the water from our front porch?"

Will grinned, meeting her gaze, then stepped behind her, wrapping his arms loosely around her shoulders.

"What is it about the sea that's so soothing?" Lorna thought aloud, allowing herself to sink back against Will's chest.

"From a distance, it's calming. Settling, I suppose."

She stared hypnotically.

"But when you get closer," he continued, squeezing Lorna

tighter, drawing her away from its trance, "you start to notice the waves crashing and the churning beneath the surface."

He pressed his lips against the tender skin on the side of her neck.

"I've never felt as still as when I'm with you," Lorna admitted, turning to look up at him.

He pressed his lips slowly and softly against hers. A gentle warmth wove its way inside her.

Minutes later, Will slid the key in the lock and turned it, revealing a little living room that flowed into a small kitchen. Dated palm-leaf wallpaper adorned the front space with a worn-out sofa plopped carelessly at the room's center. The decades-old furniture piece sat ruminating in a uniquely musty smell.

"Pretty bad, huh?" Will winced.

"Could use some love," Lorna countered nonchalantly. "No big deal. We'll fix it up in no time."

Their bungalow had just one bedroom in the back, and the bed was just as decrepit as the rest of the house.

Will's eyes widened. "That mattress has bed bugs. I can sense it. I shared my boot camp bunk with more critters than you had down Whitehall Road."

"Not possible. But I'll be right back." Lorna returned with a generous-sized quilt her mom had tossed in the truck. She spread it on the wooden floor next to the front window. "This will do until we get a bed."

"You're quite resourceful," Will said, jolting open the window before dropping down onto the quilt.

A gust of wind off the ocean came wafting in, replacing stagnant air with a tangy, salted aroma, and silence gave way to the thunderous beat of the tide crashing against the shore.

Lorna lay down beside Will, looking up at the faded white rafters as the sun slipped below the horizon.

He rolled toward her, and the tips of his fingers slid slowly down the nape of her neck. Goosebumps gathered on Lorna's skin as she turned, her hands wandering along the sloping peaks and smooth valleys of his back.

As the moon coiled forth, a soft glow illuminated their skin, and they gradually gave themselves to one another.

The following morning, a warm breeze glided through the open window, waking Will, all alone on the floor.

He checked the kitchen and front porch, but Lorna wasn't there. Turning his sights on the beach, he noticed her sitting along the water's edge, arms curled tightly around herself, eyes squeezed shut above contented lips, her face lifted toward soft rays of diaphanous light sifting through the clouds.

Will joined her on the sand. "Tell me the truth, did I accidentally marry a mermaid?"

"What gave me away?"

"You look as happy here as I've ever seen you."

Lorna beamed, opening her gaze toward the water. "One year, my grandparents took us to Rehoboth Beach. Kate and I pretended the sea was coated with magic. We'd sprint into the freezing water, allowing it to engulf our little bodies. As it made its way over our thrashing legs, they mysteriously turned into mermaid tails. I loved the way smooth, wet hair felt against my bare back and how incredible it was to frolic in those waves—fun for a girl, but exhilarating for a mermaid."

"I knew it. You do come from the sea."

As she smiled, the distant cries of seagulls filled the air.

Will continued, "Can I ask you something?"

"Sure."

"Do you ever wish you could meet your biological parents?"

Lorna's body stiffened. "Why would I? They never wanted to meet me."

"I'm sorry, I shouldn't have..."

"No, it's fine."

The wind shifted, and Lorna watched as a thin layer of sand covered her toes, but it was the rock that had wedged itself inside her throat that she felt most. "I never told you how it happened, did I?

"No."

"My dad told me I was abandoned at the hospital by my real mom."

Will placed his hand on hers. "I'm so sorry. She must have known she couldn't do it."

"I get it. But a mother...I mean, to just walk out on her own child." Lorna's gaze was on the horizon and Will saw its reflection in his wife's dark, glassy eyes. "At least take the baby to an adoption agency or something, right? But to just leave your newborn and never look back."

"I realize you know this, but, Lorna, things are rarely what they seem."

Lorna pulled her hand away. "So, you're defending her?"

"I am not. It's just, well, for a mother to leave her baby, the situation must have been dire."

She scanned the ground. "I hate how you always empathize with people, while I just see their faults."

"Come on. You're more guarded. I understand why."

Lorna silently started counting ships out on the water, tiny dots so seemingly still.

Will didn't say a word.

Lorna eventually took his hand back into hers. "Thank you," she whispered.

"For what?" Will intertwined his fingers with hers.

"For being steady. I always felt like I had to take on that role. My parents were so concerned about their own battles with each other."

"Someone had to be there for Kate, right?"

"Pretty much." She pushed her hair behind her ears, knowing full well it wouldn't stay for long. "I'm grateful I have someone to talk to about...you know..."

"The stuff you think about at night?"

Lorna nodded as he pulled her in close.

No one spoke for some time until she finally asked, "What keeps *you* awake at night?"

"Usually nothing. You know I pass out when my face hits the pillow."

"I do. And I envy you for it. But sometimes, surely sometimes..."

"Honestly, the one thing my mind seems to replay recently. Well, we talked about it yesterday. I was so selfish as a kid. I didn't take enough time to listen, especially to my grandpa."

"He knew how much you loved him, Will."

"I hope so. All I wanted to talk about was sports. Sports. Games. I did enjoy his military stories. But he didn't like to talk about those much. He loved our family, past and present. I remember seeing him in his study, looking through old letters. At least, I think they were. He looked up at me from his desk one time and wanted to show me something. I was thirteen or fourteen and said I'd be right back once I gave my cousins the football. I forgot to go back. Talk about being self-consumed."

"I believe that's the definition of a teenager. They probably should have locked us all up and let us back out when our brains finally developed."

Will looked at her and smiled. "Without a doubt."

And for a long time, they just sat, present, listening to the roar of the sea.

By summer's end, the dilapidated beach bungalow had a fresh coat of paint, despite it taking Lorna and Will a dozen more hours than they'd anticipated. It was their way of thanking his uncle for letting them stay there. But with Will's long hours of training during the week, they had to drag themselves out of bed on weekend mornings to avoid the heat and Lorna's afternoon waitressing schedule.

And because she was starting her Licensed Practical Nursing certification at Cape Fear Community College in Wilmington that fall, they pushed to finish by September, knowing her weekends would soon be filled with schoolwork. At night, they'd crawl into bed with sore backs, tanned skin and "Seashell Peach" splattered hands.

On the day they finally finished, Lorna was peeling paint off her paint-encrusted thumb when Will handed her a package wrapped in a brown paper bag. She found her way to the couch, wanting to laugh aloud at his lackluster wrapping job but decided to refrain—instead flipping it over and slipping her fingers under the multiple layers of tape.

She couldn't help but smile. "You really made sure this wasn't coming undone."

"You never know, with greasy old paper bags."

Finally making her way into the heavily fortified rectangular gift, her mouth dropped open.

A vintage wooden frame surrounded a simple pencil sketch of their tiny beach cottage. It looked exactly like the real thing, right down to the oyster-lined driveway, staggered palm trees, and unkempt beach grass.

"Will, it's incredible. Thank you. Our home."

"Our place. And no more chipped paint."

"No more chipped paint." She studied the image—they had been so busy she'd forgotten how charming it was. "And I love that you're drawing again. Please, don't stop. Your sketches always make me see exactly what I'm missing."

Chapter 11

Wilmington, North Carolina
February 2011

The following winter

Lorna watched the shops along Front Street slip by as she stared from the passenger seat of her truck, but she didn't notice their names or the people drifting past them. Her mind kept finding its way back to Will's imminent departure the following morning.

And while Lorna normally prided herself on finding open parking spots, this time she failed to notice the empty space right next to the Reel Café. Thankfully, Will saw it and swung into the spot, positioning their truck just inches from the curb.

"Did you see that?" he asked, switching off the engine.

Her head went on a swivel. "See what?"

"My parking job. I'm assuming, as always, you have a grade for it."

Lorna stepped out onto the sidewalk. "Not too shabby. B-plus."

"Come on, that's an A if I've ever seen one," he countered.

"The back tire's a smidge closer to the curb than the front."

"Really? A letter drop for a smidge?" Will wrapped his one

arm around Lorna and pulled her in as they started toward their destination. As she took in Will's scent and settled into his warmth, she momentarily ignored the tension coiling itself through her body. But the reprieve only lasted a moment, returning as they looked up at the three-story brick building they were about to enter.

The Reel Café was a place they'd ventured several times with Will's Marine buddies and their wives or girlfriends. Most of the guys were single, so it was usually a man-fest, but Lorna was glad to be with Will; plus, his friends never failed to entertain.

But when the guys agreed to meet up in Wilmington that evening, Will thought Lorna would prefer staying home on their last night together.

Normally, it would have been a no-brainer, but the jittery sensation pulsing through her veins made it hard to sit still. Distraction felt like the only option, so she suggested they hang out for a while but make it an early night.

As they entered the Reel Café's second-floor bar, fast-paced music thumped off the walls, and two strong arms clutched Lorna from behind, lifting her into the air, her arms pinned to her sides. Will grinned—his wide, radiant, familiar smile—and she knew exactly who had her in his grips.

Jack.

Right out of high school, he'd enlisted in the Marine Corps with Will. Both of their parents had pushed for them to go to college, but neither of them listened. "Jack hates school as much as I do," Will had told her. Together, they went off to basic training as Lorna accepted a lacrosse scholarship to the University of Maryland. Will and she hated being apart. As basic training was finishing up, Jack and Will had to decide on a spot to be stationed. Jack pushed for Japan or California, but Will insisted on North Carolina, to be closer to Lorna. So, Jack too listed Camp Lejeune as his first preference. Both guys also aspired to serve in a reconnaissance battalion, an elite and tightly knit unit renowned for their intelligence-gathering. The longtime friends each earned a spot as Recon Marines and were set to deploy the next day together for seven months in Afghanistan.

"Let me down, you big lug," Lorna said calmly. Jack had become so much denser than the skinny kid she'd befriended in elementary school.

Jack set her back on the floor. "Shots?" he asked, glancing between them.

The word seemed to draw Will's friends in like bees to a half-licked popsicle. Suddenly, a dozen of them were there, including a tall, thin Marine named Mike who was holding a wide tray of endless shots, high above them all. He had the platter perched on one hand, but Lorna wished he'd use both. She could tell he'd never waited a table in his life.

The tray wobbled dangerously.

It happened in slow motion: a body bumped into Mike; the tray dipped downward, succumbing to gravity's ever-present grip; the shot glasses drifted apart midair; and the shower of brown liquid splashed against unsuspecting victims everywhere.

While Lorna saw it coming, she couldn't get away fast enough, the whiskey spraying across her face and onto the cream-colored sweater she'd chosen to wear that night.

Immediately after the sound of glass shattering, Will's friends started chanting, yelling and teasing Mike—or as Lorna heard them call him, "Finn".

Will grabbed a roll of paper towels by the bar and passed her a sheet. She'd rarely ever seen him flustered, but this time his expression was saying otherwise. "Oh man, Finn, what an idiot. I'm so sorry, hun. Wanna just head home?"

It was tempting, but seeing as she already smelled like whiskey, Lorna figured she might as well enjoy an actual shot of it before making the forty-five-minute trip back to Topsail. "Let's just stay a few more minutes. I'm gonna wipe my face off in the bathroom."

"Okay." He looked around, his eyes wide, his lower lip pulled up over his top one. "Maybe we could head to the rooftop bar and air out from our Jim Beam shower," he suggested. "They have heaters up there, so we shouldn't freeze too badly."

"That sounds good. I'll meet you up there."

Will's back was facing Lorna when she made it up to the roof. He was looking out over the churning Cape Fear River in the distance.

She wrapped her arms around him and whispered, "Can we just jump on that big riverboat down there and drift away?"

"Man, am I in. I wish." Will seemed to stiffen as he turned to her. "I'm so sorry to leave."

"Don't be," she forced herself to say. "I'll stay busy with nursing school. And you obviously won't be bored. We'll get through it."

He wrapped his arms around her, a touch of her incessant tension squeezing itself out.

His lips hovered next to the smooth strands of hair that covered her left ear. "Thank you for being so strong. I knew it would be hard, but not *this hard*."

She held him tightly too, eventually reopening her eyes to the dark, turbulent waters below. "You're right. We should get outta here," Lorna confirmed before noticing Jack standing back near the rooftop bar, peaking in their direction but clearly trying to give them space. She let go of Will. "Come see us, Jack."

"Quite the party foul," Jack said as he approached them.

"Who, us?" Lorna returned.

"No—Finn. All that liquid joy is now just a brown stain on your sweater." Jack flipped his bottom lip downwards but quickly twisted it into a smile. "Have no fear, I have another round coming."

"That'll hit the spot. Then we're gonna get going, buddy," Will told him.

"So soon!?"

Will nodded.

Jack looked disappointed but proved forgiving. "I get it. I'm surprised you two made it out at all tonight. Let me grab those three shots."

He was back in an instant, passing one to Lorna first, then Will. Raising his own shot glass, he brightened. "Cheers to the two best pals a guy could ask for. Let's kick some ass in both nursing school and the AFG. We'll all be back together by fall."

"Cheers!" Lorna and Will returned in unison.

"All right, get outta here and enjoy the rest of your evening together," Jack pressed.

Will shook Jack's hand, then pulled him in for a firm embrace. As Will started toward the door, Lorna dove in to hug Jack as well, whispering to her oldest friend, "Watch out for yourself and keep an eye on him, okay?"

Jack nodded. "You know I will. I owe you both."

Chapter 12

Topsail Island, North Carolina

April 2011

Two months later

A booming knock drummed off the door.

Lorna had fallen asleep studying for an anatomy exam in her favorite dark blue, velvet chair, an aging treasure she'd found at a flea market in Wilmington. She woke up wondering if the sudden clang was part of a dream. Yet, another even louder thud from the rusty, anchor-shaped door knocker left no room for doubt. Lorna glanced at the analog clock in her kitchen, its shorthand just shy of midnight.

"Who in the world?" she muttered under her breath.

Crossing her living room with a blanket nestled over her shoulders, Lorna flicked on the pitiful porch light hanging tiredly by a thread and peeked under the blinds.

Two Marines stood side by side, immobile toy soldiers lined up for battle, until the one closest to her began awkwardly adjusting his Service Alpha uniform.

The room was suddenly spinning like that horrible rotating contraption at the State Fair where the floor drops out and everyone sticks to the wall like helpless, flattened flies. Lorna gasped for breath as her mind raced to find an escape: *maybe Will was hurt, but surely, he's fine...surely, he's okay.*

Her fingers gripped the doorknob. Should she really be opening a door at night for two strange men, regardless if they appeared to have military ties?

Probably not.

But there was no way she couldn't. If she didn't answer, she'd definitely lose her mind not knowing if Will was all right. So, she tugged at the knob and pulled the door back. Halfway, she stopped, waiting for them to explain.

The man to her left spoke first, "Are you Mrs. Lorna...Br..." He stumbled over her last name. No one had ever stumbled over Brooks.

Lorna made herself nod.

The other Marine broke in: "The wife of William C. Brooks, ma'am?"

She refused to say yes at first, unready to take on the power of his words.

Finally, she nodded again.

He continued, "We would like to ask permission to enter, please, ma'am?"

Lorna opened the door further and moved aside as they hesitantly stepped into her sandy bungalow in their pristine, deep olive-green uniforms, removing their hats immediately.

"My name is First Lieutenant Alan Briggs, and this is Staff Sergeant Ian Moore. Would you mind sitting so we can speak with you?"

Lorna's throat suddenly harbored a mysterious mass that had swelled significantly as she groped for her blue chair.

"May we sit on your sofa?" she heard a voice ask.

Lorna's lump grew larger still, shutting off any chance for speech. She put her hand out toward the couch, and the men sat in unison.

Finally, she forced out the words, "Please tell me he's okay?"

The lieutenant, with his single shiny silver bar, looked as if his throat was failing him as well, but after the longest second of Lorna's life, he gathered himself. "Mrs. Brooks, the commandant of the Marine Corps has entrusted me to express his deep regret that your husband, William, was killed in action in Helmand Province, Afghanistan, today, April 8th, 2011."

No, Lorna mouthed, trying to fend off the devastating blow. She found her voice. "No!" And a flood burst from within her. "Stop! Please, No! He can't be..."

The men could barely look at her as their faces grew blurry. She felt the force of the giant wave crashing against her body, but she was too stunned to struggle further, too shocked to move. Deep into the cold depths, it took her, where she was unable to blink, unable to breathe.

The voice above her, somewhere near the surface, continued, "Sergeant Brooks was patrolling on a night mission with two other Marines when he stepped on an improvised explosive device. All three men lost their lives. The commandant extends his deepest sympathy to you and your family in your loss."

Loss. Lost. The words swirled around her like a shadowed figured, extinguishing the last sliver of light from above.

She didn't see it happen, but the men stood, their voices distant: "Mrs. Brooks, do you have family or close friends who live nearby? Someone you could call to come over tonight?"

Lorna nodded unknowingly. She was somewhere far away, unable to return.

Chapter 13

Annapolis

July 2012

One year later

Will's mom, Morgan, kept her gaze on Lorna, who stared out at the boats parked along the inlet in downtown Annapolis.

"How was Florida?" Morgan asked.

"The weather was beautiful. And living with my cousin was fine." Lorna adjusted herself as they sat together on a bench at the water's edge. "But it's far, of course. So once my dad got sick, I came home."

"I'm sure that meant a lot to him. How's he doing?"

"Much better, thankfully."

"How are *you* holding up, Lorna?"

"Probably about as good as you are. We just finished up the worst year of our lives so, surviving."

Morgan eyes glazed over, brimming with tears.

Lorna continued, "Which is why I didn't call you back. I didn't call anyone. I was lucky if I got out of bed and made it to work."

Morgan gently laid her palm across Lorna's back. "I understand."

A plump male duck waddled his way past them, squawking forlornly. He was used to getting food from downtown visitors. That was one of the little things she missed about her old self: being so much more easily humored, laughing at random things. They were sitting close to the spot where Will and she had come on their first date. Lorna looked left and remembered the little girl with the giant loaf of bread, and Will trying to appease her by feeding the duck properly—only to get tossed on the ground, all thanks to the kamikaze flyer no one saw coming. She wanted to tell Morgan the story but couldn't bring herself to do it.

"Would you like some lunch at Dock Street?" Morgan pointed to the blue-brick restaurant just behind them. Lorna had once written a school report on how that same building served as the town jail in the eighteenth and nineteenth centuries.

"I would, but I just started picking up shifts again at Cantler's and have to leave in a few minutes."

Morgan paused a moment before speaking. "Lorna, have you thought about going back to school?"

"I'm not ready."

"Of course." No one spoke until Morgan changed the subject. "I saw Kate the other day."

"Did you?"

"She was on West Street. We got to talking. I hope this isn't too personal, but she mentioned you had to burn through most of Will's life insurance money on your dad's medical bills."

"He doesn't have health insurance, so it's just...the way life goes sometimes, you know." If that was true, though, then why was she starting to feel so bitter?

"I love that you're helping him. I just know you really wanted to be a nurse."

"Well, certain doors have closed for the time being, so I just have to accept it."

Morgan leaned in slightly. "Then you need to find new ones."

"New what?"

"New doors. They might not look the same, but they can take you in a similar direction. Besides, you've never been one to give up on anything. Why start now?"

"Why? Because I have my dad's medical bills to pay. Because I'm a twenty-one-year-old widow stuck in this town—again. As you know, I didn't come from money. I came from deadbeat parents who gave me off to...well, dysfunctional parents. I'm sort of used to reaching into my pockets and coming up short. Not everyone has money to spare."

Lorna's mother-in-law had grown up with a private-school education and a large, old house nestled comfortably inside the same upscale Murray Hill neighborhood she still resided in. Lorna immediately liked herself less for her insinuation but couldn't resist.

Morgan didn't miss a beat. "Your pockets might feel empty, but you've got something better—a sharp mind and a passion for helping others. It's okay to grieve. You deserve to grieve. But maybe focusing on something that lights a fire inside you could be the best thing for you. Listen, my brother's place..." She paused, seemingly searching for the right words. "The one you and Will stayed in on Topsail Island is open again if you want to get out of here for a while and finish up at Cape Fear Community College." Morgan pulled out an envelope, placed it in Lorna's hand, hugged her tightly, then walked away toward Main Street.

Lorna's heart sank as she slammed the heel of her hand against the bench beneath her. She fixed her gaze ahead for quite some time until she finally slipped the envelope open. A check with multiple zeros beamed back at her. The note on the card read: "You have lives to save. Please use this for your first semester back at nursing school."

Carefully, Lorna slipped the card and check back into the envelope and hid them away inside her purse. She didn't need Morgan's help. She didn't deserve Morgan's help.

Her eyes closed as several powerful gusts from the bay whipped against her face, the birds and traffic suddenly a cacophony of sounds piercing her ears.

Despite the noise, she heard a voice come to her as sure as the wind; it was a woman. “What if you embraced his memory rather than ran from it?”

Lorna spun around, but only strangers stood behind her.

A slight shiver shot down the back of her neck and took flight across her shoulders.

Lorna immediately fled to her truck. She settled into her seat and spun the steering wheel toward the small traffic circle by Market House, shot past the side entrance to Middleton Tavern, hooked a sharp left at the Naval Academy’s Gate 1, and finally took a breath beneath the red light at King George Street and Maryland Avenue.

But she couldn’t shake the feeling someone was beside her in the truck. The woman’s voice whispered again, “With winter, you will find your spring.”

Lorna tried to rationalize. “I did not just hear a voice. I did not just hear a voice.”

She froze to listen again, but only silence met her vexation.

A thick bead of sweat rolled down her spine.

It was nothing. Winter? Not even close.

Once at Cantler’s Restaurant, Emma passed by with a dozen blue crabs teetering high atop her tray.

After grabbing an apron, Lorna tied it carelessly around her waist.

Emma slowed. “What’s wrong?”

“I’m fine,” Lorna muttered without meeting her friend’s gaze, hoping to get past her into the kitchen.

But Emma stood her ground, the oversized tray blocking the doorway. “Okay, what happened?”

“I’ll explain later.”

"Promise?"

Lorna nodded, trying to hide her unsettled expression, and nudged her way past Emma.

Throughout the afternoon, she struggled with tasks, hearing the customers' voices murmuring their orders, pitifully aching to fill their bellies with fried clams and crabs—so many, miserably messy crabs—but what they said exactly, she had no idea.

After her third messed-up order, Lorna's manager sent Emma to find her. She grabbed the sleeve of Lorna's t-shirt and pulled her into a small filing room.

"What are you doing?" Lorna raged.

"You need to tell me what's going on," Emma demanded.

Lorna looked away, barely noticing the strewn papers that covered wooden crates and the single light bulb that flickered overhead.

"It's just been a strange day," was all Lorna could muster.

"You walked in here all startled and anxious and..."

Lorna finally made eye contact. "Do you believe in ghosts?"

Emma leaned in. "Excuse me?"

"I heard a voice downtown and again in my car as I was coming here."

"A voice?"

"A voice."

"What did it sound like?"

Lorna shut the door so no one could hear and kept her own voice low. "It was a woman. Do you think I'm losing my mind?"

"I'm gonna hold off on answering that, but what did she say?"

Lorna's gaze scanned the floor as she thought back, then finally continued, "Something about embracing Will's memory rather than running from it. Oh, and some garbage about winter."

When she looked up, Emma's eyes were narrow and her mouth open wide, but nothing was coming out.

Chapter 14

January 2013

Six months later

—

Two weeks after Lorna met Conor

The tattered blue comforter of Lorna's childhood twin bed became the staging area for the contents of her suitcase as she prepared to head back to North Carolina. But as she stood looking down at her meticulously folded piles of clothing, they eventually drifted from sight as the dream she'd had two weeks earlier wandered back into her thoughts.

Lorna imagined herself pushing through the hovering fog and Will standing before her. But why was it so hard to imagine his face now? Hadn't she seen it a million times?

I guess that's what happens when you refuse to look at his photo, she scolded herself.

Her mind returned to the dream and the book Will had cradled in his hands, the flames leaping from its pages.

He hated reading. I could see him holding a beer, a football, or a rifle. But a novel? I guess he knew I always loved to read. But why was it burning? Then, a thought unexpectedly glided to the surface. That time he'd mentioned Arthur's daughter, Allison, who wrote a book about some sort of notorious ancestor. *Why didn't I ask more about it? And I did have the dream that night at the inn. At the inn...*

A thump on the front door stole Lorna from her reverie.

"Conor...Hi." Lorna welcomed him inside, but uncertainty filled her. She hadn't seen him since their awkward date at Reynolds Tavern just over a week earlier. "I'm surprised you know where I live."

"I hate to brag, but I'm pretty good at uncovering mysteries."

"Apparently."

"Besides, you know it's hard to keep anything hidden in this town."

"That's a fact. So, what's up?"

"I had you on my mind. Seeing if I could get you to stay one more day. My friend has a boat. I just grabbed a six-pack of beer and thought maybe you'd like an afternoon in the sun before you rush off."

"As tempting as that sounds, I'm afraid I need to get going today."

"Uh, such a shame." He was outwardly disappointed, but continued, "I get it. Well, I won't keep you any longer. But before I go, can I ask you something personal?"

"That's always a scary question, but, um, sure, I guess."

"On our, you know, when we went out, before Christmas, you said you'd been married and he..." Conor began to fidget with his shirt. "You said that he passed away, and I never got to ask how long he's been gone."

Lorna leaned against a small counter near the sink. "It'll be two years in April."

Conor's eyes pinched at the sides. "I'm so sorry."

"Thank you."

"If I may be so bold, you said you needed to leave here. I understand how your hometown would remind you of him, but you also said you lived in North Carolina together. Won't it be equally hard to go back?"

"You're not the first to ask that." She paused, wondering where to go next. "See, when my husband first died, I left North Carolina but refused to come home. I wanted somewhere that didn't bring up his memory, as if I could hide from it. So, I dropped out of school and got a job in Florida, living with a cousin I barely knew. Guess I thought the distance and sunshine would help."

"Did it?"

"I had a nice tan and a lonely heart."

"So, you came home?"

"Yes. Mainly because my dad had gotten sick. Plus, Emma's here. My little sister too. But my dad's doing better, and I'm not living with him forever. I'm also definitely not staying with my mom and her most recent boyfriend. And with going back to school, I don't have a lot of extra cash for rent, so when I was offered Will's Uncle Rob's beach cottage that we used to live in, I said yes."

"You're brave."

Lorna couldn't look at him.

"I mean it. What you've gone through. I can't imagine. But you're still pushing forward."

"Truthfully, my husband was brave. I didn't choose the military life."

"I disagree. You chose him, knowing the risks."

"Well, I just kind of think love has a way of making choices on its own."

"I suppose so..." Conor began to twist his thumbs before crossing the room and quickly hugging Lorna goodbye. "Don't be a stranger and shoot me a text sometime."

"Sure."

The defeated look Conor left her with stayed in Lorna's mind as she threw her suitcase in the passenger seat, loaded up the truck bed with a few pieces of her life, and drove away down Whitehall Road.

Once in town, Lorna found a spot to park on Maryland Avenue and fled toward State Circle. Topsail Island was a six-hour trip south (depending on traffic, seeing as Route 95, just south of DC, was quite possibly the worst highway corridor on the eastern seaboard), and it was already midafternoon, so she didn't have time to linger at the Brooks Inn.

Narrow steps led to a heavy, black, wooden door with a weathered-brass mail slot and a matching knocker. Lorna creaked her way into the front room, where a tuft of white hair floated behind a sturdy oak desk. The pearly mane gave way to bristled eyebrows perched above thin-rimmed glasses and soft, grayish-blue eyes that eventually peeled themselves away from a leather-bound book and glanced up at Lorna.

"Hi, Arthur."

It must have taken him a moment to bring her into focus.

"Oh, Lorna! So good to see you."

"Thank you. I won't keep you from whatever story you've got yourself happily wrapped inside. I just have a quick question."

"Please do. I imagine if you trampled out in this blistering cold, it's got to be a good one." He stood. "I just hope I have a worthy answer. But first, let me grab you something warm: tea, coffee?"

"No, thank you. I'm about to embark on a long road trip, so I can't stay."

"I see."

"I'm heading back to school in Wilmington, North Carolina."

"I'm so glad to hear it. The medical field, right?"

"Yes."

"Come find a comfortable seat in the study and ask away."

He led Lorna to a room just off the foyer, where towering mahogany bookshelves lined the walls and two worn-in leather wingback chairs posted themselves proudly before a popping fire.

"Please, sit."

They both found a chair, Arthur sinking into its tall back and Lorna balancing herself on the front edge.

She decided to jump right in. "That time I stayed here a few months back...I had a dream. And in it, Will showed me a book. Maybe it sounds ridiculous to pay so much attention to a dream, but this one felt different."

"I understand."

"Of course, Will wasn't a huge literature guy. If he was, for some reason, trying to tell me something, I just can't figure out why he'd be holding a *book*."

Arthur fixed his glasses. "A book?"

"Yes, and the only novel I remember Will ever mentioning to me was the one your daughter, Allison, wrote."

The comfortability in Arthur's demeanor faded. But only for a moment. Then he rose from his chair, crossed through a shaft of sunlight to the back corner of the room. Reaching up to the top shelf, he grabbed a thin, dark, hardback book and returned to the fireplace, handing it to Lorna.

"This is it?"

"This is it."

"How much would you sell it for?"

"Not a dime. I insist. It's historical fiction based on the lives of some of our ancestors, particularly a woman named Caroline Brooks, who is a great-grandmother of ours from many generations back. I gravely regret not giving a copy to Will so he could know our family history better." Arthur rubbed the back of his neck as he gazed down at the wide pine floors. "Things were bad between his grandfather and me, as you probably know. I'm ashamed that it resulted in Will and me talking far less often than I would have liked. Everyone got caught in the middle of Bill's and my foolish quarrel—a disagreement that strangely enough began with Caroline."

Lorna noticed his shoulders hunching further.

"I'm sorry, Arthur."

"Thank you. So am I. Sadly, I would have come to know you better as well, had it not been for that."

"I'm grateful to be here now."

He nodded gently. "So glad to have you."

She peered down at the simple, black cover: *Where the Foxgloves Bloom* by Allison Brooks.

"I'm sorry that I haven't had the chance to meet Allison."

"It's unfortunate. I hope one day," Arthur said.

"Where does she live?"

He stood, retrieved the fire poker, and began shifting logs inside the blaze. "She's in London."

"Oh, wow. I didn't realize she was all the way over there."

"Yes."

She waited for him to say more, but he didn't.

"I imagine it's hard with her being so far away."

He nodded. "Have you ever heard what Roman Emperor Marcus Aurelius said about living?"

"No."

"He said, 'The art of living is more like wrestling than dancing.'"

"A lot of truth in that."

"Indeed. I will say, I was fortunate she went to college here at St. John's, but I miss her and my grandson terribly." He continued to prod the fire.

"I heard you did a lot of the research together on the book?"

Arthur returned to his chair, a slight smile forming on his lips. "We did. It was one of the best times of my life—digging together, watching her discover and grow as a writer."

"It sounds like you made a great team."

"Thank you. I think so too. It was her very first book, and of course, it was even more special since it had to do with the stories I grew up hearing."

"Did she ever publish it?"

"No. She chose not to. Allison's gone on to write and publish many other books, all wonderful pieces of literature, but this will always be one of my favorites."

"Will never said what it's about."

"Sadly, he probably didn't know. But maybe he wants you to know now."

When Lorna finally reached the old bungalow in Topsail that night, she flicked on the light, shut the door, dropped her purse on the ground, and stood, silently, taking in her—no, *their* quaint little living room. It wasn't the peeling palm wallpaper or the cheap couch they'd picked up at a garage sale that she noticed first, but that distinct smell—briny, sharp, and sacred. It sucked itself inside her. She'd told herself the entire trip to remain resolute, stoic even when it came to her arrival. Instead, it surprised her how quickly the tears began to flow—so much pent-up sorrow rising instantly to the surface. The joy they'd shared within these walls suddenly felt like a means of torture, reminding her that she'd never experience those moments with him again.

Everyone was right. She shouldn't have come. What made her think she was strong enough to return?

Exhaustion and frustration suddenly set in, and she slid down to the floor, curling her knees up to her chest with her back bending dejectedly against the door. Then, from the corner of her eye, the contents of her spilled purse suddenly came into view, mostly sprawled across the hardwoods. Next to a tube of Burt's Bees lip balm and a half empty bottle of water, the novel Arthur had given her lay open, its pages fanned out, their edges resembling the delicate feathers of a bird's wing. She hastily closed it and tossed the book several feet away.

How ridiculous and pathetic I must have looked coming to Arthur for that book. Why am I doing this to myself?

Noticing a ray of light shooting through the kitchen window, Lorna followed it across the room, only to realize it was shining off the cover of Allison's book, illuminating the word, "Bloom."

Everything inside her said to let it lie. Unpack her things. Keep moving on. She didn't have the energy to even go there.

But a quiet voice whispered, "Just one quick look."

After another intense stare-down, she finally retrieved her

newly found torment device and hesitantly turned to the first page —Part One: Catch Me If You Can.

But after reading the heading, she shut the book. *I can't do this. It's hard enough just being back in this house that we shared. I don't wanna think about his family. I need to let him go.*

She hid the novel away in her bedside nightstand and unpacked her things.

Two weeks later, just after dawn, Lorna woke suddenly. It was a Friday, and with her early-morning nursing class just a few hours away, there was no way she was falling back asleep. She could get out her notes and look over them—but she wasn't in the mood, especially since that meant getting up.

Allison's book, tucked away next to her, beckoned.

I'll just read a page or so...

WHERE THE FOXGLOVES BLOOM

By Allison Brooks

PART I

Catch Me If You Can

Annapolis
October 1774

Autumn leaves, crisp and frail, swirled among clouds of powdered dirt, trailing two stunning horses who'd taken flight down Whitehall Road.

The striking beasts stretched out side by side, their riders' bodies also bobbing in unison.

A young woman sunk low atop the chestnut mare, her silk skirts flapping violently in the wind.

Her teeth clenched as the stallion beside her shot ahead, growing his lead to four lengths, his muscles pulsing under a shining charcoal coat.

His rider's face gleamed with confidence, the young man sneaking a shot backward to assess his competition's speed.

The female rider only grinned.

She knew exactly why he had cause for concern.

Her mare was a force.

With a long dynasty of champion racing in her blood, the animal was known not for how she started a race, but for how she finished it.

Her rider's gaze was resolute. She too had also learned to prevail.

So, it was far from shocking for the woman—and, likely, her horse—when they began to gain distance on the stallion, pushing past him with prodigious speed in the final moments of their mile-long race.

Both riders, just seventeen years old, shared a youthful glow, only enhanced by the wind's flushed footprint painted across their cheeks.

"Well done, Caroline." The young man shook his head, looking down at his white knuckles, still tightly gripping the reins.

He always was a better loser than I, Caroline thought to herself.

"It's my mare whose outdone your stallion. Her grandmother, Selima, would be proud," she said as she leaned forward on the horse and, with her gloved hand, patted the sweat drenched hair on its neck.

As they neared Whitehall mansion, a sprawling brick home

perched on the edge of the Chesapeake Bay, a woman's voice called out from the back porch, "Miss Collins, make haste! Your father is looking for you!"

Caroline pulled on the reins, bringing her mare to a sudden stop. The fine hairs on her forearms suddenly sprang to attention.

Her racing partner, Thomas Pierce, halted his stallion beside her.

"I saw Grafton Brooks pull up in his carriage earlier. Your father wants your affections placed on him, doesn't he? I've heard he's after your hand."

"So it seems," she said begrudgingly.

"I assume you'll refuse him?"

"I wish it were so simple."

"Isn't it? You've never been one to worry about pleasing others. Especially a thirty-five-year-old man you've never even met."

He'd always known how to press her, even while donning that seemingly innocent expression. Caroline turned to meet Thomas's gaze. "Tell not another soul what I'm about to tell you, understand?"

"I've been your closest companion since we were both still in stays. Have I ever wronged you?"

He had a point.

Caroline looked back toward Whitehall, no longer willing to meet her friend's eyes. "My father is dying."

"What? How?"

She swallowed carefully, refusing to let even a single tear form. "His heart is failing. They say it's only a matter of time."

"That doesn't feel possible. He's a legend to so many of us. I'm so sorry, Liny."

"And there's more. You know, he was never known for his financial restraint. The house will have to go first." Somehow, saying the words aloud made them feel so much more certain—and painful. She watched as Thomas lowered his gaze. "Oh, Caroline. No."

Certainly, her father's heroics against the French and Iroquois were incredibly admirable, but the money he'd lost on miscalculated business deals and endless horse races were about to leave them penniless.

"So, he's insistent I meet Mr. Brooks today. And while I've never been one to accommodate his demands, this time there's suddenly much more at stake."

"I understand, but you're going to consider marrying..."

"What choice do I have, Thomas?" Her voice filled suddenly with indignation. What did he know about sacrifice? Born into a wealthy family with two relatively dependable parents and the complete admiration of his fiancée, the beautiful and equally affluent Virginia Pembrooke.

Sure, he could easily marry for love.

"There has to be another way," Thomas pushed.

"How I wish it were so. If only I were a man. With this brewing conflict with Britain, I'd leave it all behind and lead a militia against those lobsters if I could."

"I'll say you've got a better musket shot than most men I know."

Caroline surrendered a rueful grin. "Even with the education my father provided, I still have no other choice but to adhere to the stipulations of my sex when it comes to owning my own property, something *you've* been given and don't have to rely on *another* for. So, please don't lecture me on my choices, because they are few."

Before Thomas could speak, she was off—wispy, fallen pieces from her blonde bun lashing wildly in the wind once again.

When Caroline entered the parlor inside Whitehall mansion, she watched as several sets of eyes swept her way. She went first to her father, who stood near the fireplace sipping a cup of half-century-old madeira. His face was several shades paler than when they'd first arrived, and his expression grim.

"Do you need some air, Father?" Caroline tried to whisper, but her voice was always considerably louder than most.

"I'm quite fine," Colonel Collins returned through gritted teeth.

"Is the medicine not helping again?" she further prodded.

"Caroline. Enough." He turned toward the flames. "Have you spoken to Grafton? You know that is my *one* request."

"Yes, I was just about to..."

The Colonel drew himself next to Caroline's ear, "Well, he's crossing the room, so you'll have your chance. Please, do not frighten him away like the others."

Caroline narrowed her eyes and met her father's stare. Neither of them bulked.

She saw the ghastly bloodshot tint growing around his irises and the withered skin below his lower lids, an outside reflection of inner destruction.

For once, she turned away before he did.

That's when Caroline first saw Grafton Brooks.

He was a tall man with a sharp jawline and handsome features, unintentionally hindered by a natural scowl.

While it wasn't easy, she forced her voice to echo more joy than annoyance. "Greetings, Mr. Brooks."

PART II

What's burning

"So, *you're* the infamous Caroline Collins," Grafton said, his chin lifting upward.

Caroline responded immediately, "I'll take that as a compliment, Mr. Brooks. Infamy trumps insignificance."

Grafton's lips parted into a thin, barely distinguishable smile. "We can agree there. Miss Collins, I'm not a coy man. I prefer directness. You have a reputation of battling back suitors. I hope you won't be inclined to do the same with me?"

"It would be quite remiss of me not to vet a gentleman; however, I will be as affable and equitable as the situation requires. Do you warrant any reason for me to be especially scrupulous?"

"I suppose your father wouldn't have invited me here if he felt so." His look was piercing, but it didn't shake her.

"I do believe you've just tried to circumvent my question, Mr. Brooks."

"Caroline..." her father began to interject, but a sudden scream from the foyer stopped him.

A servant was gasping for breath as she entered the drawing room. "Miss Molly, please come quickly. It's little Horatio!"

Molly Ridout, the hostess of Whitehall—her dark hair twisted and rolled high atop her head with two thick curls trailing behind—dashed past Caroline.

Without a word of explanation, Caroline abandoned her suitor to follow Molly, soon realizing the cause of the servant's panic. Horatio Ridout, barely five years old with jet-black, disheveled hair, looked paler than ever as he lay coiled up in agony on a settee near the front door. His older sister, Anne, stood aghast by his side.

"I shouted when I saw him do it, but it was too late." Anne trembled as she buried her petrified face in her hands and wept.

Molly fell to her knees beside her daughter, gently gripping her arms, "What did he do, darling? Please, you must tell me so we can help him."

"He ate a batch of berries. Apparently, some children dared him to do so."

At Molly's side stood a teenage servant with bright eyes and a sharp, focused demeanor. The young mother looked up at the enslaved girl by her side. "What can we do, Charity?"

"He needs Bowman's root to purge the poison." Charity's voice was soft but decisive.

"It'll induce vomiting?" Molly asked.

"Yes. I'll make a tea."

"Please hurry," Molly begged, but Charity was already gone, halfway to the kitchen.

Molly hugged her daughter. "Thank you for letting us know," she whispered before moving to her youngest son, whose moans resonated throughout the home. She placed her hand on the small of his back and sank close to Horatio's ear. "Deep breaths, sweet boy. You know our Charity will help you."

"Let me carry him to his bedroom, Molly?" Caroline interjected.

"Thank you, but I need you to find Charity to tell her where we'll be."

"Of course." Caroline rushed off.

When she reached the kitchen, Charity was standing over a black kettle suspended inside a large, open brick fireplace; the water within was just starting to bubble and burst. Moving to stand beside her, Caroline watched as Charity reached toward the ceiling and pulled down a thick bushel of hanging dried sprigs, tossing them into the kettle. Dark ripples consumed the crimson stems and pointed leaves.

Caroline stared down at the steaming concoction. "How long do we wait?"

"A few minutes. The tea has to be potent."

Charity scooped the ladle off its hook as Caroline reached for a nearby copper kettle.

"It's hard to wait." Caroline eyed the door anxiously. "Poor Horatio."

"I know." Charity kept her gaze on her tea water as she stirred the Bowman's root in wide circles, making sure the two became one. As she did, Charity intertwined her arm with Caroline's, who softened ever so slightly.

The teenagers had grown up together during Caroline's and her father's frequent visits to John and Molly Ridouts' downtown Annapolis home.

Caroline suddenly remembered when they were ten years old, and she'd hastily jumped in front of a carriage while crossing Main Street. Charity had reached out and grabbed Caroline's skirts from behind, pulling her back off the road just in the nick of time.

Charity closed her eyes and whispered, "Lord, please allow this to heal the boy."

Upstairs, Molly pressed her son's forehead as he writhed in pain. Her husband, John, paced the room.

Molly turned to John, the fear in her voice multiplying with every word. "His fever is growing."

John wiped the sweat from his brow. "I sent Marcus for Dr. Hampton. He'll likely be here soon."

Horatio's arms, no wider than a small tree branch, squeezed his stomach as he rolled from side to side.

"We should have stayed in town," Molly said. "The children aren't used to this setting, and Dr. Elders is always just a stone's throw away across Duke of Gloucester Street."

The Ridouts were entertaining that day at Whitehall, the home of their good friend and John's former employer, Maryland Governor Horatio Sharpe, who'd gone back to England the year prior to take care of his affairs. Everyone in Annapolis said the bachelor governor had built the grand abode over a decade earlier to impress Molly, whom he desperately hoped to marry. But Molly fell in love with his much younger secretary, John Ridout. Despite the disappointment of never gaining her hand, Sharpe still cared deeply for the Ridouts, and upon his departure to the Motherland, urged them to enjoy his home while he was gone.

Little Horatio, the son they named after Governor Sharpe, let out a shrill scream just as Charity and Caroline shuffled through the bedroom door. Charity placed a china teacup on the bedside table as Caroline managed to steady herself enough to pour the Bowman's root tea inside it. John ran to his son's bedside, and together Horatio's parents set him up against ample pillows.

Caroline sat down on the bed next to Horatio and blew on the amber-toned brew before placing the porcelain cup to Horatio's lips. "You must drink it."

The young boy was weak and refused her.

Caroline set down the cup and placed her palms around his flushed and burning cheeks. "Horatio Sharpe Ridout, the poison is eating up your belly, so drink this tea right now, and the pain will go away."

She picked up the teacup again, pressed it to his pale lower lip, and carefully poured the tea into his mouth. The room went still, all eyes on Horatio.

Suddenly, he began to gag, hope rising inside Caroline. Charity grabbed a nearby chamber pot and thrust it under the boy's mouth just as he began to vomit. Once the poison had left his tiny body, Horatio's fever relinquished, and he was able to restfully nap.

Later that afternoon, Charity was alone in the hallway, just off the great hall, locating coats for departing guests. The notes of the harpsichord hung fancifully in the air, eventually mixing with the clinking clatter of heeled shoes tapping against pine floors. Charity turned to see Molly stopped by her side with hands raised to her heart.

"I can't thank you enough, Charity."

"It's my pleasure to help, Miss Molly."

Caroline and her father, Colonel Collins, stood nearby, waiting for their coats.

"Leaving so soon?" Molly turned to them.

"Night draws ever nearer with winter's approach," the Colonel returned. "How's little Horatio?"

"He's well, thank you. So grateful for your heroic daughter, who is always ready to act when danger beckons." Molly crossed to Caroline, gathering both of her hands.

Colonel Collins's eyebrows rose. "Well, I must say, it is often the peril she invites upon herself, so this is a rarity." A stern look grew across his face as Caroline's eyes narrowed.

"Thank you, my dear friend," Molly said to Caroline.

"It's Charity who saved the day. I was but a mere messenger."

"Not so. You are always the first to jump forth, no matter what ensues. It's one of the many things I admire about you. Remember when John's horse got spooked in town last year and went blazing up Green Street? It was you who tracked that old mare down and brought her home."

"I suppose it takes a wild creature to harness a wild creature."

Colonel Collins showed his first hint of a smile all evening as he met Caroline's gaze.

Molly interjected, "My father taught me a German phrase just before he died, 'Der Apfel fallt nicht weit vom Baume.' I was six, but I still remember it."

"Do share the translation," Caroline chimed in.

"The apple falls not far from the tree." Molly winked at Caroline, then turned to take the Colonel's hands. "Forgive me, Charles. I couldn't resist."

"And just like your own father, you have enough charm to carry off even the gravest of offenses."

"You know I meant no harm, but quite the contrary. If it weren't for your own fierceness, you never could have achieved what you did during the war. And you never could have raised our headstrong Caroline." Molly quickly turned the conversation. "Can I get either of you a chocolate drink or coffee before you leave? Of course, I wish I could offer you tea, but I suppose we won't be receiving shipments anytime soon." Molly's face grew slightly uncomfortable. "I apologize, Charles. I shouldn't have even brought the subject forth. I know this has been a horribly arduous time for merchants like you, trying to obtain your imports from England."

If you only knew just how arduous things are, Caroline thought to herself.

"We're making do. If you need tea, you let me know," Colonel Collins added.

"Thank you. We're fine for now," Molly returned.

The Colonel's expression remained unchanged, but he straightened his shoulders and placed his forearm in the small of his back. "With your husband as Naval Officer of the Port, I suppose you've heard about the large brig setting out in the harbor some days now. It's owned by our neighbor, a Mr. Anthony Stewart, and the Whig folks are pushing to dump his 2,000 pounds of tea aboard that ship into the bottom of the bay, just as they did in Boston."

"It's the right thing to do, Father," Caroline interjected, adrenaline rising inside her. "If old King George doesn't want trouble, then he should stop robbing his own people like a common thief."

"Caroline, enough. You know that could just as easily be us facing the mobs with one of my vessels. That poor man's wife and young daughter remain locked inside their home, terrified of the uproar surrounding them, not knowing if their place will go up in flames because of those angry anarchists."

"I should think Mr. Stewart would have thought of his family's well-being before he loaded a ship with cargo that's not permitted on our shores. And no, that couldn't have been us, because you wouldn't have allowed taxable British goods on your boats, now would you, Father?"

Colonel Collins's eyes narrowed while his voice deepened, "Speak not on things you don't fully understand, Caroline." He turned to Molly, reaching into his pocket. "Take care, my dear, and please give the boy this once he's awakened from his nap." The Colonel placed a gold coin in the palm of Molly's hand. "Do tell him I discovered it while serving in the Indian Wars. Let him know how grateful I am to know he's well again."

"What an honor. Thank you, Charles. This will ever so lift Horatio's spirits." Molly took in a deep breath. "I hope you know how thankful I am for you. You've been like a father to me since, well, as long as I can remember."

"Your father was the closest friend I've ever known, and he looks down on you with great pride, Molly. I'm immensely proud of you too."

Caroline watched her thumbs spin and shifted from one foot to the other as her father continued to address Molly, "Still not thirty years of age, and you have a thriving household, a host of beautiful children, and a kindness that simply cannot be matched. Furthermore, it is I who is in debt to the way you've taken Caroline under your wing all these years."

Charity handed the Colonel his pristinely folded tricorne hat. He placed it on his head and dismissed himself toward the carriage, leaving Caroline and Molly to face one another beneath the back-door threshold. Molly leaned in to kiss Caroline's cheek before moving her mouth toward her friend's ear. "Horatio's accident kept you from talking with Mr. Brooks, didn't it? I was grieved to hear that he took his leave while we were occupied with my son."

"No loss of mine. He's impertinent."

"Do be cautious with him," Molly warned.

Caroline stepped back. "Fret not over me, friend. You know I can handle my own well-being." And with that, she shot down the porch stairs, leaving Molly to watch her go.

When they reached town, Caroline peered out her carriage window to discover smoke billowing near the harbor.

What's burning?

Coming up King George Street, it was impossible to proceed any further as crowds of people gathered on the dusty dirt road. Caroline and her father were forced to go the rest of the way on foot, trudging along until they reached Hanover Street.

A man turned to Colonel Collins, filled with excitement. "The *Peggy Stewart* is burning in the harbor! They forced that bastard, Stewart, to set his own brig ablaze because of his treasonous tea."

The Colonel ignored the man, locking his arm inside his daughter's. "Quickly, let's get to the house."

Screams and chants filled the air all around them as they passed the Stewart's substantial brick mansion. Caroline could feel her heart throbbing—somehow, equal parts excitement and fear.

Suddenly, her father started gasping for breath. Fear quickly took over.

"Go, Caroline. I'll catch up. Don't stop until you reach the house."

"I'm not leaving you."

They continued to their own immense colonial with a pristine view of the bay. Caroline helped her father inside and onto a chair in the drawing room. Once she knew he was all right, she whispered, "I'll be back," and rushed upstairs to get a better shot of the harbor. From her bedroom window, Caroline's eyes were immediately drawn to the searing patch of flames breaking forth from the water's inky surface, completely engulfing the cargo ship.

Colonel Collins, too, made his way into Caroline's bedroom and stood a few paces behind her.

She could hear his heavy breathing and turned. "You shouldn't have come up the stairs, Father."

"War is coming," he said matter-of-factly. Then his voice softened slightly. "I wish I was going to be around to watch over you."

Caroline's shoulders fell slightly as she met his tired eyes, then rose again. "Rest assured, Father, I don't need protection. You've taught me to be strong."

"I didn't have to teach you anything. You came out kicking."

She turned back to the smoking ship, her stomach dropping uncomfortably as it always did whenever anything remotely related to the day of her birth was mentioned.

He walked to the window and stood beside her. Together they watched the inferno licking hungrily at the wooden hull, its heat intensifying, causing the timbers to crackle and splinter, as the blaze spread with an unyielding ferocity. The sails quickly disintegrated into swirling ashes, while the water around the boat reflected the fiery glow.

Her father's voice was low but crisp. "Just don't let your passions get the best of you, as I have."

"So, it's me you want to protect from myself?"

He turned and headed to bed.

Her answer came in his silence.

Chapter 15

January 2013

Lorna stared at the chalkboard while her instructor scribbled the words *functionalism*, *natural selection*, and *cell formation*, then rambled on about the class's first physiology quiz. The teacher's voice grew distant replaced by the sound of hoofbeats and the image of Caroline floating effortlessly as she rode her mare down Whitehall Road. *What color was the horse? I think it was chestnut. Yes, chestnut.*

"Miss Brooks?" the teacher said, startling her.

She peered up at the woman. "Yes?"

"I'm looking for an answer."

Lorna's palms grew clammy. "I'm sorry, I don't know."

"I hope all of you figure it out by Monday. Class dismissed. Study up."

Lorna shot out the door like a cannon, mortified by her inattentiveness.

Crisp air greeted her as she reached the parking lot and scurried into her truck. Given its heat wasn't working (had it ever?), she zipped up her coat and sped past the "Cape Fear Community College" sign, leaving Wilmington and heading north toward Sneads Ferry—a bite-sized shrimping town nestled beside the back gate of massive Marine Corps base, Camp Lejeune.

As Lorna coasted along Route 17, a sharp pinging noise rang out from her backpack, so she reached inside the front pocket and retrieved her phone.

It was a text from Conor: *Hi. Thinking of you.*

A restless energy rose up inside her. Conor had texted her several times a week since she'd left town. It was nice to know she was on someone's mind, but strange too. The dream with Will a month earlier and that morning spent reading about his family's past made him feel closer than he had in a very long time, and she liked it. How could she possibly be ready to move on?

When Lorna pulled into Rick's Restaurant along Highway 210 for her evening shift, she immediately recognized the white Jeep Cherokee with its faded Broadneck Baseball bumper sticker.

Jack.

A lump formed in her throat.

Lorna hadn't seen him since Will's funeral in Arlington.

She fixed her eyes on the worn, pleather steering wheel and reminded herself again what a terrible idea it had been to return.

But she had to press on. She would focus on school and work. And maybe seeing an old friend again wouldn't be so bad. Besides, at least Rick's was warmer than her freezing truck.

Jack sat alone at a corner booth.

Lorna tucked herself in beside him without saying a word, and despite his shock, he immediately wrapped his arms around her puffy coat.

"Damn. You feel like a giant marshmallow."

"Nice to see you too, Jack."

He laughed—its familiarity was comforting. "What are you doing back here?"

"Finishing my LPN degree to become a nurse."

"That's awesome. I'm just surprised as I'd heard you moved home."

"I did for a while. You can imagine how that worked out."

"I guess being home was never your jam."

"Not so much. It was nice though to have Emma, Kate, and my dad."

"Good old Kevin," Jack interjected.

"Yes, good old Kevin."

"My mom told me he was sick."

"He's doing better." Lorna had to wiggle out of her coat, considering the confined space. It was the perfect time to turn the attention off her. "How've you been, though?"

"You know."

Lorna waited.

Finally, Jack continued, "Just got back from my second deployment."

"Wow, seriously? Already?"

"Yep," he answered, throwing down half the drink in front of him.

She hesitated, before asking, "How'd it go?"

"Well, this one wasn't nearly as bad as the first, of course, but how could anything be worse?"

Lorna tried to gather herself before diving into the inevitable, something she'd wanted to tell him for quite some time. "I'm so sorry you had to be there, Jack. I'm grateful he had you, though."

"Thanks, sure..." He stuttered for a few seconds before finishing. "But let's be honest, what good was I?"

Lorna knew he was saying something that had run through his mind a million times, and a pain shot across her chest. "No, no. Please don't do that to yourself, Jack. I mean, you weren't even on the patrol that night."

"You have no idea how much I wish I was."

"Why? So you'd be gone too?" Lorna's voice began to rise, "Mike...what's his last name...Finnington or Finnler."

"Finn, we call him."

"That's right, the guy who spilled all the shots on us in Wilmington."

"That's him."

"During the battalion homecoming, he got wasted and told me

they never should have sent Will out that night with just two other Marines." Lorna could feel the heat rising inside her but pressed on anyway. "When you've got three guys walking only a few feet apart and one steps on an IED, who's there to help?"

"I'm so sorry he told you that. At the homecoming too."

"What? The truth. Why shouldn't I know the truth?"

Her words hung heavy in the air and Jack fell silent.

Lorna continued, her voice steadier than she felt. "Besides, I'm not bitter toward Mike. No one knows what to say." She began folding sharp creases into her napkin. "I just get so angry when I think about how everything went down."

"You have a right to be." Jack looked down at his drink. "I am too."

"Are you still having the nightmares?"

"How'd you know about that?"

"Mike's wife, Jenna, told me you and Finn were talking about it over drinks one night."

"Finn, what a big mouth. Yeah, still having them. The dreams are...well, you know, take a toll on a lot of us. Never a break when you're haunted through the night too." Jack took another sip. "How are you holding up, Lorna?"

"I'm all right. I keep busy. Just moved back into Will's Uncle Rob's place."

Jack's eyebrows rose as he began to speak, but Lorna interrupted, "Maybe you could see someone—to talk about the dreams."

"I'd rather pull out my arm hairs than rehash my nightmares to some shrink."

Lorna met his gaze. "I'm so sorry you had to see what you did. Your mind needs a rest, though. Talking it through will clearly be brutal, but nothing's worse than what you're already living with."

Jack looked down at his drink. "Yeah, we'll see."

She stood and wrapped an apron around her waist. "Better start my shift, but it was great to see you. Let's grab a drink soon."

Jack raised his glass. "I'll stop by the old pad sometime."

"Do that."

By the time Lorna made it back to her quiet bungalow, she smelled like beer-battered fish and ached for a scorching shower.

After scrubbing away the day's exertions, she wrapped herself in a fluffy towel and slipped into flannel pajama bottoms and an oversized hoodie. The lingering aroma of lavender shampoo clung to her skin, and a rare sense of tranquility washed over her as she settled into her worn blue chair. She relished the rare escape she was about to take. On the wooden side table sat Allison's book, waiting.

Lorna peeled the cover open and slipped inside the story.

WHERE THE FOXGLOVES BLOOM

By Allison Brooks

PART III

SECRETS BENEATH THE SURFACE

DECEMBER 1775

CAROLINE STUDIED THE ICE-CAPPED HARBOR, the panes on her bedroom window sharing the same frosted sheen. Just over a year had passed since she stood in that very same spot, spellbound, watching as fire erupted across the water—the *Peggy Stewart* consumed by a wave of anger that continued to surge throughout the colonies.

For a moment, Caroline imagined herself stepping out onto the barely frozen river, pausing to hear the sharp cracking beneath her feet. It would only be a moment before the current mercifully dragged her down into its depths, sweeping her body far, far away.

A faint knock echoed off her bedroom door.

"Come in." Caroline turned as Charity entered.

"You look lovely." Charity's eyes narrowed when she smiled. "Molly asked me to check on you and see if you needed anything."

"I'm fine." Caroline stiffened her back.

Charity crossed the room, reached into the deepest pocket of her linen dress, lifted a closed fist to Caroline, and uncoiled her fingers to reveal a small, gold locket.

"What's this?"

"A wedding gift." Charity transferred it to Caroline's hand. "Hopefully, it will bring you good luck. I think it also complements your yellow dress."

Caroline drew it closer, flecks of sunlight bouncing off its gleaming surface.

"It's exquisite."

"Are you wondering how I got it?"

She wasn't. "I've seen you unearth thimbles, whirligigs, shutter latches, and more coppers and shillings than a wealthy man possesses." Caroline shifted her gaze from the locket to meet her friend's eyes. "However, this is undoubtedly your most impressive find."

Charity grinned shyly and stepped toward Caroline. "May I put it on you?"

Caroline handed the shiny oval and delicate chain to her friend and sat down on the bed, her back toward Charity. "You polished it up with one of your concoctions, didn't you?"

Charity fastened the clasp at the back of Caroline's neck. "It was charcoal gray and coated with mud when I found it buried at the edge of an alley along Main Street."

"How in the world did you see it?"

"One link in the chain had a single speck of gold left."

Caroline's eyes met the floor.

"I don't want to do this, Charity."

"I know you don't." She bent down on the floor in front of Caroline, so their eyes met. "But if you can teach me to read, surely you can teach Mr. Brooks to be an adequate husband."

Downstairs, thick, drawn drapes forced away the sunlight in Colonel Collins's study. Grafton paced. His friend and fellow merchant, Andrew Moore, leaned against the fireplace mantle, twiddling his thumbs.

"Surely, there's some way we can profit from the ensuing madness." Grafton's gaze never left the rich burgundy rug.

"You mean the conflict between Britain and the Colonies?"

"Obviously, Moore. The rebels just sacked Norfolk because they're terrified a British fleet will come sweeping up the Chesapeake and capture city after city." Grafton paused and looked up at the portrait of Charles Collins's father, proudly perched atop his white gelding, the serene English countryside a striking juxtaposition to his vibrant-red uniform. His features twisted and relaxed into a satisfied grin. "Interesting."

"Pray tell." Andrew shifted his weight from one foot to the other, his nose rising in the air like a fox trying to calculate his surroundings.

"We both know fear can be a beautiful thing, if preyed upon properly."

"And what do you have in mind?"

"Everyone has heard whispers of what war brings. Entire cities ransacked by the Redcoats. Yet the wealthy seem more afraid of losing their prized possessions than their lives. They'll do *anything* to protect their money."

Grafton crossed the room and drew close to Andrew, his voice lowered. "That old underground tunnel we found a few years back, the one that connects my cellar to the Maryland Inn's. Since you're managing the place now, you have perfect access to it. Imagine if we arched the roof on it properly to avoid cave-ins. Paca, Carroll, Brice, and every one of their rich cronies will pay a fortune to store their precious heirlooms where cruel King Georgie can't find them."

Moore's face brightened. "Brilliant."

"The moment this ceremony is done, we begin on that tunnel."

Both men turned toward the doorway as Mrs. McGregor, the Collins's Scottish indentured servant, stepped confidently into the room. "The Colonel 'twould like ye to join him in the parlor. Miss Caroline will be joinin' ye there verra shortly."

Grafton nodded ever so slightly before turning his back on her.

She was far from fond of the gesture. "Did ye hear me, sir?"

"Yes, yes." He swatted effortlessly into the air, looking to dismiss her at once, but she didn't move—eyeing him carefully, the wrinkles under her eyes drawing closer together.

After Mrs. McGregor finally pulled her gaze away from Grafton, murmuring something under her breath about a "Bubbly-jock," she returned to the parlor.

The Colonel was sitting alone at the far end of the room, his head resting against five spindly fingers as they dangled limply. Mrs. McGregor eyed his fading frame. Her much-loved stews and shortbreads weren't sticking to his ribs like they used to.

"You don't like him, do you?" the Colonel asked without looking up at her.

"What I think tisn't of much importance."

"I wouldn't have asked if I agreed with that."

Mrs. McGregor studied the floorboards, and he turned to study her.

"It isn't like you to hold your tongue, Agnes." The Colonel motioned toward the adjacent chair. "Sit, please."

"Uh, but the other guests'll be arrivin' shortly, sir, and..."

"I don't care a lick about them. Please, sit."

She wedged her wide hips between two armrests. "Caroline's a clever lass. She'll figure out how tuh navigate 'im."

Colonel Collins plunged his fingertips into his temples and lowered his eyelids. "I left her little choice."

Footsteps clattered across the foyer.

"I'll watch out for her, Colonel."

"Promise me?"

"That I do."

Guests began to fill the parlor, chatter quickly accumulating. The furniture had been removed, as everyone would remain standing throughout the ceremony. Colonel Collins covertly clung to a bookshelf while he greeted his company. His face remained solemn, but those in attendance were used to his somewhat severe disposition.

Caroline entered the room, and all eyes turned toward the bride. Only then did a faint smile finally grace the Colonel's lips.

Grafton's chest protruded proudly as he pivoted to see his soon-to-be wife.

Caroline's gaze shot straight ahead at the priest, whose cloak swayed ever so near to the flames in the fireplace.

Colonel Collins stepped in to take Caroline's hand, squeezing it tightly before he passed it on to Grafton.

All that Caroline would remember from the ceremony was a small child peeping in the parlor window, his flushed apple of a nose pressing firmly against the glass. When he finally drew himself back, his eyes met hers, and he grinned before running off.

After dinner, Grafton discovered Caroline alone in the dining room, hoping to grab a moment of respite. She tucked herself into a lone armchair concealed in the shadows of a back corner.

"Hiding from something?" He tilted his neck slightly.

"Never."

"You know, you may not realize it, but you and I are quite suitable, Caroline."

"How so?"

"We are both well-acquainted with our desires in this life, and neither of us shies away from pursuing them."

"What are your desires, my dear husband?"

"I'm going to be the wealthiest man in Annapolis."

"I see. And why would you require *me* for that?"

"It is said that a wife renders a man upright in character. Yet, of greater significance, she bestows upon him the *appearance* of integrity."

"So, it's all about appearances, then, is it?"

He stepped closer to her so no one else could hear. "My dear wife, please don't try to play the virtuous lady. We all know you find yourself in need of coin due to your father's indiscretions."

"There's only one person I see lacking discretion."

Grafton took a step back. "Uh, let us not quarrel on this, our very first evening as man and wife."

She stood. "Very well. Shall we take a walk, then? There's somewhere I'd like to take you." Caroline grabbed a thick shawl that hung near the back door before heading outside. Grafton followed curiously behind.

PART IV

A Surprise Encounter

"It's a bit frigid out, don't you think?" Grafton pressed.

Caroline stopped walking and turned to him. "Were you not in the Royal Navy before becoming a merchant? I imagine the ship's deck was a tad blusterier than this?"

"Yes, but circumstances forced me to remain there. On the day of my nuptials, I wish to keep warm."

"Well, I require some air. I'm fit to go alone if you would prefer it?" Caroline said while trudging on.

Grafton stopped and stared at her. Perhaps he was considering what the guests would think if they knew he'd allowed his new wife to venture out alone with evening's light casting a haunting glow down Hanover Street. He was likely weighing that fact against the deep chill coiling its way under his linen undershirt. Regardless, he chose to follow, catching up with her as they reached Maryland Avenue.

"Tell me about your mother," Caroline said without looking at him.

"She was troubled."

"In what manner?"

"Tis a lengthy tale," he said coolly.

They walked in silence all the way to State Circle and past the home they would soon share. Caroline felt the bitter air biting at her ankles as they briskly wandered through the dim, stretched shadows of the State House, finally arriving at adjacent Church Circle. Despite the demolition of St. Anne's Church earlier in the year to make way for a new one, the cemetery remained untouched.

Caroline led Grafton to her mother's gravestone. "I never made her acquaintance. She died on account of my birth. Yet, I trust her with my life's dealings. Not a word of ill repute have I once heard spoken about her."

Grafton was silent as the wind forced its way up Main Street, striking them with a punch.

Finally, he spoke. "You know, you mustn't believe everything you hear."

Caroline turned abruptly. "Are you referring to my mother?"

"I'm referring to myself."

"This has not a thing to do with *you*."

"This has *everything* to do with *me*."

Grafton leaned forward and pressed his lips firmly against Caroline's.

In shock, she stilled momentarily. *The nerve*, she then thought, kicking him directly in the shin. "How dare you plant a kiss right after insulting me!" she yelled.

Grafton began hopping on one foot, grabbing the tender, throbbing bone on his lower leg. "Good Lord! You bloody..." When he finally gained his composure, he turned to Caroline, "Clearly, I am the one who should be doubting my trust regarding *you*. What kind of *lady* does such a thing?" He turned and hobbled back toward her house without looking back.

Caroline took a seat on a nearby bench overlooking her mother's grave. Another frigid gale swept itself through her tightly wound bun, causing it to suddenly unravel. The lonely strands lashed against the tender, exposed skin on her face as she peered down at a single wooden cross holding itself up on the tombstone.

The fury inside her only grew. "How could you, Lord? Had she remained, Father never would have piddled our money away. She was his anchor, they say. Her worth surpassed us all combined. But you had to claim her for yourself. Damn you."

A soft snow began to fall, dusting the hillside and leaving a thin coat of milky-white across Caroline's shoulders.

"If you're looking down at me, Mother, I imagine what you're saying: 'Why are you always messing up, Caroline? How dare you curse God and scare away your husband on your own wedding day.'"

"That's not the sentiment your mother would have expressed," came a voice.

Caroline stood abruptly and turned to face a woman with a woven shawl wrapped loosely over her head. Caroline guessed her to be middle-aged, though her smooth face bore few wrinkles—she was quite beautiful. Snowflakes melted against her cheeks and onto the tip of her nose. Her eyes remained soft. "I didn't mean to startle you," the woman said.

"Do I know you?"

"No, but I am acquainted with you, as I knew your mother well. May I sit?"

Caroline nodded. From the bench, they both peered down at the small tombstone engraved with the words: *Lydia Collins, wife and mother, 1738-1757.*

"My name is Mary Reynolds. I'm the wife of William Reynolds, who owns the Beaver and Lac'd Hat Shop across the street."

"Uh, yes. My father frequents your shop."

"He's a close acquaintance of my husband."

"How did you know my mother?"

"Before our home became a tavern as well, we were simply a hattery and ordinary store. Your mother used to come for sundry goods each week. At that time, I was but a housekeeper for William, as his first and second wives had not yet passed. Many of the townspeople looked down their noses at me—a girl with no means. But not your mother. She'd ask about my day and go on complimenting how nicely I kept the place. I will never forget her kindness."

Caroline pulled her cloak in tighter but remained quiet.

"I'm so sorry you never got the chance to know her," Mary added genuinely.

"I appreciate your sentiments."

The snow began to plunge forth, spiraling around them mischievously.

"Come." Mary placed her hand on Caroline's shoulder. "The weather's turning. We must hasten back to my house."

"I need to make my way home."

Caroline turned toward the small lane that led toward the State House—a wall of white now separating her from it. "Not in this storm," she said. "Your father will understand."

"Uh, but what you must not realize is my father is already undoubtedly displeased with me, having the privilege of entertaining my wedding guests for quite some time now."

"Your wedding is *today*?"

"I see you hadn't heard."

"I was told you were marrying Mr. Brooks but did not know as to when. I understand your hesitation, but you mustn't walk home in this. What could be worse than a bride catching some awful ailment on her wedding day?"

Both of their lips were growing bluer by the second.

"Please, come warm your frozen limbs, and you can head back as soon as it passes."

"Very well," Caroline said, sighing loudly as she marched toward the Beaver and Lac'd Hat Shop, which would one day become known as Reynolds Tavern.

Caroline stepped into the sitting room and immediately felt the comfort of a roaring fire.

She melted into a small armchair that sat comfortably close to the hearth.

Mary handed her a steaming cup of mulled wine, then settled into the chair next to her, breathing warmth into what Caroline noticed were strong, weathered hands, before she spoke. "If it's any consolation, my wedding day didn't go as planned, either."

"How so?" Caroline asked as the distinct aromas of cinnamon, clove, and nutmeg filled her instantly.

"I had every last detail sorted through. I knew that even if others didn't agree with me marrying William, at least I'd make sure the rooms were scrupulously cleaned and there was not a speck of muttering that they took home even one flea or bedbug."

"I'd make sure they took home *both* if they were going to put up a fuss over who I chose to marry," Caroline assured her, pressing her lips to the porcelain cup and savoring the spiced, woody flavors. A soothing heat spread throughout her body.

Mary grinned. "Maybe I should have been more like you, my dear, not always so precise in trying to prove myself. But that is neither here nor there. So, after William and I had said our vows, we passed out tea. One of our guests, Mrs. Mildred Wilkins, was a close friend of William's second wife. She *accidentally* spilled tea all over the front of my pale-sage gown, and the entire room gasped. I was told later she'd been boasting about her plans to do so for weeks."

"What did you do?"

"I rushed to clean it and changed into a dress I cared not for. Do you know what I remember thinking as I exchanged gowns?"

Caroline didn't answer but waited for Mary's response.

"Either I allow a pathetic old woman to ruin my wedding, or I refuse to do so."

"Please tell me you spoiled her dress in return."

Mary laughed. "Don't presume the notion didn't cross my mind. Yet, if I returned to the wedding, *my wedding*, and acted out my desires, I would have forever been remembered as the vengeful bride. But if I rejoined the guests and enjoyed myself immensely, I would be seen as the joyful, unshaken bride. Plus, that doesn't mean I didn't slip a few cockroaches from the basement into someone's bed that night," she confessed, winking.

Caroline couldn't help but smile. "Clever. I'll speak candidly, though. I give little heed to how those attending my wedding will remember me."

Snowflakes in the window slowed their descent, as if hoping to gaze at the inviting fire, swaying and popping as it pleased.

"You hold your father's opinion in esteem, do you not?"

"Previously, I did not."

"He's grown unwell, hasn't he?"

"He attempts to conceal it."

"I've observed as much. My condolences, Caroline. I am always here if you need anything."

"Thank you."

"The storm has slowed, and I know you need to get back. I'll have a carriage readied for you out front. Can you yet sense your fingers?"

Caroline set down her cup and squeezed her hands together. "Thawed at last."

Just before walking out the front door, she turned to Mary. "I appreciate your hospitality immensely, Mrs. Reynolds."

Mary smiled and bowed her head.

"And for speaking about my mother. None wish to utter her name, as if discussing her is a grave sin."

"I imagine that's difficult. None desire to cause you pain."

"It wounds me deeper to behave as if she never existed."

Mary nodded. "I understand."

Caroline turned away quickly and entered the carriage, her horses clomping away through heaps of white powder.

When Caroline made it back to her home on Hanover Street, she hadn't left the carriage before Mrs. McGregor rushed out into the snow to greet her.

"Uh, lass, tis good to see ye back. Yer da is verra—"

"Concerned," she finished for her. "Yes, I imagine he is. Please tell my father I'm quite fine. I must change my shoes before I join the others, as they're soiled through from the weather."

"Aye, Miss."

Caroline hurried up the porch stairs before anyone saw her through the front windows. But when she opened her bedroom door and stepped inside, she startled.

Grafton was standing in her room.

Chapter 16

Topsail Island
January 2013

A soft knock vibrated through the front door, jolting Lorna from the story. She froze. A cold sensation shivered through her veins.

It's nine p.m. Surely Jack wouldn't have come so quickly.

Who in the world could that be?

She crept toward the front window.

The still dilapidated porch light was glowing as Lorna peered through her blinds and gasped.

She rushed back against the wall to avoid being seen. Her eyes widened as she cupped her hand over her mouth, trying to suppress any sharp, guttural sounds. Another knock came, and her cell phone shrieked on the coffee table.

Why would he show up like this? Ah, I hate surprises! I guess I have to answer it. Do I have to answer it? Oh, man—he drove all the way here. But I never agreed to this!

Half a minute passed, which felt like an eternity as Lorna deliberated over what to do.

Finally, she pulled the door open.

"Conor. Wow."

"Surprise." He slid his red, swollen hands in his pockets.

"I'm shocked."

"Is it good shocked or bad shocked?"

"Um...kind of just...super shocked."

"Not the answer I was hoping for, but I guess that's fair."

When Lorna was little, her father repeatedly warned her about letting someone into her home or into her life who she didn't truly know or trust.

But I do trust him. She combed through her uncertainty. *Don't I?*

"Can you just give me two seconds?" It was more of a statement than a question. Lorna closed the door in his face, slipped into jeans, grabbed a coat, and retrieved her car keys.

When she returned to the door, Conor was seated in a chair on the porch, blowing into his icy palms, his head bowed forward.

"That might not have been the kindest welcome—I'm just a bit surprised. Up for a drink?" Lorna tightly twisted the hair behind her ear.

"Sure," Conor returned, but his face looked like he was questioning everything.

They poured into Lorna's truck, and the scent of his cologne sucked itself inside her. Conor barely said a word on their way to a nearby dive bar. The place was practically empty with just a few locals braving the cold. Lorna chose two seats at the bar as that felt less intimate than a confined booth.

"I feel like I've totally freaked you out," he finally said, after shooting back a massive gulp of whiskey.

"No...no. I mean...it's just...well, how did you even find my place this time?"

"Once on the phone, you mentioned your next-door neighbor's lovely giant seahorse statue and how much you hated it. But that its only redeeming quality was it matched your peach-colored siding."

Lorna's eyebrows rose to attention. "That is true."

"I figured, how many pink cottages could there be in North Topsail? Not to mention with a huge matching seahorse beside it. And you said you could see the ocean between two beachfront properties, so I knew you were on Island Drive."

Lorna had no words.

"Okay, I probably should have asked. I've just always kind of preferred the element of surprise."

"Right. I just don't do as well with...surprises. But it is good to see you."

Conor rested his elbow against the bar and his fist against his cheek. *He certainly doesn't avoid eye contact*, she thought to herself while both hating and enjoying her attraction to him.

A song on the jukebox echoed in her ear, its lyrics whispering of inevitable goodbyes.

Suddenly, she was back riding in her truck with Will, about to drop him off on base for his deployment. Neither of them spoke the entire way. She wished she had said something-anything. But what was there to say? He already knew how much she'd miss him. Why did it have to be so damn cold that February morning? And why had that painfully sad song played on the radio, making it impossible to speak?

Lorna snapped back to the present and anxiously excused herself to the restroom. Once there, she locked herself inside a stall, turned her back against the door, and cradled her face in her hands. *Slow, deep breaths*, she tried to tell herself.

When she finally made it back out to the moldy restroom sink, Lorna eyed her makeup-free face in the mirror. The door creaked, and a petite, older woman with a short, cropped haircut and a soft Southern accent entered the narrow, two-stall bathroom.

"How ya doin', honey?"

"I'm all right, thanks." Lorna watched the bright-bubblegum-colored soap slide and slosh between her fingers, hoping to delay her return to Conor.

The woman stopped beside her, set her purse on the counter, and pulled out a tube of lipstick. "You don't have to be all right, you know. People are allowed to be upset."

"Is it that obvious?" Lorna replied without looking up.

"Not at all. I'm a mama and grandmama, and we just have a wayuh knowin'."

Lorna finally looked up at the reflection beside her in the mirror. The woman's lipstick matched the soap.

"Man problems?" the lady continued.

Lorna reached for a paper towel and crunched it into a ball. *I almost forgot how friendly and forward people are down here.* She forced a smile. "I guess you could say that."

"Always is. Time passes quickly. Why waste it on someone who brings you grief? Now, I won't lie—most of them *do*." The woman's laugh was genuine.

"You're right on that one." Lorna flipped her crumpled paper towel into the trash can. "Have yourself a good night."

"Poison and Wine" by the Civil Wars now played on the jukebox as she approached the bar, the slow, methodical echo of an acoustic guitar drifting forth. While Lorna was receiving an unsolicited bathroom intervention, Conor had finished another cocktail, which seemed to mellow him. He stood up to greet her. "Would it be too forward to ask for a dance?"

"You, too forward?" Her lips twisted to one side of her face.

He laughed aloud.

Despite his smile reminding her of how much she was drawn to him, Lorna still had no desire to dance. She was tired. Tired of being tired. Tired of being pushed into replacing someone irreplaceable.

But she finally agreed, telling herself that one dance wouldn't hurt.

Conor wrapped his arms around her, and Lorna's entire body stiffened with his touch. But a few moments later, with his breath gently warming the side of her neck, she slowly softened, and the tightness in her jaw gradually began to ease.

When they returned to the house and Conor started to get in his car to head to a hotel, she stopped him.

"You don't need to pay for a hotel. My couch is open."

"Are you sure? I know this was all a lot. I can come back in the morning?"

"Yeah, I'm sure."

Once inside, Conor found himself a spot in her blue chair while she foraged through the fridge and eventually came out with two bottles of water.

Conor looked at the side table next to him and lifted Allison's book. "What's this?"

"It's...it's something I've been reading. My husband's great-uncle gave it to me. Oh, you said you know Arthur?"

"Yeah, he's a little crazy."

"He is not crazy."

Conor smiled back at her. "What's the book about?" He twisted the bottle top until it clicked open and sucked down the water.

Lorna found a spot on the couch. "Well, it's a story about Arthur and Will's family, I guess you could say." She curled up on the couch with a blanket. "But it mostly focuses on one of his ancestors who lived during the American Revolution; her name was Caroline Collins. Then she became a Brooks—Caroline Brooks."

"She must be an interesting lady to get the key role in the history of someone's family."

"She is. It's funny and kind of weird. I can't seem to keep my mind off her."

"Wow. Should I be jealous of a dead woman?"

"Um, that would be even weirder, but based on previous conversations we've had, I think you'd find her intriguing too."

"Do tell..."

"Where to begin. Well, we first meet her on Whitehall Road, which is the road I grew up on."

"That's right. I almost passed it when I came to see you a few weeks ago. Just sort of hidden back there off Route 50."

"Yep, my friends and I used to drag race down it. Apparently, they did the same thing on horseback in the 1700s. The book describes how Caroline was racing a man on his stallion all the way to Whitehall mansion, which still stands today."

"I like her already."

"Yes, she didn't fit the status quo, that's for sure. It's sad, though..."

"What is?"

"She married this asshole she didn't love. It had to do with money. Her father was apparently a big-shot war hero, but he managed to gamble it all away, and she was left with nothing."

"Until she found herself a rich asshole she didn't like."

"Right. Except he wasn't especially rich when she married him. He had means, but he was very ambitious and aspired to be the wealthiest man in Annapolis."

"I see. Then what happened?"

"I don't know yet."

"Well, read on, then." He tossed Lorna the book.

"Seriously? Now? As in, read-aloud time?" She grinned awkwardly.

"Absolutely," he pushed. "I wanna see how she does with the asshole."

WHERE THE FOXGLOVES BLOOM

By Allison Brooks

PART V

UNPREDICTABLE

"What are you doing in here?" Caroline crossed her arms across her chest as she studied Grafton, lurking near her bed.

He turned to her. "I just wrote a letter at your desk. There's not a proper drafting spot in your father's guest room."

"Why are you not downstairs with our guests?"

"I could ask you the same."

"I got caught in a snowstorm atop the hill. Remember, it was where you left me."

"Yes, I recall, because it's the very same spot you struck me on our wedding day. Clearly, your temper is menacing."

"As are your words."

He stepped closer to her. "Let's make something properly straight. I am your husband and will not tolerate disrespect."

"And I am your wife. I will not tolerate any dishonor."

Grafton laughed, adding with a snide tone, "You speak like the women up north. All sorts of backward ideas about a lady's standing in society." His voice lowered. "And in her home."

Caroline stepped toward him, inches now all that separated them. "Then you understand what I need. Civility begets civility. I will make an honest man out of you to the rest of the world if you show me the courtesy assumed by a partnership behind closed doors."

"A partnership? Is it in order that I pass my ledger on to you too?"

"I've helped to maintain my father's. I would handle it with care."

"You are something, Mrs. Brooks."

His face drew closer to hers, so near she could feel his breath.

Surprising even herself, she leaned in and touched her lips to his.

His posture stiffened as she pulled back, releasing herself from him, but their eyes remained locked.

Grafton grabbed her wrists, but Caroline twisted out of his grasp, squeezing his hands into hers instead. Their bodies moved magnetically inward, their lips drawing together again—so tightly this time, they gasped when pulling away.

She lowered his pants, and he, her undergarments. They never undressed fully or desired the comforts of Caroline's bed, the cold floor suiting them both just fine.

When Grafton shuffled to his room across the hall afterward, Caroline noticed the necklace Charity had given her had fallen from her neck and into the crack between two floorboards. She retrieved the dainty chain and locket, clutching them tightly, fully aware that her heart was still throbbing violently in her chest. Caroline had reminded herself before the wedding not to grow attached to Grafton in any way, particularly concerning intimacy. She intended to fulfill her expected duties as a wife but understood that desire could be perilous.

It left oneself unimaginably vulnerable.

This was why, following their encounter, she resented both the tingling sensation that had spread across her skin, as well as the unbridled passion she had drawn from Grafton's lips. Their combined intensity felt as rapturous as it was terrifying. A formidable knot tightened inside her stomach as she pulled on her stockings and returned to the guests.

When Caroline descended the steps, she noticed a man at the bottom looking up at her. He had skittish eyes and a forced smile. "May I dare to be the first to call you Mrs. Brooks?"

"As long as I first know what to call you?"

"My name is Andrew Moore. I will be your neighbor when you move into your new home by the State House. I manage the Maryland Inn and live there with my wife, Rebecca."

"And how do you know my…How do you know Mr. Brooks?"

"We're both merchants. Our paths cross often."

"Apparently so if he invited you to our wedding."

Mr. Moore laughed sheepishly. "We've known each other for many years now."

"Oh, then you can attest to his character?"

"Quite so."

"And...?"

"Are you asking me to vouch for your husband, ma'am?" He stepped back, mouth agape.

"I am."

"Is that not customarily done prior to the nuptial ceremony?"

"It seems you're having trouble applying a proper compliment to him, which is telling in itself."

"I beg your pardon. I meant no offense." The color abandoned his face.

Caroline began to snicker. "I jest with you, Mr. Moore. I am quite aware of Mr. Brooks's merits and feel indelibly honored to be his wife."

"As you should be," Mr. Moore returned.

"I do have one final question," Caroline added.

"Inquire freely."

"Does he always have a way of sneaking up on people?"

"Predictability is not his natural tendency. I suppose it's why he and I excel in our business dealings with one another. I also prefer it not."

"Good. Nor do I."

Chapter 17

January 2013

Lorna looked up from the book to see Conor slouched in her chair, asleep. She stood, spread a thick blanket across the couch, and found a spare pillow in the closet. Finally, she touched his shoulder and whispered, "Why don't you try the couch? You'll sleep better."

Conor's eyelids slowly peeled open, and it seemed to dawn on him where he was. He then rose and fled to the sofa. Lorna watched him fall back to sleep before turning off the living room lights, brushing her teeth, pulling on pajamas, and slipping into bed.

Despite the overwhelming nature of her day, she disappeared into a dreamless sleep somewhat easily.

But a few hours later, a sound in her bedroom startled her.

Lorna's eyes shot open to discover a shadowy presence looming over her.

The nearest nightlight cast a soft glow in the room, just slightly illuminating a man's distinct profile, silhouetted beside her dresser.

There was the distinct sliding rattle of a zipper unfastening.

Was he undoing his pants?

Though incredibly bewildered, Lorna switched on her bedside lamp. "Conor, what are you doing!?"

He didn't respond but stepped toward her dresser and began urinating in an open bottom drawer.

"Stop!"

But he didn't.

She jumped out of bed and forcefully shoved him from behind. "You're peeing on my socks!"

Conor suddenly pulled back, his eyelids fluttering, confusion marked across his face.

Lorna sighed heavily and shook her head. "So, you're a sleep-walker. Great."

"Wait, what?" Conor's eyes began darting around the room as he instinctively zipped up his pants.

She took his shoulder and led him back to the couch, where he thankfully fell back to sleep immediately.

Lorna threw all nine pairs of her socks in the wash and went straight to bed.

She pulled her comforter up to her neck, rolling from side to side, her body tense. She found herself unable to sleep.

So many thoughts swirled, but as always, they landed back on Will. Wouldn't he just be howling? She could almost hear him: "That's what you get for letting this random dude in."

You're the one who woke me in the night with the weird dream that led me to Galway Bay! she nearly said aloud.

Lorna reached for her cell phone. While she recognized the desperation in a 3 a.m. Google search, she also believed that distraction might be the only way to quell her inner imaginary fight with her deceased husband.

She clicked inside the Google search engine and quickly typed "Conor Delaney."

"Only 1.5 million results," *Annoying.* One was a doctor, one a farmer, and one a murderer. *Guess we're gonna need to break this down a bit.* She knew he wasn't from Annapolis. *Where did he move from, though?* She'd have to pry that out of him tomorrow.

Still certain sleep would be a fight, Lorna wondered who else she could Google. She clicked back to the search engine and typed "Author Allison Brooks."

Much better. Photos of one woman immediately popped up. Long, dark hair and bright-blue eyes stared back at her. But Allison's smile was where Lorna's gaze lingered. In every single photograph (her professionally done headshots, her author-event group shots, the snapshot of her signing a copy of her book for an adoring fan), her smile was flawless. Genuine. Perfect. Happy.

Arthur said Allison had a son, so likely there was an adoring husband too.

Next was a photo of Arthur with his arm wrapped snuggly around Allison, the two of them grinning from ear to ear. Of course, she had the luxury of growing up with a father who was one of the nicest, most put-together men Lorna had ever met—an accomplished and respected professor who desperately loved Allison, his only child.

She clicked on her webpage. The words "Bestselling Author" caught her eye first.

Scrolling down, all of Allison's book covers popped up. *How in the world does someone write this many novels?*

Suddenly, something annoyingly uncomfortable crept up inside her, but she couldn't stop herself from feeling it. *Her life. I want her life.*

The more Lorna scrolled, the worse she felt, so she set her cell back on the nightstand, rolled onto her side, and curled into a tight ball.

Just as she was about to give up on sleep, she sank into a deep, dream-laden slumber. Darkness gave way to sunlight, which poured across her skin. The rhythmic echo of waves uncoiling at their breaking point reached her ears as she peered out at the ocean, her toes nestled in the warmth of the sand—just shy of the water's edge.

After a few moments of taking in the new scenery, she turned left, then right.

Will always wanted to head right—south, toward Surf City.

He loved grabbing a drink at Daddy Mac's, a laidback restaurant on the water.

Lorna, on the other hand, had always preferred the other direction. She liked the leisurely pace of North Topsail, where winsome beach homes lined the coast, serenaded at all hours by the sea. During the cooler months, one could stroll for miles without seeing a soul.

But on this occasion, an aching for Will led her south.

As she strode along, a sudden gust of wind came skimming off the emerald-blue water, spiraling her hair about her head, stopping her in her tracks, and leaving the path before her sightless.

When she finally cleared her eyes, the outline of a man became clear in the distance. He was staring out at the horizon. As she drew closer, her stomach plummeted. Will. It was Will.

She started to sprint, gliding across the wet sand where the waves broke, but with every step, he slowly began to fade, his body slipping away into the midday haze.

"No! Come back!" Lorna begged as she finally reached the spot he'd been standing. She fell on her knees, gasping for breath.

Then, just beyond her, something appeared from the corner of her eye. What was it there, half buried in the sand with its corner sticking out? A book? Possibly, but it seemed too thin. Maybe a notebook? She immediately crawled toward it, her chest heaving, and peeled it from the beach. Its bleached-gray cover was simple and unassuming. Opening it, Lorna realized the pages were completely blank. An empty sketchbook? What did that even mean? She flipped through it to be sure, stopping halfway—well, not entirely empty. A penciled sketch filled the space, its lines decisive yet delicate. The face of a little girl, so simple and soft, yet profoundly beautiful. Lorna's finger drew itself like a magnet to her sweptback hair, narrow eyes, and rounded jaw—tracing the lines carefully. Her gaze turned back to the girl's eyes, fixed sharply off to one side as if on the alert. Watching. Waiting.

Lorna looked around, hoping he'd somehow appear again. And yet something inside her shifted. The desperation and frustration—always so tight within her chest, lessened ever so slightly. "Who is she, Will?"

Could it be Caroline as a girl, or someone else I haven't read about yet?

Without warning, another penetrating breeze came dashing off the tide, covering her and the sketchbook in a layer of mist, which shifted into a piercing black as she awoke, disoriented and alone under her sheets. The glowing digits on her bedside clock read 3:56 a.m.

After realizing what a lonely hour stretched before her, Lorna groaned and rolled deflated onto her back. Still uncomfortable, she curled restlessly onto her side, and when her eyes adjusted to the dark, she noticed the book on her nightstand. After gathering enough energy, she turned on the lamp and immersed herself in Caroline's world for nearly an hour. Eventually, she drifted back to sleep and didn't awaken until 9:00 a.m.

When Lorna entered the living room, she found Conor asleep on her couch, with his long legs squeezed inward. He sprang up, though, when the coffee began brewing and insisted on fixing them breakfast.

Lorna jabbed her fork into the airy pancake he'd just slid her way. She hesitated, then spoke without looking up, "So, was this the first time you peed in someone's sock drawer?"

"I'm sorry, what?"

"Last night..." she began, but stopped, allowing his brain to search for the memory it had so willingly buried.

Shock filled his face. "Oh no. I told myself that was a dream."

Lorna continued chomping on her breakfast, a slight grin growing gradually.

"I am *so* incredibly sorry."

"It could have been worse."

"How?"

"Well, you could have been awake and just had a weird fetish for peeing on people's things."

Conor pressed his palm against his forehead. "Wow, I

shouldn't have had that last drink. Alcohol tends to bring out the sleepwalker in me."

Lorna pressed her teeth together. "Noted."

"I'm surprised you didn't kick me out."

"I considered it. But that felt like a lot of effort."

"Right." Silence filled the space until Conor finally spoke again. "Okay, I'd desperately like to change the subject."

"Fine by me."

"Did I also fall asleep during the story?"

"I wish I could say you didn't miss some good stuff."

"I remember the bedroom scene," Conor smiled. "But nothing after that."

"You missed quite a bit." Lorna squeezed her fingers around her coffee mug. "Including everything I read last night when I couldn't sleep."

"Going on without me, I see. That hurts."

"In my defense, I had to do laundry at three o'clock in the morning."

"Okay, I suppose I deserve it, then. Will you fill me in at least?"

"I'll reread what I just read. After Grafton and Caroline's wedding, the next chapter is a year later. The war is in full swing, and we're thrown aboard a British warship for a moment to get a feel for some super secretive and vitally important package. Then we connect back with Caroline for a deadly fire that doesn't seem to have been an accident."

Conor's eyebrows rose over the brim of his coffee mug. He swallowed quickly. "Do tell."

WHERE THE FOXGLOVES BLOOM

By Allison Brooks

PART VI

A Mysterious Package

Chesapeake Bay
August 1777

"GUARD IT WITH YOUR LIFE," the British admiral whispered sternly, his wide palms tightly gripping the small tin box.

The midshipmen nodded slowly, his white neckcloth glowing in the lantern light, its fit suddenly more constricting.

The admiral continued, "I would have delegated this critical undertaking to a higher-ranking officer, but I need someone as dependable as they are strong and agile."

As well as slightly more expendable should anything happen to me after the drop-off, the midshipman couldn't help but surmise. "I understand, sir."

A commanding breeze shot across the choppy water of the Chesapeake, sweeping over the wide, swollen floor planks of the ship before slipping itself between the two men and mischievously dashing off toward the nearest sleeping town along Maryland's sandy coast.

The midshipman looked out into the night; a Royal Navy frigate loomed inside the fog on HMS *Eagle's* port side—just one of the 270 British ships traveling north with them.

The admiral continued, "Our mission to transport the army toward Philadelphia is certainly paramount, but how I despise having to leave this behind."

What could he possibly have in there? the midshipman contemplated, trying to remain focused. "I assure you, no one will find it, sir."

The admiral nodded. "I'm counting on it. As dawn breaks, the front echelon of our fleet will pass Annapolis. At that moment, deploy a longboat and look for a pointed strip of land jutting out into the bay, just east of the city; they call it Greenbury Point. A Loyalist farmer owns the property. Bury the box there and prepare a map to assure we know the precise location. Secure three of the farmer's horses and hasten with the map northward to Maryland's Elk Landing where we'll be making landfall. You will retrieve my possession on our way back down the Chesapeake."

Letting go proved to be an insurmountable task for the admiral. However, with austere hesitation, he finally entrusted the small metal container to the midshipman. "Two armed sailors will escort you on your journey."

The young officer pulled the parcel into his chest. He could feel his heart thumping adamantly against it. "Yes, sir."

"The fate of the war rests on your shoulders. If this is lost—all is lost."

PART VII

An Anonymous Contributor

Annapolis
Ten days later

"Have you read the Maryland Gazette?" Molly inquired as she watched a heaping scoop of liberty tea leaves travel from the tea canister to the caddie spoon and into the large silver teapot.

Caroline then poured a steaming kettle of water into the pot. *Of course she's inquiring. She can't help but check up on me.* "No, not recently."

"Are you all right, Caroline?"

"I'm fine." She stood straighter with an impassive expression, refusing to take her eyes off the task at hand.

"You seem a bit out of sorts today." Molly hesitated when her friend didn't answer and continued, "As for the gazette, an anonymous contributor to the paper wrote about a courageous sixteen-year-old girl named Sybil Ludington, who just this past spring, allegedly rode forty miles atop her horse to muster militia after a British attack on the town of… Oh, what was the name?"

"Danbury," Caroline quickly explained.

"Uh, yes, Danbury." Molly surreptitiously eyed her hostess as Caroline passed her a teacup.

Molly pulled the newspaper clipping from the pocket of her dress and began to read aloud, "Press on Patriot. For our cause, we must choose to sacrifice a million-fold. What greater gift can we give to one another, and our children, than the birth of freedom? This astounding opportunity has arrived, so may we seize it."

Molly placed the slightly crumpled paper next to her cup and saucer, while Caroline tightly gripped the teapot's handle and filled her friend's porcelain cup, releasing the fragrant aromas of locally grown peppermint, rosehips, lemon, and raspberry leaves into the parlor air.

Lifting the teacup, Molly peered at her friend from behind its rim before clinking it quietly down in her saucer and whispering, "You wrote it, didn't you?"

Caroline poured herself tea without saying a word.

Molly looked behind her to make sure no one had entered before continuing, "Most of the men wouldn't have brought up Sybil. You're trying to rally the women. I applaud your bravery, but I beg you to be careful. As much as I admire your fervent enthusiasm for the cause and your willingness to inspire other patriots, Caroline, you are with child, and the risk you take writing those words against the crown is more dangerous than you know."

Caroline finally spoke. "You'd say the same if you could."

"But I cannot. You know our ties to England. We have no choice but to remain neutral. It would be foolish otherwise."

Caroline took a seat, sipped her tea, and peered back at Molly. "I understand, but I, for one, will not sit back and watch as something incredibly egregious is happening to our people."

"Caroline, what would Grafton say if he found out you were secretly writing to the gazette?"

He would lose his wits, Caroline couldn't help but imagine, yet said nothing.

Molly pulled her seat in closer to Caroline and again checked to make sure no one had entered the room. "I realize Grafton presents himself as a Patriot, given the city's current allegiance, but there are whispers everywhere that he's spying for the British." Molly clutched Caroline's hands and continued, "Then there's this business with Isaac Abbott's valuable painting of his late wife suddenly going missing from Grafton and Mr. Moore's tunnel. I'm afraid you suddenly have more enemies than friends because of your husband's diminishing reputation. You saw it four years ago when the *Peggy Stewart* went down. The mob is merciless. They grow uneasy once more, and curiously, your own gazette writings may push them closer to insurrection. Imagine if your own rallying cry shows up at your door. What if they turn on you and harm your unborn child?"

Caroline's eyes grew fierce. How little Molly understood about the rage she felt toward England. Naturally, the motherland helped make Molly's family "known" and incredibly wealthy. Her grandfather had been a member of Parliament, and her father, a former captain in the British Army, had been appointed governor of Annapolis three times over. But Caroline's own father was the son of an injured English military man who left his family with little means when he died, just as Colonel Collins had done to her. She understood that authorities often took more than they gave and that one had to make their *own* way in the world.

"Molly, what sort of life will I be passing on to my child if we allow the British to possess us like mere livestock, telling us what we can and cannot do, stealing our coin on a whim? Full control without even a single representative in Parliament. I'd sooner die than abandon our cry for freedom."

"I understand, but..." Molly took in a shallow breath. "Please come with me back to Whitehall. Your child might make an early appearance. Please, Caroline, this town is full of peril. You don't have to abandon your beliefs by choosing to seek refuge. John and

I believe in the same principles as you, but we choose to keep the safety of our family paramount."

Caroline glanced inconspicuously down at the sizable bump on her midsection and stood. She adjusted her dress, which had grown tighter by the day, then looked back at her friend. "I cannot. You've always looked out for me, Molly, and I am forever indebted. But I will not leave."

"I told your father, before he passed, that I'd be here for you. Now let me be here for you." Molly rose and stepped toward Caroline. "You must come. I feel it deeply and gravely."

Clumsy footsteps clomped across the wide-plank pine floors.

Caroline turned. "Yes, Mrs. McGregor?"

"Uh Mr. Isaac Abbott tis at the front door lookin' to see Mr. Brooks."

What dreadful timing. "Please tell him he's not home."

"I told 'im nay an' he tisn't leavin'. He's verra insistent on seein' someone. Says he's not leavin' til he gets the piece uh priceless art that's been stolen from 'im—that tis a Charles Peale piece or somethin' or other."

Caroline felt her stomach tighten. *Of course, he's angry. Why wouldn't he be enraged that someone stole a Peale painting of his deceased wife? Especially considering he's not nearly as well-to-do as the other men who'd paid to put their belongings in Grafton's tunnel.* She lifted her chin. "I'll speak with him."

Molly stepped forward. "Caroline, this man sounds irate. I advise you not to get involved."

"Don't ye worry, Miss Caroline, he won't be gettin' beyond me," Mrs. McGregor assured her.

But Caroline fled past them both toward the front door, flinging it open to a well-dressed, middle-aged man with disheveled hair, a flushed face, and livid eyes.

Caroline spoke first. "Mr. Abbott, I heard the painting of your wife has gone missing, and I assure you my husband and Mr. Moore are combing the city to figure out who has taken it."

Mr. Abbott drew himself a step closer to Caroline, as if his raised voice weren't enough. "I'll tell you who. We've all noticed several unknown visitors entering this very doorstep, many of which are rumored to have Tory leanings and would undoubtedly enjoy stealing from a local Patriot. Any of them could have learned of the tunnel and entered it through *your* basement."

It was Caroline's turn to take a step closer to her visitor. "Mr. Abbott, I watch over this entryway like a hawk. Whoever confiscated your painting did not possess it during my watch."

"So, you accuse Mr. Moore of purloining it from his end of the tunnel?"

Caroline's voice rose as she said, "I have not."

Mr. Abbott's scowl grew menacing. "I want the rest of my goods from that tunnel this very instant."

"I cannot allow you to enter it until my husband returns, as the tunnel is *his* endeavor."

"I want nothing to do with your lying, crown-loving husband."

"Then I suppose you won't be able to collect your things."

"Oh, I'll be back, I promise you that."

Caroline slammed the door shut and stepped into the dining room, fuming as she watched Issac Abbott stomp angrily away. Passing him, but headed toward Caroline's home, was another man, this one taller with a far more fluid gait, yet he too made no attempt to hide his own formidable scowl.

Caroline's breath caught. She knew he was heading straight for her doorstep, but once again, with Molly there, the timing could not have been worse.

She rushed back to the front door, hoping she could speak to him alone, but Molly was already there, standing flustered in the foyer. "Is everything all right?"

Hoping not to look unnerved, Caroline kept her reply short. "Of course."

A sharp, inevitable knock resounded off the door.

"Another visitor?" Molly pressed.

Caroline drew her shoulders back. "I need you to return to the parlor."

Molly's brows pursed together. "What *else* are you trying to hide?"

A heaviness descended on Caroline's shoulders. "I would explain more, but..." Her heart rate rose rapidly, and before Caroline even knew what she was doing, she reached toward Molly and grabbed her forearm with an unrestrained fierceness, pulling her into the parlor. "Honestly, you need to await my return."

"Caroline! Unhand me!"

The pitch of Molly's voice both shocked and somehow simmered Caroline's rage, at least momentarily. She hadn't heard Molly yell like that since she was a girl. Thirteen-year-old Caroline had stolen a piece of venison from the open market near the docks. Unfortunately for her, Molly didn't miss a detail. So, when Caroline showed up at the Ridouts' downtown home with a tightly bound fist, Molly swept her into the dining room, away from her father's gaze, and reprimanded the teenager for her unlawful behavior. Caroline was accustomed to her father's constant anger, but without a mother to admonish her, it all felt strange, foreign really, yet oddly comforting—just as it did at this very moment.

Caroline released Molly's arm.

Although slightly enraged, Molly took a breath and continued, "You do know about the giant fleet of British ships that passed by our shores just the other day?"

Caroline straightened. "Indeed."

"Those standing near the bay said it looked like a sea of red, and it could have been a sea of red on our shores had they chosen to stop here. Rumor has it Britain's General Howe and his brother, Admiral Howe, considered attacking Annapolis. Thankfully for us, they have instead headed north toward Philadelphia. But our time is likely coming. Writing anonymously in the gazette is one thing, but having involved parties coming directly to your home is another."

If she's fretting now, wait until she finds out just how entrenched I am, Caroline ruminated.

Mrs. McGregor entered the foyer, looking slightly confused. "Miss Caroline, I heard uh knock. May I let in yer visitor?"

"Thank you, but I'll manage myself."

As Mrs. McGregor excused herself, Molly pressed, "When is Grafton returning?"

"In a few hours. All is well," Caroline said, once again fixing the midsection of her gown just before pulling on the brass doorknob to open the door.

The man's face was pale, his eyes darting.

"Good day, sir." Caroline stepped back so he could enter.

"Good day, ma'am." He stepped inside, reaching for his tricorn hat and bowing, but his sneer remained.

"Why so troubled?" Caroline pushed.

"I've heard rumors."

"I am not my husband," Caroline assured him confidently.

"That's not for me to decide." The man lowered his voice to a whisper. "I am only here because Captain Pierce insists on it."

The man reached into an interior coat pocket and pulled out a folded slip of paper. He passed it to Caroline, bowed again, and was gone.

Molly's cheeks grew further flushed. "Captain Pierce? You're working with my cousin, Thomas? You're directly aiding the Continental Army?"

Caroline peeled apart the creases of paper, studying the note as she spoke. "I cannot explain the particulars."

"Of course not." Molly huffed, eyeing a magenta shaded bruise on Caroline's wrist.

"How did you harm yourself this time? Last month it was a swollen eye. You ought to be more careful."

"I fell from my horse."

"You're still riding?"

Caroline's gaze remained on the note until she hastily refolded the paper and tucked it away in her dress pocket.

"Caroline, if Thomas knew you were carrying a child, he would never entangle you in such matters."

"I'll make that judgment."

"My friend, you are telling me you're aiding the Continentals from this very home while your husband may be corresponding with the enemy? This will not conclude favorably."

Mrs. McGregor, utterly breathless, having just entered the house from a side entrance, returned once more to the foyer. "Miss Molly, yer carriage awaits ye out front."

After grabbing her cloak, Molly made her way back to Caroline. "Bring it."

"Bring what?"

"The note he gave you. I'll take the risk. I cannot leave you here. Please come with me. You have a child to protect."

"Which is exactly why I have to act, and I cannot do it while hiding away at Whitehall."

Molly's face grew solemn. "I only wish to protect you."

"And I you. You must go now to reach home before nightfall."

Molly slipped away, unable to hide her defeated expression. If only she could understand, it was Caroline trying to protect her.

PART VIII

A Fright in the Night

Caroline climbed the stairs to her bedroom, swiftly shutting the door behind her and pulled the note from her dress. A hand-drawn map filled the bottom half of a wrinkled sheet. On it, a few curvy black lines wove around a single square, and near the map's center were three large circles with a smudged "X" just beneath them. Above the map was a brief letter from Thomas.

For months, Caroline had pressed her childhood friend—now a captain in the Continental Army and one of Gen. George Washington's intelligence officers—to allow her to help the rebel cause. Despising the idea of putting her in danger, Thomas pushed back. But Caroline was relentless and assured him she'd prove valuable. He finally acquiesced, but only on the condition that she agreed to employ a technique to encode messages within their correspondence.

. . .

Dear Caroline,

I hope you are well, my friend. I am filled with plentiful remorse that I could not attend your father's funeral. His indomitable spirit and courageous military career will live on in our memories.

I know not how my mother is doing as she is unable to write because of her condition. Graciously stop by and see her, won't you? I've attached a map of where she's staying with a friend. Though it's quite crude, I know you'll recognize the location.

When you see my dear cousin Molly, send her my love, and please let her know I think often of her, John, and the children.

With heartfelt gratitude,
Thomas

Immediately, Caroline surmised the map was not there to find Thomas's mother, but its purpose and location remained a mystery.

She grabbed a small taper candle, lit it quickly, and steadied the flame just below the letter, close enough to heat it, but far enough away for the paper not to catch.

At that moment, Caroline knew not that the map had to do with the much talked about event around town, the one Molly had just reminded her of, which had occurred just ten days prior when the waters along Annapolis received surprise visitors. The British Royal Navy's 270-ship fleet shocked locals as it traveled up the Chesapeake and passed their homes on August 21st.

Fear had spread throughout town. Were they coming for *them*?

Gen. William Howe, commander-in-chief of the entire British Army, was part of the fleet, riding aboard the HMS *Eagle*, a massive 64-cannon warship. Joining him on deck was his older brother, Adm. Richard Howe, who oversaw the British Royal Navy. He was there to escort his younger brother's immense army to Elk Landing in Maryland so they could march north and overtake the city of Philadelphia.

When the Howe brothers left New Jersey six weeks prior, the Continental Army assumed they were heading to Philadelphia through the Delaware River. While that would have been the fastest route, the brothers knew that rebel troops had heavily fortified the banks of the Delaware. So, instead, they chose to surprise Washington's army by taking the much lengthier route and heading up the Chesapeake Bay with their 17,000 soldiers and sailors.

As the British fleet passed Annapolis early on that summer morning, a local elderly man, who lived just east of town on the Broadneck Peninsula, noticed a longboat carrying three British sailors to shore. He immediately sent a letter to his son, a Continental soldier, stationed nearby with Captain Pierce.

To maintain secrecy, Pierce dispatched a spy to track down the British sailors in Annapolis. The spy serendipitously encountered the trio at a tavern just outside town. Posing as a Loyalist, the Rebel operative befriended them over drinks and learned that one of the sailors, a midshipman, possessed a map. In his inebriated state, the naval officer disclosed to Pierce's agent that Adm. Richard Howe had tasked them with concealing a highly important package. Despite being unaware of its contents, they had buried a locked metal box on Loyalist property and crafted a map that they were taking to Elk Landing. Admiral Howe intended to retrieve the box on his journey back down the Chesapeake.

The spy bought the midshipman a final drink and quietly pocketed his map.

Word reached Captain Pierce that the map was in their possession and that it represented a rural area just east of Annapolis. Thomas, who was busy trying to determine which route the newly landed British soldiers were taking toward Philadelphia, instructed them to take the map to the one person who knew that area best—Mrs. Caroline Brooks. With her father often away on military campaigns, she spent most of her childhood riding her grandfather's horses along those same dirt roads on the Broadneck Peninsula.

As Caroline continued to hold the candle below the letter, she noticed nothing new had emerged on the paper. Had he not used the hidden-ink technique he told her he would? She raised the candle's amber tip just slightly closer. *Oh dear, this map is likely to take fire if I draw any nearer.* Suddenly the door slammed. Grafton was home. She buried the letter inside the top drawer of her dressing table and waited silently at the top of the stairs.

Judging by the heaviness in Grafton's footsteps, she could tell he was in a foul mood. Caroline was far from surprised, as this was often the case. It was the sound of Andrew Moore's voice that she didn't expect, as he never accompanied Grafton home in the evening.

Caroline glided quietly down the steps and into the foyer, stopping just short of Grafton's study to listen.

"Damn it, Moore, we're going to lose considerable income over this. They'll all pull their possessions out now!" Grafton groaned, slamming his palms against the desk, causing Caroline to shudder slightly. "I need this money. I've lost so much in my shipping ventures on account of these privateering scoundrels."

In a softer tone, Andrew said, "I assure you Abbott's painting was not stolen from my end of the tunnel. It could not have been. Like I've always told you, the basement door of the Maryland Inn is kept bolted and I am the only one who possesses a key."

After throwing back a glass of sherry, Grafton scoured the *Maryland Gazette* instead of responding.

Caroline entered the room, eyeing the crimson liquid on his desk then turned to their guest. "Mr. Moore, shall I have Mrs. McGregor fetch you a drink?"

"Thank you, but I am just leaving," he answered.

"Your wife," Grafton interjected, still holding the newspaper in front of his face.

"Pardon me?" Andrew turned to him, something in his eyes suddenly shifting.

Grafton lowered the paper, staring straight at his business partner and slowly pronouncing each word: "Your wife has a key to the tunnel."

Caroline felt an ominous presence forcing its way into the room, extinguishing any hint of the goodwill they'd once shared.

Andrew's face paled. "Why would you presume I'd given her a key?"

Caroline knew exactly what Grafton was doing—preying on the man's insecurities with his wife. Rebecca was a fine woman, but she did not love Andrew the way he loved her.

"I didn't presume. She told me," Grafton said calmly.

He's slowly twisting the knife.

Mr. Moore stood as still as a stone, his lower jaw jutting suddenly outward. "And when were you talking to *my* wife?"

"Rebecca told me she keeps her canned goods inside the tunnel because you ran out of room in the inn's basement." Grafton stood abruptly, tossing the newspaper onto his desk. "Why would you lie to me? What is a partnership without trust?"

Andrew fumed. "That's an excellent question. One I'm wondering myself." Without another word, he grabbed his coat and fled from the room.

Caroline squeezed her fists as the front door slammed shut. "Are you still heading north in the morning?"

"Yes," Grafton returned, a haughty expression etched across his face.

A chill swept through her. "Well, I'm off to bed." Caroline started for the stairs.

Grafton's voice boomed behind her, "Who was the man who entered our home this afternoon?"

Caroline stopped, her body stiffening and spoke without turning, "He had a letter from my old friend, Thomas."

"I wish to see it," Grafton countered coldly.

"Whatever for, dear husband?" Caroline asked through gritted teeth, her palms growing moist as she pressed them stiffly together.

"Just get the letter, Caroline."

She trudged up to her bedroom, taking Thomas's letter in her hand and studying it carefully to make sure its brief encounter with the candle hadn't changed the paper's coloring. Eventually returning to Grafton's study, she realized he was no longer there, his sherry half drunk on his desk. Caroline reached inside the pocket of her dress.

A few moments later, Grafton approached her from behind and snatched the letter from her grasp. Immediately, his gaze fell to the map.

"What is this?"

"His mother. He asked me to visit his mother at that location?"

"Where is she staying?"

"I haven't had the time yet to discern *where*."

Grafton chewed on his lower lip as he scrutinized Thomas's words. "He says you'll know immediately where it is from the map."

Shoving the letter back toward her, she gratefully rescued it from his grip.

Her hand shook slightly as she drew the paper behind her back. "I'll have to delve deeper into it, but for now I'm fatigued and needing to retire. First, I aim to catch myself a cup of warm milk."

Grafton explored her face, the fine line between his eyebrows coiling inward. "Milk?"

"Since I've been with child, it's been a comfort to ease myself to bed." Without another word, Caroline dashed to the cellar and returned to her bedroom with the milk she'd purchased for such an occasion. Dusk was slipping through her windows, so she lit several candles which faintly illuminated her bedroom in flickering light. *Focus*, she told herself and opened the map. *To send me this letter, considering his courier's mistrust of Grafton, this must be of considerable importance, and time is likely of the essence.*

She once again placed a candle just inches below Thomas's letter, moving it ever so slowly, her hand still shaking under its transformative glow.

What are you trying to tell me, Thomas?

He'd had a messenger explain to her several weeks prior to hold a candle flame near a piece of correspondence so that its heat would activate the invisible message he'd be writing to her, but this was her first time actually having to do so.

Sweat formed along Caroline's hairline as she stared at the jet-black ink twirling itself across the page. She continued to circle the flame beneath it, listening for Grafton's footsteps.

I must be doing something wrong.

Then came a single letter, shooting up at her like the first star to pierce the night's sky. It was a rich brown "T" appearing between the already visible lines of text. Caroline held her breath as she continued to heat the note, other letters suddenly emerged as well, the line breaks now filled with the newly formed words:

IDENTIFY THE LOCATION OF THE MAP AND LEAVE IT AT THE SPOT. IT IS SOMEWHERE EAST OF TOWN. MAKE HASTE.

Make haste.

East of town.

I must know this.

Her heart quickened as she scanned the map once again, taking in every line, shape, and potential marker.

Drat! What a dreadfully drawn sketch!

The roads were sparse, and just one simple square was hard to go by. But the circles. Her eyes kept returning to the circles. Their size—so large, and...*three* of them.

She gasped. *Could it be?* Her eyes darted to one of roads as it split suddenly to form a "Y"—how had she not noticed it before? A fork in the road next to the square which was placed northeast of the circles. *Yes, it must be.* A spark lit inside her.

Sitting down promptly at her desk, albeit farther from it than normal considering her sizable midsection, she retrieved a single sheet of blank paper from the drawer and slipped the quill inside the clay cup of milk. Near the center of the parchment, she wrote:

UNDER THE THREE BOULDERS WHICH LIE NEAR THE PIPPIN FARM.

Blowing on the paper until the milk was dry and completely invisible, she then folded the sheet and slipped it into the pocket of her bedgown. Thomas's messenger had advised her to write secret messages with an acidic substance like milk, lime, or lemon juice, ensuring they could only be read when carefully heated. But Caribbean and European fruits were hard to come by, especially because of the war. She remembered her father saying his sailors amassed citrus fruits on his ships to prevent scurvy. In recent days, she'd even gone down to the docks to see if limes or lemons were available but came home empty-handed. Thank goodness for the milk she'd purchased at the market earlier that morning.

When should she take her own hidden message to their spot near the dock? Pacing near the door, she weighed her options. She could drop it off immediately under the cover of darkness. It was what she wished to do, considering Thomas's messenger was likely staying at Middleton Tavern until he received word from her. But she loathed the idea of going downstairs to face Grafton. She would have to take care of things come morning.

And while restlessness seized Caroline, her mind spinning relentlessly, she still managed to curl up on her bed and, out of utter exhaustion, drift into her dreams.

A full, hollow moon glowed boldly against an ebony backdrop as the middle of the night inched slowly toward morning.

"Miss Caroline, get up! Get up! Yer house is on fire!" Mrs. McGregor's voice suddenly resounded off the walls.

But Caroline remained still beneath the covers.

A cloud of thick, silver smoke advanced through the open doorway, invading the room and curling its way around her cannonball four-poster bed.

"Ye must wake up!" Mrs. McGregor violently shook Caroline's body as the smoke pressed in on them.

Caroline's eyes finally peeled open to discover her housekeeper hovering above her.

What in the world is she doing?

"A fire, Miss Caroline! Ye have tuh get out!"

Caroline rolled onto her feet, coughing as the suffocating haze slipped into her lungs. She instinctively staggered to the window. "We should jump."

"Ye can't with the bairn."

Eyeing the open doorway and the thick charcoal-tinted smoke flushing in through it, she stiffened but knew the old woman was right. The fall was substantial. "To the door, then."

They fled blindly down a dark and smothering stairwell, the housekeeper stopping halfway to cough repeatedly. "Go on ye, I'm comin'."

"I'm not leaving without you!" Caroline yelled as she grabbed Mrs. McGregor's arm and pulled her down the rest of the steps.

They burst through the front door into the street; the crisp, night air filling their burning lungs as they gasped for breath. Both women turned just in time to witness the roof of the Brooks home implode inward, with every wall consumed by flames.

Caroline cried out, a shrill moan from the pit of her being.

The rest was a blur. Neighbors with wooden buckets scooping water from the harbor and tossing it hastily on the blaze. Mrs. McGregor's piercing sobs. Sheriff Stone announcing, "I'm sorry, Mrs. Brooks, but your husband is gone. Smoke overcame him." Menacing heaps of gray vapors rising toward the rapturous glowing ball in the sky. Someone placing a blanket over Caroline's shoulders, desperately trying to calm her shaking body.

Though no one was speaking, suddenly Isaac Abbott's voice rang out in Caroline's mind, the deep, indignant cries of a forsaken man. She had tried to sympathize with him, but he was too enraged to listen. Had his vexation turned to flames?

She dug down deep inside the pocket of her bedgown.

Her trembling fingers still managed to grasp a small slip of paper.

All felt lost, but her message for Thomas remained.

Chapter 18

January 2013

"Who started the fire? That guy who had his wife's painting stolen?" Conor took a sizable gulp of coffee, his gaze fixed on Lorna.

A strong gale from the ocean swept against the front of the cottage.

Lorna pulled the blanket up over her shoulders. "I don't know. This is as far as I got."

Conor's eyes widened. "Or was the Moore guy involved?"

"Strange that Grafton knew Andrew's wife had the key, right?"

"Something was going on between them. Pretty low, Grafton."

Lorna studied Conor while she nibbled on an already chewed strip of nail. "You really get into stories, don't you?"

"I've done therapy. It's not cheap. Reading's my next best thing. Keep going."

Lorna tried to ignore the strange feeling in her stomach. But perhaps it was justified. After all, this was about Will's ancestors. And Will himself had seemingly led her to this book. Was it a mistake to share it with this random person she barely knew?

Yet, having Conor there also helped distract her from the fact that every time she read Allison's book, she thought of Will. That gnawing feeling inside dissipated ever so slightly when sharing the story with someone else.

"Come on," he smirked. "I have a thing. I need to know the ending."

WHERE THE FOXGLOVES BLOOM

By Allison Brooks

PART IX

LOST AND FOUND

OCTOBER 1777
ONE MONTH AFTER THE FIRE

Caroline's high-pitched shriek resounded off the walls of Whitehall as fear and guilt echoed through her mind. *I'm going to die. Just like this. Of course I am. It's what I deserve after robbing my own mother of life.*

"Please...deep, slow breaths." Charity sat positioned on a wooden stool at the bottom of a four-poster bed, near Caroline's feet.

"No!" Caroline belted.

"Yes. Focus on the sound of your breath," Charity's voice was slow and steady.

"All right, all right, I'll try. Meanwhile, tell this child to come out already!" Caroline cried out. The color had already drained from her face.

Molly paced near the back windows of Whitehall mansion's first floor, inside the guest room where Caroline lay, watching for a carriage. "We've sent two men. I'm sure the doctor will be here soon."

Mrs. McGregor sat perched beside the bed, the housekeeper's hand trembling as she pressed a moistened cloth against Caroline's forehead.

Charity examined Caroline, feeling for the child within her, before sending an alarming gaze toward Molly.

"What is it, Charity?" Caroline was panting, sweat pouring down both of their foreheads.

Charity met Caroline's eyes. "The baby is backward. I need to get the child in a better position."

"Have ye ever done this afore?" Mrs. McGregor tried to whisper, but everyone heard.

Charity answered immediately: "Twice."

Caroline's eyes narrowed. "One of Molly's babies?"

"A horse's actually..."

Caroline bit down as another contraction rolled in faster than the previous. When it passed, she asked, "And the second delivery?"

"A cow," Charity answered without making eye contact.

"Dear Lord," Caroline said between gritted teeth.

The color drained from Mrs. McGregor's face as well.

Caroline's fingers clung to the bedsheets. "And were you successful?" she practically yelled.

Charity straightened her back and drew her chin up. "I was." She hid her bloodied fingertips below the mattress.

John Ridout heard Caroline's haunting screams all the way from the broad front porch as he stared out at the bay waters, white caps furiously churning and shifting, warning of the coming storm. The skies darkened within minutes, only illuminated by the crack of lightning that burst forth through Caroline's window.

Molly lit several candles throughout the room and quietly sent out just as many urgent prayers—for the child, for Caroline, for Charity, and for the doctor to get there.

Caroline bit down on a rag that Molly had supplied.

"The child turned!" Charity's relief pulsed forth. "You can push now, Caroline."

John had come inside when sheets of rain sprayed in sideways, soaking the covered portico. He was standing in the grand entry hall, looking up at the carved golden phoenix on the ceiling—its wings spread wide, its body risen from the ashes—when the crisp sound of an infant's cry broke forth, the tiny human's very first proclamation to the world. The innocent babe knew nothing about the dark circumstances leading up to his arrival but simply cried out because for the first time, he felt cold and alone. And while the child was quite dismayed, the sound of his voice set the home ablaze with thanksgiving and joy. For despite all the inauspicious happenings, Providence had granted him life.

When Dr. Hampton finally arrived, Caroline was peering down at the child's face with complete wonder.

"Gabriel. I'll name him Gabriel after my mother's father. I owe him the world for teaching me to ride."

"It suits 'im." Mrs. McGregor placed her hand on Caroline's shoulder as several bulbous tears slipped down her cheek. "Yer ma t'would be proud."

"Who delivered the child?" the doctor asked.

"Charity did," Caroline announced proudly as Dr. Hampton's gaze followed hers toward the young woman cleaning up rags strewn across the floor.

"She was magnificent," Molly added.

A fortnight passed.

Caroline held her son in the front parlor, its walls covered in hand-painted Chinese wallpaper with lush ornamental trees surrounded by frolicking birds and butterflies. Petal-pink doors, trim, and drapes popped in every direction, while a deeply veined marble fireplace perched itself at the center of the room. Outside, the noonday autumn sun lingered high in the sky, casting an aureate glow across surrounding fields.

John Ridout slowly entered the room.

Something inside Caroline stirred. "Have you just arrived from town?"

"Yes. The Sheriff declares they have tracked down Isaac Abbott. They found him concealed near Williamsburg."

Caroline turned to him. "At last."

Molly entered the parlor next. "Blessings be. He surely set the fire. Any man who departs town in such haste is as guilty as if he'd been caught with the torch in hand."

John rubbed his palm across a tightened jaw line. "One would suppose, but Mr. Abbott insists he only ran from town because he was certain everyone would suspect him, considering his outburst in front of Caroline's house that very day."

"Likely story," Molly added.

"The only problem is, he now possesses a witness to attest to his innocence. Mr. Abbott was allegedly down by the docks, helping to unload a late-night shipment at the fire's commencement. Initially, he fled town, but later resolved to locate the merchant ship's captain in order to vindicate himself. The captain did, in fact, accompany him back to Annapolis and told Sheriff Stone he was with the accused at the fire's onset." John paused as the sound of pounding hooves suddenly filled the room.

Caroline turned toward the window to see a dark carriage emerging in the distance. She pulled the baby to her chest.

John cleared his throat before speaking. "The sheriff."

Molly turned abruptly. "Why is he here?"

PART X

A Brooding Storm

"He wants to speak with Mrs. McGregor," John explained as he studied Caroline. Her expression hardened as she watched Sheriff Stone crawl down from the carriage and fix his gaze on Whitehall.

"Mrs. McGregor?" Caroline turned to him. "What does she have to do with anything?"

John's face grew graver. "I cannot say for sure, but he is on the hunt, and you need to warn her."

Caroline handed Gabriel to Molly and fled to her guest room. Mrs. McGregor was hanging Caroline's petticoats in the wardrobe.

"You must come promptly. The sheriff seeks to question you."

John told Sheriff Stone he could meet privately with Caroline's housekeeper in the library.

Mrs. McGregor squeezed her apron under an expansive desk as she sat across from the lanky, emaciated sheriff, who barely took up any room on John Ridout's stately, green-leather chair. "You were the one who awakened Mrs. Brooks the night of the fire. Why were you not sleeping?" he prodded.

"I twasn't. Havin' takin' care uh' Miss Caroline since she was uh lassie..." She struggled to swallow, let alone speak. "I sleep as uneasy as a broody hen sittin' atop her eggs."

"You can play the hen all you like, Mrs. McGregor, but know you have now awoken the rooster. Someone must sound the alarm. This case has quickly moved from arson to murder. As you know, a neighbor pulled Mr. Brooks's body from the fire just before the house collapsed. We presumed that smoke inhalation had taken his life, but I had my own misgivings. Upon further examination of Mr. Brooks's body, I noticed a foaming substance around his mouth, indicative of arsenic poisoning."

"What exactly are ye implying, sir?"

"Slaves have done it to their masters. Why couldn't you, his agitated servant, have murdered him?" His hollow eyes widened.

Mrs. McGregor cupped her mouth. Then shock turned to anger. The housekeeper rose from her chair in one swift motion, her face filled with rage. "How dare ye come in carryin' such accusations when ye have not a bit uh proof. I've been uh loyal servant. Ye should be ashamed uh' yerself. As God as my witness, I did not poison Mr. Brooks."

The sheriff studied her carefully. "If you are blameless, then who did it?"

"Ye want me to be doin' yer job now?"

"I need people to speak the truth, ma'am. I'm certain two visitors entered the Brooks home that evening, and they barred another man from going inside. Isaac Abbott, who Mrs. Brooks turned away, was our most notable suspect. Thus, we didn't delve deeply into investigating the others, but now that we've acquitted Mr. Abbott, we must continue our search. The second man, a tall gentleman, came into the home. What can you tell me about him?"

"An acquaintance uh Miss Caroline an' I know naught more."

"An acquaintance, eh? And what do you know of the third

man's relationship with Mr. and Mrs. Brooks?" The Sheriff began tapping his eight bony fingers against the shiny desk surface. They jolted and jumped like the wiry legs of a spider until, without warning, Sheriff Stone's sharp, shrill voice rose forth again. "Mrs. McGregor?"

"Aye, Mr. Andrew Moore came later that evenin'. He had uh working relationship with Mr. Brooks. I saw 'im leave, but he seemed uh bit vexed."

"Do go on."

"I witnessed it not, but merely saw 'im huffin' and puffin' as he left."

Sheriff Stone stood, towering over Mrs. McGregor, his gaze penetrating. "Please tell Mrs. Brooks I need to speak to her directly."

"Remember that lass has just had herself a bairn and lost both her home and her husband. She has done naught to deserve yer ire." With that, Mrs. McGregor stood and shuffled away.

When Caroline returned, she too sat across from the sheriff at John's desk.

"Ma'am, there's no way to approach this lightly. Someone murdered your husband on the night of the fire. It was not the smoke that took his life, as the fire was likely a ruse. I suspect the murderer had already poisoned Mr. Brooks, and I am quite certain that arsenic was involved."

Caroline stared at something on the wall beyond him as a shadow fell across her face.

"I regret to say it, but everyone is now a suspect—even you."

She returned her attention to him, her eyes hardening. "You don't appear sorry. The way you rode in here accusing my old maid of treachery, and now me."

Sheriff Stone glared back at Caroline, the center of his face pinching together. "You and your maid have suspicious manner about you. That is not my fault, Mrs. Brooks."

"You mean because we speak what's on our conscious?"

"You speak outside of your place."

"And you speak without cause or consideration. You prey on the broken. Now, what do you need to know so you can be on your way?"

Sheriff Stone's chest burst outward, the bright-blue veins along his temples bulging in tandem. "Who was this acquaintance of yours who entered your home the same evening as the fire?"

"I knew him not. He was bringing me a letter."

"Would he have any reason to want to target your husband?"

"Grafton did not know him either."

"But possibly this man knew of him? Mr. Brooks's reputation as a clandestine Tory spy was becoming known. Not so much appreciated in a town of Patriots," the sheriff pushed.

"The man was a letter carrier and was quickly on his way."

"Mrs. McGregor believed you knew him."

"I had never seen him in my life."

Sheriff Stone leaned in, and Caroline refused to look away.

"What about Mr. Moore? I understand he had a business acquaintance with your husband. Certainly, the entire town knows all about their *tunnel*. Mrs. McGregor said Mr. Moore looked displeased when leaving your residence on the evening of the fire. Any idea what could have caused his irritation?"

"You should probably ask him."

"And I shall. But first, I need to find out about your relationship with your husband. Was he benevolent toward you?"

"Grafton was not an affectionate man, but I didn't require such accommodations."

"I understand. Yet surely having different sympathies toward the cause created animosity?"

"I will never imply we agreed on everything. Does matrimony ever prove to require such?"

"Do you admit he was a Tory spy?"

Caroline looked down at John's desk as she considered her options. Either admit Grafton's traitorous ties and open his murder investigation up to an endless list of enemies, including herself, while blemishing the Brooks family name for Gabriel forever...or lie and let Grafton look like an innocent man who did not betray his country, which he certainly was not.

"What my husband did behind closed doors was of his concern."

"You walk a fine line, Mrs. Brooks, but if you want me to find your husband's *murderer*, you need to tell me everything you know."

A knock echoed off the door. John entered the room as Caroline quietly gasped for breath. She heard John's voice, muffled and direct, but barely made out what he said. It was all hitting her at once. Finally coming to, Caroline forced herself to listen.

"It seems a long line of dark clouds are building from the west," John warned the sheriff.

"I'll be getting on my way then." Sheriff Stone stood. "The only thing more dangerous than aggrieved humans are angry storms."

Caroline looked out the window at the thick, foreboding storm clouds while John led Sheriff Stone out of his office. Just as they reached the threshold, the sheriff turned to Caroline. "I'll be back Mrs. Brooks. I plan on doing you the *honor* of finding your husband's murderer."

His pale cracked lips spread into a thin line as he observed her carefully. Caroline refused to look away until the sheriff turned to fasten his cloak.

She didn't feel the air lighten until Sheriff Stone's carriage was gone. Yet, as he departed down Whitehall Road, unbeknownst to her, a new, unexpected visitor was heading straight toward the house. The sheriff saw the lone horseman through his carriage window, but the immense beast soared by so quickly, all there was to see was a flash of darkness against a profuse mass of upturned dirt.

While the Whitehall servants were scattered, preparing for the storm, the approaching guest knew precisely where to conceal his tired horse and how to sneak up on the unknowing household.

PART XI

Three brothers

The newly arrived guest didn't realize, as he slipped along the side of the Whitehall portico, that someone was huddled in the corner of the grand front porch overlooking the bay. As he tried to get through the door, a woman's voice startled him: "Look who's gone and run away from the army."

Thomas Pierce paused in his tracks as a slight grin grew across his face. Straightening his blue, wool coat, he knew exactly who it was even before he turned to see Caroline sitting in a rocking chair, sheltering a baby in her arms. Thomas quickly crossed the porch toward her but stopped a few strides short, his smile turning solemn.

"I'm so sorry to hear about your husband, Liny, and your home. I cannot imagine how you've grieved."

She looked down at the baby nestled tightly in a blanket, then back up at her childhood friend. "Thank you, Thomas."

He joined her in an adjacent rocking chair. "What's the child's name?"

"Gabriel, after my grandfather."

"I imagine he'll be as courageous as he was. And as brave as his mother too." Thomas gazed out at the water, its charcoal-toned ripples reflecting the ominous clouds above. "I only wish his mother would have told me she was with child. I surely would not have had her risking both of their lives for the Continental Army." Thomas scanned the porch before turning back to Caroline. "I know of several occasions when you were riding that horse to our drop-off location."

"What's done is done. We all risk much to gain our freedom. And the child is fine, so please refrain from lecturing me. And do tell—was I right or wrong about that spot on the map?"

Thomas's eyes suddenly came alive with excitement. "It was *exactly* at the spot you suspected!"

Caroline felt her stomach flutter as if the child were still within. "Truly? It was there? Do tell—what was it they were hiding?"

Thomas pulled his chair closer to Caroline. "Apparently, the British sailors, who my men stole the map from, created it after burying a vital package on the farmland of a local Loyalist who was a trusted acquaintance of Adm. Richard Howe, the commander of the British Navy. Howe's massive British fleet sailed up the Chesapeake in August. I'm sure you heard about them passing?"

"Quite so. It's all anyone has discussed, and they are *still* speaking on it two months hence."

Thomas grinned. "I imagined so. Admiral Howe was transporting his younger brother, Gen. William Howe, on one of the ships called the HMS *Eagle*. William just so happens to be the commander-in-chief of the British Army."

"Yes, I've sense heard much about the Howe brothers. I was told they came up the Chesapeake to capture Philadelphia."

"The devils. They outmaneuvered us. I won't begin to discuss my frustrations with Philadelphia. It enrages me to know they have control of another of our cities. We'll regain that ground as we have before, though. But regarding the Howe Brothers, it appears they have connection to the royal line in England. Their grandmother was the half-sister of King George the First. There were actually three famous Howe brothers, all gifted military leaders."

"What happened to the third brother?"

"The oldest, George, a British general, was killed during the Seven Years War on American soil. Back in the 1750s, before hostilities arose with England, our people loved George Howe, who died valiantly, a genuine war hero. Because of this, British authorities appointed his younger brothers, Richard and William, to lead the Royal Army and Navy in hopes they could negotiate peace with the colonists."

"An impossible task."

"Indeed. So arduous an endeavor that the Howe brothers brought a *good luck charm* with them from England."

"What kind of *charm*?"

"An immensely valuable one that kings and queens have worn for centuries."

Caroline's gaze tightened. "You jest with me?"

"I do not. And guess which queen loved it most?"

"Surely not..."

"Surely so."

"Thomas Pierce, I am certain you quip with me."

"I assure you for once, I do not."

Caroline stood up from her seat. "Queen Elizabeth?"

Thomas was on his feet now, nearly shaking with excitement. "There are several portraits of her wearing it. In fact, Elizabeth loved the necklace so much they carved it into the marble sculpture of her on her tomb at Westminster Abbey. Beyond that..."

"How can you possibly go beyond that?"

"Daringly enough, I can. This jewel has the most fascinating history. Created in the 1300s by a duke in Burgundy, stolen in war, owned by one of the richest men of all time—a German banker—purchased by the legendary Henry VIII's son, then of course adored by his daughter Elizabeth and her predecessor King James, who wore the massive piece on his hat before passing it on to

James's son to charm a Spanish princess. It was the most coveted jewel in all of Renaissance Europe—reputed to bring immense luck and prosperity to its possessor!"

Caroline's eyes widened.

"Then suddenly, in 1645, it went missing."

"What happened?"

"King Charles the First of England became embroiled in a civil war, and as a result, he entrusted his queen, Henrietta Maria—known as Queen Mary—to sell their crown jewels to raise funds for the war."

"She was the woman they named Maryland after, right?"

"Correct."

"Did she sell the piece?"

"She sold the others, but secretly held on to the necklace."

Caroline stared down at Gabriel, peacefully lulled to sleep by the pounding of her heart. "Isn't her husband, King Charles, the one who got his head chopped off?"

"Yes, I believe so."

Caroline touched the tender skin on her neck. "So much for good luck."

"I suppose, but lest you forget, *her head* remained well intact. Maybe she didn't like him much anyway." Thomas grinned. "For 130 years, it remained a hidden British Crown Jewel. The Howes, being descendants of the royal family, eventually inherited it, and so it became their little secret. I've been told they *thoroughly believe* they need this lucky charm to win the war."

"Truly? Why didn't they want people to know they had it? Weren't they proud?"

"They were afraid it would disappear—as it has." Thomas stepped closer, his eyes alit with excitement. "Come! Meet me in the carriage barn quickly, before I burst."

She felt a thrill shoot through her. "Wait. You possess it now?"

"I suppose you'll have to come and find out."

"I'll place Gabriel in his cradle and arrive before you!"

Moments later, Caroline grabbed a lantern and slipped out the back door, finding herself sprinting across the lawn just as the sky opened, thick sheets of rain shooting at her sideways and soaking her down to her petticoats.

The wide barn door creaked as she drew herself inside. Caroline held up her dripping lamp, its flame still burning, and saw Thomas's long silhouette against the far wall. Skirts clinging to her skin as she approached, she wondered momentarily if it was all just one of his pranks.

Thomas turned, completely dry, holding a satchel over one shoulder. "Such a shame you couldn't beat the storm."

She reached him and wrung out her dress on top of his boot. He jumped backward. "Liny!"

Caroline smirked. "Oh, but I know you're aware it was warranted."

Thomas led her to an old wooden worktable where they gathered next to one another. He pulled from his satchel a dark-metal box with a thick, gold clasp wrapped around the side. When Thomas set the box down, Caroline placed the lantern beside it.

He placed his thumb under the gold clasp. "Blast it! It's stuck."

She went for the box, and he pulled it away.

"Forbear your efforts to torture me," Caroline pressed.

"But it's richly amusing."

Again, he placed the box on the table, this time peeling apart the clasp and slowly opening it. Caroline's breath caught, her eyes first landing on the pointed, deep-blue diamond at the center of the necklace. But it was all its parts combined that made the piece especially stunning, forming a unique triangular pattern. Set in gold and surrounding the diamond were three wide rectangular rubies interspersed with three pale white pearls at each point. An even larger, raindrop-shaped pearl hung from the bottom, dangling like a delicate pendulum.

"They call it the Three Brothers," Thomas whispered, sending a chill up her spine.

Caroline bent in closer. "It's magnificent."

Thomas turned to her. "I'm leaving it here...with you."

"Have you gone mad?"

"You're the reason we found it. Sell it to a wealthy Whig and purchase yourself a home. Or keep it for luck. Couldn't you use a little, presently?"

"You cannot fathom how greatly I stand in need of good fortune right now, yet how might I accept such a gift? You should be presenting this to your wife."

"I would be severely reprimanded by the Continental Army should word ever reach them that Ginny was wearing stolen British goods. Especially an item of such worth. It is *you* who needs it most."

Caroline blew the air from her lungs as an intense thrill coursed through her. "Thank you, Thomas. I have one final question, though. Why, after hauling the jewel all the way from England, was Admiral Howe worried about taking it to Philadelphia?"

"Elizabeth Lloyd Loring is why."

"And she is?"

"Mistress to William Howe. The wife of a Loyalist who he encountered in Boston. She later joined him in New York and once more in Philadelphia. My informant says that William confided in his brother Richard, expressing his wish to dazzle Mrs. Loring by permitting her to adorn herself with it at a dinner party upon their seizing of Philadelphia. Richard was livid and said someone might recognize the necklace, but William was adamant. In the end, big brother prevailed, having it hidden near Annapolis before his love-smitten younger brother could seize it and carry it north with his army."

Caroline spun around suddenly. "Did you hear that?" she whispered.

"Hear what?"

She tiptoed to the wide carriage-house doors, gently easing one open to glance among the shadows.

Nothing.

Caroline returned to Thomas. "I swear I heard Molly's little spaniel barking."

"That dog barks at everything," he tried to assure her. "Now, I have a question for you. How did you determine the necklace's location from that dreadfully drawn map?"

"My grandfather."

Thomas's face grew fierce. "You showed him?"

Caroline crossed her arms over her chest. "Thomas, he's been gone for years."

"Of course. My apologies."

"My grandfather often took me down the roads depicted on that map. I have perhaps mentioned he is the one who instructed me on the art of riding. He was my primary caregiver after my mother's passing and used to remark that I inherited her passion for horses, and my father's stubbornness." Thomas laughed and Caroline continued, "One summer, we were out riding, and the sun was beating down on us mercilessly, so we took a back road to reach his home faster. We passed the Pippin Farm, which sat near a sharp split in the road. Shortly after, he slowed his horse. We'd come upon three boulders congregating near the forest's edge. My grandfather smiled and proclaimed it was my mother, him, and me, all having a jolly chat up in heaven someday. He was a preacher —and the only reason I have any faith at all."

Caroline's gaze reached beyond Thomas, where she saw herself surrounded by the immense stones, her grandfather by her side. She could see his gentle, crinkled eyes as if he was standing before her, and that smile which could soften even the most jaded of hearts. Caroline's focus snapped back to Thomas. "Yes, but when I first observed the three large circles on the map, the boulders did not come to mind immediately. It took time. In thankfulness, though, the fog eventually lifted, and all became apparent: the fork in the road by the farmhouse and, of course, those three massive stones."

"Remarkable how that one ride prepared you for such a

moment as this. I have to say, I had other theories of what those circles may have been, but boulders—that I failed to imagine."

"Thomas, this necklace could raise money for the war effort."

"Selling it off is not an option. I don't believe in luck, but some of my superior officers do. They won't risk it ending up back with the Lobsterbacks."

"Then use it for negotiations with England."

"We are, sadly, quite past the point of negotiating. The necklace is meant for you, Caroline." Her pulse quickened as Thomas continued, "It's not safe inside the house, though. If the Redcoats come, the jewel will disappear and even worse, they'll label you a thief and a rebel."

"Then what should we do with it?" Caroline looked down at the necklace, still in shock.

"You tell me. Show me a good spot to bury it."

Chapter 19

January 2013

"I'd sell it," Conor said as Lorna closed the book.

"No way. Caroline was fascinated by its history," Lorna insisted.

"Its history can't buy you a new house. Think how much that thing was worth."

Lorna's eyes remained on Conor, but her mind wandered elsewhere. "How selfless."

"Selfless of who?" Conor questioned.

"Thomas. He could have just buried it himself and kept it."

"I'm sure his wife would have preferred it," Conor said, grinning.

"I looked her up. Virginia something or other was her name. Anyway, her family was loaded. Big time. As Thomas said, he knew Caroline needed it more. He loved her like a sister, it seems."

"I wouldn't give my sister a dime. But I do wonder where the necklace is now?"

"I know. I'm so curious."

"Wanna take a walk on the beach?"

She hesitated. "It's a little chilly, but...sure, why not?"

Stepping outside, a brisk, unwelcoming breeze greeted them,

frigid and unwelcoming, causing Lorna to cinch her coat's hood tighter.

Conor stiffened. "Wow, it's colder than I thought."

Finally, they reached the sand.

"Which way?" Conor glanced over at her.

"Let's go north." Lorna took a sharp left.

The tide had swept out, revealing a hundred little sandbars peeking above the surface. An unexpected smile grew across Lorna's lips as Kate came to mind. That summer at Rehoboth Beach, how they loved to spring across the tiny islands during evening's low tide, belting out songs as their shadows followed like little lost ghosts. Neither one of them even remotely carried a tune, but in the company of a sister, it never much mattered.

Conor stopped, gazing at a ship barely visible across the horizon. Lorna paused as well, her boots sinking steadily into the sand.

"My father was a merchant mariner," Conor shared.

"Oh really? Did you ever get to spend time on his boat?"

"Once." Conor started walking again, and Lorna joined him. "He took me to the helm. Showed me how to steer, which was incredible for a kid who'd barely left his neighborhood."

"I imagine. Were you close with your dad?" Lorna asked.

"Never had the chance to be. He was always on the water."

"I'm sorry."

"It's okay. He was kind of a bastard anyway. Every time I see my son, I try to make it count."

His words felt sincere. "What's your son's name?"

"Charlie."

"And how old is he?"

"Six going on sixty. Oldest soul I know. Such a fantastic kid. He truly is. I got lucky. I just wish I saw him more."

"Why can't you?"

"His mom has custody. Man, do I miss him."

"I'm so sorry."

They walked on silently. Lorna opened her mouth to speak,

but Conor beat her to it. "So how about your family? Are you close with them?"

"More my dad than my mom. But yeah. And my little sister Kate and I are close."

"So, you're the big sister. I can see it."

"How so?"

"You have that *protective older sibling* thing about you."

"Okay, I'll take your word for it."

"I'm really glad you have them. Especially with everything you've been through."

They walked on, the water biting at Lorna's ankles. "Yeah, me too. I should probably lean into them more."

"Of course you should. Anything that helps."

"It's been almost two years and I'm still...well, not the person I wanna be."

Conor stopped and turned to her. "Well, let's see—you've been through an incredibly traumatic event, so why wouldn't you be struggling?"

"You know, you read about someone like Caroline, so brazen, strong and self-assured, and I just...I just wish I were more like her sometimes."

"Be careful what you wish for. Sure, Caroline was a badass chick, but she's also a murderer."

"What? She didn't murder Grafton."

"Yeah, well, I've changed my mind about it being that Andrew Moore guy. It was Caroline."

"I mean, I don't get the sense she and Grafton were a match made in heaven, but to murder her husband and the father of her child?"

"You just wait. I bet I'm right."

"I don't think so. Because why on earth would she burn her own house down too?"

"To cover it up, of course."

"No. She sacrificed too much for that home. She married a

man she didn't even love because she needed a roof over her head. She wouldn't give that up."

"She had Whitehall to fall back on. She knew she could always stay with Molly," Conor pressed.

"No, Caroline was too independent. She loved Molly, but she wanted to do her spying without Molly peering over her shoulder."

Another forceful breeze tore across the sea, flattening it out like a smooth sheet of velvet.

"Wanna head back and read some more?" Conor said, while not so successfully concealing a shiver.

Lorna didn't answer right away. She saw a figure sitting alone farther down the shoreline, staring out at the ocean. "Sure, let's head back."

Once she was home, Lorna found a spot on the couch, expecting Conor to once again take the chair, but he didn't. He grabbed the book off the side table and sheepishly stepped toward the sofa instead. "Mind if I sit?"

"Are you making a move on me?" Lorna said, smirking.

Conor's eyes sprung open as he threw his palms up toward her, as if she'd just pulled a gun. "Just looking for a soft spot to lay my tush," he said.

Lorna laughed. "Sure. But you get to read this time."

"Fair enough."

Lorna felt something tightly bound and unyielding inside her begin to unravel as he settled onto the couch next to her.

He kept his eyes on the book, dimples flexing, and dove into the next chapter.

WHERE THE FOXGLOVES BLOOM

By Allison Brooks

PART XII

Foxgloves and Fear

Bitter gales blew off the bay as late fall succumbed to winter and a restless darkness took over Caroline as well. Charity watched her roam the halls late at night, even though the baby lay sound asleep.

"I'm fine," Caroline always insisted.

Even Charity's homemade tea, which Caroline had once consumed abundantly, didn't seem to calm her.

The letters from Thomas, asking for help from the Continental Army, had ceased. Caroline knew it was because of the child —so Thomas's communications would no longer endanger them. She found it infuriating.

Yet, somehow, when spring broke forth, she seemed to settle too, as if the chill in her demeanor finally thawed. Caroline stopped watching for a letter carrier and started noticing the baby in her arms. She became enthralled by his dimples and his distinctive infant smell. And when he cooed, she couldn't help but kiss his soft, squishy cheeks.

One late May morning, eastbound breezes blew fiercely through tall, tailored windows in the parlor, chilling Caroline's skin and keeping Gabriel amused as the curtains danced playfully like the skirts of ladies dancing.

Charity entered the room, believing she was unnoticed, and watched from the unlit corner as she gathered teacups from the table. The woman Charity had held dear since childhood seemed genuinely content for the first time in her life. Where once losses and trials had locked and barred the doors shut, love had finally become the key to unlatching them.

Caroline kept her eyes on the baby. "Let's get some fresh air," she practically shouted, making Charity jump and nearly spill her tray of porcelain.

"I'd almost forgotten you had ears like a fox," Charity murmured as she rearranged the scattered saucers.

"I need a keen sense of hearing with you always scurrying around as quiet as a mouse." Caroline rose from her chair with

Gabriel wrapped snuggly in a light sheet that Charity had sewn and embroidered with the letters *GB*.

"Please walk with me," Caroline said. "Show me that patch of foxgloves you always loved."

Dishes needed scrubbing, and Charity had promised one of the Ridout children she'd mend their socks. Caroline noticed her initial hesitation. "The china won't tell, Charity. And with Molly and John visiting her brother at Belair, it's the perfect time to sneak away. Come on, I have something I need to show you."

Caroline slipped Gabriel into the crook of her left arm so she could open the back door. He smiled up at her, his neck finally secure, and spun toward the light, feasting his eyes on the wide-open world before him.

Charity tickled his toes as Caroline drew a full breath of air into her lungs, taking in the sweet, fragrant smell of honeysuckles bursting over horse fences in the pasture. Charity lifted a woven basket off the front porch, carrying it with her in case any of her medicinal herbs had recently bloomed.

A vibrant sun glistened at their backs as the trio headed for a patch of trees near the water.

"All right, there's something you need to share with me, what is it?" Charity said with eagerness, but she looked over to discover Caroline's suddenly unsettled expression. "Caroline?"

"There are murmurs in town. The sheriff, they say, has fixed his mind that I murdered Grafton and set my house ablaze. He is apparently intent on coming for me."

Charity stopped, as still as a stone. "Why do you remain here, then?"

"I have a child to protect."

"Indeed. So, make haste."

"And go where?" Caroline pushed back.

"Anywhere but here. I'll watch your boy 'til you secure a dwelling."

They came to a patch of low-lying foliage and stopped just before the indigo blooms. Caroline saw them first—Charity's foxgloves. They'd bloomed—tall, fragrant sprigs of peach, pink, white, and crimson, teetering restlessly in the wind. Just beyond them was a thick oak, its branches drooping solemnly toward the earth.

"If I'm ever apprehended, return to your foxgloves. And should it be winter, and they have not bloomed, look for a small triangle carved into that oak."

"A triangle?" Charity's face twisted ever so slightly.

"It represents the Three Brothers, a renowned, three-sided jewel worn by kings and queens alike since the 1300s. Thomas gave it to me after his men seized it from the British. We buried it behind the foxgloves and below the oak. Please, allow no one to know, including Gabriel, until he's of age. Then, have him dig up the necklace to sell, seeing as the fire took all our possessions and now I've failed to leave him a home.

"At the bottom of the jewel is a giant pearl. I want you to take that to help procure a home for yourself once you've been given your freedom. I've heard whispers that because you saved the Ridout family's lives on more than one occasion, that John plans on manumitting you once he passes."

"That's not the only reason." Charity turned toward her foxgloves.

"Why else?"

"I've heard whispers too. There is talk that Molly's uncle is my real father. He oversaw the plantation at Belair."

"Molly's mother's brother? Colonel Benjamin Tasker?"

"Yes."

"Oh, Charity."

"It would explain why my skin's lighter than my mama's."

"And that would make Molly your..."

"Cousin. But as far as the necklace goes, I won't take the pearl. It was given to *you.*"

"I don't know what will become of *me.*"

"You cannot speak in such a way."

"But I must prepare us both. Even if you wish not to sell the pearl, keep it to remember me. Above all, I beg you to protect Gabriel."

"I promise, should anything happen, I'll guard him with my life. And I'll make sure he receives the jewel."

"And you the pearl."

"Thank you, Caroline, but I cannot take it. Something that special should never be broken apart."

"But the necklace is all I have left. Grafton owed more than we possessed, and what we did have, the fire claimed."

"I don't want your *things.*" The gentleness in Charity's eyes shifted—an alertness taking shape. "What I want is for you to be safe. Now, please listen." She took a step closer. "There is no reason for you to be caught, nor part from your child. Return here tonight, dig up the necklace so you can sell it, if need be, take Gabriel, and be on your way. Go somewhere they'll never find you."

Caroline studied her. "I do not wish to leave you. Nor Molly." Her voice grew emphatic. "I am finally...happy."

The powder-blue sky grew suddenly shadowed as a host of sparrows fled overhead and the thundering sound of hoofbeats filled the air.

"We aren't expecting anyone." Charity's face tightened as she turned toward the house.

Caroline's eyes widened like a hunted animal sensing danger.

Charity grabbed her by the shoulders and spoke as calmly and deliberately as she could muster. "You cannot carry Gabriel on horseback. I will protect him. Hurry through the woods."

"I won't be able to reach the horses without the sheriff seeing me. And if he sees Gabriel with you, he'll be suspicious. He knows I have an infant and Molly does not." Caroline scanned the landscape, searching for other options. An old, wooden rowboat bobbed by the water's edge, a single rope all that prevented its voyage into the open bay.

Caroline turned to Charity. "Distract the sheriff. Please."

She fled to the boat with the baby, her heart pounding, and

jumped immediately inside. Caroline unwrapped the tethering cord, despite her shaking hands, and with Gabriel on her lap, she rowed hastily toward cover along the tree-lined shore. Moments later, Molly's spaniel let out a shrilling bark from the yard, and Caroline dropped to the damp floor of the boat, curling her body around her son. The tall, swaying grasses in a nearby cove concealed their tiny vessel.

Sheriff Stone and two of his men fanned out across the house and property. They found Caroline's clothing in the guest room. Charity said Caroline was visiting friends, but that she didn't know who she was calling on.

Sheriff Stone's brows, like two woolly bear caterpillars, rose quickly toward his hairline. "Quite the coincidence you aren't aware of her location. No matter. The other colonies will know her description. She shall not find refuge afar, especially once word spreads that we possess evidence proving she murdered her husband."

When the sheriff's men finally departed, Caroline emerged from the boat with her bundled baby. She retrieved a basket to lay Gabriel inside and readied her carriage. As the sun dipped below the horizon, she, too, quietly faded into the night. But even Charity was never told whether Caroline and her son were heading north or south, east or west.

Chapter 20

January 2013

"She never said she did it," Lorna said immediately when Conor closed the book.

"She never said she didn't either," he returned.

But Lorna's mind was already elsewhere. "She seems so different in this chapter, doesn't she?"

"How so?"

"Less...fierce. Not in a bad way. She just seems..."

"Happy?" Conor interjected.

"Yes, her baby. He settles her. And, of course, she's far from timid still. Especially now when it comes to the boy. I mean, escaping alone in the night like that."

"People do things they never dreamed they would to protect their people."

Lorna shifted in her seat. "Wanna take a trip down to Wilmington today? It's about forty-five minutes south of us. Or would you prefer to stick around here?"

"Probably just lie low, since I'll be traveling tomorrow."

"Makes sense."

"I'll head out in the morning, if that's okay with you?"

"Sure."

Looking back, she wasn't sure why she did it. Loneliness.

Curiosity. Attraction. All she knew was she was tired of being a pathetic blend of sadness and predictability.

And mostly she wanted to forget.

Lorna carefully laid her head on Conor's chest. As the warmth of his body spread into hers, she looked up and pressed her lips against his. A longing inside her ignited. She spread her fingers around the curve of his neck, and he, in turn, placed his palms against the soft skin on her lower back.

Then, unexpectedly, a firm knock reverberated off her front door.

Lorna rose, straightening her clothes as she headed toward the window, and peeked under the blinds.

Jack.

He was shifting back and forth on her porch, squeezing his hands together.

Her mind immediately went into panic mode. *Oh no. This is bad. And he sees my truck, so how can I ignore him?*

Lorna hesitated, then finally opened the door and stepped outside.

"Hi, Jack."

"Hey, Lorna, I can't find your number because I got a new phone but...well, I felt like all we did at Rick's the other night was talk about my struggles. You're the one who..." Jack paused, unable to finish his sentence. Finally, he continued, "I got home and felt like a real ass that, you know, I didn't ask more about you."

Why does it feel so hot out here? It can't be January, spun itself through Lorna's brain, "No, please, Jack. I was asking you a bunch of questions—you hardly had a chance to do the same. It's just that..." Her thoughts bounced back inside the house to Conor. *What am I gonna do? Should I tell the truth? This is so awkward.*

Jack's face looked confused.

She needed to start talking again. "We're all struggling."

"Yes, but you're..."

"Jack, we're all struggling." Lorna used her fingers to press the sides of her lips together. "Listen, I have someone visiting, but you're welcome to come in."

"I don't want to intrude if..."

They stared at each other, wide-eyed.

"Come in. It's...it's totally fine, really." But really it wasn't.

The moment Jack made eye contact with Conor, she fully recognized her folly. Turning him away would have been better for everyone.

Jack shook Conor's hand, despite the uncomfortable presence that suddenly filled the room, choking Lorna's insides as if all the oxygen had been sucked outside the moment he entered.

"This is Conor. Conor, this is Jack, a friend of mine since we were kids."

"Wow, pretty cool," Conor's tone wasn't convincing.

"Do you live around here?" Jack returned.

Here it comes, Lorna thought to herself.

"No, I live in Annapolis."

"Oh, really?" Jack's eyebrows rose instantly. "Strange, I never ran into you before."

"Well, I've been there about ten years. Wasn't born and raised there like so many of you."

"Right..." Jack stared at Conor.

Lorna began to search desperately through the fridge. Maybe a midday drink could curb the awkwardness? She felt like Mother Hubbard with a single bottle of Budweiser sitting all alone in the back.

"I'm out of beer. Let's go grab a drink." She forced a smile.

Jack finally looked away from Conor, his gaze shifting to the cloth-bound book on the couch. "Does that say *Allison Brooks*?" Jack picked it up, gently grating his rough fingertips against the smooth cover.

Suddenly, Lorna hated Jack's ultra-observant side, a trait she'd previously admired, but not as much as she despised the guilty feeling rising up in her chest again for reading a book about Will's family *with* Conor. So, she pretended not to hear Jack, swiftly squeezing into her thick coat. "Well, let's get going."

Jack unexpectedly had selective hearing as well and continued on about the book. "I've seen this before..."

In the middle of zipping her jacket, Lorna froze. "Not likely. It was never published."

He paused, his face going blank as if he was searching for a memory. "No, I remember it. Will had it during our deployment." Jack's face seemed to grow a shade paler, and he hesitated before he spoke again. "I saw him reading it just before he left for...the patrol that night."

Lorna felt her stomach tie itself into a tightly bound knot. "But Will's Great-Uncle Arthur said he never gave it to him."

"No, it was Arthur's daughter, the one who wrote the book—Allison. She lives in London, I think, and she sent him a care package while we were over there with that book you have inside it. Will told me she used to babysit him sometimes before Arthur and Will's grandpa got in some huge fight. I guess she'd heard that a lot of Marines like to read books when they have downtime on deployments, so she sent it to him with some snacks. Will said Allison wrote it about their ancestors."

Lorna's body went numb. Even her tongue refused to speak. *Will actually read the book. Part of it anyway.*

"Are you okay?" Jack asked her.

"I'm fine." Something as thrilling as it was overwhelming filled her. But on the outside, she remained impassive. "Let's get going."

Jack started for the door, as did Conor.

"I'll follow," Jack said, making his way outside and toward his SUV.

"Perfect," Lorna replied as she and Conor headed to her truck.

She considered going to Rick's Restaurant, but having her coworkers around to witness their interaction felt unbearable. So, back to the nearby dive bar they went. Lorna sat between Conor and Jack at the bar. She ordered a Bloody Mary before disappearing to the jukebox. *Maybe an upbeat song will help the mood,* she hoped.

On her way back, she heard Conor speaking. "So, you guys go way back."

"That's right. We had a lot of good times together growing up."

"That's great," Conor returned. "It sounds like you were good friends with her ex too."

Jack sat up straighter. "I mean, he's not her *ex*. It's not like she broke up with Will or something. He died, dude."

"Right, I know. I didn't mean anything by it, man." Conor raised his palms in the air.

"It's easy not to understand when you don't know what they had," Jack pressed further.

Lorna grabbed her drink off the bar, which the bartender had mistakenly placed on the other side of Conor instead of in front of her stool between Conor and Jack. Lingering for a moment behind Conor, she fidgeted with the tiny straw, bobbing it aimlessly in the spicy, opaque-red concoction.

"I'm sure they were great together," Conor said defensively. "I said nothing to show otherwise."

"You called him her ex." Jack's voice was jagged and strained. He stood up suddenly, and Lorna stiffened but instinctively moved back to her seat, coming between the two men. She'd been around enough Marines to know it didn't take long for a fight to ensue.

Even the dust in the room ceased moving as Jack and Conor peered around her, eyeing one another.

"Listen, buddy, your issue shouldn't be with me," Conor said.

Jack turned quickly to Lorna. "I gotta go."

"Listen, Jack, I think this has just been a big misunderstanding."

But Jack was insistent. "I can't." He grabbed his coat and headed toward the door. Lorna wanted to follow but knew him better. He needed time.

For the rest of the weekend, a low-grade tension settled itself between Lorna and Conor, leaving her eager for his departure. When he woke Monday morning, Lorna had already escaped to her 8:00 a.m. class. She'd left a note instructing him to grab a bite to eat before he headed out, but Conor never set foot in her kitchen.

The North Topsail Beach Bridge led him into Sneads Ferry, where he passed a restaurant adorned with a massive marlin, mounted above the front entrance. Below it, a vibrant-blue sign proudly proclaimed: "Rick's Restaurant and Sports Bar."

Conor slammed his palms against the steering wheel, floored the gas pedal, made a sharp right turn, and sped northbound back toward Maryland.

Lorna could barely focus in class that morning. When it finally concluded, she rushed back home to dig back into Allison's book. One thought lingered in her mind: what happened to Caroline?

WHERE THE FOXGLOVES BLOOM

By Allison Brooks

PART XIII

A Very Important Guest

December 1783

Five years had passed since Caroline Brooks and her baby quietly slipped into the night, hastily fleeing Annapolis. In that time, the nation had triumphed over England and achieved its hard-earned quest for liberty. However, while many Americans appreciated their newfound freedom, for others, nothing had changed.

Charity gently stirred a pot of simmering bone broth, undaunted by a fat rat that skittered by her feet. Her mind slipped back to the days when she and Caroline used to run errands together as children. Back then, the Ridout family still lived downtown, just across town from the Collins home. When visiting, Caroline always asked if she and Charity could pick up supplies. The two girls loved dashing across the through town, only pausing to collect a few eggs at the market or to procure Molly's chosen remedies from the apothecary. Charity could still hear Caroline's unrestrained laughter resounding off the buildings near the harbor. Colonel Collins objected to the amount of time they spent together, considering Charity to be nothing more than a mere servant girl. However, Molly could be trusted not to disclose the details of their days, and the Colonel was too busy to ask.

The rhythmic plodding of John and Molly's footsteps on the stairway drew her back to the present. Knowing it was an immeasurably significant day, Charity slipped from the kitchen into the main hall to see them off.

Molly stood over the threshold, gazing out at the light—her slender silhouette outlined by the back door frame as the sun attempted to calm winter's chill. Did she sense she'd remember the day forever? Charity certainly would. She watched as Molly turned back toward her, offering a wave of farewell before gliding down the porch stairs to join her husband inside their frost encrusted carriage. Even the horses seemed anxious to grow warmer, their hooves rising and falling repeatedly in place until the coachman finally granted them permission to dash away down Whitehall Road.

Molly adjusted her cloak, pulling it taut against her neck as she and John reached town and drifted down King George Street, passing her childhood home, which now belonged to her brother and would later be known as Ogle Hall. They made a sharp right turn onto Northeast Street, later to be renamed Maryland Avenue, and headed toward the towering State House.

The road was bustling with dignitaries and prominent citizens, all thrilled to be present for the resignation of the acclaimed Gen. George Washington. The ceremony marked the culmination of several balls and dinners held over the previous few days to honor the Revolutionary War hero, who had just secured victory after seven excruciating years of fighting.

As the Ridouts stepped inside the State House, Molly marveled at the exquisite marble floors and vaulted ceilings, despite seeing them numerous times as a little girl when her father served as governor.

"Madams to the ladies' balcony please," a voice rang out beside her. She squeezed John's hand, then, letting go, made her way alone to the top of a narrow set of stairs leading to a modest-sized balcony that overlooked the larger room below.

A dozen other women, most of whom Molly recognized, were already standing along the railing looking down at the men seated in a horseshoe shape below. The excitement loomed so palpably, she felt as if the air could spark at any moment.

As more ladies gathered on the balcony, she listened as the entire space became infused with chatter. Then, out of nowhere, a single voice boomed from just outside the room's entrance, "Introducing the Honorable Commander-in-Chief of the Continental Army, General George Washington."

Every onlooker seemed to hold their breath as Washington's tall frame glided into the room and stopped, poised just at its center. The fifty-year-old war hero tucked his left arm into the crook of his back and addressed the crowd with a soft-spoken, yet commanding delivery.

Molly had hosted the general at her downtown home a decade earlier, growing immediately fond of his kindness and gentility. She noticed he still had that unpretentious air and grounded humility about him, even now, despite being admired by an entire nation.

"I resign with satisfaction the appointment I accepted with diffidence—a diffidence in my abilities to accomplish so arduous a task, which however was superseded by a confidence in the rectitude of our Cause, the support of the supreme Power of the Union, and the patronage of Heaven."

When he spoke his final words, not a dry eye could be found.

As Molly floated down the balcony stairs, she whispered to an acquaintance, "I think the world has never produced a greater man and very few so good."

The woman nodded as she dabbed a cotton handkerchief to her flushed cheek.

Once Molly reached the grand foyer, she searched the room for John, but when a single finger jabbed forcefully against her shoulder, she knew immediately the poke was much too cold and sharp to be her husband's.

Molly turned to find the gray, sunken skin and puffy, wrinkled under-eyes of Sheriff Stone before her. "Mrs. Ridout, what a coincidence to see you today."

The smell of moth balls and decay suddenly overcame her. "Good day, sir," she managed.

His lips curled ever so slightly, revealing a mosaic of crooked, yellow teeth. "I thought you may be interested to hear that I have at long last pursued the whereabouts of your friend and her young lad."

Molly remained still, concealing her torment, while Sheriff Stone seemed to relish every passing second, his features contorting into a churlish smirk. In the months following Caroline's disappearance, he had become a dim shadow stalking over Whitehall, relentlessly visiting the estate in pursuit of her.

"Are you all right?" he inquired.

"I am *fine,* Sheriff Stone," she pushed back.

"Uh, but you appear as though you've seen a ghost, ma'am. I had hoped you'd be considerably more delighted."

Molly gathered herself. "Where are they?"

"I have a carriage bringing them up from Wilmington, North Carolina, at this very instant. Can't hide forever by the sea. Not from this sheriff."

"Please permit me to take the boy into my care while Caroline awaits trial."

"You can fetch him on the morrow, but she remains with me."

PART XIV

To Touch the Gates of Heaven

Christmas Eve, 1783

Molly and Charity arrived at the downtown dock early the following morning, Christmas Eve, awaiting Caroline and Gabriel.

"We could be sitting for a considerable span," Molly said, turning to face Charity, their reflections hovering over the frigid, steel-blue water. "I need to inspect our tenant houses. Would you prefer to accompany me, or do you wish to remain here?"

"I'll stay," Charity answered immediately. "I wish not for Caroline's boy to enter inside that place, even for the briefest moment." Her eyes were fixed on the jail just in front of them, its decaying shiplap facade staring out dolefully at Dock Street.

"Thank you," Molly said before heading toward Duke of Gloucester Street.

Charity found a spot to wait by the water's edge. The nearby marketplace wasn't bustling, as it had been in warmer months. A few vendors braved the chill, hoping to sell their goods before Christmas: a ragged woman cradling a basket full of brown-and-white-speckled eggs, a lanky man with wide-eyed dead fish languishing over ice, and the butcher's boy whose sausage strings were slung around his neck. However, mostly the streets were empty, bewitched by a thin sheet of pearled white as wandering flurries continued to blow in from the bay.

Just across the street from the market, Charity's eyes met Middleton Tavern. Molly once mentioned General Washington liked to stay there when he visited town, but it was Charity's mother's account of Middleton that stuck out to her most. Rachel was a masterful storyteller, weaving tales that never failed to capture her children's attention. When Charity was a young girl, she struggled to fall asleep in the crowded, dingy cellar of Belair Mansion, Molly's childhood home, where Rachel and her family were enslaved. Charity, her brother James, and their mother shared the space with twenty other bondservants, six horses, and fifty hogs.

"Tell me the story about the scary ships and dark taverns, Mama," Charity used to whisper, her high-pitched voice breaking through the blackness.

Exhausted from endless household chores from dawn to dusk, Rachel still managed to indulge her daughter. "I'll tell you, child, but only if you rest your tired eyes."

Charity would shut them immediately, allowing Rachel's soft, soothing voice to fill her mind. "The ships our ancestors came to the colonies in were much, much scarier than this here cellar. Cruel men took our ancestors' clothes, chained their arms and legs, and crowded them in so closely, they could barely move."

"And remember how even the ships were sad for our people?" six-year-old Charity would interject.

"Oh yes, even the ships cried for them. All night long, they screeched and wailed. And would you believe they even tried to rock them to sleep? Back and forth, back and forth, those ships swayed."

"All the way to Annapolis," Charity added, trying to overcome a yawn.

"All the way to the docks in Annapolis."

"That's when they had to go to those scary taverns, right?"

"Sometimes, baby girl. Often, they sold them right there on the ships, but other times, like for Granny, they took them to places like Middleton Tavern and the Beaver and Lac'd Hat Tavern. Granny said she always hated the bitter, smothering smell of ale 'cause it brought back the fear she felt the day the bosses bid on her and her family."

"But she didn't give up, did she, Mama?"

"No, child, she didn't. No, she did not. You see, she knew that the shackles our people have had to bear represent one dark chapter of God's story for us, *but* there will be many more chapters to come. In time, she said, her children's children will walk back into those taverns, places that housed so much shame and brutality, and they will be *free citizens*, never forgetting the bloodshed but always looking forward, refusing to trade hate for hate, and *always* remembering the strength they came from."

"Strong minds and grateful hearts," Charity would say quietly, her eyes still closed, the message imprinted inside her.

"Indeed, my Charity. To bravely cast your eyes on the hidden joy in *every* circumstance is to touch the very gates of heaven."

Charity's eyes grew wide again as she processed her mother's words. "I'm glad I have you and James down here."

Rachel kissed her daughter's smooth cheek. "Oh, me too, baby girl, me too." Her lips then hovered beside Charity's ear, "And you know what else, that *free citizen* Granny was speakin' of...is going to be *you*. I just know it to be so."

Suddenly, the sound of clomping horse hooves drew Charity back to the docks. A black carriage carved narrow lines in the stark, white snow as it passed, pulling up right in front of the jail. Charity rose quickly and ran toward it, stopping just a few yards short as the door opened sharply and one of the sheriff's men stepped out.

She could feel her heart throbbing as she let out a chilled exhalation that lingered before her. Beyond her frozen breath, she made out little Gabriel, now six years old, being lifted from the carriage. Charity instinctively ran to him, but another one of the sheriff's men intervened, pushing his arm in front of her. "Stand back!"

Stepping suddenly from the carriage door was Caroline, her wrists chained together, her fierce eyes immediately finding Charity's. Caroline's expression softened when she saw her, but Charity hated the despair laid bare across her face.

Turning toward the guard who'd been traveling with Caroline, Charity willed herself to speak. "Sir, please know Sheriff Stone agreed that Mrs. Molly Ridout could take the boy."

Thankfully, Molly came running up at that moment, panting. "Yes, I've come to fetch the boy while his mother stands trial."

The guard studied them both. "Very well, if Sheriff Stone approved it."

Caroline looked toward Molly and Charity, releasing a deep, detained breath before speaking. "Thank you for taking him."

Gabriel curled up beside his mother, leaning his soft, blonde curls against her shackles, his tense blue eyes gazing up at these women who he certainly didn't remember.

"These ladies once held you as a baby, Gabriel." Caroline stooped down beside him. "You can trust them. I promise."

Charity crouched next to the boy, pulling a carved wooden yo-yo from the flour-sack bag she carried over her shoulder. She smiled. "This is for you."

Gabriel reached his hand out carefully, allowing Charity to place the smooth, round toy in his upturned palm. He studied it thoroughly.

"They're going to take care of you until I see you again." Caroline kissed his forehead, bottling his scent inside her. "I love you."

"I won't go," Gabriel whined.

Caroline's heart felt as though it would burst. She bent down to meet his eyes. "You must."

Gabriel shook his head.

"My boy, you have to be brave for me." Caroline stood, forcing herself to flee as Charity took Gabriel's hand.

He cried out, "Mama!"

Caroline told herself she could only handle one last look—but meeting his eyes, the sadness in them nearly doubled her over, so she turned back toward the jail. But just before walking inside, she needed to see him one final time. His slight frame, speckled with snow, reached out to her. Caroline closed her eyes and turned away before the tears could fall. She stepped into the jail, wiping her eyelids, and the noxious smell of urine and blood overwhelmed her.

"Greetings, Mrs. Brooks." Caroline straightened her shoulders as Sheriff Stone emerged from the gloom. "As the new year commences, you are to face trial for the murder of your husband." His eyes narrowed. "In the meantime, Merriest Christmas."

PART XV

The Jury has Reached its Decision

January 1784

Caroline, wrapped in a thick wool cloak with a wide hood draped over her head, stopped momentarily to gaze up at the imposing State House, looming high above her, its newly constructed pillars a classical representation of strength and order —the furthest thing from what she felt at that moment. She then transferred her eyes to the path ahead—the final stretch from the city dock jail to the murder trial that would decide her and Gabriel's future.

"Keep moving," Sheriff Stone pressed, disdain pouring from his glare. A frigid gust swept across the cobbled lane as she stepped forward, aware of the onlookers staring down reproachfully from their frosted windows. As they reached State Circle, her eyes cut across the ashes of her former home; the sounds of shouting and piercing pops filling her mind, vivid remnants of that dreadful night.

Despite her wrists being bound, she still managed to raise the hem of her dress as she ascended the steep, icy steps of the State House. The immense doors at the top felt like portals of judgment as she slipped herself inside them. Once through, her defense lawyer, Jonathan Caldwell, a well-postured man with a commanding presence and meticulously combed salt-and-pepper hair, greeted her.

"Mrs. Brooks, we face a formidable challenge today, but rest assured, I am here to advocate for you with every fiber of my being."

Caroline, refusing to remove her hood, slowly nodded. He guided her to a room off the main hall where court proceedings took place. Wide windows cast an eerie glow across rows of wooden benches and an elevated platform, where she imagined the judge would soon deliver the verdict. A chill spiraled up her spine.

Mr. Caldwell and Caroline found their way to counsel tables that sat just feet from the judicial bench. The seats behind her began to fill.

Unbeknownst to Caroline was the arrival of Molly and Charity, who'd slipped quietly onto a back bench in the courtroom. But a stone-faced constable noticed them both. "The mulatto woman stays out," he grumbled.

"Greetings, Mr. Cummings." Molly stepped closer so others couldn't hear. "Please allow her to remain. I beg of you."

The aging officer with thick brows and a thicker waistline studied her carefully. "Oh, Mrs. Ridout, I didn't realize it was you." He'd served as town constable for many years, dating back to Molly's father's governorship. Mr. Cummings surveyed the room. "Remain concealed here in the rear, and if anyone inquires, it was not I who granted permission."

"I owe you, sir, and will return the favor if ever I can."

Within minutes, the courtroom thrummed with anticipation.

Caroline lifted off her hood just in time to notice Prosecutor Richard Hastings gathering at a counsel table next to hers. He stood with an air of stern authority, ready to present the case against her.

Also, just arriving was Judge Robert Sinclair, with his silvered hair, neatly powdered and held back in a queue. His tailored, dark-hued robe cut an imposing silhouette on the elevated bench.

And finally, the twelve male jurors filed into a dozen chairs in the courtroom's front corner, disparaging looks painted across their faces.

Judge Sinclair asked Caroline's counsel to begin.

The room fell silent.

Mr. Caldwell addressed the jury. "Ladies and gentlemen, my client, Caroline Brooks, stands accused of a heinous crime. But I implore you to listen to the whole tale before casting judgment. I call first to the stand Mrs. Molly Ridout, daughter of our esteemed former governor, Samuel Ogle." Molly stood and elegantly drifted to the stand, her unwavering eyes a source of solace for Caroline.

"My dear friend Caroline is a woman of virtue, devoted to her husband Grafton. Their love was steadfast, as I witnessed with my own eyes," Molly testified.

The courtroom tension escalated as the prosecution called Andrew Moore to the stand, casting shadows on Caroline's character. "On the night Grafton Brooks met his end," Andrew spoke gravely, "Caroline offered us sherry. I denied her, but Mr. Brooks was not so fortunate."

Mr. Caldwell rose, objecting vehemently. "Your Honor, insinuations without evidence have no place in this courtroom!"

The judge upheld the objection, and Andrew continued with a sly smile, "My apologies, but it is true Grafton had a difficult time bridling his outspoken wife."

Caroline felt a surge of unease as Mr. Caldwell furrowed his brows. Andrew Moore's insinuations lingered, casting doubt on her innocence, which was further threatened when the town's apothecary, Dr. Samuel Goodwin, took the stand.

Prosecutor Hastings addressed him first. "Dr. Goodwin, did Mrs. Brooks visit you at any point before Mr. Brooks's murder?"

"She did. The morning before the fire."

Whispers rippled through the courtroom as the crowd exchanged speculative glances.

But hope flickered in the cross-examination when Mr. Caldwell questioned Dr. Goodwin about her visit.

"Mrs. Brooks sought arsenic to rid their home of rats from the dock. It was a dire necessity, I assure you," Dr. Goodwin testified.

Mr. Caldwell addressed the jury. "As you can see, Caroline sought a solution to a problem that plagued her household, not a sinister plot."

As Caroline's fate hung in the balance, Judge Sinclair announced the jury's decision with solemnity. "The jury has reached its decision."

Caroline held her breath, her heart thrashing in her chest, the room rocking and spinning around her—a treacherous sea of trepidation.

"Caroline Brooks, the court finds you *guilty* of the grievous crime of murder. You shall be taken from hence to the place whence you came, and from thence to Gallows Hill, where you shall be hanged by the neck until you are dead. May God have mercy on your soul."

Caroline gasped, a wave of horrifying nausea washing over her. Before she knew it, they were leading her from the courtroom, the crowd stunned into silence. Sheriff Stone perched himself by the back door, waiting, his arms crossed, a snide satisfaction sculpted across his face. Gathering the last morsel of strength she had left, Caroline straightened her neck and glared back at him, only lifting her hood once she passed and stepped back into the blistering cold.

———

The day before Caroline was to be taken to the gallows, Charity slipped inside the jail. The guards gave her a few moments to speak to her friend. Several bars at the top of a solid wooden door separated them.

Something deep inside Caroline gave way when she saw Charity, but she barely showed it. During the trial, and in the days that followed, she'd forced herself to grow stoic and hardened in her movements and emotions.

It was the only way she could face her fate.

A tear raced down Charity's cheek.

Caroline reached through the slight opening and took her hand.

"I've known this day would come."

"Oh, Caroline, how even now can you stand tall?"

"I learned it from you."

"No." Charity wiped her cheek. "You were *always* stronger."

"It's not so. Anger has made me weak. It has taken *everything* from me. It's you whose steadiness reveals genuine fortitude. Do you remember when we were five years old, and my father took me to Belair Mansion to visit Molly's family? I found you with your family in the basement among the hogs. I tried chiding Molly's father, much to the disdain of my own. You told me not to let bitterness take hold, saying everyone finds hardship, but only those who actively seek it will find a lantern to guide them through the darkness."

"I can't believe you remember that. Those were my mama's words, not mine. She was a faithful woman."

"And you listened to her. Can't say I ever heard a word my father uttered. I was far too proud."

"You know, I recall thinking all those years ago that you were the bravest girl I'd ever met, coming down into that basement alone, though you knew you weren't permitted. You never did abide by the rules."

"Which explains why I'm here."

"You are here because you refused to let a man harm you, your child, and your country. I saw the bruises you hid. I should have pressed you."

Silence crept its way into the cracked walls around them.

"I should have told you...that I did it," Caroline finally said, loud enough for even the guards to hear. Charity's eyes widened as Caroline continued, "Worry not. They can't deem me guilty twice."

"I hate that he was violent with you."

"It wasn't about the blows, for I endured those. But when his fists struck me on that morning before the fire, I vowed he'd never lay hands on the babe again. I'd also learned, through a letter I intercepted, that Grafton was, in fact, conspiring with the enemy and had information to give them. I felt I had no other choice."

"Couldn't you have proven that somehow to the judge?"

"Not since my house burned down."

"But didn't you..."

"I would never ruin my home, especially right before the birth of my child."

Charity's eyes drifted toward the ground, her mind searching. "Then who did?"

"I wish I knew because I'd make sure they hung from the gallows next to me."

Charity's voice dropped to a murmur. "You should have sought my aid rather than the apothecary's. My foxgloves are straight poison."

"I could never embroil you."

A tall, muscular guard with a natural scowl stepped forward and told Charity she had just one minute longer.

Charity turned back to Caroline. "I so desired to bring Gabriel but..."

His name alone sent chills through Caroline. It was more than she'd allowed herself to feel in weeks. How she missed his wee fingers wrapped in hers. His mischievous smile. She forced away the images.

"No, I wish not for him to lay eyes on me in this condition. I trust with every part of my being that I will clasp him once more in the hereafter. But that doesn't mean I'm not torn apart knowing I won't be here to see him grow."

Charity's eyes and shoulders fell as if all breath had escaped her.

"Do not pity me, friend," Caroline continued. "I held an angel in my arms and saw him turn into a bright, reckless little boy for far more days than I deserved. Watch out for him. Please, Charity."

"Always."

The guard was back. "You must depart. Your time has expired."

Yet Charity couldn't release her grip. The expression in her eyes pierced Caroline's heart. She, too, would deeply miss her dearest friend. The guard seized Charity's arm, forcing her to leave. Caroline watched as the sunlight beckoned her friend back into the world, only to vanish abruptly as the door sharply shut.

Hours later, evening's glow poured itself through Caroline's compact jail cell window.

She felt its warmth against her face. *My last sunset.*

The guard from earlier interrupted her thoughts. "You have one more visitor."

Caroline's body went numb.

Don't let it be Gabriel. I can't bear...

A tired, sheepish face stepped in front of her cell.

"Mrs. McGregor..." Caroline stood up, shocked to see her old housekeeper.

"I'd heard ye was back in town..."

"Not the homecoming I'd hoped for, but yes. Here I am."

The graying woman's eyes welled with tears. "I'm so sorry, Miss Caroline, that I didn't come to the trial to plead for ye. I knew what he..."

"Please, no. It was best you refrained. Recounting his brutality would have only deemed me more culpable of his undoing."

"There's somethin' else ye need to know."

"Yes?"

Caroline watched as Mr. McGregor pulled on her fingers and shifted in place before finally speaking. "I found Mr. Brooks...well, gone...lyin' there in his study that night. And I saw the drink spilled right beside 'im. I heard yer fight earlier that mornin' too. I saw 'im hit ye from behind the parlor door. I'd seen 'im hit ye afore as well." Mrs. McGregor's face fell to the ground. "I dreaded they'd seize ye. I knew they'd catch ye."

Caroline pressed her face against the bars. "What are you saying?"

Her frightened gaze turned back to Caroline. "In Mr. Grafton's dyin' moments, he scribbled yer name in ink. Covered the wall with his words: 'Caroline did it.' It was nay time to ponder." Tears streamed across her rosy-plucked cheeks. "I knew his carriage was takin' leave at dawn, and they'd find 'im. They'd witness it all and take ye in haste."

Caroline felt the heat rising inside her. "So, you set the house ablaze?"

"I did."

"Why would you not wake me first?"

"I panicked when I saw that Mr. Brooks's new manservant 'twas awake. I knew ye'd be finished if he found 'im.

Anger surged within Caroline. It burned without warning. She turned away and paced the cramped cell, sweat forming on her forehead.

Caroline glanced back at Mrs. McGregor's grief-stricken eyes, the same ones that had safeguarded her since childhood, and clarity struck her. She realized that their remaining time together was rapidly diminishing. It also became apparently clear that Mrs. McGregor was likely the reason she was able to escape to Wilmington and witness Gabriel's childhood for as long as she had.

Caroline forced out the words, "You made the right decision," then lowered her voice, "but speak not of it again. Do you understand? You will not hang for my transgressions."

The guard was back. "Your allotted time has elapsed, madam."

"Thank you for your loyalty," Caroline told her.

"Yer the dawther I never had." Mrs. McGregor's voice was stern, but her eyes bore tenderness. She bit her lip and bowed her head before shuffling away in tears.

Poor woman. I should not have remained in bed that night, filled with fear. It's my fault she was compelled to do the unthinkable because I was too afraid to descend the stairs to face my actions.

As the sun began to finally surrender its light, Caroline noticed a thick host of gray, hollow clouds sweeping in from the west. Snow soon poured down like powder, coating the soiled earth. Her grandfather's words, delivered in a sermon a decade earlier, as she sat in the back pew, suddenly came to her: "Thou your sins be as scarlet, they shall be white as snow."

The following day, a brief statement in the *Maryland Gazette* announced that on January 18, 1784, the sheriff and his men took Mrs. Caroline Brooks to the gallows in Annapolis, where they privately executed her on account of the snowstorm, after being found guilty of murdering her husband, Mr. Grafton P. Brooks.

Chapter 21
January 2013

"Hello, this is the Brooks Inn. Arthur speaking."

"Hi, Arthur, it's Lorna."

"Lorna, what a pleasant surprise. How are you?"

"I'm doing well, thanks. Just wanted to let you know I finished the book."

"I'm so glad to hear it."

"I couldn't put it down."

"Allison will be so pleased to know, as am I."

"The scene at the end where Caroline and Charity have to say goodbye, it tore me apart. I realize she killed Grafton, and it's messed up she took his life, but I mean, let's be honest, he was an abusive spy. And how I hate that she had to leave Gabriel."

"Certainly. The boy makes everything...harder."

"Considering Caroline was assisting the Rebels, and Grafton was spying for the British, I thought some of the Patriots in Annapolis might have found a way to prevent her execution."

"You would think. They had no evidence of his espionage, though, particularly after the house had burned down. Another problem seems to be that Thomas was gone. He would have pleaded in her defense without a doubt."

"Thomas died?"

"Yes, he came down with smallpox a few years after he gave Caroline the necklace."

"How awful. He seemed like such a good man."

"I know. And Thomas, of course, was one of the few people who knew Caroline was secretly aiding Rebel missions. As you know, she wrote her Patriot sentiments in the *Maryland Gazette*, but they had to be unanimous because she was a woman."

"So barely *anyone* knew how much she actually gave to the cause."

"Sadly."

"What about the Ridouts? Molly seemed to be putting the pieces together. And didn't John have some clout?"

"He lost a lot of it because of the war. Although John and Molly held strong Patriot sympathies and deeply admired Continental leaders like George Washington, they also made earnest efforts to maintain neutrality, given their close family and political connections back in England. I imagine they were profoundly torn. It's the reason they eventually relocated from town to Whitehall mansion. Yet, by not taking a side, they fell out of favor with some authorities who might have potentially influenced Caroline's fate."

"Tell me about those five years she spent with her son in Wilmington, after she fled from Annapolis."

"Unfortunately, Allison and I know very little. We searched and searched but couldn't find any records of her living down there."

"Really? None?"

"None. I mean, certainly she would have kept her cover low, knowing Sheriff Stone was combing the colonies for her. I suppose it's incredible how long she stayed hidden. From what I've read, the sheriff was obsessed with finding her, constantly traveling the coast."

"Where did that come from?" Lorna switched on the light to her bedroom. "Such a fixation on apprehending her. I mean, I realize he wanted to do his job, but to take it to such lengths."

"I'm sure Caroline enraged him—how she spoke her mind, even to him, a complete megalomaniac."

"Absolutely. But to take away his attention from the town he was supposed to protect, I don't know, it just feels like something's missing." Silence drew itself between them until Lorna finally continued, "Interestingly enough, I'm heading to downtown Wilmington tonight to have drinks with a friend from my nursing program."

"How nice. You know, Allie and I traveled down there one time, many years ago. I'd found an address in one of Gabriel's letters: 14 South 3rd Street, I believe it was. But no town name was given. Gabriel wrote it as an older man to his daughter Penelope. The address was at the bottom of the letter with no explanation. Regardless, when I discovered there was no such address in Annapolis, I immediately thought of Wilmington, since I knew Gabriel lived there as a boy. We went so far as to visit the house on 3rd Street, but it was in ruins, sadly, and no one had ever heard of a Caroline Brooks."

"Hmm...14 South 3rd Street. It's worth a try to check into again. Thank you, Arthur."

"It's my pleasure. I hope you discover more than I was able to. And please, do visit when you get back to town."

"I will. Bye, Arthur."

"Goodbye, Lorna."

She put her cell phone down and picked up Allison's novel on the nightstand. Lorna wrote the address on the inside cover, placed the book in her purse, and grabbed her conglomerate of key chains, linked with two small keys, then headed out the door.

Front Street Brewery in Wilmington was a bustling spot on Saturday nights. Lorna, never one for crowds, considered this carefully when choosing a restaurant, but her craving for chicken nachos and a craft-beer sampler won out in the end.

She popped open the door and scanned the restaurant for Tess, who lived close to downtown and had agreed to arrive first to ensure they had a table.

Lorna spotted her in a nearby booth, but Tess was staring down at her phone.

"Lookin' to find yourself a good time tonight?" Lorna said, watching surprise turn to elation when Tess looked up.

Pushing herself off the cushioned pleather seat and onto her feet, Tess coiled her arms around Lorna. "Hellooo, darlin'!"

Lorna felt a contagious warmth rising through her body. Being with Tess always had that effect on her. A divorcee with three teenage children, she'd been through a laundry list of heartbreak and had more than twenty years on Lorna, but life certainly hadn't stolen her zeal.

Tess stepped back and met Lorna's eyes, her voice lowering and the tone of her smooth southern drawl further softening Lorna's edges. "So glad we could get ya out tonight." Then her pitch rose once again. "I was afraid you'd wanna stay home and work on all that dadgum nursing homework she gave us! What does she think, we're tryin' to be brain surgeons or somethin'?"

"Seriously, it's gonna take me all day tomorrow to finish that. Might as well have fun tonight," Lorna returned, looking down at the beer sampler in front of her.

Tess smiled, "I remember you said in class you were cravin' it."

"I sure am. Thank you!"

Tess raised her own glass, a lemonade. She didn't drink anymore. "Cheers to our night on the town."

Two glasses clinked together, rising above the noise in the room.

"How'd you get off work at the news station? I thought you always worked on Saturdays now that you have nursing school."

"I told them to leave me the heck alone tonight." Tess smirked. "And a gal I work with wanted some extra hours, so I obliged."

"I'm glad. I'd love to see you in there working your video editing magic and ordering all those young reporters around."

"Oh, dear me. Suppose they call me 'Mama Tess' for a reason. I prolly look like an angry old bitty forcin' my rule on those absent-minded weenies when they don't get their scripts and video in on time, but *merrrcy,* someone's gotta do it."

Lorna grinned. "Will you miss WECT once you get a nursing job?"

"I won't miss the paychecks cause there's nothin' to miss." Her boisterous laugh filled the room. "But yeah, I'll miss a few of those ninnies, I suppose."

After dinner they strolled along the Cape Fear Riverwalk, a wooden deck that stretched along its banks for several miles. The sun had almost set, and a cool fog gathered over dark waters. Lorna wrapped a scarf snugly around her neck.

"There's an eerie feelin' out tonight," Tess said as she zipped up her coat.

"I have to agree."

Lorna filled Tess in on Caroline Brooks and the Three Brothers. Tess agreed they should stop by 14 South 3rd Street to check if the house might be linked to Caroline.

Taking out her cell phone, Lorna opened the map app. "Looks like the house is right across the street from St. James Parish."

"Let's walk by and investigate, then," Tess suggested.

"Sounds like you should have been a reporter, Tess."

"Oh no. I do not do well with crazy people. But I've got your back, my friend."

"Thank you. It's way more fun to have a partner in crime," Lorna smiled.

"Batman, you have found your Robin."

Lorna laughed. "Thank you. Although I must say, I saw myself as more of an Indiana Jones/Agatha Christie-type. But your direction leads us to an entirely more badass costume, so let's stick with that. The place is just off Market Street."

"Oh, I know exactly where it is. Been walkin' these streets since I was a little scrap. My brother and I used to ride our bikes through the St. James Cemetery. Ohhhh did my mama get mad when Mrs.

Thomas the neighbor lady told her she'd seen us using those gravestones like obstacle-course cones. Oh my, did we get a lickin' that day!"

"Ouch." Lorna snickered. "I didn't realize you grew up down here."

"Yes, ma'am."

As they strolled toward the house on 3rd Street, they passed a crisp-white, stately home first. Lorna stopped to stare up at the towering mansion.

Tess turned around. "Oh, that's the Burgwin-Wright House."

Double porches swept along the entire front facade with a wide staircase leading off the lower one. At the bottom of the steps, a sign read: "Night Tour: Saturday at 9 p.m."

Lorna looked down at the map on her phone. "Looks like 14 South 3rd is just around the corner." Then she checked the time. "But it's two minutes till nine o'clock. Wanna pop inside here first, do a quick tour, and get warm?"

"Oh heavens, I don't do well with creepy old homes in the dark, but if you wanna check it out, honey..."

"I need you, Robin. Plus, it's warm."

Tess smiled. "All right, then. Warmth does sound nice."

On the ground level, they entered a gift shop. A college-aged girl, probably working to pay off her UNCW bills, wore colonial attire, her hair neatly tucked in a tight bun. A name tag pinned to her chest read: "Jane". She stood behind a cash register. "Two for the tour?"

"I suppose," Tess said apprehensively.

"Yes, please." Lorna handed Jane two twenties.

Jane gave Lorna her change. "Head back outside, up the porch steps, and the tour will start just inside the front door."

The lights were switched off inside the foyer, but several candelabras flickered, casting a soft, hazy glow throughout the space. Half a dozen others shuffled around near the main staircase and in an adjacent study, waiting for the tour to begin. One man asked when the house was built.

"1770," Jane answered. After introductions, she led them through the downstairs, which included a large sitting room that Jane called the parlor, two smaller offices, and a host of oversized portraits with haunting eyes looking down at her. It was upstairs, though, where things got more interesting.

Jane stopped at a closed door. "All the employees have a least favorite room in the house, and this is it."

Lorna and Tess looked at each other. Lorna grinned while Tess pursed her lips.

"You can do it. I'll protect you," Lorna whispered.

"You best," Tess said, not so quietly.

Chapter 22

Jane swung the door open, revealing a walnut four-poster bed with an ornate, white canopy that glowed in the candlelight.

She stayed outside the room and motioned for the group to head inside, but Tess stood her ground. "Why don't people like being in this room?"

"There's this strange air in the main bedroom. A lot of people get an uncomfortable feeling when they're in it. I feel it myself. When I need something in this room, I kind of hurry in and out," Jane explained.

Tess looked straight ahead into the eerie space. "Why we goin' in, then?"

"Well, it has a lot of beautiful eighteenth-century furniture and..."

Tess crossed her arms. "Oh, y'all can go for it, but I am staying right here."

"You won't get to see the notorious spinning wheel, then. It was stuck in place for years. But one night a tour group saw it suddenly begin to turn until it started spinning faster and faster." Jane was bubbling with excitement. Tess wasn't. Jane continued, "Until suddenly, the wheel just stopped. The group walked over, and someone tried to move it, but it was stuck tightly in place again."

Lorna eyed Tess, who stood frozen in place. "Tess, I'm sorry this stuff makes you so uncomfortable. Let's go."

"Oh no, I am holding my ground. We are on a mission. I'll just let you deal with the ghosts." Tess howled in laughter, causing half the people in the bedroom to spin around nervously.

When everyone came back out into the upstairs hallway, Jane shared another story about the "man in the hall," who even she, of course, had seen clopping around early one morning. "I could tell by his knee breeches that he was wasn't from our century."

"Maybe the knee-breeches guy was yet another victim of that Caroline woman," Tess said with a chuckle.

Lorna knew she was joking and tried to smile, but it wasn't a convincing grin. Her attachment to the past, to someone she never even knew, felt strange—ridiculous even. Lorna forced her lips to widen further, thinking to herself, *I must look like a complete loon to Tess—chasing ghosts like this.*

Jane went on, "One very sad reality about homes like this during the Colonial Period is that they used enslaved people. Some of them slept on the floor outside these bedroom doors so they could be available when needed."

Lorna's stomach dropped. Standing next to Tess, whose ancestors went back many generations in Wilmington, possibly as enslaved workers, Lorna imagined how painful it must have felt for her friend to envision the arduous life they'd led.

Tess eyed the wide pine floors, which clicked and moaned as the group trailed into the final upstairs room of the tour. Lorna took in the sage green walls, ornate dining table, and vast openness of the room.

"Here we have the dining room—likely put on the top floor to avoid foul and pungent smells from the street. Now for years, people around Wilmington called this the Cornwallis House because the British general entertained guests here in April of 1781, during the Revolutionary War. The Redcoats had taken over the city two months prior, and Cornwallis hoped to reaffirm alliances with American Loyalists and boost the morale of his officers."

"I'm guessing this is the room he wined and dined them in," Tess said, eyeing the massive crystal chandelier dangling above them.

"Great guess," Jane replied. "Yes, this is where guests would have been brought for dinner—as you can see, plenty of room and a beautiful view of the city up here."

A few minutes later, Jane concluded the house tour. "Thanks for coming, folks." She pressed her palms together. "I know it's frigid outside, but anyone who wants to do a quick browse through the English-style gardens out back, y'all are welcome to join me. I also know it's late, so no judgment if you'd rather head home." Her voice rose slightly. "Or we have a wonderful gift shop too!"

Tess tightened her scarf as she turned to Lorna. "I won't let you be gettin' lost all alone in the shrub mazes out there."

"You wanna see the gardens? I've dragged you through the cold long enough, though."

"Nah, come on. I said I got your back, so I got it. Unless you take me to that ghost room again."

Lorna laughed. "No more ghosts...I promise."

The extensive garden was broken into separate sections. They entered the orchard portion of it first. Moonlight broke through the bare, stretching branches of fig and pomegranate trees, casting jagged shadows across the ground. Sturdy limbs proudly protruded over two perpendicular brick pathways that converged into a circular patio.

Jane stood near its center. "This beautiful orchard actually used to be a jail yard—complete with gallows for hanging prisoners, whipping posts, and stocks. The city jail stood on this property from 1744 to 1768, then Mr. Burgwin built his house on its original ballast-stone foundation two years later in 1770. Hard to imagine all the death and sorrow considering how serene it feels now, isn't it?"

After leaving the orchard and passing through two terraced areas, they moved on to the dipping pool portion of the garden. The small group surrounded a round, brick water basin.

"The perfect spot to gather rainwater for the horses to drink from. This used to be where a large, brick carriage home stood in the 1700s."

Jane started fielding questions from others in the group, which provided Lorna the opportunity to meander toward an ivy-covered brick wall dividing the garden from an adjacent yard.

After checking the map on her phone, she returned to the group and asked Jane, "Do you know anything about the house behind this garden? The white one, there through the trees, with the metal roof."

"That's the Dubois-Boatwright house. Second oldest home in the city. They built it just before this place in the 1760s. It's under construction because the current owners are restoring it."

"Any chance you may have heard of a woman and her son who lived there during the Revolutionary War?" Tess chimed in.

"Actually, I do know of someone who lived in the home around that time. She was the innkeeper there, and her name was Alice, Alice Gates, I believe it was. She's buried across the street in St. James Cemetery."

"Uh, well, that isn't the woman we're trying to track down, but she may have known her. Caroline Brooks, who I'm interested in learning more about, died in Annapolis. Authorities arrested her and took her back to Maryland on murder charges in 1783.

"I don't recognize the name, but there is a story from the Revolutionary War period about a woman who once stayed in the home. They called her the horsewoman fugitive."

Lorna's eyebrows shot up as Jane stopped strolling, her lantern continuing to rock back and forth, casting a scattered glow off the spike-leafed holly trees that refused to abandon their greenery, despite winter's chill. "I was told the authorities traveled into town searching for a female fugitive. When the sheriff showed up at the house, the woman fled into these gardens, where she hid until nightfall. She then stole a horse from the Wright family carriage house that used to sit on this part of the property."

Lorna perked up further. "Do you know what happened to her?"

"Apparently, she rode off down Front Street and made it as far as the Cape Fear River until she decided she had to go back. I'm pretty sure she didn't want to leave her child. So, she came back to the house, and that's when they caught her."

Lorna's hand automatically landed over her lips. *It had to be Caroline.*

"What name did the horsewoman fugitive go by?" Tess added.

"I don't know. One of the other tour guides just recently told me the story. Sarah, the director of our museum, is here tonight. We could ask if she knows about her. I can see if she's still in her office?"

"Please, if you would. We'd really appreciate it," Lorna said before turning to Tess. "Look at you, Ms. Detective."

Tess threw her shoulders back. "Oh, I'm just gettin' started."

While the rest of the group dispersed, Lorna and Tess followed Jane back inside the house. A woman was buttoning her winter coat and looked a bit anxious.

Jane introduced her to Lorna and Tess. "This is Sarah, our director."

"Hi, Sarah, I'm Lorna. Wondering if you can confirm the name of the lady they called 'the horsewoman fugitive,' who stayed next door when it was an inn?"

Sarah slid her fingers inside a fleece-lined, leather glove. "I'm afraid I don't know her name. But I'm sure Jane mentioned in the tour how the British seized Wilmington during the Revolutionary War and General Cornwallis entertained guests here. In letters they found while renovating this house, multiple Redcoats described a woman who came to his party from the house next door. They said she was asking a lot of questions, even to Cornwallis. They seemed suspicious of her. Now, I'm pretty sure this happened several years before the horsewoman fugitive was arrested, but maybe she stayed at the inn on multiple occasions?"

"Did any of the letters describe what she looked like?"

Sarah thought for a moment. "No, but there's a sketch from April of 1781, when Cornwallis was here. She looked to have blonde hair, and it was pinned up high."

"There was a drawing of her?"

"Yes. One of the British soldiers drew it." Sarah pulled a second glove from her coat pocket. "I'd love to tell you what book I saw this in. Or was it an online source? I'll try to remember. Unfortunately, I'm late picking up my thirteen-year-old from a party, and I have to run."

"Of course. But quickly, before you go. Jane told us about the innkeeper, Alice Gates, who's buried across the street. Do you know anything about her?"

"Very little. Just that she's in the cemetery. But I do know the current owner of the house." Sarah pulled out her cell phone. "Would you want to give me your number, and if she knows anything, I can text you?"

"Oh, um, sure. Thank you." Lorna told Sarah her number.

"I'll shoot you a message, then you'll have mine too. Next time I see the owner, I'll ask what she knows about Alice, as well as the horsewoman fugitive. Have a good night!" Sarah sprung toward the front door but turned just before she reached it. "Oh, and Alice's gravestone is under the only crepe myrtle in the cemetery, if you'd like to stop by." She waved goodbye then turned back once more, slowly this time. "One last thing. The woman at Cornwallis's party—I remember her necklace catching my eye. It was stunning. And massive."

Lorna, her face frozen, stepped toward Sarah. "Was it a triangular shape?"

Sarah's features pinched together. "Yes, actually, I think it was. With a massive pearl hanging down from the bottom." She waved and finally disappeared out the door, leaving Lorna dumbfounded.

She turned to Tess. "Could Caroline have taken the necklace to Wilmington the night she fled from Annapolis? If so, the audacity to wear it in front of the British officers and their Loyalist friends. I can't wait to tell Arthur."

Tess grinned. "The girl at the ball with the biggest balls of all."

Lorna and Tess eventually made their way around the corner on Market and 3rd Street.

The place next door, similar to the Burgwin-Wright House, had a white exterior and appeared to have been there for several centuries; but that was where the similarities ended. It was sizably smaller, with just one wide front porch. And unlike the Burgwin-Wright House, that had been beautifully maintained, this home's neglect spread from the ivy-covered siding to the dilapidated back wall that could have and should have toppled at any moment.

"I prefer this place, actually." Lorna cocked her head as she looked up at the home.

"This one?" Tess studied it. "Are you sure?"

"Yes, it's...simple."

"Sure is. But the other was at least taken care of, despite its creepiness."

"Yeah, this one needs work. But it'll be charming when it's renovated."

Tess didn't look convinced as she continued to peer up at the crumbling abode. "Guess I'll have to take your word for it."

They made their way onto the wide front porch. Lorna began to read the plaque beside the door, until Tess suddenly twisted the brass doorknob and popped it open. "Guess the construction crew forgot to lock up."

"Tess! Why'd you do that?"

"Darlin', you'll never get anything accomplished in life unless you're all in."

"What has gotten into you? You're getting way braver than I am now."

"I mean, you're still going in first."

Lorna eyed the bleak, black opening beyond the doorway and took a deep breath. She looked back toward 3rd Street. Because the front porch sat on cinders, high above the road, they were mostly hidden from view, but Lorna was still on edge. "I know no one is living here right now, but it's still trespassing. We could get into big trouble if someone sees us." She sighed. "Maybe just a quick look?"

"Real quick. Didn't you say this Caroline lady placed some symbol where she hid the necklace in Annapolis? Now that we know she brought it here too, isn't it worth a look?"

"A triangle."

"Say what?"

"A triangle," Lorna repeated. "That's what Caroline wrote on the oak tree where she buried the necklace at Whitehall. And you make a good point; you never know." Lorna pulled out her phone, opened the flashlight app, and before turning it on, stepped inside.

It took Tess longer. She waited in front of the doorway, trying to step through the threshold several times, but continuously retreating.

Lorna called out in a mock whisper: "Psst. Hey, this is Batman, Robin. Let's go. And close the door behind you."

Tess cautiously pulled out her cell phone too, held the flashlight up, put her left hand over her eyes, and stepped inside. When she opened them, Lorna was already studying one of the fireplaces.

The pine floors appeared to be original, with plastic coverings protecting them. Paint cans and spackling containers were scattered throughout the front rooms, which faced one another with matching fireplaces. The stairs were tucked away at the rear of the house, alongside what seemed to be a small, unfinished kitchen.

"Do you hear that?" Lorna looked up at the ceiling.

Tess's eyes bulged. "What?"

"It's like someone's scratching?"

They turned to face each other.

Tess's mouth dropped before whispering, "Maybe someone doesn't like us being here."

Chapter 23

Out of the corner of their eyes, back near the stairs, both Tess and Lorna saw a movement. It was like a fleeting wind, or a woman's dress, shooting right past them and turning them both instinctively toward it. But when their flashlights reached the steps, nothing was there.

The scratching sound grew louder.

Tess started backing toward the front door and felt frantically for the knob. "What in the..."

Lorna turned around to face the fireplace opening just as a dark creature emerged and thrust itself at her. She toppled backward, slipping on plastic wrap and tripping over several scattered tools as she collided with the floor.

Tess let out an ear-piercing scream.

Through the darkness, Lorna couldn't see what had come straight at her, but she wasn't going to stick around long enough to introduce herself.

Rolling onto her side, Lorna crawled hastily across the floor until she reached the open door, where Tess yanked her onto the front porch. They sped down the steps and didn't stop running until they were across the street, gasping for air in the church courtyard.

"What in the world was that!?" Lorna finally made out the words through her panting.

Tess, holding herself up on Lorna's shoulder, turned to look back at the house, the streetlights bathing it in a spectral glow. She pointed a shaky finger, and they both watched as an enormous raccoon slid its way across the metal roof, slipping as it neared the gutter, toppling into the grass below, and waddling toward the gardens next door.

Together they began to howl, laughter pouring from inside them, so unbridled it took them simultaneously to their knees as tears came streaming from their eyes.

It was several minutes before they finally gathered themselves.

"Lord, I haven't laughed like that in ages," Tess said, the two of them sitting on the grass. "Nor have I been that terrified in as much time."

Lorna agreed wholeheartedly as she peeked up at the enormous white church looking down at them—St. James Parish. The main building reigned proudly on the corner, its four gothic revival spires soaring high into the sky. A courtyard lay off to its left with multiple smaller buildings and a covered walkway sprawling out behind it.

Tess pointed. "Back there, that's where the cemetery is."

Lorna rose to her feet, helping Tess up too. "All right, one last stop before we get the heck outta here."

They strolled, arms interlocked, into the graveyard. Lorna pulled out her cell phone flashlight once again to illuminate the way ahead. Small, weary headstones and large, coffin-sized slabs peppered the ground.

"Good, there aren't many trees here. She said this Alice woman's grave was under a crepe myrtle, right? Do you know what they look like?" Lorna asked.

"Honey, was I born in the South or was I born in the South?"

"Fair enough, but you'd know it even without its blooms?"

"Who needs the flowers? When the leaves are gone and all is stripped from it, even its bark, those trees still glow."

They wove their way through stone after stone.

Tess finally stopped in front of a cluster of vertically bound branches, its trunk patterned with every shade of cream, tan, and cinnamon, like a paint-by-number portrait. "This is it," Tess marveled.

Simultaneously, they looked down at the tiny gravestone set before them.

Here lies Alice Gates,
keeper of the Inn,
mother, and friend,
who died July 1st, 1799,
aged 41 years.

Lorna grinned, "It's neat to think she might have hosted Caroline at the inn. Maybe they were even friends." She looked back up that the tree. "And look at that crepe myrtle. I never noticed how beautiful they are, even in the winter. You see the beauty in things no one else notices, Tess."

"Thank you. We all have our gifts. You know what I've noticed one of yours is?"

"What's that?"

"You're more of a survivor than you realize. It's why you like that Caroline so much. She had grit and a lot of it. Now, don't go knockin' anybody off like she did, if you can avoid it."

"No murdering. Noted."

"Good, 'cause I don't wanna be visitin' you in jail. You know I'm not that brave."

"I don't buy that. You grew up here at a time when I imagine it was far from easy to be a little black girl in the South."

"And you know what? It made me a heck of a lot stronger, just as all this heartbreak is gonna do for you—if you let it. I always found Greek mythology captivating, especially the story of the phoenix rising up from the ashes of its former self, emerging renewed and far more powerful than it was before."

Lorna looked back down at the gravestone. "As much as I'd love to become a far better version of myself, I just don't know that chasing ghosts is in any way helping."

"Sure, it is. Because you're doing it for Will. And the strongest thing in this big, old, crazy world is, without a doubt, love. We are created to love and be loved—it's that simple. All the rest is just hogwash."

"You're right. I just think I feel a bit ridiculous taking myself, and now you, on this wild goose chase."

"Tell me this, why couldn't Will, by the good Lord's grace, use a woman you've never met, this side of heaven, to guide you toward something momentous? *Follow her*. And don't let anybody make you think you're crazy for it. You understand?"

Lorna nodded.

Tess went on, "The only thing crazy is not listening to your instincts."

Chapter 24
Annapolis
April 2013

A few months later

Light trickled through ethereal clouds.

Puddles on the road reflected the light.

Lorna's tires spun through the murky pools, softly speckling a "Welcome to Maryland" sign with rainwater.

She'd contemplated staying back in Topsail for Spring Break, but Kate and Emma were relentless, eventually convincing her to travel back home. And maybe even Conor had mentioned it a time or two.

Yet, none of them would be the first person she'd see.

Lorna and Will had a tradition when they'd come into town, and she wasn't about to trade it in just because her world had crumbled before her. So, she found a parking spot just barely wide enough on Maryland Avenue and slid her truck inside it.

Will's Nana lived in an ancient brick colonial on Hanover Street close to the Naval Academy's Gate 3. Lorna knocked a few times before carefully opening the front door.

The acrid odor of something charred assaulted her senses, and a hazy mist enveloped the foyer. She rushed into the kitchen, but thankfully, the oven was off, and a solitary, blackened, shriveled morsel (*Is it meat?*) sat forlornly on a porcelain plate at the center of the table. Lorna couldn't help but laugh quietly, knowing Nana's reputation for culinary mishaps.

As she turned the corner, there was Nana, nestled into her favorite chair in the living room, her eyelids closed, and a serene smile etched across her face.

Lorna wondered where Nana's dreams were taking her. Was she anxiously awaiting her fiancé's ship from Europe at the close of World War II? Or maybe she was nearing midlife in the 1950s with three rambunctious boys, who took pleasure in hurling stones over the towering wall of the Naval Academy, much to her chagrin.

Lorna sat down across the room on the well-worn, pin-striped sofa that had been there as long as she could remember. It was where she and Will had always settled in, as they shared memories with Nana and Pop. Will's grandfather had been as dear to her as his grandmother, both the kindest and most genuine people she'd ever known.

Nana stirred.

"Hi there," Lorna said softly, afraid to frighten her.

"Evelyn?" Nana's eyes didn't open.

"It's Lorna."

Nana finally looked up, confused at first, then a smile overcame her.

"Lorna dear, oh, forgive me. My sister and I were playing near the stream behind our house. And she was singing. I loved when she used to sing to me." She beamed but swallowed hard as she continued, "So interesting how someone's spirit can leave the earth but still feel so close."

Lorna nodded. "Such a gift to still feel her. And yet I'm sure you miss her dearly."

"Every single day. But I'm happy for her. She always wanted to meet God. I have a feeling she's driving him mad with her questions, though."

The two women laughed. Inside Lorna wondered, *Is heaven real, and if so, what is Will doing there other than tormenting me with his crazy clues*?

"How are you, my dear Lorna?"

"Doing well, thanks."

"But how are you really doing?"

Lorna touched her right hand to her temple and began to sift through the tiny strands of hair near her ear.

Nana continued, "Something's on your mind."

"You know it's strange, Nana. I feel like Will's been trying to tell me something."

His grandma's eyes narrowed, but she didn't speak.

"Do you remember ever hearing about one of his and Pop's ancestors named Caroline Brooks?"

"She used to sit in this very room."

Lorna inched toward the edge of the couch. "What do you mean?"

"Caroline grew up in this house. When her father passed, she married and moved to a home on State Circle where the Brooks Inn is now. Apparently, her father lost this home to his debtors, just before his death, but it ended up back with the Brooks family about a hundred years ago. Pop grew up in this house too."

"I had no idea."

Nana leaned toward her as if someone else could hear them. "Legend has it, Caroline put her own cruel husband in the grave, and what's worse, she turned my husband into a wannabe treasure hunter," she said, rolling her eyes.

"Oh, really?" Lorna asked.

"Oh, yes. It tormented him. He and Arthur both. One of them got wind that Caroline once buried a famous crown jewel at Whitehall, and they could talk of nothing else. You know, *at first*, they seemed to really enjoy discussing the necklace. It bonded them."

"The phrase 'at first' never ends well."

"Isn't that the truth? Just before his death, Pop and Arthur's father took all the letters that had been passed down from his own parents and split them between Pop and Arthur. Then, one night when comparing notes and after a few drinks, the two of them got into a horrible fight. It had been building for many years. Pop was the hardheaded but loving military man. Arthur, of course, was the smart and sophisticated professor who saw the world quite differently than his older brother. So, their argument about the lost necklace was the straw that broke the camel's back." Nana's eyes saddened. "Would you believe they never spoke again? And, after that, they refused to share their letters with each other. Instead of digging into the mystery together, neither of them could ever solve it alone."

"So sad. Did you or Pop ever read Allison's book that Arthur helped her research?"

"No. And I feel bad saying it, as Allie spent a lot of time writing it and I'm sure it's wonderful, but I had no desire. The whole feud just made me bitter toward all of it."

"I understand completely."

"So, how is it Lorna, that Will led you to Caroline?"

"He comes to me in...well, it seems so silly to even say... but...dreams."

"Don't ever doubt the tenacity of a loved one. In life or death. What did he say?"

"He can't seem to speak in the dreams. But he opened up a book, and when he did, fire engulfed the pages. He'd mentioned Allison's novel briefly, so that's the only book that came to mind. Once I read it, the fire certainly makes sense. I think maybe he's guiding me to Caroline."

"Hmmm. And why do you say that?"

"Well, the book is all about her."

"Why Caroline, though?"

"I'm not sure. The only thing I can think of is he wants me to find the necklace and finally solve the mystery."

"Well, if anyone could manage to pass along messages all the way from heaven, it would be Will." Nana peered at a light shaft that had suddenly discovered her through a front window, took a deep breath, then turned back toward Lorna. "Honey, my only fear is that it'll take you down with it—like it did to Bill and Arthur. All their toiling in vain. Maybe it does bring luck to those who possess it, but it only seems to bring misery to those trying to find it."

"I understand. But what would you do if Pop was asking the same of you?"

Nana's eyes combed the ceiling, her lips and palms pressing simultaneously together. Finally, her gaze returned to Lorna. "I'd go to the only people I thought could help."

"Do they live around here?"

"Oh no, they aren't living. The dead, of course, know far more about the past than we do." Nana exerted all her strength, pressing both hands into her armrests, and slowly raised her frail body from the chair. Lorna stood and helped her up. Nana immediately started toward the office. "If you'd like to see them, I still have the old letters that Pop's father gave him years ago."

Lorna's pulse quickened. "I'd be so honored, Nana, thank you."

That evening, Lorna spent hours in Pop's study, curled up on a small chaise, looking through two centuries' worth of correspondence between relatives. Pop had even hidden a few of the earliest letters inside his favorite novels. Lorna thought it was special, but Nana had different sentiments. She believed her husband did it out of paranoia and fear that someone, namely his little brother, would find the letters and get to the necklace first.

Lorna also found a more recent letter from Pop to Nana during the war dated May 8, 1943.

. . .

Darling Beatrice, I hope this letter finds you well, safe and healthy, and sporting your breathtaking smile. I'm lucky enough to see it every day when I pull out your photo. The edges are torn and bent from being in my pocket, but I refuse to let you leave my side.

The ping of a text message instantly pried Lorna away.

Conor: *Just saw your truck on Maryland Avenue.*

Lorna's stomach caught, but she resisted the urge to text back, tossing her phone onto the red-and-gray Persian rug at her feet. She continued reading Pop's letter to Nana:

Will you make me the happiest man alive, Bea, and become my wife when I return?

Lorna gasped.

How a single sentence can change a life.

Nana walked in with a steaming cup of coffee. She placed it on Pop's desk, near Lorna. "To help you with your search."

"Thanks so much, Nana." She held up the thin piece of paper with a wide, beaming grin. "Pop just asked you to marry him."

"How about that...I'd forgotten about that letter."

Nana sat down beside Lorna and scanned the handwriting she knew so well. Her cheeks suddenly flushed with color. Lorna placed her arm around Nana and took a mental note to remember that moment always.

When Will's grandma left the room a few minutes later, Lorna continued to read. So much hope, sadness, love, and strength in all their stories and spirits.

Lorna was about to call it a night when suddenly the book *Twenty Thousand Leagues Under the Seas* caught her eye on the shelf. She remembered it was Pop's all-time favorite.

"I thought it was the word 'Sea' in the title and not 'Seas,'" she'd once said to him after seeing his ancient addition of the story years earlier. She and Will were still in high school and just over for a visit.

"Uh, that's what you'll find on most of the modern copies,"

Pop had told her. "But as you probably know, Jules Verne was French, and his original title should be translated to 'Seas'—the reason being that it refers to the distance traveled under the various oceans and not the depth of the ocean, as most people think. When you realize that 20,000 metric leagues is equal to 40,000 nautical miles, it makes sense that he wasn't talking depth. That distance will take you around the world twice!"

She rubbed her thumb slowly across "Seas" and opened it slowly. Lo and behold, in the front inside cover sat an ancient piece of parchment that was clearly older than the rest of the letters she'd delved into that evening.

January 13, 1818

My dearest Penelope,

How deeply I've missed you, my daughter. Your love and loyalty all these years have been indelibly marked on my spirit. And how I've longed to meet your child, my precious granddaughter. Please tell her I love her from afar.

If you're receiving this letter, that means you've made it home to America and I am no longer earthly bound and here to welcome you back. It pains me even to write this, yet considering my current ailments, I've deemed it necessary to make the proper arrangements for this letter to be given directly to you upon your return from England, as at this present moment you have departed London and I have not received word of your newest whereabouts.

Please do not grieve my passing, but know that your grandmother awaits me in heaven, where the two of us will one day joyfully await your arrival.

My darling, Penny, how you've always reminded me of her: bold and fearless, adventurous as the day is long, and quite impossible to harness. So, while my far more sensitive soul has continuously grieved your departure, I can't help but admire your willingness to cross an ocean in order to follow your heart. I pray you continue to live fully and cast your burdens on our loving creator.

For my final request, please do recall your grandmother's necklace and the writing lessons I told you about, which she learned from her dear friend Thomas. It is essential that you use the one to procure the other. Upon doing so, may this piece forever remind you of the powerful link that lies between us, three points, forever bound.

All my Love,
Father

Lorna reread the line: *"Please do recall your grandmother's favorite necklace and the writing lessons I told you about, which she learned from her dear friend Thomas."*

She also studied the sentence: *"It is essential that you use one to procure the other."*

Lorna ran into the living room with the letter. Nana startled as she looked up from a newspaper she'd been grazing through.

"Could Caroline's son have written this?" Lorna handed Nana the letter.

She looked it over. "Hmmm. Yes, that's right. Penelope was Caroline's granddaughter, so it must be from Gabriel." She studied it further. "You know, Pop always found this letter peculiar."

"Why is that?"

"He believed Gabriel was trying to convey something to her without saying it."

Lorna's hands were moist, her throat suddenly parched.

"You said Pop never read Allison's book, right?"

"That's correct."

"Nana, I'm sure you've heard of invisible ink, right?"

A puzzled look gathered across her face, but she answered, "Yes."

Lorna's mind was reeling as she began to doubt herself. *Maybe he's talking about something else. His mother died when he was just five years old. How would he have known about her use of invisible ink during the war? Could someone else have taught him? Thomas was gone, so it couldn't have been him.*

"What about invisible ink, though, Lorna?"

"Allison's book explains how Caroline used it during the war to write to Thomas, and he to her. She revealed the invisible writing using the heat from a candle."

"So, you believe Gabriel has a hidden message somewhere in this letter?"

Lorna felt her stomach doing somersaults. "It's possible that's what he means."

Nana's eyes lit up. "There's only one way to find out."

"How can we heat up the paper like Caroline did? Do you even have a taper candle?"

"Pop made me promise not to keep candles in the house because I almost accidentally lit the place on fire...a few times."

Suppressing a laugh, Lorna decided she'd rather not risk an open flame near a 200-year-old piece of paper anyway.

"Maybe I could look up another way of heating invisible ink on YouTube," Lorna said, pulling out her phone.

"I actually saw a piece on the History Channel one time," Nana began, drawing Lorna's attention back to her. "It talked about how the use of invisible ink goes back to ancient Greece and Rome."

Lorna, nibbling on her fingers, feared a long explanation was coming and longed to draw a much faster answer from Google.

Nana continued, "They used vinegar and milk to write with because it dried clear, but when heated, a chemical reaction made it turn brown."

"Yes, apparently, Caroline used milk!"

"Oh really? They said milk has proteins and fats that caramelize when they get hot enough. Anyway, they used to use candles, but they showed how now you can activate it using an iron or the oven."

Within minutes, Lorna was holding Nana's decades-old clothes iron just inches from Gabriel's letter. They'd read online to use a low heat setting. Lorna held her breath as the warm iron descended toward the paper. *What if it singes the sheet and ruins everything?*

She froze. "Let's try the oven."

"The website said 200 degrees, right?" Nana asked, making her way to the not-so-new Whirlpool oven in her kitchen. Following closely behind with the letter was Lorna, her mind spinning. "Maybe this is something we ask the historical society about instead?"

"Whatever you think, honey."

Lorna eyed Nana's oven then turned her gaze toward the letter. *I'm dying to know what you wanted Penelope to know, Gabriel.*

"Do you want me to turn it on?" Nana stood beside the stove, her fingers barely touching the temperature nozzle.

The heat was already rising inside Lorna. "Yes. Please make sure it's not above 200 degrees."

Moments later, Lorna carefully laid the paper on the wire rack inside the oven and closed the door before she could change her mind.

She opened it back up every twenty seconds or so but eventually determined the old stove would never heat up while doing so. She began to pace across the kitchen instead as Nana watched from the corner.

Suddenly, the distinct acrid smell of smoke pierced Lorna's nostrils. Her eyes widened in panic. "Nooooo!"

She sprinted for the oven door and, in one fast swoop, had it open. A cloud of gray came wafting out. Lorna felt like she could vomit.

When it finally cleared—thank goodness, the paper was intact.

Nana waved away the smoke. "Must have been some of my homemade mayonnaise burning at the bottom of the oven."

Why Nana was baking mayo, she wasn't even going to ask.

Her mind had something much more important to think

about. The paper wasn't only intact, there was now brown-shaded writing between the lines that Gabriel had written with invisible ink.

Lorna grabbed the letter, which was hot to the touch, but she barely noticed. "Nana, there's a hidden message!"

"Oh, my dear heavens, what does it say?"

Lorna read the newly formed words aloud to Nana:

The necklace is halfway through the tunnel under a loosened floorboard. Make haste!

Chapter 25

"Do you think it's even remotely possible that it's still there?" Lorna pressed.

Nana pulled her hand away from her mouth. "You won't know until you see for yourself."

Studying the letter, Lorna finally asked, "Can I show this to Arthur? I'll make a copy on your printer and leave the original letter here with you."

At first Nana hesitated, then changed gears. "Oh my, of course. He'll be exhilarated to find out."

Arthur and Nana spoke every so often. They'd apparently reconnected at Pop's funeral.

"Are you sure? It's Pop's letter, and I know they didn't share..."

"It's time, Lorna. Work together."

It was settled. Lorna would head over to the Brooks Inn first thing in the morning.

She planned on avoiding Maryland Avenue, though. It might be a few minutes longer to take a back street, but it was best not to pass Conor's apartment above Galway Bay. She'd text him soon. Maybe grab coffee. They'd kept in touch that spring, and something inside her actually kind of missed him. Despite that low-lying instinct to run the other way, there was also a lightness inside her when she thought of him, a touch of happiness she rarely experienced anymore. Their connection might even have been part of why she had come home, though she'd never admit it to anyone, especially herself.

But now was not the time to think about Conor.

She had to stay focused.

The next day Lorna made a copy of Gabriel's letter in case anything happened to it and left the original on Pop's desk. Nana handed her *Twenty Thousand Leagues Under the Seas*. "Go ahead and keep it. It'll remind you that Pop's always with you."

"Oh, Nana, but it's part of his book collection."

"He would want *you* to have it."

Lorna was overcome with gratitude and hugged Nana tightly. As she headed outside, her joy shifted to excitement at the thought of showing Arthur what she'd discovered. But in her eagerness, she mistakenly sprang straight toward the State House.

Halfway down Maryland Avenue, she noticed a woman opening the back seat of her car to place an overnight bag inside. Lorna recognized her from her last visit to Reynolds Tavern. She could almost hear narrow heels clicking across cold, brick floors.

Trying to avoid eye contact, Lorna looked down at Pop's book, which contained the copy of Gabriel's letter to Penelope with the hidden message revealed.

Just when she thought she was in the clear, a high-pitched voice shot through the air, "Lori! Lori!"

Oh no.

Maryland Avenue was one of those streets that went to bed early and woke up late, so with no one else around, Lorna couldn't help but acknowledge her.

The woman was hurrying toward her now, her clothes casual, but her face adorned with a full mask of makeup. "It's me, Tara. I remember meeting you with Conor. Sorry that it was an awkward intro. You probably already know this, but Conor has a way of making things uncomfortable."

"Um, yeah. I noticed." *Must be what drew you two together*, she wanted to say. Instead, she just fidgeted with the book in her hands.

"I just have to ask..." Tara paused, smoothing the edges of her mighty mane. "He's not calling you anymore, is he?"

Lorna could feel her breakfast suddenly churning uncomfortably inside her. "Barely. I live in North Carolina now."

"Oh, got ya, because we're back together."

Tara seemed to be watching for Lorna's reaction, so she refused to give one, even though her full stomach now felt wedged inside her throat. She needed to escape. Quickly. "Well, nice seeing you, Tara. I'm on my way to meet someone."

Tara scanned her watch. "Yep, and I have to get to work. Just wanted to say hi, Lori."

"It's Lorna."

"Oh, sorry. But yeah, wanted to warn you he's back with me, in case he claims otherwise."

Lorna inched backward. "Right. Right. Perfect."

Tara flew off as quickly as she'd come.

What was that feeling settling itself in Lorna? Jealousy... embarrassment...self-loathing. Maybe a lovely combination of them all. It's not like she and Conor were officially dating or even in the same state, so she had no reason to keep tabs on his love life. Even so, they'd talked a few times a week for several months, and he'd repeatedly said how excited he was to see her again.

Lorna decided it was mostly her fault. She knew all along pursuing him was foolish. Why would she ignore her gut?

So here she was—deservedly disappointed.

And officially *done* with Conor.

Then came her name again. This time from a much deeper voice and, shockingly, her actual name. "Lorna!"

She stopped and dropped her face for a split second toward the pavement. *Double whammy.* Turning around slowly, she finally drew the courage to look up.

He was jogging in her direction.

"Hi, Conor."

Why did he have to be so annoyingly cute? No matter, she was done wasting her time with him.

"Where are you heading?" he asked breathlessly.

"I...I'm meeting up with someone."

"Do you have two minutes? Hop into Galway with me for a sec. Please. Haven't seen you in months."

Her body tensed. "I would, but Will's Uncle Arthur is planning on me coming and..."

"Right, okay. I get it. But not even one cup of coffee?"

She looked back toward the Brooks Inn. *Really should have taken the long way.* "All right, one quick cup."

Lorna hadn't been back inside Galway Bay since the night she first met Conor four months earlier. While it felt a lot less dark and moody in the daytime, the lengthy, abandoned bar reminded her of that frigid night in December.

"Grab a seat." Conor took his time pouring black coffee into two mugs. "Listen, I fully understand why you don't always get back to my calls."

"I've gotten back to most of them. Just not the ultra-late nighters."

Conor tapped his lip with his pointer finger. "Yes. About those..."

"Listen, it sounds like you've got a great thing going again with Tara, so let's just..."

"What? We aren't back together."

Every nerve in her body ignited. "Conor, I just saw her leaving your place. And she told me you were back together." He started shifting from one foot to the other, and she dove back in just before he could speak. "You know what? It's fine. I don't need to know anything. We are not...anything."

"Okay, but Tara and I...we're not..."

Lorna's phone vibrated in her bag. She pulled it out. Arthur to the rescue. She placed Pop's book and her purse on a nearby table, stepped from the bar into the attached restaurant, and answered his call.

Arthur's low, soothing voice calmed her a little. "Hi, Lorna, how are you?"

"Oh, I'm good." *And I'll be better once I get out of here.*

Arthur didn't answer immediately, always the empath. He seemed to sense she wasn't...good.

He must have decided not to push her, though. "I know you said you were coming soon. Just wondered if it would be before noon? I have a couple coming to check into the inn around then."

"I'll be there in just a few minutes."

"Great, I look forward to seeing you."

"You too...and Arthur, I have something pretty crazy to show you."

"I'm intrigued. Come quickly."

"Will do. Be there soon. Bye."

"Goodbye."

Lorna slipped into the restroom before heading back to the bar.

"I have to run," she told Conor as she grabbed Pop's book off the table and slipped it into her purse.

He was wiping down a nearby table. "Any leads on your little mystery?"

"Maybe we could talk about it some other time?"

Conor stepped closer to her, tossed his rag onto the bar, and leaned back against a nearby booth. Something in his eyes changed. "You'll never let me in, will you?"

"What are you talking about?"

"Your past haunts you, so you'll always just stay inside your brokenness and push everyone else out, won't you?"

"Conor, excuse me?" Lorna wanted to say more, but her mind was spinning, unable to land on one significant sentence.

"I drove all the way down to Topsail to see you, and that meant nothing to you."

"I really have to go." Lorna nearly sprinted for the door. Pushing it open, she spilled out onto Maryland Avenue.

Hearing him talk about her *brokenness,* the very word Lorna felt so intrinsically about herself, left her feeling unimaginably vulnerable and hurt. Yet she wouldn't let him distract her with his ruthless desperation. She forced her mind to regain focus.

When she finally arrived at the Brooks Inn, Arthur was sitting on his wingback chair by the fireplace. He looked up, "Hello, hello! Do share what you have for me. I've been so anxious to hear."

Lorna sat down on the chair next to him, pulled Pop's book from her purse, peeled it open, delicately retrieved Gabriel's letter from inside it, and passed it to Arthur. He balanced his readers on the bridge of his nose and studied the note carefully.

Lorna couldn't contain herself any longer. "Do you see the brown words? They were hidden between the lines of black writing until Nana and I heated it to reveal the invisible ink."

"Absolutely...remarkable." Arthur seemed to have trouble gathering his words, but the unspeakable exhilaration on his face was salient. Lorna was bursting to say more, but she held herself back.

Finally, he asked, "Oh my goodness, how did you know how to decipher it?"

"From Allison's book! I read about Thomas and Caroline writing with invisible ink and how heating it revealed the message. We used Nana's oven. Go on, read what it says."

"Truly?" He pulled the letter closer to his face and read aloud, "'The necklace is halfway through the tunnel under a loose floor-board. Make haste!'"

Arthur studied her, then laughed, a jovial echo booming off his vast shelves of books. He then seemed to remember something as he placed a hand across his open mouth. It took him a few moments, but Arthur finally spoke again. "Caroline's son, Gabriel, rebuilt this home years after the fire when he returned from Wilmington. Sadly, the database shows his wife died in 1811, so he was a widower for almost a decade. One thing I've read is that his only child, Penelope, was away living near her husband's family back in England for several years before and after Gabriel's death in 1820. Another family moved into the Brooks Inn before he died. So, it would make perfect sense if Gabriel had hidden the Three Brothers in the tunnel for her to find once she returned."

"Wow."

Arthur brightened further. "You may know this, but my parents owned this inn when we were children. Bill and I used to play down in that tunnel as boys, racing each other up and down the corridor."

"I'm sure you had so much fun."

"Oh, we did." Arthur looked back down at the copy of the letter. "Where did you find the original of this?"

She held up the book. "It was right here inside Pop's copy of *Twenty Thousand Leagues Under the Seas*."

Arthur continued to study it. "I never should have let things come between us." He shook his head. "Regardless, thank you for coming to me with this, Lorna. This means a lot."

"You showed me the book. Otherwise, I never would have known about Caroline and her coded letters."

Arthur's eyes grew ever impassioned. "Let's follow this lead for Will, who led you to me in the first place."

Lorna's heart quickened. Arthur believed her. She nodded. "And for your brother."

Arthur smiled back sadly and handed Lorna the letter so she could place it back into Pop's book and safely inside her purse.

Lorna followed Arthur to the basement where a musty smell instantly filled her lungs, yet she barely noticed it, her eyes glued to the choppy stone foundation. Caroline had stood in that very space before the house burned. Did she view the tunnel with dread because of all the anger and betrayal that had come from it?

"I haven't been inside it for years, so we'll have to be careful," Arthur warned.

"Certainly."

Lorna set down her purse and helped him push a small bookshelf away from one of the basement walls, revealing a short, locked wooden door. He undid the bolt and pulled it open.

The vast darkness before them felt as petrifying as it was thrilling.

Chapter 26

"How do you feel about spiders?" Arthur turned to Lorna before entering the tunnel.

"I like them more than rats."

"Try to be loud, then."

Lorna's skin prickled. "Right."

Arthur stepped through the tunnel door first, and Lorna followed. She carried a cane from Arthur's antique collection to swat away cobwebs and her cell phone flashlight to navigate the dark, dingy space. Arthur gripped a rusty crowbar to pull up the floorboard in one hand and an ancient flashlight in the other.

Hand-cut brick walls reached far off into the distant black. Arthur shot his flashlight beam upward. "If you wonder why this tunnel has lasted several centuries, just look at those beautifully fortified, arched, brick ceilings." He then angled the beam downward. "And yes, being that we're just a breath from the bay, they lined the floors with cypress wood, which can take on water without being damaged."

"Someone knew what they were doing."

"They sure did."

"I suppose we need to find the halfway point. I'd be glad to count footsteps," she said loudly as her eyes darted across the floorboards.

"That would be incredibly helpful." Arthur continued to scan the ceiling once more.

"How is it, by the way, that *you* feel about spiders, Arthur?"

His eyes grew in size. "I'd like them more if they didn't have eight creepy legs, fangs, and venom."

Lorna couldn't help but laugh. "How about I go first and swat the cobwebs?"

"I'd be forever in your debt. Besides, I'm not opposed to letting a brave lady lead. I'll count paces, then."

She paused and turned to Arthur. "You know what, let's both count silently. Then we can compare numbers." He nodded, and Lorna walked back to the very beginning of the tunnel and began again, focusing on each step she took.

They proceeded through the musty corridor, where it felt as though time had come to a standstill. Suddenly, the sound of creaking wooden floorboards within the lurking shadows ahead shattered the silence. Lorna quickly turned back toward Arthur. "Did you hear that?"

Arthur, focused on counting paces, paused. "Hear what?"

"Could anyone else be in here?"

"There's only one other entrance," he answered.

"Where?"

"From the Maryland Inn. We should be nearing it soon."

"That's right...Andrew Moore's side of the tunnel."

"Good memory."

Half a minute later, the glow of Lorna's flashlight uncovered the door to the Maryland Inn's basement. She continued counting until she was exactly in front of it. "I've got 565 feet. You?"

Arthur kept his flashlight aimed at the ground. "That's strange."

"What is?" Lorna looked down.

"See the footprints in the dirt there in front of the door? This entrance has been closed off for years." He reached for the doorknob and rattled it. "Locked. All right, well, let's find this midway mark. I got 548 feet. Let's use yours: 556. How'd you do in math? What would the halfway mark be."

"At 278," Lorna immediately returned.

"Not bad. I always preferred words over numbers, so I'm thankful to have you around."

Lorna grinned, but an uncomfortable feeling settled inside her as she stepped ahead of Arthur and began swatting the air for any cobwebs she'd missed on the way there. *Those footprints.*

Together they retraced their steps back through the tunnel, the worn floorboards creaking with each step: "276...277...278." Arthur paused. "All right, this crowbar marks the spot." He wedged it between two pieces of wood. "These guys aren't budging." He stepped back to where they'd just walked. "Look at this piece, though, I think it's loose!"

"Seriously?" Lorna reached down and easily peeled the wide plank from the ground.

Their eyes grew wide as they peered under it.

A hole had been dug beneath the piece of flooring. It was big enough to hold something the size of a shoe box, but nothing was inside of it.

"And the tomb was empty," Arthur said.

Lorna could feel the excitement draining from her.

He added, "Absolutely remarkable that something was once here, though."

Getting down on her knees for a closer look, Lorna shoved her flashlight into the hole. "What's this?"

"You see something?"

"There's a flat rock wedged down into the dirt at the very bottom." Lorna gasped. "I think there's something carved in the stone."

"Honestly?"

Lorna practically had to lie on the ground to decipher the words: *Reynolds kitch firep.* "It says Reynolds kitchen fireplace."

Her eyes shot up at Arthur. "The kitchen at Reynolds Tavern doesn't have a fireplace."

"Remember, whoever wrote that may have done so in the early 1800s. Back then, Reynolds Tavern had their kitchen in the basement."

Lorna's face lit up. "The 1747 Pub fireplace!"

Arthur's grin grew quickly. "It's worth a look!"

As they started back toward the Brooks Inn entrance, Lorna stopped suddenly. "Wait. You said the Maryland Inn basement is the other entrance to the tunnel."

"Yes, the coffee shop." Arthur's pale skin looked almost ghost-like when it caught shafts of illumination from the flashlight.

Her mouth felt parched. *The coffee shop. Conor's favorite spot.*

"Lorna, are you okay?"

The look in her eyes showed she wasn't. "I need to get to Reynolds Tavern—now."

"Then what are you waiting for? Go. I'll catch up."

Lorna wasn't worried about swiping for cobwebs as she rushed back through the tunnel, hurried through the Brook's Inn, and dashed around State Circle. The governor's mansion was straight ahead as she hung a left on School Street, her feet pounding across an aged mosaic of red bricks. Looking for the most direct route, she scanned left then right, before crossing Church Circle, her lungs blazing, but she wasn't slowing down.

Her mind flashed back to *Twenty Thousand Leagues Under the Seas,* sitting there on the table at Galway, left behind for several minutes when she'd taken Arthur's call and gone to the restroom. How foolish of her to not take it with her, especially with the copy of Gabriel's letter peeking out on all sides of the book. Those five or ten minutes would have been just enough time for Conor to see the deciphered ink and know that the necklace was halfway through the tunnel. He was cunning. Conor had figured out where she lived on more than one occasion, and now he was angry after their embarrassing interaction that morning.

Lorna's nerves buzzed, and a cold dread washed over her as she imagined him opening Pop's book.

Conor was best friends with the owner of the Maryland Inn and spent every morning there. Of course, he would have known that it, too, had an entrance to the tunnel, where Andrew Moore once accessed it.

Once on the sidewalk in front of St. Anne's Church, Lorna sidestepped past slow-treading tourists, too busy to notice as they studied their maps and brochures. She sped back across Church Circle once more and made her way down a flight of steps that led to the 1747 Pub tucked inside the basement of Reynolds Tavern.

With everything she had left, she swung the door open.

Chapter 27

Someone was crouched down in front of the fireplace, facing away.

But it wasn't Conor.

Lorna slowly trudged toward the person, her chest rising and falling with labored breaths. All she could see was a long curtain of blonde hair hanging down a woman's back.

Confusion filled her. "Did you lose something?" Lorna asked.

The woman turned quickly and stood. Her disheveled bangs skimmed the top of her thick, dark-rimmed glasses.

"Yes. I was looking for an earring."

Lorna noticed the woman's earring-free earlobes. Maybe she'd taken the other one off already. "Can I help you find it?"

"Thanks, but I need to get going. I have to get to work." The woman then grabbed her purse on the ground and hurried out.

Lorna watched her rush away then turned back toward the fireplace.

"Lorna, is that you?" came a voice.

She spun back around to see a familiar face. "Oh, hi, Marie."

When Lorna went in for a hug as floral perfume filled her instantly.

"How are you, lady?" Marie asked. "You look a bit flushed."

"Yes, well, it's been an interesting day."

"I can see that." Marie studied her. "How about a table and a tall glass of water?"

"Make that two." Arthur huffed from the doorway, considerably out of breath.

Lorna turned. "Arthur, are you all right?"

He strolled slowly toward them, shaking his hand in the air but not looking up. "I'm good. I'm good."

"Are you sure?" Lorna insisted. "Please sit."

"Yes, here's a chair." Marie directed him to the four-top right in front of the fireplace, then grabbed two glasses of water. She returned to their table and sat down beside them.

"Marie, this is Will's great-uncle, Arthur Brooks, who manages the Brooks Inn. Arthur, this is Marie Adams. She's the boss lady around here and a very close friend of my mom."

"I recognize you, Marie. I've seen you around town, I'm sure."

"You as well, Arthur. You look very familiar. It's nice to meet you, though. I'm just so sorry for your loss. I don't have to tell you, but Will was a genuine hero, and I'm proud to have known him." Arthur shyly smiled as Marie continued, turning her gaze on Lorna. "Proud to know this incredible lady as well. I've been fortunate to be around Lorna since she was a little girl. Her mother and I have been friends forever."

"You are fortunate, then. I've only more recently come to know Lorna better."

"I have to ask, were you two running a marathon together? You both seem quite worn out?" Marie inquired.

Lorna and Arthur looked at one another and laughed.

"Yes, well, it's an interesting story," Lorna said.

Marie's eyebrows shot up. "Do tell."

Surrounded by low lighting and a hodgepodge of centuries-old stone, brick, and plaster walls, Arthur and Lorna told Marie about Lorna's dreams about Will, who Caroline Brooks was, and how her long-lost necklace was quite possibly lying under or inside the fireplace right next to them.

Marie listened carefully, her eyes narrowing and widening in a repeated melody until the end of their story. She then closed them altogether and pushed a slow breath from her lungs.

Arthur and Lorna met each other's gaze. Lorna noticed he looked as nervous as she felt.

Their next move depended on Marie.

As her mom's friend peeled her eyes open, they could tell the wheels inside her mind were still spinning. Finally, she spoke. "What a thrilling family story. Wish my ancestors were that exciting. Listen, I would love to let you look under and inside that fireplace—really, I would—but you realize I'm the manager, not the owner. I could get in serious trouble."

"*If* someone found out," Lorna added, shocked by her own forwardness.

"*If* someone found out," Marie mimicked, her eyes once again narrowing.

Arthur adjusted his glasses.

"Then they would fire me," Marie continued.

"Then they would fire you." Lorna pressed her bottom teeth to her top lip.

"But..." Marie stopped, and the only sound was that of china cups clattering upstairs. "If we just wanted to admire the fireplace for a few minutes, maybe see what kind of bricks they used back then, I suppose that would be all right."

Arthur's weary expression regained its vitality. "Thank you, Marie."

Lorna and Arthur stood immediately and bent down to study the fireplace.

Marie began talking quickly, as if she were just educating customers on the home. "The basement was the main kitchen for the tavern in the 1700s, which is why the hearth is so substantial."

"Uh, that makes sense. It's a shame that none of the bricks on the ground look moveable." Lorna fidgeted with them, but nothing budged.

Arthur turned to Marie. "Would it be all right if we grab a chair and very delicately look up inside the fireplace?"

Marie looked around. Still, no one else in sight, so she pulled a dining chair into the fireplace, and Lorna quickly crawled up on top of it.

"There's an opening and a ledge where the flue is," Lorna explained with a thrill in her voice. "But it's too dark to see. One sec."

She reached inside her pocket and pulled out her cell phone. One battery bar left. *Yikes.* Lorna turned on the phone's flashlight, held her breath, and aimed it above the small hidden ledge inside the chimney.

The space glowed.

But it, too, was empty.

Her heart sunk, and Arthur's face fell. Even Marie looked disappointed.

Lorna climbed down and thanked Marie repeatedly for allowing them to check things out before they said their goodbyes.

Back out in the light of day, Arthur and Lorna began their crestfallen saunter back toward the Brooks Inn.

"I know it was such a long shot, but in my mind it all seemed possible," Lorna admitted.

"It was a thrilling hunt, at least," Arthur returned.

Lorna stopped and looked up at the billowing clouds shifting forlornly behind the giant cross at the top of St. Anne's Church.

Arthur took notice. "It's about more than just finding the necklace for you, though, isn't it?"

Lorna remained silent.

He continued, "It's about finding Will."

Lorna looked down at the pavement and nodded. She eventually found the strength to turn to Arthur and speak. "If we'd found the necklace, it meant he really did, in fact, lead us to it, you know?"

"Right. And if he led us to it..." Arthur paused waiting for her to answer.

Lorna's shoulders felt as if they carried an immense weight. She forced out the words: "Then his spirit lives on."

"Lorna, I can only imagine how hard it's been to lose him. I just think you're putting way too much pressure on these dreams."

"I realize that. But does it even seem remotely possible that he could be connecting with me?"

"Einstein once said, 'The most beautiful thing we can experience is the mysterious.' I don't specialize in the beyond, but let me tell you, if you *can* visit loved ones in their dreams in the hereafter, I am so incredibly in." A smile drew across Lorna's face as Arthur continued, "And above all, I love that you sense he's guiding you."

"Thank you, Arthur. I needed that."

"Now, I imagine you're wondering where to go from here."

"How'd you guess?"

"What would Will tell you to do next?"

Lorna thought for a moment. "He'd say, 'Stop stressing.'" She searched her memory more until another phrase suddenly came to her: "And 'Don't fall in love with your plan, Lorna.' I used to hate when he said it because it always meant my system of doing something wasn't working."

"'Don't fall in love with your plan.' I like that. Plans fail. Often. That doesn't mean we can't find a new one."

Lorna's face brightened slightly. "Good, because I'm not ready to give up."

They continued back toward the inn as Arthur assessed things. "So far, you've followed the trail beautifully. As I mentioned before, Penelope was in England the last few years of her father's life."

"That's sad she was away, especially in the end."

"I imagine it was incredibly hard for them both. They seemed to have a wonderful relationship. Now, Gabriel wrote that letter to Penelope nearly a year before another letter, one which my parents passed along to me. At that point, Gabriel likely knew he was selling his home, so maybe he put the necklace in the tunnel, wrote the invisible ink letter to his daughter, and then things changed."

"What changed?"

"This other letter I'm talking about, written a year later, was to Gabriel from the owner of the Maryland Inn."

"Did Andrew Moore still manage the place?"

"No, he was long gone by then. The new owner told Gabriel he was adding another section to their tunnel. He said a large group of influential lawmakers in town were willing to pay him a substantial fee to have the Maryland Inn/Brooks Inn tunnel expanded to the State House. The lawmakers wanted a secret way to slip away for a drink at the tavern beneath the Maryland Inn. They eventually filled in that part of the tunnel, but for years, they used it."

Lorna added, "I'm sure Gabriel was nervous about keeping the necklace in the tunnel then, given the expected increase in foot traffic and the uncertainty of when Penelope would return home."

"Precisely. So, he likely moved the Three Brothers. I also know Reynolds Tavern used to be connected to the first bank in Annapolis. I've read that whoever held the title of Cashier of the Bank got to live in the house. And I know for a fact that Gabriel Brooks was close friends with Jonathan Pinkney, who at one time was the Cashier of the Bank. Maybe Gabriel moved the necklace from the tunnel to his friend's fireplace for safe keeping until Penelope returned."

"Then he carved 'Reynolds kitchen fireplace' into the stone so she could still read the invisible ink letter that he left here in America for her to receive when she got back to find the necklace based on that. And do you suppose, in the end, Penelope discovered it in the fireplace when she came home?" Lorna asked.

"She couldn't have. Penelope never made it home. She died in England in her twenties, a year or so after Gabriel passed." Arthur adjusted his button-up sweater, which had acquired its share of muddy splotches throughout the previous hour.

"How sad."

"It really is."

"So, there was never anything written about the necklace after that?"

"Not as far as I know. Gabriel seems to be the last person to have had it. The necklace once again disappeared from history."

Lorna pulled a piece of hair from behind her ear and twisted it around her pointer finger. "We're definitely missing something here, Arthur."

"Don't I know it."

They stopped walking and stood together in front of the Brooks Inn.

"Have you ever been in the back courtyard here?" Arthur asked.

"I haven't."

"Do you have a little more time? There's something I'd like to show you."

"Sure."

"I need to use the restroom, but I'll join you in a moment. It's just through there." Arthur pointed to a wrought-iron gate several yards away.

"Great, I'll head there in a second. I just need to make a quick call," Lorna said, pulling her phone from her pocket.

As Arthur ascended the front steps, she dialed Conor's number, nerves piercing through her body. Lorna had no idea what she would say, but she hoped he'd act suspicious so she could confront him about the tunnel.

First ring...nothing.

Second ring...still no answer.

Third ring...nope.

Conor's voicemail picked up. *Coward.* Lorna ended the call and bitterly traipsed down the narrow sidewalk that led to the backyard of the Brooks Inn. It was small, but sheltered and welcoming, wrapped on all sides by a wooden fence, almost completely engulfed in a layer of crisp, green ivy. At Lorna's feet, a weathered stone path traversed its way through tiny pebbles as it guided garden dwellers to a wooden bench surrounded by an expanse of vibrant spring flowers.

She stepped from stone to stone until she reached the bench, curling up comfortably on it. That's when she noticed them: butterflies everywhere. Lorna grew still, marveling at the kaleidoscope of fluttering wings hovering over nearby petals, beating rapidly around her. In time, they flew away—all but one, a stunning striped swallowtail. Its intricate yellow pattern transfixed her. Then she noticed the flower it rested on: a flame-colored foxglove.

A sudden warmth filled her. Caroline, she was the foxglove—bold and alluring but dangerous when crossed. And Charity, she was the swallowtail—tenacious and...free? *Did the Ridouts ever free her?*

"Allison planted those several years back," Arthur said, his voice catching her by surprise. He sat down on the bench next to her.

"They're stunning. Charity's favorite, right?"

"That's right."

"Whatever happened to her? Was she ever given her freedom?"

Arthur smiled. "She was."

"Actually?"

"Charity went on to purchase her own home right where we were just standing ten minutes ago—on South Street and Church Circle, just across from St. Anne's Church."

"Right between the Maryland Inn and Reynolds Tavern?"

"Exactly."

"Why did the Ridouts finally free her? Was it because of who her father was, as Charity suspected? Or because Charity had healed the family so much, as Caroline mentioned?"

"Likely the latter. But possibly the former too. Many believe she was, in fact, Molly's uncle's child. Benjamin Tasker Jr. was mayor of Annapolis and a powerful man, so no one would have written that he'd fathered a child with one of his enslaved workers. As for Charity's care for the family, John Ridout wrote in his last will and testament that she was incredibly faithful to his wife and helped his family through many sicknesses, even saving his grandson when he had smallpox. He arranged for Charity to be freed in 1807 and receive an annual stipend from his sons. When John died in 1797, Molly freed her immediately. Charity went on to become one of the first African American women to own property in Annapolis."

"Amazing."

"You know what I admire about her most?"

"What's that?"

"Her patience. Her mother believed she'd gain her freedom one day, but she had to wait forty years to get it. It's a wonderful reminder—sometimes the wisest thing we can do is give it time."

The following day, Lorna stepped inside the coffee shop beneath the Maryland Inn. Her mother, Maggie, who worked for a downtown real estate company, had asked if they could meet.

Lorna chose the spot, as she wanted to try to locate the tunnel entrance that she suspected Conor had snuck through the day before. She circled the shop, unable to stop thinking of him going behind her back like that. Then, to ignore her phone call and never get back. *What a jerk. Should have seen all this coming.* But she tried to push her frustrations aside and focus on her surroundings.

Much like Reynolds Tavern, the basement of the Maryland Inn was filled with character—hand-fired brick walls shadowed above by dark, splintered beams. In a back, hidden corner, a few stairs led down to a short corridor, which ended at a wooden door. A plaque on the wall explained how the coffee shop was originally a tavern and that statesmen used the door to enter a clandestine tunnel to the State House, just as Arthur had told her.

Lorna envisioned Conor reading those very words and using them to his advantage. An unsettled feeling churned inside her. *There's no way Conor could have actually found the Three Brothers, is there? The Maryland Inn is slightly closer to Reynolds Tavern than the Brooks Inn, but still, he was nowhere to be seen when I got there. Surely, he's not that fast. Besides, that woman was standing by the fireplace...*

Her mind then skipped to the other reason she was there, so Lorna went to grab two caffeinated drinks, including her mom's caramel macchiato with soy milk, hold the whipped cream.

A distinct voice rang in her ear.

The one and only Margaret Jones.

Maggie knew everyone in town, and their brother's sister's cousin too. She had a gift for making conversation and wasn't afraid to talk to anyone. Lorna's mom was also talented at telling people what they wanted to hear, which helped tremendously when selling homes.

Spotting her daughter, Maggie came in for a hug. They embraced quickly. Maggie smiled as she stepped back and studied Lorna. "Love your shirt. That color looks pretty on you."

"Thanks." Lorna handed her mom a drink, and they simultaneously dropped into a nearby booth.

Maggie also liked to cut to the chase. "Fill me in. Why were you at Reynolds Tavern with Will's great-uncle? Marie said you were looking for some famous, long-lost necklace?" She snickered as she started answering someone's text message.

"It's a long story." Lorna lowered her eyes.

"Can I have the abridged version? I've got a two o'clock showing on a gorgeous waterfront in Bay Ridge."

"Mom, clearly you've got a lot on your plate."

"Come on. I'm curious."

Lorna hurried through the backstory as Maggie nodded, her gaze bouncing around the room.

"Are you even listening, Mom?"

"Of course, honey. It's just that, well, this seems a bit like you're searching for a needle in a haystack."

"I figured you'd say something similar."

"Lorna, I'm just being honest, and I truly don't want to upset you. But trying to get to the bottom of Will's family folklore won't bring him back."

Nerves stood suddenly on end. How desperately Lorna wanted to leave. *Why even try with her?* "I am fully aware that he's gone, Mom. Thanks for the news flash. But I still think he's trying to tell me something, and I should have been wise enough to know you wouldn't understand."

Lorna stood.

"Honey, where are you going? I still have a few minutes before my showing."

"I don't. I left my purse at the Brooks Inn yesterday and need to grab it before work. Bye, Mom."

"Lorna..."

But she wasn't turning back.

Around both Church and State Circle she fled, past the blooming cherry blossom trees, then up eight steep steps and into the Brooks Inn.

Arthur wasn't at his desk.

"Arthur!" His name bounced off the foyer walls and echoed up the main staircase. "Are you here?"

Suddenly, she smelled a hint of something burning.

She opened the kitchen door, and a plume of hazy gray assaulted her instantly.

Lorna took a step back, her hands falling to her knees, which she cupped as she choked repeatedly.

When she finally drew a clean breath, Lorna looked back toward the kitchen. Smoke engulfed every inch of the room, and flames shot forth at its center. She shut the door, hoping to contain it momentarily.

"Fire!" Lorna yelled forcefully, trying to warn guests. She grabbed her cell phone, dialed 9-1-1, and headed back toward the entryway.

"9-1-1, what's your emergency?"

"There's a fire at the Brooks Inn on State Circle in Annapolis."

The smoke had pushed its way under the kitchen door and was at her back, stalking her like some sort of lonely spirit.

She opened the front door and sucked in fresh spring air. But the thought of Arthur's study stopped her in her tracks. Those towering bookshelves, covered from floor to ceiling with his beloved novels, cemented her feet in place. In just a few moments, they'd be nothing more than kindling. And what of his endless array of prized antiques scattered throughout the inn? His vast collection of family letters? They'd survived decades, some of them centuries. Could she really let them disappear now?

Lorna spun around and bolted back toward the kitchen.

There has to be a fire extinguisher somewhere.

The tea kettle was screaming by the time Lorna opened the kitchen door a second time. She started coughing again but forced herself to enter. Dropping to her knees, she crawled toward the sink. The blaze at the room's center raged too rampantly for small amounts of water to expel it, but hopefully, an extinguisher was in the cabinet below. Beads of sweat broke free on her forehead as she reached below the porcelain farm sink and dug inside. A red fire extinguisher appeared through the haze. Relief filled her.

She grabbed it and turned toward the popping at her back. The inferno on the oven was reaching toward the tall ceilings, dancing gleefully as it sought to devour all. Lorna pulled the pin and squeezed the handle, but the force inside the extinguisher shot her backward. She rebalanced and aimed directly at the stovetop. As the foamy substance connected with flames, giant heaps of white joined the suffocating smoke. Lorna started to feel nauseous, her head pulsating. She drifted down to her knees, once again gasping for breath. When she looked up, the tea kettle was still blaring, but the white smoke from the extinguisher had cleared, and the fire was gone too. Relief slowly eased the heaviness inside her chest.

Lorna pulled herself back up to her feet. She noticed the electric stovetop burner was still red under the tea kettle, so she switched the range knob off. Her eyes searched the room to make sure nothing else was burning. Incredibly relieved that the fire was doused, Lorna fled the kitchen and returned to the front room where Arthur's desk was. She reached inside her pocket and grabbed her phone.

Arthur must have stepped out, but then who left the kettle on?

She dialed his number. As the call rang in her ear, she heard another phone buzzing in a nearby room. Lorna turned her head toward the study, her heart sinking with a growing sense of dread.

Chapter 28

Arthur sat slumped in one of the wingback chairs by the fireplace, his eyelids drawn. Lorna rushed into the study and bent down, nudging his shoulders.

"Arthur...Arthur. Wake up!"

But he wasn't budging.

Please tell me he's alive.

She looked down at his face. The answer was right there—was he breathing? Still, she hesitated for a moment. Then, knowing time was critical, she forced herself to lean down and listen.

He was still breathing. *Thank God.* His pulse was faint but detectable.

Lorna called 9-1-1, answering all the operator's questions quickly.

"Please hurry," she urged before ending the call and setting down her phone.

She fell to her knees, pleading, "Please, wake up, Arthur."

Every few seconds, she'd check his pulse and try to stir him. *Still there, but barely. Come on, ambulance.*

Finally, a fire truck's siren cut through the air.

The vehicle had to sit on a side street, thanks to State Circle's narrow accommodations.

Lorna ran out to the two firefighters coming toward the Brooks Inn. "We need an ambulance. The fire is out, but a man is unconscious, and his pulse is incredibly slow."

She sprinted back inside to be by Arthur's side. The next few minutes were a blur; firefighters rushing into the house, two of them attending to Arthur, the others heading into the kitchen. After they placed Arthur on a stretcher and wheeled him toward the front door, Lorna slipped down to the basement and retrieved her purse. She instantly dug inside it, grabbing Pop's book, which she hastily opened and found the copy of Gabriel's coded letter safely inside. A sense of peace washed over her. Making her way back upstairs and into the front yard, she found half a dozen guests standing dumbfounded outside the inn. Lorna briefly explained to them what had happened. Minutes later, she was off to the hospital.

At Anne Arundel Medical Center, a nurse with thick, black curls drawn up in a claw clip, led Lorna to a room in the emergency department. "He's still unconscious," she told her.

"What happened?" Lorna asked.

"We can't say until more tests are done." She leaned in closer to Lorna and lowered her voice. "But if I had to guess, it looks like a heart attack."

Tubes and cords were everywhere. Arthur lay atop crisp bleached sheets, his complexion a similar shade. Beeping machines chirped away, but she didn't hear them.

This is all my fault, dragging him through that stupid tunnel yesterday and then rushing him over to Reynolds Tavern. What was I thinking?

Lorna eventually found a seat in the corner, its padded cushion clearly used to cradling distraught visitors, judging by the frayed strands of cloth brushing out on all sides. She dropped her face into her palms.

"God, I know I haven't been much of the praying type lately, but please let him live," she whispered.

Lorna had swung by Nana's house on the way to the hospital, but no one was home. She pulled out her cell and called Nana's house phone, only to get the answering machine.

There was only one other person who needed to know immediately—his daughter, Allison.

And surely Nana would have her niece's phone number.

But where was Nana?

Wasn't she always home when they'd stopped in the past?

Lorna heard Will's laugh, as if he were standing right there, and remembered his warning from several years prior when they had to skip the usual stop at Nana's house. "Don't come driving into town on a Monday and expect to see Nana," he'd told her. "She'll be far too engaged in a cutthroat card game at Anna Jean's house.

That has to be where she is, Lorna thought begrudgingly to herself.

She looked up and noticed Arthurs's flip phone sitting on the side table next to her. He must have had it in his pocket when they brought him in. Certainly would be a good time to call his daughter and let her know what happened, but it felt strange digging through his contacts list.

Lorna thought of her own father, though. If he was in the ER, wouldn't she want to know right away? So, without further ado, she grabbed the phone, snapped it open, and hit "Contacts." Allison was the first name, but as Lorna went to press it, something stopped her.

Delivering heart-wrenching news to someone she'd never met before was a daunting task in itself. But beyond that, this wasn't just Arthur's daughter and Will's relative. Allison was a highly accomplished writer whose story had meant so much to Lorna. She'd introduced Lorna to Caroline, who, despite her flaws, was somehow bringing something alive inside her again. And Charity, the healer, who reminded Lorna that she was making the right choice by studying medicine. They were exactly the people, it seemed, Will wanted her to meet, and none of it would have happened if it weren't for Allison.

Lorna finally touched her name but struggled to press her number.

As she gazed over at Arthur, she couldn't help but notice his trembling hand. Blue veins wound like a jagged mountain range beneath his delicate, almost translucent skin. In the middle, a weary beige bandage clung tightly, holding the IV needle securely amid the peaks and valleys of his fragile flesh.

She pressed Allison's number. It rang just one time.

"Hi, Dad," came a voice on the other end.

"This is actually Lorna Brooks, Will's wife."

"Oh, hi," her tone changing just slightly.

"It's a shame we've never met."

"Right."

Words caught in Lorna's throat, and she hesitated before finally speaking. "I'm sorry to have to tell you, but your father is in the hospital."

Allison's pitch heightened. "He is? Why?"

"He's unconscious." Lorna took a breath. "They're doing tests. A nurse told me it looked a bit like a heart attack, but she wasn't sure yet."

There was silence on the other end.

"I'm so sorry," Lorna finally broke in.

"I'm just a bit taken back."

"Of course. I stopped by the inn, and he was in a chair in his study hunched over, so I called the ambulance."

Allison didn't respond, so Lorna continued, "The Brooks Inn somehow caught fire too. I believe it had to do with the stovetop, which was turned on when I reached it. Thankfully, there was a fire extinguisher, but the kitchen still suffered a lot of damage."

"Holy shit. All right, well, I'll take it from here."

"But with you having to come all the way from London, I can stay here at the hospital until I get a hold of your Aunt Bea."

"That won't be necessary. You've done *enough.*"

The line hung up.

You've done enough, repeated itself inside Lorna's mind. She couldn't shake the memory of how Allison had said it, with a sharp and somewhat disdainful tone.

Lorna's entire body went numb, overwhelmed by anxiety to the point of nearly becoming sick. Instead of throwing up, something else spilled out: "What the hell?" she exclaimed before composing herself.

The woman's in shock, Lorna reasoned. *Her father could die at any moment. People don't think rationally in these situations. But still, she didn't have to be so...cold. I'd done enough? What did she mean by that?*

Oh, stop Lorna. Just stop.

So, she sat and started counting magnets on a nearby dry-erase board but kept losing track of where she was due to a newly arrived headache. Lorna couldn't decide what was worse—the throbbing sensation behind her eyes or the sudden surge of nausea.

Had she said something that offended Allison?

Unable to sit still, she walked out to the waiting room. If she couldn't get a hold of Nana, what did Allison want her to do? Just leave Arthur there alone?

An older man reclined in a stiff chair, facing the window as he peered out into the night, his silver streaks illuminated by harsh overhead lighting. Lorna found a spot on one of the sofas, and suddenly she was seventeen again, sitting next to Will, terrified, on the night Jack nearly paralyzed himself at Greenbury Point. But the sound of Allison hanging up the phone—without a simple thank-you or even a goodbye—kept bouncing like a pinball through the dim and lonely corridors of her mind.

Okay, surely, she was being too sensitive. Allison feared for her father's life. It was no wonder she rushed off the phone. *Come on, Lorna, get over yourself.*

She walked back into Arthur's room, shut the door, and watched through the window as cars sped by on the highway. Her mind drifted away again. *She made me feel almost bad for being here, though. Maybe she knows I'm interested in her book...and Caroline...and the necklace. Maybe Arthur said something. Doesn't she have better things to occupy her time with in London, like writing the next bestselling novel? Regardless, I can't leave him. I'm not leaving, at least until I get in touch with Nana.*

Lorna turned the chair toward the window and tried to get comfortable. A half-hour passed, but Nana still didn't answer her phone.

Suddenly, the door peeled open behind her, and a chill ran through her.

Just the nurse again, I'm sure, she convinced herself.

Lorna turned slowly and saw a woman, but she wasn't the RN from earlier. In fact, she wasn't a nurse at all but wore jeans and a Creedence Clearwater Revival T-shirt. Why did she look so familiar?

The visitor's face was flushed, like she'd been crying.

"Hi," Lorna said awkwardly.

The woman didn't speak but walked over to Arthur's bed and took his hand.

Lorna suddenly felt as if she were a ghost, unseen but still there to witness an intimate moment. Then, as if the pieces of a disheveled puzzle suddenly began to clasp themselves together, Lorna saw things more clearly. And it took her breath away.

The earring lady. From Reynolds Tavern.

It was her.

She wasn't wearing those distinct tortoise-shell glasses she'd had on the day before, but Lorna remembered her thick, blonde bangs and petite frame.

But how did she know Arthur?

"He won't give up," the visitor abruptly said aloud.

Lorna didn't know whether she should speak or not.

The woman then turned to her. "Hi, Lorna."

"Hi," Lorna returned. *But who was she?*

Likely noticing the perplexed look on Lorna's face, she clarified things. "I'm Arthur's daughter."

"Allison?"

"You sound surprised."

"Uh, yeah."

"We spoke on the phone, remember?"

"I thought I was talking to you from London."

"My dad didn't know it yet, but I just got back into town. I'm staying with my mom."

How strange she wouldn't tell him she was in Annapolis.

"I see." Lorna immediately felt foolish for sounding so confused, so she attempted to explain. "It's just that, well, I hope I don't sound like a stalker, but I searched your name online and you looked...different."

"It's called hair dye and thirty pounds."

"Apparently, I'd be a poor FBI profiler."

"Probably not your calling."

Lorna stood and pushed the chair out. "Would you like to take a seat?"

"No, I just wanted to stop in and see him. My son's in the waiting room with my mom."

"Of course."

"Listen, I need to give you a heads-up. I don't know how you suddenly got so interested in the necklace bullshit, but my dad doesn't need this. And I know you've been through a lot the last few years, so good Lord, don't torture yourself chasing something you'll never find, like the rest of them."

A million thoughts swirled through Lorna's mind, but she couldn't find anything worth uttering, so all she managed to say was, "I'll leave you with your dad." She then shuffled into the hallway.

The refrain "Don't torture yourself...like the rest of them" echoed in Lorna's mind as she entered the waiting room. But what about Allison? Hadn't she been the one standing inside Reynolds Tavern looking at the fireplace, therefore likely the person Lorna had heard in the tunnel too, instead of Conor? Why was *she* still chasing the necklace if it was just so ridiculously foolish? And how did she find out about the tunnel clue? Lorna had only told Arthur moments earlier. He couldn't have called Allison that quickly, especially since Lorna was by his side the entire time.

A little boy was standing just feet from Lorna in the waiting room, his round face framed by a shock of brown hair, and his eyes bright blue and uneasy. He couldn't have been older than five or six.

Lorna went to walk past him.

But he drew himself in front of her, forcing eye contact. "Hi, do you know my grandpa?"

Lorna startled and stepped back. "Um, is your grandpa named Arthur?"

"Yes, that's him."

"Oh, wow, yes, he told me he had a grandson."

"What else did he tell you?"

"Well, that you're very smart and brave and that he missed you very much."

"I missed him too. I told my mom I didn't want to move to England, but she didn't listen."

"Moms have to do hard things sometimes."

"What's your name?"

"Um, Lorna. How about you?"

"I'm Charlie."

"Hello, Charlie."

Lorna watched Charlie's mouth carefully curl into a crooked smile, a grin that felt instantly recognizable.

"My mom says I can't go in to see Pappy yet because he's sleeping and she doesn't want to wake him. But why, then, is she allowed to go in? You know?"

Lorna heard what Charlie said, but her mind was spiraling elsewhere.

Seagulls suddenly screamed overhead; the ocean rushed forth.

Conor talked proudly about his child as one side of his lips bent at a distinct angle. And *Charlie*. Wasn't his son's name *Charlie*?

The floor felt as if it had begun to tilt sideways.

She forced herself back. "I'm sure your mom will be right back, Charlie. Where's your grandma?"

"She went to the bathroom."

"Oh, okay."

Lorna quickly debated whether to ask the question. It was burning a hole inside her head, but she was terrified to hear the answer.

It's now or never, she reminded herself.

"Charlie, does your dad live around here?"

"Yep."

"And what's his name?"

"Aloysius."

The air returned to her lungs.

"Oh, okay. Not who I thought." She felt lighter. "But listen, I have to get going. It was so nice meeting you."

"You too, Lorna."

"Goodbye, Charlie."

Lorna headed toward the exit.

Charlie's voice rang out behind her, his squeaky tone suddenly sharpening in her ear, "Oh, by the way, my dad goes by his middle name: Conor."

Chapter 29

That unrelenting ache was back in Lorna's head as she fled the hospital.

Once in the parking garage, she scanned the cars. Her truck always had a way of standing out from the rest. She sprinted to it, popped open the door, thrust herself inside, buried her face, and began mumbling, "I am such an idiot."

Conor and Allison. They'd been a couple. How didn't she realize it earlier? Conor didn't like Arthur, and everyone liked Arthur. Why hadn't she asked more questions?

And, of course, Conor wasn't actually interested in Lorna. He'd simply used her.

That first night in Galway Bay, he'd realized her connection to the Brooks family. It explained why he was so adamant about forcing his way into her life. He wasn't intrigued by her but likely still talked to Allison. Maybe he was spying on Lorna for her? They were all probably obsessed with finding that stupid necklace.

Her mind churned with anger as she contemplated Conor's manipulation. Then, gradually, her irritation shifted toward Will. After all, wasn't he the one who'd guided her straight into this hornet's nest?

Or had she done it herself?

Of course, Will had come to her persistently in dreams, but she was the one who let Conor into her life, against her better judgment.

She grew furious with herself.

As she slammed the steering wheel with the base of her palms, the horn's blaring sound echoed through the confines of the parking garage, blending with her own cries of anger and frustration.

How could she have so easily let him in?

It was all coming together. He must have seen her copy of Gabriel's letter that she foolishly left for several minutes sitting inside the book on the table at Galway Bay, then immediately called Allison. It would explain how Allison got into the tunnel while she and Arthur were lollygagging around at the Brooks Inn.

The parking garage suddenly felt as if it were caging her in. She needed to get out. Should she head back to Nana's house? She still didn't know about Arthur. Probably best to go there, but at that moment, she wanted nothing to do with anyone from the Brooks family, even sweet Nana.

Home. She would go home to wallow in her sorrows.

Lorna scrambled through her purse to find her car keys.

Where was her ridiculous conglomerate of keychains?

Then it torturously dawned on her. She'd pulled the keys out of her purse when she went to check her phone in Arthur's room and had probably left them on the small table next to the chair.

Lorna pounded the steering wheel again, reluctantly slid out of the driver's seat, and made her way back into the hospital.

When she reached the room, Allison, Charlie, Arthur's ex-wife Deborah, and two nurses were standing around Arthur's bed, facing his body. Lorna could see his feet shooting up under the white sheet like two rabbit ears, but everyone else hid the rest of his body and face.

Allison was speaking, "Dad, you're in the hospital. You passed out. Do you remember anything?"

"Yes, I think so," came a dry, groggy voice.

Lorna, in a state of apprehension and disbelief, floated to the end of his bed where Arthur's eyes were opened slightly. *He's alive. Thank you, God.*

Allison was holding his hand, tears streaming down her face. Charlie had crawled up on the bed, his knees drawn up close to his grandpa as he watched nervously.

"You scared us, Dad."

Arthur was trying to grin as he spoke. "I just wanted a visit from my daughter and grandson, that's all."

"Very funny, Dad. How about, next time, just call?"

A nearby nurse interjected, "We need to get some vitals, but you can continue talking as we proceed."

"I remember smelling smoke," Arthur said suddenly.

"Yes, Dad. There was a fire in the kitchen."

Arthur started to say more, but only garbled sounds came out.

"Hold on, I'll grab you a drink." Allison hurried into the hallway and returned with a plastic cup of water.

Arthur seemed more relaxed after he drank it, but his hand still shook as he returned it to Allison. "Who found me?"

"Lorna did," Allison said, her voice uneasy.

Arthur's eyes circled the room, as if trying to make sense of everything.

Charlie chimed in. "Lorna's right there, Pappy." Arthur's eyes followed his grandson's finger to the foot of the bed.

"Oh, I'm so happy that the three of you have finally met. Lorna, thank you," Arthur said.

Oh yes, we've met. As much as she wanted to escape the room, she smiled, beyond grateful he was okay.

Allison fidgeted with her fingers. "Do you remember what happened just before you passed out, Dad?"

"I'd been in the kitchen, I think." Arthur paused and hesitated.

"Making a large pot of tea for the guests, maybe?" Lorna tried to help.

"Yes, that's right. I always read a book while I'm waiting for it to steam, so I went to get one in my study, but I started to feel dizzy. Right as I got to my chair, the chest pain started. It grew worse and worse. Finally, I had to sit down. I suppose, eventually, I slipped from consciousness."

"We're just glad you're better," Charlie whispered.

A lanky doctor with a disappearing hairline entered the room. "Folks, I need to check on this fine sir. Would you mind moving over there for a few moments?" He motioned toward the chair and table where Lorna's keys sat.

When everyone dispersed, he grabbed the hanging curtain and pulled it around Arthur's bed to conceal his patient.

Allison's mother, Deborah, cupped Charlie's hands in hers. "Let's go find a snack." Charlie agreed, bouncing out of the room, with Deborah trailing behind.

Slipping into the only chair, Allison leaned her head back, a sigh of relief tumbling free.

Lorna reached for her keys.

So much she wanted to say to Allison. So much anger still inside her. How desperately she needed to explain that this was all more than just about the necklace. And how deeply she wanted to know why Allison had gone inside both the tunnel and Reynolds Tavern without even telling her own father what she was doing. And why had she come back to Annapolis without contacting him in the first place?

But how could she bring everything up, considering all the gravity that moment already had to bear?

So, she slipped from the room and ran back to her truck, just in time for the tears to stream down her face.

Some of them were from sheer relief—Arthur was awake and okay—while others came from the hurt and shock of Allison's treatment and Conor's betrayal.

And worst of all, Lorna feared she had become so wrapped up in the mystery that she'd lost track of the one person she had opened the book for in the first place.

Even the date had slipped her mind, momentarily—April 8th.
No, she couldn't go home yet.
There was somewhere else she needed to get to first.

Chapter 30
Arlington, Virginia

A sea of marble headstones spread out in flawless rows as far as the eye could see; one silent, unified army. High above, thick clouds swelled and swayed. Lorna gripped the grass below as her gaze lifted upward, her mind drifting to Will. While his body lay six feet below, she imagined him there on the blanket beside her.

"Why, Will? Why drag me into all this? Sure, I probably got myself too wrapped up in the hunt, but isn't that what you wanted me to do? Weren't you leading me toward it?"

The wind shifted, and Lorna noticed a little girl standing beside a nearby grave. *Where are her parents?* Then the girl slipped behind a thick elm and disappeared. Concerned, Lorna stood, strolled in her direction, and peeked behind the tree.

But she was gone.

Lorna made her way back to Will's grave, her eyes combing the vast cemetery, but not another living soul appeared.

Finally, her attention shifted back to Will's small headstone and settled on the date: *April 8, 2011.* She knelt before it. "Exactly two years since you left us."

"But I never really did," she heard him say.

"I feel you here now. Yet, you're not there lying warm next to me in our bed, and I hate it"—her voice began to break—"or standing there grinning with your cup of coffee in the morning."

"I'm sorry, Lorna."

"You shouldn't be." She steadied herself. "They never should have had you go out that night with just two other guys. No one was there to help you, and that kills me."

The clouds started shifting to a steel gray.

"I know it does, and I hate that you have to hurt because of me. But please, let your anger go, my love. People make mistakes."

A single raindrop dabbed at her forehead.

"A mistake that cost you *everything*." More beads of rain fell, then the sky opened, soaking her black t-shirt. "I just miss you so much," she added, pinching her eyelids shut tightly.

"And I'd do anything to keep you warm again," his voice hummed.

Lorna lay down and curled onto her side. As the rain pelted itself against her, she felt a heated sensation pressing up against her back. Then, once more, his voice murmured in her ear, this time closer than before, "One day, you'll make it back to me."

She sat up, listening for him to say more, but all she could hear was an unwavering drizzle beating against the earth. She noticed something else: water droplets falling steadily from a rosary that dangled from his gravestone. *Nana, of course. Oh, to have faith like her.*

As Lorna drove back to Annapolis, she felt Will's presence once more, as if he'd tucked himself there beside her in the passenger seat. When the storm started to fade, she even put the window down on his side, knowing he loved to feel the wind surge against his face. And somewhere between the bursting sound of traffic and the steady, rushing air, Lorna could have sworn she heard his laughter. The distinct echo instantly caused the hair on her forearms to stand on end. She didn't brush them back down. She needed the moment to linger.

If only she could perpetually live in her daydreams.

When she turned down Whitehall Road and eventually pulled

into her driveway, an unfamiliar car was sitting there. Walking toward her from the front porch was the last person she expected to see.

Allison.

Lorna stepped down from her truck. "Hi." She hoped the porch light wasn't successfully illuminating the look of shock on her face.

"Hi. My mom's place, where Charlie and I are staying, is just down the road. She lives in the Amberley neighborhood," Allison said.

"Oh, right."

"My mom said your dad lives here."

"Yeah. I...I didn't realize your mom was just over in Amberley."

Allison hesitated, then finally spoke. "I talked to my dad a bit more when you left. He told me about your dreams. And, well, I've been hard on you, Lorna. I jumped to conclusions."

You think? Lorna nearly spoke the words aloud but decided to listen instead.

"It felt like you were chasing down our family's heirloom and nothing more. And maybe you, growing close to my father, felt strange to me too. Especially since I've been a world away, not necessarily here for him."

It was shocking to see Allison's hardened exterior give way to vulnerability.

"I can see how it looked, but it was so much more than that," Lorna said. "Your book, Allison. It brought healing to me."

Allison looked surprised.

"As far as the necklace," Lorna continued, "I never intended to get so wrapped up in it. I'll admit it was a nice momentary distraction, but I also feel...well, I know it sounds strange, but I feel like Will's trying to tell me something through all this."

"Maybe he is."

"I'm just not sure what, though." Lorna dug her shoes into the gravel driveway.

The two women studied each other.

It was Lorna's chance to ask the question that wouldn't let her rest. *How can I? Should I even go there when she's come to apologize? I'll always wonder if I don't.* "Can I ask you something, Allison?"

"Sure."

"Did you ever find your earring?" Allison said nothing, so Lorna continued, "At Reynolds Tavern—downstairs in the pub. You said you'd lost it by the fireplace."

Allison's expression hardened. Lorna wondered if the passive-aggressive route had been a bad idea. She held her breath, waiting.

Finally, Allison spoke. "I'm a terrible liar, aren't I?"

"I've seen worse."

"Thanks, I guess. Of course, you had the disadvantage in the tunnel, choosing an old man for your ally." Allison smirked. "Not to mention the Maryland Inn's the easier access point."

"Conor told you about the letter I found, didn't he?"

"Conor?" Allison laughed. "You overestimate him. He and I can't stand each other. I'd be the last person he'd share that with. Nor does he take much time to think about anything beyond alcohol and women."

"Then how did you know about the coded letter?"

"Aunt Bea."

"Nana told you?"

"Charlie and I stopped at her place yesterday morning for a quick, unannounced visit since we'd just gotten into town. We were going to surprise my dad next. Anyway, you'd just left her place, and she told me you'd gone to tell my father something about a letter you'd discovered."

"And she told you what it said?"

"No, *you* did."

"What do you mean?"

"The letter was still out on Uncle Bill's desk. I, of course, read it and talked to Aunt Bea, who explained what happened. I didn't like that you were meddling, so I asked her to look after Charlie for an hour, and I went straight to the Maryland Inn, knowing I could get into the tunnel from there."

Lorna almost wanted to laugh at it all. "Well played. Wow, after I found out Conor was your ex, I thought I had it all figured out—that he only came to North Carolina to spy on me for you."

"Again, you give him far too much credit. He's not that cunning. I never told him anything about the necklace while we were dating, so I imagine he truly was learning about it for the first time. He's chasing after you because he likes you, Lorna. Good luck with that."

"Can I ask what happened between the two of you? And why you moved all the way to London?"

"It was a rough situation with Conor and me. He's eight years younger than I am and, at twenty-four, was *not* ready to have a kid. But most of all, he had serious drug and alcohol problems. I caught him driving drunk and high with Charlie in the car."

"So scary."

"It was awful. I was always on edge, and once we broke up, I never knew what kind of girlfriends Conor had him around either. But I will say, Charlie adores him. And man, does Conor love Charlie. It's a shame it wasn't enough to end his addiction. One day, he got caught with a box full of pills he was selling...with Charlie in the backseat. He'd gotten into a fight with some guy downtown standing by his car on Main Street. Among his many charges, he was found guilty of child endangerment, and I got full custody."

"So, you took off."

"I did. Nearly broke my mom and dad's hearts. And Conor's. And Charlie's. But I couldn't risk having him anywhere near my son."

Lorna felt numb. "I understand."

"I've been told he's cleaned up his act with the hard stuff. Who knows, though? Listen, I need to go. It's been a long day. I really am sorry I deceived both you and my dad."

"I should have talked to your dad about notifying you once I started digging into finding the necklace. Even if you were in London, this is your family history. Not mine. I wouldn't know any of it without your book. Trying to figure out Will's dreams or not, I was thinking about myself first. So, I'm also sorry."

"None of it matters anymore. All that's important is you found my father and likely saved his life. I owe you a thank-you."

"Just grateful he's okay."

"Me too. Well, I need to get back," Allison reiterated before narrowing her eyes. "It's funny. You remind me of someone, but I can't place who."

Lorna shuffled in place.

"Anyway, take care," Allison continued.

"You too."

———

Curled up in bed that night and about to fall asleep, Lorna's mind finally settled. With her cell phone's ringer already turned off, it vibrated annoyingly on her nightstand. She rubbed her eyes, reached through the dark for her phone, and glanced at the glowing home screen.

It was Conor.

Suddenly wide awake, her heart drumming, she turned on the lamp, took a deep breath, and answered with, "Hi."

"Hey, I noticed you called yesterday." Conor's tone was flat.

If only he knew that call was to accuse him of going behind my back and sneaking through the tunnel. Thank goodness he didn't pick up. "Yeah, I called."

"Listen, Lorna, I was angry. It wasn't right that I said you'd never let me in."

"Actually, you weren't wrong." Her mouth dropped open. *Did I just say that aloud?*

He paused before speaking. "Excuse me?"

She had to force herself to keep going. "It wouldn't be fair for me not to be honest, Conor. Am I broken? Absolutely. Can I be fixed? I don't know. But I do know I don't see 'us' in the end."

"Let me guess, Allison told you about some of the issues I've had."

"How'd you know we spoke?"

"I called her mom's house, and Deborah told me you saw them at the hospital."

"So, yes, Allison told me you had addiction issues. She said you were young when you two first had Charlie and you'd made mistakes. She also said that you love your son."

"So, this is about Tara, then?"

"It doesn't help that I ran into her leaving your place."

The line went silent.

Conor finally spoke. "I mean you and I...we talked on the phone a lot, but you've been so far away. It wasn't like we were dating. But you're moving here soon. Things could be different."

"Right. But I'm not ready to be your next Tara."

"It wouldn't be like that. Give me a chance," Conor muttered with a hint of frustration

slipping between his words and rolling uncomfortably off her skin.

Give me a chance. He sounded a lot like her mom when she'd first betrayed her dad.

"I'm grateful we connected, Conor. You helped open up something inside me again. Something I was fighting to find. But as hard as it is, I know I'm supposed to step back."

There was a long pause, then, "Guess I *was* right then. You won't let yourself move on."

"Not when it doesn't feel right. Bye, Conor."

Chapter 31

Topsail Island
May 2013

One month later

It was a balmy morning, but Lorna felt herself drawn to the ocean. She stepped out of her sun-bleached bungalow and made her way to the dunes. Her bare feet slowly sank into the baking sand, and she didn't pause until water was gently curling around her toes.

Lorna looked up and noticed where the sky met the sea.

"God, if you're there, remind me how to laugh again, truly laugh, the way I used to, without this awful tightness in my chest."

She felt the familiar clench of grief but also the rays of light, raw and warm against her back.

"And I miss loving someone as deeply as I did him."

When Lorna finally fell asleep that night, she was standing on a cliff, a deep chasm just inches from her feet. As her heartbeat began to race, a sudden tap prodded at her shoulder. She turned to see Will's face. He reached out his hand, and she took it, stepping toward him, away from the jagged precipice.

Immediately, he pulled her into his arms, and although she wasn't prepared for the rush of emotion, she allowed his love to envelope her, a rare moment of conscious surrender, with every piece of her cocooned in his embrace.

Finally setting her free, he handed her a book as they began to walk side by side. She drew it to her chest and slipped herself in next to him, remembering how easily her shoulder tucked beneath his arm. When she looked up, they were standing by the ocean.

"Want to swim?" he asked.

Lorna's eyes met the water, and for the first time since childhood, she saw the purple layer of magic glowing across its surface. "It's stunning from afar, but man, is it cold once you get in. And you know, I started having a thing about sharks a few years back," she confessed.

"You didn't worry about any of that before. You just dove in."

Lorna pressed her lips together and grimaced. "Sure, it's easier before you understand what's in there."

"It's time, Lorna. Life's about more than watching from the shore."

She turned to him. "Listen, I've jumped in deep enough. I almost killed your Uncle Arthur in doing so. What more do you want from me?"

He met her gaze. "I need you to keep going. I know it's not easy, but you've got this, Lorna." His voice was steady. "I'm here for you, but ultimately this discovery is something only you can make."

She swallowed her disappointment and nodded. Will continued, "Don't be afraid to answer hard questions, and don't get sidetracked—stay focused on what truly matters to you. It's going to take time, but you'll get there. Pop once told me, 'Our most remarkable finds are often far beneath the surface.'"

The following morning Lorna slipped her spatula under a sunny-side-up egg, flipping it onto its fleshy uncooked underside.

What exactly is he trying to help me find—far beneath the surface?

An emotional cocktail stirred within her—frustration laced with a splash of annoyance.

Nothing made sense anymore.

She didn't remember even eating her eggs, but her legs were suddenly guiding her back toward the water, across the coarse pavement, and onto the early morning's cool, powdered sand.

Lorna noticed a boat crawling across the horizon. While she wanted to further unravel her dream with Will, the vessel reminded her of Conor. How he'd gotten to climb aboard his dad's boat, but just that once. His conflicted expression as he'd told the story came to her, and she saddened, thinking about that little boy who must have craved his father's love. It wasn't hard to imagine. After all, he must have looked just like Charlie. Sweet Charlie, with his giant eyes and crooked smile. While in London, he, too, must have missed his own father terribly.

But distance was the only thing that had kept them apart. Conor had certainly made mistakes, but he wasn't the neglectful dad his own father had been. He loved Charlie and showed it. Lorna wasn't sure how long Allison was staying in Annapolis, but she was happy Charlie could be with his dad for the time being.

As far as her relationship with Conor went, Lorna didn't miss their phone calls as much as she'd thought she might. Sure, she'd enjoyed the way he made her laugh unexpectedly and the tingle across her skin when his name popped up on her cell. But when he'd have to slip off the line in a hurry, which happened quite often, her stomach inevitably would twist uncomfortably. As she stood there looking out at the single boat, now just a speck in the distance, she reminded herself that the laughs and excitement just weren't enough.

Did Allison ever miss Conor? she wondered.

Allison. What a strange thing that Conor had strong ties to her

—and that Lorna's dream about Will had led her to not only Caroline, but also to Allison.

Without a second thought, a rarity for her, Lorna dug into the back pocket of her shorts, pulled out her phone, scrolled through her contacts, and dialed.

The voice on the other end sounded slightly surprised.

"Hi, Lorna."

"How are you, Allison?"

"Doing well, thanks."

"And Arthur?"

"He has days where he's more tired than others, but overall, he's doing a lot better. He's more than ready to move back into the inn, that's for sure. Nana has been an absolute gem allowing him to stay in her guest room, but as you know, that inn's his baby."

"Absolutely. How's it going, trying to repair it?"

"It's been...slow. The contractors come when they please. It's a bit maddening, really, but we'll get there. It's been kind of fun, though, getting to work with my dad on the project."

"Remind you a little of the old days?"

"Yes, in many ways. Except he knows a lot more about our family history than he does about kitchen design."

Lorna laughed.

"How are you doing?" Allison asked.

"Pretty well, thanks. Classes just finished. I'm moving back to Annapolis in a few days. Finally coming home with my LPN degree."

"Congrats! You should be truly proud."

"Thank you." The line fell silent. "Any chance we could meet up next week when I get back?"

The following Saturday, Lorna pulled her truck into the Cape St. Claire shopping center, a well-kept strip mall with Graul's Market —a locally owned grocery store, Cape Ace Hardware where all the friendly retirees worked, and several of her favorite restaurants where t-shirts were the chosen attire.

After Lorna had asked to meet, Allison suggested brunch at a new place called Blue Rooster. When Lorna walked in, the smell of fried bacon and freshly brewed coffee filled her instantly, taking her back to weekend mornings in Topsail when she'd wake to the same two mingling aromas. Will knew she had a weakness for both and always picked them up on his trips to the little market in Surf City.

She found a table tucked away in the corner, free of shifting bodies and steaming dishes.

Lorna had just wrapped the handle of her purse around the back of her seat when she heard the door spring open. Allison drew herself inside, and she wasn't alone.

Charlie shot around his mom and made it to the table first.

"Good morning, Miss Lorna. Would you mind if I sit?" he asked.

What six-year-old arrives with pleasantries? "I'd be honored," Lorna returned with a smile.

Charlie had already slipped into the seat next to her by the time Allison made it to the table. "My mom couldn't keep Charlie this morning, so we have a very handsome date for breakfast," Allison explained before finding a chair across from them.

"How lucky are we, then?" Lorna said.

"The luckiest," he returned, a wide grin exploding across his face. He then stood abruptly. "I'll be back. Gotta use the men's room." And with that, he was off.

Lorna watched him disappear into the narrow hallway behind her. "He's something."

"Don't I know it," Allison added, eyeing the giant rooster painting looming above Lorna on the wall behind her.

Lorna started to flick the corners of the laminated menu. "Thanks for meeting up."

"Of course. It's great to see you."

"You too."

Allison continued, "You have something on your mind, don't you?"

"I don't think it's the necklace I'm supposed to find."

"Then what is it?"

"You," Lorna said, shifting in her seat.

"Me?"

"Sorry if that sounds a little...creepy."

"Only slightly, and I'm listening."

"You know how when multiple things are leading you toward something or someone, you have to ask yourself why."

"And...why are you supposed to find me?"

"I haven't figured that part out yet," Lorna admitted, trying not to notice or dissect the puzzled look on Allison's face. Eventually she couldn't resist. "You think I'm crazy, don't you?"

"I haven't figured that part out yet," Allison replied casually, one corner of her mouth rising ever so slightly into a mostly hidden grin. "Of course I don't. Listen, Lorna, I realize how much this means to you—to figure things out because of Will. But few answers in life come as soon as you ask them. I have a feeling you'll understand down the road when you least expect it. Aunt Bea likes to say, 'You'll find God's peace when you let go of trying to make all the pieces fit perfectly.'"

Charlie's squeaky little voice rose up behind Lorna. "What are you trying to figure out, Miss Lorna?" He squeezed back into the seat next to her. "Maybe I can help."

Lorna felt the spot where her shoulders met her neck tighten. Where to even begin with a six-year-old, however precocious he might be.

Allison handed him a menu. "Pick out what you want for breakfast, okay, bud?"

But Charlie was not interested in being redirected. "Pancakes and bacon, please. So, what is it you need help with?"

"First of all, I'm sad you didn't get to meet Will, Charlie. Certainly, since he's your relative, but mostly because he would have loved you, and I just have a feeling you would have loved him back. He told me in a dream that I need to stay focused on what matters truly matters to me."

"So, the people in your life," Charlie said instantly.

"Well, yes. But I have this feeling he also wanted me to read your mom's book and learn something from it."

"Did you?"

"I did."

"Then what are you worried about?" Charlie asked, buttoning the top of his baby-blue, collared shirt.

"Well, I don't think I'm done. It feels like there's more I need to know. I haven't gotten to the bottom of what he's trying to tell me."

"Okay," he said, tapping a finger to his lips. "Well, the people in mom's book are from our family, but are you paying attention to your own family?"

"Charlie..." Allison started in.

But Lorna stopped her. "No, it's okay."

Suddenly, she was back beside the ocean, its roar raging before her, seagulls yapping above, and Will by her side. They'd just moved to Topsail, and he was asking her about her real mother.

Then Charlie's bright-blue eyes were back, gazing up at her, begging for answers too.

"I'll be honest, Charlie, I don't know my biological parents, but my adoptive parents...I mean..."

She had almost felt it coming, Charlie interrupting with, "Why don't you know who your real parents are?"

"Because I never met them."

"Oh, I didn't know that," Allison said, looking up from her menu. "Were you born here?"

"Yes."

Lorna watched the hesitation draw itself across Allison's features, but naturally, Charlie didn't miss a beat. "Then what happened to your Mom?"

"I guess she was young and decided she couldn't take care of me." Lorna tried to distract herself by eyeing the menu. Finally, her gaze returned to Allison, who appeared suddenly uneasy.

When Allison started to speak, she seemed to be choosing her words with careful consideration. "But...you...don't know...who she is, even?"

That feeling was returning. The burdensome weight that liked to unload itself right on top of Lorna's chest. "No, I have no idea who she is. I think she was in high school."

"Broadneck High School?" Allison asked immediately.

"No clue."

Charlie started to break in, but Allison interrupted with her own question. "Do you mind if I ask how old you are?"

"I'm twenty-two."

Allison's eyes gained an alertness as she nibbled on her thumb, her mind seemingly slipping off elsewhere.

Lorna could feel something shifting inside her, like microscopic jolts of electricity darting across her skin. Her amygdala, they'd taught her in nursing school, was the ancient part of her brain that sent out warnings. It signaled danger. In early humans, it alerted them, saying something like, *Yes, I sense it, that shuffle in the brush. It smells you, so run! A tiger is coming!*

She stood up suddenly. "I need to use the restroom."

"Yeah. Of course," Allison returned.

While rubbing the scratchy, beige paper towel over the tops of her hands, Lorna decided she should probably get something quick to eat, then get going. She had a lot of unpacking to do. The heaviness on her chest was still there, but she didn't acknowledge it. Lorna had grown so used to the feeling, it almost seemed like it would just never leave.

"Oh, look, they have smoothies," she said when she returned to the table. "I might get one of those. What are you guys eating?"

"Are you okay?" Charlie said.

"Yeah," Lorna quickly returned.

"Your hand is shaking, though," he added.

Lorna lifted her fingers, watching them vibrate. "I'm fine. They do that sometimes. Nervous twitch, I guess."

Allison was quiet as she sipped on her steaming cup of black coffee. She then pulled out her phone and began scrolling.

"What are you looking at, Mom?"

"Facebook."

"Why?"

She looked up at Lorna. "There's something I need to throw out there."

Lorna's throat tightened, and she braced for impact, fearing the force of what Allison's next sentence might bring.

"I realized who you remind me of. I don't know how I missed it before, because you're a carbon copy of her."

The clanging in the room grew louder. Lorna's mind zeroed in on the awful howl of the blender: part vacuum cleaner, part hair dryer, part circular saw. Someone really needed to invent a quieter way to make a smoothie.

"I grew up with her," Allison continued. "We were friends when we were young. In high school, she...she got pregnant. I'm not saying it's her..."

Her. Her. Her.

"I don't think you're old enough for me to be..." Lorna started in.

"I'm thirty-eight, Lorna. The same as Hailey."

Hailey. She has a name. It can't be, though.

"We're sixteen years older than you. It would make sense. Do you want to see her photo?"

Every nerve was pulsing in Lorna's body. *I don't want to see her. Do I?* Curiosity began to surface, but she shoved it back down. *Why should I even go there?* Then came anger. *Why is Allison doing this? She has no idea if it's even her.*

"Can I see?" she heard Charlie's voice saying.

Allison, still holding the phone, her eyes locked on Lorna, was waiting for a response.

"I don't know," Lorna said, uneasily. "I mean, it might not even be her."

"It might not be." Allison's eyes softened. "But I think it is."

Lorna's arm reached out slowly, her palm curling open before her mind could even make the decision to say "yes."

Allison placed the phone inside Lorna's hand. The photo on the screen screamed 1980-something. A teenage girl with a permed, brown mane peered back at her, dark eyes gleaming with excitement, a smile as wide as the ocean, and an oversized pink sweatshirt engulfing her midsection.

Even Lorna could see the undeniable resemblance.

And she was sure the entire room could hear the throbbing of her heart.

Charlie was suddenly there at her side, peeking over her arm at the woman who certainly appeared to be *her mother.*

"Are you okay?" Allison asked.

"I'm fine." But what was she really? As she saw the young girl's face for the first time, what was that undeniable emotion worming its way inside her? It was sneaky and discomforting. It was not what someone wanted to feel when they initially laid eyes on the woman who likely brought them into the world.

And yet she said the last thing she ever expected to come out of her mouth.

"I need to meet her."

Chapter 32

Four days later, Allison was driving Lorna north to Baltimore in Arthur's Volvo. At a downtown traffic light, a man appeared next to Lorna's window. A grizzled beard nearly cloaked his cracked, downcast lips. Meanwhile, the sun peeked its way over the red brick Camden Yards baseball stadium, illuminating his face. His eyes seemed hollow, lonely, and rimmed with exhaustion; and his clothes, caked with dirt, had split at the seams.

When the light glowed green, and Allison pressed the gas pedal, Lorna watched his ghostly countenance diminish slowly until it vanished behind the fast-paced flurry of vehicles, each striving desperately to get ahead of the pack.

"Lorna, there's something I want you to know about Hailey."

"Okay."

"Well, she's a bit...quirky."

"Quirky?"

"Yes, I don't know how else to say it."

"Well, if you're a writer and you can't find the right words, she must be unique."

"She's that too. Hailey's always marched to the beat of her own drum, which is what I love about her most."

"How'd you meet her?"

Allison searched her memory. "We were ten years old at a Navy football game, actually."

"Really? I never took Arthur for the sporty type."

"He's not. Will's grandpa—my Uncle Bill—took me."

"Now I'm even more shocked. I thought..."

"This was before the big feud."

"Got ya."

"Uncle Bill and Aunt Bea's boys were grown, so he asked if I wanted to join him. We were watching the game from a blanket on the hill by Navy's end zone. He was super focused on the field while I chomped away at my popcorn. Out of nowhere, my buttery box goes flying through the air, kernels flinging in all directions. I squealed like a pig, and when I turned, there was a girl about my age, sprawled out on the ground next to me. 'Why'd you do that?' I yelled immediately, but when I looked over, her face was molded into the mud next to me. Uncle Bill stood and asked her if she was all right. He was a big man, with big hands, but I remember him ever so gently helping her to her feet."

"And was she covered in mud?"

"Completely. Her mom had bought her this Navy cheerleading outfit, and it was brown."

Lorna couldn't help but laugh. "Oh, my goodness. How did she manage to trip over you?"

"She was staring off into space, I imagine, which is definitely her."

"So, did she go running back to her parents?"

"No, apparently her mom had dropped her off at the game and left. You know how the stadium sits on that flat field, and in November, when the wind whips across it, it feels like you're in Antarctica. But Hailey didn't even have a coat. My dad put me in about twenty layers, so Uncle Bill asked if I could spare one of them to give to her. Kind of his way, I think, of not only covering up the mud but also keeping her warm."

"How'd you feel about that?"

"I remember giving Uncle Bill a death stare. But when I looked at Hailey, her skinny little toothpick legs standing there, all cold and pathetic, I gave in."

"So, she hung out with you guys?"

"She did."

"How'd that go?"

"She grew on me. She was unlike anyone I'd ever met—incredibly endearing, whether you wanted to like her or not, with this wild imagination, and oh, how she made me laugh."

Allison and Lorna continued into the city, weaving under the shadows of towering buildings with people bustling anxiously across wide streets.

At another stop light, Lorna watched a woman emerge from an Italian restaurant, its striped, crimson awning matching her lips. Flawlessly put together, she exuded an air of confidence that lingered with Lorna as they drifted away.

Skyscrapers turned into shaded streets where homes pressed together like the folds of an accordion, tightly bound, with black bars braced against windows and doors.

Lorna was grateful for pops of green, white and red where Japanese maples and dogwood trees had found their footing on the grassy knoll at the road's center. Even an occasional towering sycamore managed to survive among the endless expanse of cars and concrete.

Allison peered down at her phone before making a quick right into a tight parking lot. Two police cars were parked haphazardly, as if they'd rushed onto the scene in a hurry, but the officers were nowhere to be seen.

After squeezing the Volvo into a tight spot, Allison turned off the ignition.

Lorna exhaled slowly. "Thanks for bringing me."

"Of course." Allison's face squeezed together ever so slightly. "Are you okay?"

"I'll be fine."

Lorna got out of the car first, and Allison followed.

A woman, likely in her fifties, with hair knotted high in a

messy bun, loitered near the front door of the apartment complex, sucking on a cigarette. "Who ya looking for?" Her voice was deep and raspy. "I'm the landlord."

Allison kept walking. "We're good, but thanks."

"Suit yourselves."

A jagged hole, a bit larger than a fist, was in the front door of the building, with shards of glass scattered on the ground inside. In the dim and musty hallway, a bitter, overpowering smell permeated the air.

They exited the elevator on the second floor.

Neither of them spoke.

Moments later, they were standing in front of Apartment 20B. Something inside Lorna wanted to turn around and run. Allison tapped her knuckles against the door. When no one came, she pounded harder with the side of her fist. The door creaked open slowly, but a security chain stopped it. Just past the three-inch opening, deep brown eyes looked back at Lorna.

Someone fiddled with the chain until the door sprung open, and a woman stood before them, her hair dyed an unnatural black —a sharp contrast to her pale complexion. "Come on in, but hurry...there are a lot of odd ducks around here."

Lorna complied, urging her feet to move forward, even though they felt as heavy as cinderblocks. The room was dim, with a red sheet covering the sole window, and a small lampshade struggling to illuminate the space from its table in the corner.

Once seated on the couch, Lorna couldn't tear her gaze away from the coffee table, which was completely covered with an array of plastic pastel bowls, a bib, an empty baby food container, and a soiled rag.

"Sorry, the place is a bit messy. I've got a little one."

Another little one, Lorna thought to herself. *Since things worked out so well with me.*

Allison joined her on the couch.

Lorna watched Hailey as she found a seat on a wooden dining chair near a small television set across the room from them.

No one seemed to know what to say. Finally, Allison grabbed for a sentence. "I saw photos of the baby online. She's beautiful, Hailey."

"Thank you. She's taking a nap." Hailey's lip flattened into a smile.

Lorna was relieved that Allison was making conversation since she suddenly wasn't feeling like it herself.

"What's her name?" Allison asked.

"Who?" Hailey returned.

"Your daughter?"

"Oh, right," Hailey laughed awkwardly. "I call her Winnie."

"Winnie. How sweet," Allison said. "Listen, I know you have your hands full with a baby, so thanks for letting us come over."

"I'm glad you could make it." Hailey's eyes met the ground as she nibbled on a fingernail.

Lorna noticed a trail of chalky gray on the side table where cigarette ashes had been hastily wiped away.

"Would you guys like some Pepsi or something?"

Allison shook her head. "I'm good."

Lorna hesitated. "Oh, um...I'm fine too."

Hailey shot up from the chair. "I think I'm gonna grab myself something. Are you guys sure?"

Lorna watched as Hailey squeezed her wrists, one after another.

"You know what? A Pepsi would be great," Lorna finally managed.

Hailey slipped into the nearby kitchen.

"She's nervous," Allison whispered.

Lorna nodded.

Hailey returned with two small glass cups, one featuring Garfield with an impish smile standing next to Odie, and the other cup covered in blue Smurfs. Both were half full of soda.

Lorna took a sip. It tasted flat so she set the cup on the ashy side table next to her.

Hailey took a huge gulp then spit it back into her cup. "Ugh, super flat. So sorry about that." She looked at Lorna with puppy-dog eyes.

"Really, it's all right," Lorna tried to assure her.

"No, it's not," Hailey pushed back.

"Listen, this is far from the first time I had a flat soda," Lorna added.

"I know, but you come all the way here to meet me, and this is the best I can do. I wanted to get out to the store, but with the baby and all, well, I just..."

"I don't need anything from you, Hailey. I just thought it was time."

"You're brave. Braver than I am." Hailey laughed in a way that seemed like it hurt. "I wanted to stop by your place a million times, but I never could. I wasn't really supposed to, either. But that's never stopped me from not doing something." She paused. "I was mostly just scared."

"Then why'd you agree to meet me now?" Lorna crossed her legs, then uncrossed them, surprised the words had slipped out of her mouth.

"You want the truth? I'm finally clean. It's the first time in a long time."

The baby's shrill cry broke free from the bedroom.

Hailey didn't rise to get her, and she wouldn't look at Lorna either. Instead, she stared down at a pink bracelet wrapped tightly around her wrist, separating and jiggling the beads.

There she is, Lorna thought, stealing a look at her mother. Her entire life, Lorna had imagined her, envisioned how she spoke and smiled, wondered if the woman thought of her too, angered at the way she'd never returned to find her.

"Can I grab Winnie?" Allison inquired over the baby's cries.

Hailey nodded.

Allison returned quickly with the baby, the tiny thing's honey-brown eyes framed in red.

"She was born on a snowy December night, just like you, Lorna," Hailey timidly shared.

"Really?" Lorna tried to act pleased.

"Isn't that crazy?" Hailey smiled.

Lorna forced a grin.

"This time, I'm gonna do it differently, I told myself." Hailey bit down on her heavily lined lower lip.

"I'm glad," Lorna heard herself saying. She stood and asked to use the bathroom.

"Just through there. The room right after my bedroom."

Lorna barely noticed her reflection in the toothpaste-splattered bathroom mirror. Her focus was on the unbearable sensation that had just expanded inside her. The baby was her half-sister, and yet she felt only bitterness when she saw her.

On the way back to the living room, Lorna realized the door was ajar in Hailey's bedroom. She couldn't resist a peek. Inside, a Pack 'n Play squeezed next to an unmade queen bed, but her attention went immediately to the handmade baby mobile hanging from the ceiling. From it dangled three delicate origami animals: a tiger, a lion, and an elephant—all folded meticulously, and each catching a subtle hint of sunlight seeping through the plastic blinds. For the first time since she'd walked in Hailey's door, a calm sensation settled inside her.

On the way home, few words were said as they wove their way out of the city.

Lorna turned toward the clouds outside her window. They were beckoning her. She started to count them silently. "No," Lorna finally said under her breath.

"No what?" Allison asked.

"Oh, nothing."

"You sure?"

"It's just, I have this weird thing where I count. I feel so ridiculous even saying it. I guess I do it when I'm overwhelmed, but I hate that I can't stop."

"Don't be embarrassed. It's how you cope, and it could be much worse. I used to drink like a sailor when I got stressed. It's how Conor and I met."

"How'd you stop?"

"It was a long road to recovery. A road I'll probably always be on, but one that's gotten smoother in time."

"Do you think Hailey will ever stay clean?"

Allison switched lanes. "I hope so, but I honestly don't know, Lorna. I mean, it's good to hear she's kicked it for now, but...well, she's been hooked on some heavy stuff for a very long time."

The image of the baby's flushed face rushed into Lorna's memory, and instead of jealousy, this time she felt only pity. But this emotion was even harder to bear, so she searched for something new to think about. "Not to change the subject, but can I ask you something about your book?"

"Which one?"

"The first one. Foxgloves. Caroline."

"Sure."

"Did you not publish it because you didn't want people to know about the Three Brothers, since the necklace is still missing?"

"You know, it's crazy. I used to almost wish someone would find the stupid thing. I had myself believing that would allow my dad and uncle to suddenly grow close again. But no, that's not why I didn't publish it."

"Why, then?"

"Because I never had my ending. Most of all, I never had Caroline's ending. I always felt like something was missing."

"Like what?"

"Well, the biggest problem was I couldn't find a death record."

"But they announced her execution in the newspaper," Lorna reminded her.

"I suppose. Yet, why no burial plot for Caroline?"

"Maybe considering her crime?"

"Yes, I read sometimes they put criminals in unmarked graves.

Or I could see Molly fighting to bury her at Whitehall, but she's not in their cemetery."

Lorna watched as an endless row of pines flashed by on Route 97.

The Burgwin-Wright House gardens suddenly flickered through her mind. She'd never heard back from the director there, even after texting to remind her twice. Lorna pulled out her phone, then hesitated. *Maybe the neighbor lady didn't know anything*. It felt a bit much to bother her again. But something inside her said to do it one last time, just to be sure.

So, she pulled out her phone and texted: *Hi, Sarah. This is Lorna Brooks again. Just wanted to check in one more time to see if you ever heard anything about the Horsewoman Fugitive or Alice Gates. Thanks.*

Immediately, Lorna saw dots.

Sarah was writing back.

She started tapping the center consul awaiting her reply.

The seconds dragged on.

Finally, a paragraph popped up: *YES. So funny you should write, Lorna. Your friend Tess stopped by the other day. The woman, Nancy Barnes, who owns the place next door, is rarely there since it's being remodeled, so I couldn't ask if she had information about the women. But when Tess reminded me, I walked over and noticed Nancy in front of her place talking to contractors. She told me she'd seen a letter Alice Gates had written in the Wilmington newspaper and was going to send it to me. It sounds like something you're really going to want to read. Nancy gave me her number that day, so let me text and remind her to send it.*

Lorna filled with anticipation as she replied: *Thank you so much for speaking with her!*

She then passed along her email address as well.

Five minutes later, Sarah sent another text that read: *Check your inbox!*

Immediately clicking on Sarah's email, Lorna began to silently read Alice's letter.

Suddenly, she gasped.

"What?" Allison turned to her.

"You will never believe this." Lorna's gaze remained fixed on the letter. "Can you drive us back to Nana's house so I can share this with her and your dad as well?"

Allison's forehead wrinkled. "What is it?"

Lorna finally looked up at Allison. "Your ending."

Chapter 33
Annapolis

Arthur and Nana were in the living room when Lorna and Allison sprung through the door.

"Welcome!" Nana exclaimed.

Arthur perked up too.

"I'm glad you're both sitting." Allison's grin was wide and radiating. "Tell them, Lorna!"

The corners of Lorna's mouth inched toward her dimples as she sat down on the edge of the couch. "We came to tell you about a letter written by a woman named Alice Gates who lived in Wilmington, North Carolina, in 1799."

Arthur offered a broad grin. "I'm intrigued."

"You should be," Lorna returned. "Of course, we know from the *Maryland Gazette* that Caroline died in January of 1784, shortly after Washington's resignation speech."

"Right. Her execution was private and carried out during a snowstorm," Arthur remembered.

Lorna clenched her teeth. "More on that to come." Pulling out her phone, she quickly clicked on her email and began to read Alice's letter.

The Wilmington Gazette
February 8, 1799

Dear Reader,

There's a certain allure to truth, isn't there? Like a locked treasure, it beckons to be set free.

I feel compelled to unburden myself while still possessing breath and a hand to wield this pen.

You may know me as Alice Gates, the innkeeper. What most don't realize is I was also the Horsewoman Fugitive. On the night of my attempted escape, I concealed my identity beneath a hat and scarf, fearing the loss of business should anyone realize I was a fugitive and not just the kind keeper of the inn.

But even "Alice Gates" isn't my real name.

I was forced to become her.

Drawn into a corner by the looming threat of arrest for my husband's murder, I fled to Wilmington. I confess to his death. He was a cruel man, a danger to both me and our unborn child. Moreover, he secretly aligned himself with the British during the war, jeopardizing our country's future.

As a young woman, filled with rage, I believed his removal was imperative. Now, in my later years, I find myself questioning my actions. Though I believed I acted to safeguard my nation, myself, and above all, my son, I cannot ignore the cost. To face life without a father should not be a young boy's lot. Yet, what kind of cruelness would he have witnessed had his father survived? And was his secret correspondence with the British worth taking his life over? In the end, I've come to accept these are unanswered questions I shall carry to my grave.

When the sheriff from my town eventually tracked me down here in Wilmington, I thankfully had just one guest at my inn, a dear friend. Before my flight into the night, I instructed her to spread the tale that Alice, along with her son, had temporarily left town, so they did not realize I was, in fact, the Horsewoman Fugitive.

The sheriff's men took my son and me back to where we'd come from, and I knew I'd hang. But on the very day I was supposed to be sent to the gallows, my fate took an unexpected turn.

Years prior, following the loss of my home in a fire, a childhood friend bestowed upon me an immensely valuable necklace. He did so while I was staying at the estate of another dear friend. The sheriff also happened to be visiting my friend's home that day to question me about my husband's death.

As he was riding away, the sheriff noticed the friend who was about to give me the necklace, traveling toward the estate. Being a man who always needed to know everyone's comings and goings, he promptly turned his carriage around and returned to the house. I came to find out that he eavesdropped as I was shown the necklace in a nearby carriage barn. And later, as we were on our way to bury the necklace by the water for safekeeping, the sheriff attempted to follow us. Thankfully, a small spaniel started barking at him, forcing him to flee. But for years, he'd clearly been tormented by not knowing where the extravagant jewel was hidden.

Around midnight on the day they were going to execute me, a guard visited my cell and escorted me into a waiting carriage outside the jail. With my arms still bound, I was pushed inside, only to be met by the sheriff's malicious grin. He transported us back to my friend's estate, where I'd buried the necklace years prior. Upon our arrival, the driver concealed the carriage while the sheriff, with a gun pressed to my back, forced me to walk toward the water at the far end of the property.

Now, allow me to let you in on another little secret.

Unbeknownst to him, the necklace was no longer buried there.

All those years before, on the night I fled town for Wilmington, based upon the advice of a wise friend, I decided to dig the jewel up myself and then wore it under my shawl as I traveled.

At that very moment, the necklace remained hidden in my neighbor's extravagant English garden in Wilmington.

I was not about to reveal this to the sheriff.

I needed the intoxicating allure of the necklace.

It was my only hope.

The air was frigid, tiny crystals emerging white against the black night, the first sign of a snowstorm rattling in from the west. The earth was too frozen to dig, but he desperately needed to know the spot we'd buried it so he could return come the first thaw of spring, or so he mockingly alluded.

I asked him how he knew about the necklace, and he admitted sneaking up on us when it was gifted to me years earlier.

He was breathless as he spoke about it, his eyes filled with a frenzied fervor. This concealed fixation with finding such a valuable prize had clearly consumed him.

I knew my life was about to be claimed at the gallows, if he did not dispose of me sooner, so my mind searched desperately for an escape. As we approached the site where the necklace had once been buried, my hands remained securely bound in front of me.

My entire body shook—certainly from the biting cold, but even more so from the plan I knew I had to enact. Several times, I willed myself to take action, but in every instance, I faltered, knowing everything rested on that moment, and one false move would mean my sudden demise.

"Stop walking," he whispered abruptly. When I froze in place, he drew his chest to my back, his lips curled up beside my ear, his fetid breath pouring forth. "Tell me now. Where is it?"

"Right over there," I assured the sheriff, stepping forth once again. That's when I acted—veering directly in front of him, halting suddenly, and then bending low. He stumbled over my body as I had hoped.

His gun went off, a sharp, piercing crack exploding into silence.

Was I hit? I waited for a throbbing pain to emerge.

But somehow, nothing.

The sheriff reached out for my gown, but I took off running. I could feel a portion of it tear in his sharp, bony-fingered grasp.

The icy waters both beckoned and haunted me in the distance. I knew it was my only chance at freedom, yet meeting those frigid depths could also mean immediate death.

Still, the crashing tide beating off the bluff called to me, a far more alluring fate than what lay behind me.

And so, I dug in, sprinting as fast as my feet dared to carry me. I could feel the throb of my heart pounding furiously in my chest and the thrash of my skirts against my ankles, threatening to unbalance me at any moment. With my hands yet bound tightly, I felt the weight of my peril pressing against me. A single misstep, and I'd seal my fate.

He was at my heels, his raspy breaths maddeningly close.

Then another gunshot cracked forth from behind me, barely missing me to the right.

Finally, I reached the cliff's edge, the end of the line, stopping only for a moment to peer down at the frantic, rippling abyss. I closed my eyes, saw my son's face, and leapt forward.

The impact of my body against the bay waters stole my breath away as they sucked me down into their lonely, ice-cold depths, piercing me with a thousand knives. Surely, I'd met my end. But something deep inside me remembered to kick. And while my skirts clung desperately to my legs, cocooning them cruelly in a thicket of drenched cloth, the constraint made me thrash harder. Slowly, upward I climbed until finally my face broke free across the surface. I gasped, sucking air so intensely into my lungs it was as if I'd taken in my very first infant breath. Filled with oxygen, my body began bobbing in the current. That's when the frigidness struck me again, the wintry air cutting into my wet skin.

"Don't move," a stern whisper echoed in my ear.

When I was a girl, my father used to bring me to the deck of his anchored merchant vessels before a journey back to England. I'd stand at the helm, pretending to steer, as he spoke to his crew. My father would always warn them, "I wish you safe passage. However, shall you ever collide with that great beast of the Atlantic—do not move. Allow yourself to float for the first minute or so and force your breath to steady. Your body must adjust to the bitter tempera-

tures. Remember, shock and panic in cold water are the fastest ways to go."

Still, every part of me wanted to flail; to beat back against the current.

But I forced myself to heed my father's advice, just this once.

There, in the darkness, I lay, bobbing in layers of soaking wet fabric. This afforded me a moment of contemplation. I knew from the beginning that the shackles around my wrists were far too large. So, with the aid of the water, I slipped one of my hands free.

Thankfully, too, the moon was but a thin crest of light, concealing me from the sheriff's sinister gaze, likely scouring the bay from his precipice above.

Unbeknownst to me, because of the gunshots, several servants had emerged from the house, forcing my adversary to flee.

However, as I was not aware of his departure, I lingered in the water for a considerable span, afraid he'd meet me at the banks. I could scarcely feel my extremities, yet somehow eventually kicked my way to shore, fighting the choppy waves. Then, expending every vestige of vigor that remained, I hauled myself up the steep precipice and collapsed on the rock-hard soil.

Would you believe that same little spaniel, who had scared away the sheriff years earlier, my tiny guardian angel, smelled my scent on the wind, whipping up from the water, and his nose led my dearest friend to me.

My friend then dismantled my shackled wrist, wrapped me in blankets, and helped guide me to the fire, where I shook continuously for what seemed an eternity.

Fortunately, my son missed the commotion, lying serenely in his bed, enfolded within the reverie of his dreams.

When I finally entered his bedroom, I fell beside his bed and wept like a child, as silently as I could muster.

I had believed with certainty that I would never behold him again.

His eyelids slid open, and I kissed his cheeks over and over, then again and again.

The following day, the gazette declared my execution. They termed it a "private exhibition" on account of the snowstorm. The sheriff must have convinced himself that I would not survive the icy waters, and he was in dire need of veiling his actions.

But my son and I had already departed before the newspaper ink had set, journeying back to Wilmington where we'd built a life. On my more vengeful days, I secretly hoped the sheriff would fear I had lived and proceed in search of me. A bitter fate would have awaited him. Yet, it was not necessary to wish for such things. He met his end from a heart ailment that very year. This allowed me to raise my son in tranquility, here, by the sea.

I was so fortunate to receive a second chance. The Almighty spared my life through another man's greed.

Let my closing sentiments not merely enter your mind but burrow themselves deep down inside you. I learned life's greatest lessons the hard way; I pray better for you. Please know this beloved reader, there is so much to consume us in this world: anger, pride, vanity, grief, ambition, and fear. They prey on us like circling raptors, and when we allow them to seize hold, we sacrifice all that we cherish most.

Wake up every morning and remind yourself what truly matters, then refuse to let it from your sight.

My Best Regards,
Alice

Lorna looked up at Arthur and Nana, shock painted across their faces.

Arthur's frail hand covered his mouth. He released it and spoke. "She lived. Caroline lived."

"She did. And it's remarkable what she risked writing this. The authorities in Wilmington easily could have taken her in. She was admitting murder," Allison assessed.

"I guess telling her story and setting the record straight was worth it to her," Lorna added.

Allison nodded. "So it appears. She was never a predictable one, that's for sure."

"And what was the date of the letter?" Allison asked.

"1799," Lorna returned. "I saw her gravestone when I was in Wilmington but, of course, thought it was 'Alice Gates.' Caroline died the same year she wrote the letter."

"It's likely she wrote it knowing she was dying then," Arthur interjected.

"Likely," Lorna answered. "Even though 'Alice' didn't mention names or places in her letter, it's astonishing to me that no one realized Caroline Brooks was Alice Gates. Wasn't the Brooks murder case talked about throughout the colonies?"

"You would think," Arthur chimed in. "But I don't believe so, and here's why. Allison and I combed the *Maryland Gazette* archives from the summer of 1777, when Grafton was murdered, to January of 1784 when Caroline had her trial, and barely anything was written. I know for a fact that Sheriff Stone was deeply connected to the *Maryland Gazette*'s publisher. I imagine he knew all that time he wanted the Three Brothers, so the quicker and quieter he got rid of Caroline Brooks, the better."

Lorna's mind was racing. "Can you believe she jumped into the freezing bay?"

"She did it for Gabriel," Allison said. "She knew it was her only chance to see him again."

Nana looked at Allison. "What a mother won't do to protect her child."

Allison pressed her lips together tightly. "Lorna, thank you for sharing this with us. Knowing Caroline lived on and raised her child..." She paused as her voice caught. "It's incredible. And the piece we were missing."

Less than an hour later, Allison pulled into Lorna's driveway, put the car in park, and peered out her window down Whitehall Road.

Lorna watched her. "I'm sure you visited Whitehall while you were writing your book, right?"

"Wish I could say I did. I couldn't get access. I tried persistently, but, as I'm sure you know, it's privately owned, and no one ever got back to me."

"Wow, such a shame you weren't able to see it."

"It was."

Lorna sat up straighter. "Then we're going."

"How?"

"Come on." Lorna flew out the car door.

"But we can't even get past the electronic gate," Allison yelled from the driver's seat.

Lorna showed up at Allison's window. "Then let's take a different route."

Afternoon was fading into evening as the two women strolled down Whitehall Road.

"What will we tell the family who lives there?" Allison insisted.

"They don't live there anymore."

"So, no one should be there on a Friday afternoon?"

"Well, I didn't say that," Lorna said casually.

"*Who* will be there?"

"I never took you for a rule follower," Lorna laughed.

"But I did take you for one," Allison returned.

Lorna grinned. "Well, I make exceptions."

Chapter 34

"I'm thrilled you're taking me to see it, but again, *who* won't want us to be there?" Allison pressed.

"His name is Mr. Moretti," Lorna explained. "He's the groundskeeper. Kind of the snarly type. He oversees the property for the owners and lives in a small cottage near the main house. There's a camera on the main gate. The moment you try to open that thing, he's there."

"Sounds more like a Doberman than a man."

"There's an uncanny resemblance."

Allison's eyes sprung open. "So, how exactly are we going to deal with him?"

"We aren't." Lorna made a sharp right turn into a low-lying meadow with pops of purple and yellow wildflowers dusted throughout. "We'll just take the long way."

"Over the river and through the woods. It appears you did a lot of childhood exploring."

"This was one of my favorite places to wander. How about you? You grew up at the inn, right?"

"Yes. I mostly wandered around downtown. Could explain my alcohol issues."

"You did a lot of wandering after the Three Brothers, as well, I imagine?"

"Oh, yes, that too. Man, the places my dad and I went in search of that thing. At first, when I was a kid, I was mesmerized by it all. I felt like a real treasure hunter. But over time, I grew to resent it. I mean, not the necklace itself, but my dad's obsession with finding it. It's what tore my family apart. First, he began to hate his own brother. Then, once that relationship unraveled, my parents started arguing more frequently, and of course, they eventually divorced."

"I'm so sorry."

"It's all in the past, anyway."

"Is it, though?" Lorna questioned, surprised by how forthright she'd been lately. *Is it too much, though?*

Allison kept walking without saying a word.

"I didn't mean to..." Lorna began.

"No, it's all right. Listen, I know I struggled at first with it all, but I'm glad now that you and my dad enjoyed the hunt together. I really am. When we did research for the book, I never wanted to talk about the necklace as much as he did because I was just so bitter."

"I understand why. Do you still even want to see the house?"

"It's not the home I care to see so much. It's the bluff."

"The bluff?"

"The spot where Caroline leapt into the bay to save herself from the sheriff. It's been on my mind since you read her confession letter. And I'm curious about the distance between the house and the water. How far Charity had to go that night to save Caroline."

"Oh, you think it was Charity who saved her?" Lorna questioned. "Because it could have been Molly too. In her letter, Caroline just says her dearest friend found her with the help of a little spaniel, which was Molly's dog."

"That's true. It could have been either of them."

As they reached the end of the meadow, Lorna stepped first

into the woods. "The path we used to take is still here. I'm shocked. Must be a favorite among deer as well."

Allison followed Lorna on the narrow trail, where frail twigs snapped underfoot. Lorna remembered the giant pines, beeches, and hickory trees that soared toward the sky on both sides and reminisced about playing in the same trickling stream with Kate.

When they finally reached the end of the tree line, Allison could hear the bay waters lapping against the shore. They emerged from the woods onto a thick lawn that dropped off sharply to their right, nothing but churning gunmetal-gray water for miles. Lorna's finger shot up in the opposite direction. "There's Whitehall mansion."

"Farther from the water than I imagined," Allison said.

"It's a good thing the sheriff fired his gun," Lorna added.

"He saved her life in the end by taking those shots."

"Otherwise, they likely wouldn't have found her until it was too late."

Both women's eyes went to the house, its red-brick facade and sturdy white columns loomed above them. Its shadow stretched across a carefully manicured yard, spread out like a wide, green blanket and dotted with ancient trees.

Lorna turned to Allison. "Let's check out that bluff before our Doberman finds us."

Together, they stepped onto the edge of the cliff that peered over the untamed bay.

Lorna inched backward. "Now, that's quite a jump."

"A long way there, and even worse when you reach it." Allison watched the waves smashing against jagged rocks that rimmed the coast.

Lorna pointed left. "Over there, it's not as steep. I wonder if that's where Caroline eventually crawled out."

Allison's eyes shifted. "Very possible. Maybe it's even where they used to keep the rowboat she hid in when Sheriff Stone first came to question her and Mrs. McGregor. Remember when she and Charity were talking near the water, when she first showed her where she'd buried the Three Brothers?"

"Oh, that's right. I do. How'd you know that happened? Or was that part fiction?"

"No, it happened. Caroline kept a detailed journal before she left for Wilmington."

"Amazing it still exists. Even with the fire."

"Apparently, she'd accidentally left the journal at Whitehall when the fire took place. I know this because Caroline wrote about it. She also left the journal at Whitehall when she left for Wilmington, and Molly gave it to Gabriel many years later."

"Wow, it's so neat that you were able to get such a detailed first-hand account."

"Yes, I'm so grateful they kept it, and that Caroline loved to write so much. You know, growing up, she fascinated me. She was such a badass, right? But in time, I realized that I admire Charity just as much. Someone who's steadfast and a bit predictable usually isn't the protagonist in my books. They're my secondary characters. But when faced with hard stuff, Charity showed up courageously. She made calculated decisions. She was a master at persevering. People like her are who you want in your corner for the long haul. Wish I was a bit more like her, actually."

"Well, Miss Bestselling Author, I imagine you know a thing or two as well about making calculated decisions."

"Oh, Lorna, I've been so impulsive too. I plunged headlong into dating Conor when I knew I shouldn't have. As I told you, he was eight years younger than me and not ready for a relationship, let alone being a father. So, we bring this beautiful child into the world, who my parents absolutely adored, and I take him away, far away. I truly did want to protect him from Conor's poor choices, but if I'm being honest, I also wanted to punish Conor for not being a trustworthy boyfriend. And perhaps even my dad a little for not being the husband and father I thought he could have been. But doing so came at such a cost. Charlie ended up losing his father *and* his grandparents."

Lorna peered down at the water, grasping for the right words. "You had to make some terribly tough decisions, Allison. And we all have regrets, but it's never too late to dive in and start anew."

They made eye contact, and Allison nodded, a calm, contemplative expression settling across her face before she turned her gaze back toward the bay.

Suddenly, the sound of a small-scale motor being pressed to its limit filled her ears. She turned to see a golf cart cutting across the lawn, heading in their direction.

"That's him! Let's go!" Lorna grabbed Allison's arm, and they sprinted for the woods.

"Hey, this is private property!" a man's voice boomed.

Lorna felt like she was a kid again, with Mr. Moretti chasing her and her friends off the property. She couldn't help herself from laughing out loud. Allison joined in.

When they reached the wooded trail, which, thankfully, was too narrow for a golf cart, Lorna took the lead, and they disappeared into a sanctuary of trees.

Lorna eventually stopped, forcing down her laughter so she could listen, making sure the groundskeeper hadn't tried to get to them on foot. Allison froze, too, and covered her mouth. The only sound was the wind whistling through leaf-covered branches.

"I think we're good," Lorna said, melting onto a wide stone near the stream. Allison joined her, their backs nearly touching and their breathing equally labored.

"Why was that so much fun?" Allison asked.

"Seriously, though." Lorna lifted her gaze toward the treetops, which shifted and swayed above. Spots of light broke through the canopy, speckling the ground, their arms, their legs, and their faces.

Allison's expression fell slightly. "We didn't get to look for the large oak where she first buried the Three Brothers."

"Did you want to? I kind of assumed you're over anything related to the necklace."

"Oh, I am. But for you..."

"I'm fine. In all honesty, I got myself a bit too wrapped up like the rest. I mean, I had your seventy-five-year-old father slogging through a dilapidated tunnel, then rushing across town on a whim."

"And I wish I could say you two were the only ones trudging through that moldy tunnel or turning into creepy fireplace-stalking patrons at the Reynolds Tavern pub."

Lorna laughed. "Yes, but you weren't foolish enough to take your dad. I still feel awful about his heart attack."

"Before you continue beating yourself up about it, Lorna, there's something I need to tell you." Lorna shifted her body around on the stone to face Allison, who exhaled slowly and continued, "My father found out Conor went to see you in North Carolina, but he didn't call to warn you about what a deadbeat Conor can be."

"Why wouldn't he say something to me?"

"Well, to be fair, he did contact Conor and tried to scare him away from you. Conor asked him not to tell you about his prior drug issues."

"Why would your dad choose to protect him over me?"

"Conor told him the two of you were reading my book and that you were starting to wonder about the necklace. He promised my dad that he'd let him know if you found any..."

"Any what?"

"If you found any major leads regarding the stupid thing."

"So Conor was technically going behind my back too. Fine—we're done talking anyway. But what hurts even more is your dad pretty much chose the necklace over being honest with me?"

"Initially. Then you came back to town and confided in him about what you'd found, and knowing my father, I'm certain he felt awful for not telling you the truth about Conor."

"Your dad admitted to you that he and Conor had this conversation?"

"No. Conor told me."

"What?"

"Charlie wanted to talk to his dad a while back, so we called.

After they spoke, Conor and I started talking—a rarity for us. I mentioned to him how I'd heard from a friend that he was chasing after you. That's when he revealed my dad knew too."

"Why would your father give me your book in the first place if he was so nervous I'd start looking into the mystery?"

"I'm sure he felt conflicted. You essentially asked him for it, right?"

"Well, yeah."

"I suppose he knew it meant a lot to you because of your dreams. He loved Will. He loves you. I'll never deny that he's a good man. He is, and I love him terribly. But he also can't let go of his obsession with finding the Three Brothers. I'm certain he worried the moment that book left his hands. He struggled with me writing it in the first place."

"But I thought he helped you do all the research for it?"

"He did. And for a while it was exciting to partner on it together. It bonded us. He loved that we were passing along our family's story. However, in time, he started pressing me to exclude the part about the necklace. But it was a meaningful piece to Caroline's story, so I refused."

"Of course. Can I ask you one more thing?"

"Sure."

"Why would you tell me the truth about your dad making a deal with Conor?"

"One, because you need to stop blaming yourself for my father's heart attack, as he's no innocent bystander. And two...well, listen—I realize I haven't handled this situation perfectly. I let my pride get in the way the day I started traipsing through that tunnel. But my dad also needs to be held accountable. Yes, he's a wonderful man. He just can't let go. There's nothing wrong with loving the chase, but the moment it causes you to make poor decisions and not help the people you should be protecting, that's when you have a problem. Please find forgiveness with him, but keep your guard up too."

By the time they reached Lorna's driveway, the sun had disappeared altogether.

Lorna leaned against Arthur's Subaru. "Wow, I'm suddenly incredibly over the necklace. Whatever it's worth, the pain it caused is far greater."

Katydids chirped from every direction, and the darkness encompassed them both.

"Lorna."

"Yeah?"

"Thanks for taking me to Whitehall."

"You needed to go. Caroline would have wanted you to."

"Well, I think there's also something she'd want me to show you. I know it's been a long day, but are you up for a five-minute drive down the road?"

"Honestly?"

"I promise. It's worth your time. Plus, the situation has created quite the predicament for me, and I need your help."

Chapter 35

Allison didn't slow as St. Margaret's Road snaked itself back toward town. Lorna watched the headlights searching for what lay ahead. She wondered where the yellow lines were taking them.

"You're killing me over here, you know," Lorna finally announced. "Where are we going?"

"Last week, I stopped by St. Margaret's Church. I know you pass it all the time on your way into town."

"Sure."

"My mom used to take me to services there sometimes when I was growing up. So, I visited it on a whim with Charlie. I wanted to show him the stained-glass windows. Plus, if I'm being honest, I needed help. I've been struggling to find answers on my own. I'm torn about whether I should move back to Annapolis. On the one hand, my parents could help with Charlie and watch him grow up. He really misses them too. And occasionally, Charlie could even have supervised visits with his dad. Or do I stay in London where *my* life is? My literary team is there, and Charlie and I have friends who treat us like family. I don't have to worry about Conor doing something stupid, and I don't have to face the resentment I sometimes still feel toward my dad. Back there, things are less..."

"Complicated?"

"Exactly. So, anyway, Charlie and I went inside the church, and we were sitting there in the quiet. I said a little prayer asking for guidance on where we should live, and Charlie had a lot of questions for me. That mind—always going. He wondered about everything from how they made the stained-glass windows to what type of wood the benches were made from. Wow, is he my dad's mini-me. Then when we were driving home, I remembered that my dad had a letter from Caroline's son, Gabriel, that he sent from Wilmington to relatives in Annapolis, telling them that his wife had just given birth to a daughter, Penelope Lin, in 1798. Do you know why that date's significant?"

"Caroline didn't die until 1799."

"Precisely."

Lorna smiled. "She got to see her granddaughter."

"Yes. Then Gabriel moved back to Annapolis with his wife and daughter after Caroline's death and rebuilt the Brooks Inn. Also, based on the letter you found; we know Penelope moved to England with her husband before 1818."

Lorna added, "Right. Sadly, your dad said she died there before making it back to America."

"Correct, but we also know Penelope was still alive when her father, Gabriel, died in 1820. And she was his only heir. Also, her mother had already passed. So, put yourself in Gabriel's shoes. You're a widower and dying, but you want to leave the necklace in the safest spot possible for when your daughter returns. The Brooks Inn has new owners, as Penelope has said she'll live on her husband's land when they return to America. So, you can't hide the necklace at the inn. The tunnel's been compromised, thanks to the inebriated statesmen pushing to connect it with the Maryland Inn's tavern..."

"Yes, so the tunnel's out too," Lorna inserted.

"Exactly, and Gabriel's banker friend was moving out of Reynolds Tavern, so he had to take it out of the fireplace as well. Where would you put the Three Brothers, then?"

Lorna stared straight ahead, her mind churning, as they pulled into the St. Margaret's Church parking lot, headlights illuminating the adjacent cemetery.

Allison continued, "Where would you assume your loved one would surely come to see you?"

Lorna stared ahead. "My grave."

Allison parked and got out of the car.

Lorna followed.

Allison hit the flashlight on her phone, heading for the graveyard.

They wound their way around headstones of every shape and size until they reached three massive magnolia trees that formed a triangular shape in the center of the cemetery.

Underneath one tree, Allison shined her light onto a moss-covered, ancient gravestone that read:

Gabriel Brooks
October 18, 1777 - July 8, 1820

Lorna studied it carefully. "Wow, I didn't realize he was buried here. He was forty-two. I don't see anything else significant, though."

"We didn't either, for years. But when Charlie and I stopped by to put flowers on Uncle Bill's grave the other day, he saw Gabriel's headstone next to Bill's and said, 'Man, this cemetery's old. I wonder how far these headstones have sunk into the ground over the years. Pap taught me about erosion.' But I didn't hear anything Charlie said after that. I immediately started digging down several inches into the earth in front of Gabriel's tombstone, just to see."

Allison got down on her knees, moved a loose chunk of grass away, and clawed her fingers into the dirt, shining her flashlight toward the bottom of the gravestone, which judging by the discoloration, had been underground for quite some time.

Lorna gasped.

Deeply etched into Gabriel's headstone was a tiny triangle.

Chapter 36

"Do you think it's possible? That Gabriel would have had the necklace buried on top of his own casket?" Lorna pressed Allison.

"Gabriel was a longtime member St. Margaret's Church and a close friend of the pastor. From what I've read, there seemed to be a lot of trust between them. It's certainly possible."

Lorna's skin prickled. *Could the necklace be lying just under our feet?*

Allison rose and wiped the dirt from her knees, checking her watch.

"I lost track of time. My dad is babysitting Charlie and I told him I'd be back by now."

Lorna also stood, looking down at the ground. "Did you tell your dad about this?"

"No."

"Will you?"

"I haven't decided." Allison combed through her purse and grabbed her keys. She started back toward the car as Lorna followed, utterly dumbfounded.

Just as they neared the parking lot, Lorna caught up to her. "You seem so underwhelmed, Allison. I mean, I realize I just said I was over it all. Even so, this is an incredible find."

Allison unlocked the car doors, and they both crawled inside. "I won't say I'm not excited at all. It's just that I'm, well, torn more than anything."

"Because of your dad?"

Allison turned the wheel onto St. Margaret's Road. "Yes. I've seen this play out so many times. He gets himself all wound up. He'll likely push the church board to dig a few feet down. We could be wrong, and then what? We look crazy once again, and besides, who knows how deep they buried their dead back then? What if we run into poor Gabriel's bones?"

"Maybe the church board wouldn't let you do it. Then you can tell him the truth, but no digging is ever done."

"If they won't let him, and I love my father, but I would not put it past him to ask us to show up one night and be standing under those trees with three shovels. Then we'll feel like creepers in the graveyard with broken backs and likely still nothing to show for it. And of course, we'll all be disappointed, once again—especially him."

"Listen, I'm annoyed with him, for sure. But I must say, he handled the Reynolds Tavern fiasco quite nicely," Lorna said.

"I'm glad to hear it. Still. You know there's this weird thing when your parents start getting older, where you begin feeling like the adult and they start feeling like the child. I worry about him more and more."

Lorna watched the familiar homes disappear outside her passenger seat window. "I get it. My parents always kind of felt like children."

"Oh." Allison looked over.

Lorna sort of smiled. "I joke. Well, not entirely. I do understand about worrying, though. When my father got sick, I felt paralyzed by fear."

"I'm so sorry."

"Thanks. He's in remission though, so everything's good."

"So glad to hear it. Here I go worrying about my dad getting his feelings hurt over a stupid necklace that may or may not still exist, and your father's been through cancer."

"It's more than that, though. Your dad's been through a lot health-wise too lately. And there are a lot of emotions and history going into this decision. You're left with a really hard choice, and I don't envy you for it."

Allison pulled the car into Lorna's driveway. Lorna stepped out and walked around to the driver's side.

Allison rolled down the window. "The choice isn't as hard as I'm making it. Hearing you say that about your dad, I know what I have to do."

"What?"

"Come to brunch at Aunt Bea's tomorrow, and you'll find out."

"That is *not fair* to make me wait. Besides, I'm kinda pissed at your dad and don't really feel like seeing him."

"Join the club."

Allison hit the gas and gravel sprayed out behind her back wheels.

"Hey, that's your move," a voice broke forth from behind Lorna, one that she'd recognize anywhere.

"Sorry Subaru, but our truck does it better." Lorna grinned as she turned toward her dad.

"Hands down. How was your trip to Baltimore? Were you visiting friends?" Kevin asked.

Lorna didn't answer but wrapped her arms around her dad and squeezed him tighter than she had in a long time. He smelled like cologne and cigarettes and when his arms, still incredibly strong for all he'd been through, hugged her back, she never wanted to let go.

Chapter 37

The following morning

Lorna hesitated for a moment before entering Nana's front door.

The idea of confronting Arthur about his contact with Conor exhausted her. Besides, what would it accomplish now? It was such an awkward thing to bring up. What would it change, anyway? It was water under the bridge. Wasn't it?

Suddenly, the door opened.

"Oh, hello, Lorna."

"Hi, Arthur."

"I'd come to get the morning paper. Didn't realize you were joining us today. So glad to see you."

"You too." She avoided eye contact, retrieved the thick, curled-up newspaper, and handed it to him.

"Thank you."

They stepped inside Nana's house together.

"It smells incredible in here," Lorna said, trying to ignore the millstone in her stomach.

"Bea's got the coffee brewing, and Allie's frying up some eggs for everyone. Oh, and Bea's good friend brought some homemade cinnamon rolls over last night. They're plumping up in the oven right now. Charlie's staring at them, hoping it'll speed up the process."

"I hope so too. It all sounds delicious. I'll see if they need any help." She started for the kitchen.

"Lorna," Arthur said unexpectedly.

She turned back, and he was looking at the foyer rug.

"What's up?"

He finally drew his gaze back toward her. "Allison and I had a long talk last night. Would you mind sitting down for a second?"

"Sure." Lorna walked slowly to the striped couch while Arthur found a seat in Pop's old chair.

"I'll cut right to the chase. I'm sorry I never warned you about Conor."

Lorna said nothing, hoping he'd continue.

"Allison believed I held back on telling you Conor had drug and alcohol issues so he'd let me know if you found anything out about the necklace. I admit, there's some truth in that; however, I also did try to help you. See, I contacted Conor after I heard he'd traveled down south to see you. I told him you'd been through enough already. He knew my weakness—somehow, he found about my fascination with finding the necklace. He said he'd read some of Allie's book with you and that you mentioned to him on the phone one night you were curious about where the Three Brothers might be hidden. This was before you came back to town and I came to understand you wanted to work with me and not... well, you know."

"Against you."

"Right. I admit I'm far too attached to it all, and that's taken so much away not only me, but most importantly, the people I care about most. I shouldn't have let that cloud my judgement over telling you about Conor's issues. Truthfully, though, I also didn't want to scare you away from him because, well, even if

Conor is far from perfect, he does have a good side, and I wanted you to find..."

"A distraction?"

"Well, sort of. I didn't think Conor needed to be your Prince Charming, just someone to help you move on. The day you first came to me at the inn, asking about the book and your dream about Will, of course, the paranoid part of me thought you might be after the necklace. But the more logical, loving side of my brain was heartbroken for you. I assumed you were struggling to move on."

Lorna jumped in, saying, "Right, because the perfect answer for someone who's struggling with the loss of their husband is someone with significant addiction issues."

Arthur took out a handkerchief from his pocket and wiped his brow. "I've heard he's doing better. But, yes, you deserved to know the truth, and I'd do it very differently if I could go back, Lorna. To think I could have avoided hurting you. You know my hand was shaking as I made that tea kettle the day of the fire. It wasn't because I was upset we didn't find the necklace. It was that I hadn't been entirely truthful with you."

Something inside Lorna began to soften. "I know you were watching out for me when you first called Conor, and I understand why you got protective of the necklace. You didn't know me very well, or my intentions."

Arthur paused to take in her words before speaking again. "I didn't know you very well because I ruined my relationship with my brother. And I'm sorry for all of it."

"It's all right. I forgive you, Arthur. Thank you for being honest with me now."

"No...thank *you*, Lorna. That means more than you know. Hearing Caroline's letter the other day, it truly hit home: 'What we give up is everything we hold dearest.'"

Allison emerged from the kitchen. "Hey, Lorna. Didn't hear you come in. Brunch is ready. Come on back guys." She disappeared, a filled plate in each hand.

Lorna stood and crossed the room, hugging Arthur, a lightness finally settling inside of her.

Arthur, Allison, Nana, Charlie, and Lorna all gathered around the dining table.

"Will you say the prayer, Charlie?"

"Sure, Aunt Bea." He bowed his head quickly, clearly itching to dig into his food. "Thank you, God, for cinnamon rolls and family. They are the best things in life."

"Amen," everyone said in unison.

After brunch, Charlie convinced Arthur to head out into the backyard. Lorna, Allison and Nana remained at the dining table, sipping a second cup of coffee as they watched Arthur and Charlie play wiffle ball through a large bay window.

Nana turned to Allison. "I can't take it much longer. Please tell Lorna what happened."

Lorna's eyes widened. "I don't know if I can take any more surprises."

Allison jumped in. "I promise it's the good kind. Last night, I told Dad about the triangle on Gabriel's gravestone."

"You did?" Lorna slid forward on her chair. "What did he say?"

"He grew incredibly quiet, then he whispered, 'Well, I'll be damned.'"

Nana and Lorna laughed.

"I'm sure he's really proud of you, Allison," Nana finally said.

"He said 'Good work, Allie.' And I told him Charlie gave me the idea, which made him even prouder."

Outside the window, a popping sound startled them. They turned toward the yard to see Arthur erupting in excitement, his hands flinging through the air. Charlie had just smashed the ball over Nana's fence. His first home run.

"I suppose it's a good thing Arthur bought him a set of twenty balls. My poor neighbors." Nana smiled. "Go on, Allie, tell her what your father said next."

"He said we shouldn't dig."

Lorna's mouth dropped open.

"He said he wouldn't go toying with a dead man's grave," Allison's eyes began to water as she continued, "and he said he has all he needs above ground." Lorna beamed as Nana took Allison's hand in hers.

Allison finally added, "I got the answer I needed. Charlie and I are moving home."

Chapter 38

Annapolis

June 2018

Five years later

Will's mother, Morgan, was standing at her kitchen sink when a steady knock resounded off her front door.

She opened it to discover a familiar pair of dark eyes peering back at her.

Morgan placed her hand against her chest. "Lorna, please come in. It's so good to see you."

A little girl with strikingly similar wide-set eyes stepped out from behind Lorna.

Morgan had to catch her breath. "Oh, and I get a big-time bonus visitor," she added. Lorna noticed a slight quiver in her voice. "Both of you, come in, please."

She led them to her living room, where the child curled up beside Lorna on the couch.

Dropping to her knees beside the coffee table at the same eye level as the girl, Morgan spoke to her, "It's so nice to meet you. What's your name?"

"Everyone calls me Winnie, but my real name is Winter."

"Winter. How beautiful."

"Win, this is Miss Morgan. Her son, Will, and I were married before he went to heaven."

"Hi, Miss Morgan. I like when she tells stories about Will."

Tears welled in Morgan's eyes. "I'm sure she has lots of good ones. Those two sure had fun together. I imagine you're just as funny, strong, and smart as your mom."

"My mom had to go away."

Morgan's eyebrows fell, though she didn't pause for even a moment. "I'm so sorry to hear that. I'm glad you're in wonderful company with Lorna while she's gone."

"I'm glad too." Winnie grinned, her honey-brown eyes beaming as she looked up at Lorna, who cupped her hands on each of Winnie's deliciously squishy five-year-old cheeks.

"Oh, as am I," Lorna added, the contentedness she felt being next to the little girl momentarily settling her nerves.

Winnie pulled gently on her double braids as she whispered to Morgan, "Lorna told me you have a basement with a whole bunch of toys where your grandkids play."

Following her lead, Morgan spoke softly, as if it were the world's best-kept secret, "Would you like to see it?"

Winnie nodded in a bobblehead sort of way that made Morgan and Lorna laugh.

"Follow me, follow me." Morgan took her hand, and they disappeared together.

Lorna sunk back into the white-slipcovered couch, exhaling deeply before taking in the room: just as it used to be—blue-and-white-trellised wallpaper, a large, painted brick fireplace with a wide, rectangular mirror hanging above it—its thick frame, a deep salmon color with a modern design mimicking some sort of coral reef. Below it on the mantle stood a small Greek bust and a simple brass frame filled with Morgan's three sons, their arms wrapped around each other, cheeks flushed, beaming at the camera. Will was on the end. Lorna's eyes lingered for several seconds, memories rushing back—the day they met, his bronzed back flipping through the air at Greenbury Point, and the look in his eyes on their wedding day beneath origami-adorned Grandma Tree as she walked down the makeshift aisle. Finally, she looked away.

On the other side of the mantle, two white taper candles stood proudly inside shiny brass votives Morgan had likely picked up at one of the downtown shops.

"She's absolutely precious," Morgan said as she entered the room alone, finding a seat in one of her patterned chairs.

"Thank you."

"I'm sorry I mistook her for your daughter."

"Don't be. Most people do. She's my sister."

"Your sister?"

"Five years ago, I went to Baltimore to meet my real mom—Hailey. She reached back out to me a few weeks after we got together and asked if we could meet up again. I got to know her and her daughter, Winnie. She's my half-sister. When Hailey got arrested a few years later for drug possession and couldn't care for Win, she asked if I would take her."

"And you agreed."

"Not at first. I was terrified. I could barely take care of myself. And what did I know about raising a little girl?"

Morgan's gaze intensified. "Why'd you change your mind?"

"A good friend once told me our purpose is to love and be loved." Lorna couldn't help but allow the corners of her mouth to rise as she thought of Tess. "And that the rest is just hogwash."

"I'm assuming a Carolina friend?"

"How'd you guess?"

Morgan grinned. "She's right, though."

"It got me thinking about my own parents, good old Kevin and Maggie, who I've always judged pretty harshly. But looking back, they gave me a better life than I would have had. I realized Win deserved someone to try for her too."

"I love that. And I'm proud of you, Lorna, to take on a child with everything else you've been through. I'm so grateful you pushed past your fear and said yes."

"Thanks, Morgan. So am I. In time, she ended up bringing me out of a pretty dark place. She's been with me three years now while Hailey's been in and out of jail."

"That has to be hard..."

The air rushed out of Lorna's chest as that same old, terrifying thought forced its way back in—*when will Winnie have to leave? Sweet, well-meaning Hailey...but such an incompetent caregiver.* "Honestly, it's dreadful knowing she could..."

"Return to Hailey?"

"Yes."

"Oh, Lorna, I can only imagine."

"It would kill me to let her go. She's my girl. But I've realized there are no guarantees in life—when you get to hold someone's hand, just take it."

Morgan nodded, dabbing the inside of her eye with her fingertip. "Absolutely. I can tell there's a special bond between you."

"Now that I know that bond, Morgan..." Lorna had to stop herself momentarily. "Now that I, well, in many ways, have a child of my own, I just can't even imagine what you had to endure." She couldn't meet her eyes. "I was just so stuck inside my own pain I couldn't see past it to yours." Lorna finally forced herself to look up at Morgan. "I'm so sorry I wasn't there for you after Will died and that I didn't reciprocate your attempts for us to have a relationship after he was gone."

Morgan stood, crossed the room, and sat down on the couch beside Lorna. "A young person shouldn't have to deal with what you did."

"Nevertheless, I would have done it differently."

"We all would have. Grief is a 300-pound bear on your chest, and most of the time, it hurts just to breathe."

Lorna nodded, her gaze combing the pale-blue rug tucked beneath her feet, but her mind stretched back to the many days where just functioning took everything she had.

"I was so glad to hear you're working at the hospital," Morgan continued. "A NICU nurse, right?"

"Yes, I love it. And you need to know that all those years ago when you gave me that check to help pay for school, I may not have cashed it, but I heard what you said, that I needed to pursue something I was passionate about. It was a big reason I went back to get my LPN degree, and now I'm a registered nurse."

Morgan's face lit up. "Incredible. Thank you for sharing that with me. If I had a little one again, I'd want them in your care. Is it difficult getting in the long shifts with Winnie?"

"My parents help take care of her when I'm working. Kate and Emma fill in a lot too. They've all been amazing. Plus, it'll be easier now that Winnie's heading to elementary school."

"Windsor Farm Elementary, like you?"

"Yep. I have a little place just down from my dad on Whitehall Road."

"I love that."

"Morgan, I also wanted to tell you that I'm working on a project with Allison."

"A project?"

"A book, actually."

"Wonderful. May I ask what it's about?"

"Will. His life. His story."

Morgan smiled—though it looked like it pained her slightly, she also seemed proud.

Lorna felt her throat tighten but continued, "And part of that is writing about the war he grew to despise. Will hated how they had to go into the Afghan homes late at night and kick the families out, children screaming and crying, just so they could have a place to draw the Taliban in. And all for what in the end? It's hard to imagine 500,000 people died in the wars in Iraq and Afghanistan, including 7,000 of our own."

Morgan slowly shook her head but didn't speak, so Lorna continued, "We're incorporating my dad's military experience into it too, specifically his struggles after losing so many friends in Vietnam—something he only recently began to share with me. I'm sure you've seen the numbers—more than a *million* people lost their lives there and over *58,000* were Americans. And that doesn't count the endless men and women who came home from both wars but were never the same. Like my dad. And Jack. My hope is their stories will serve as needed reminders. That their sacrifices will encourage us all to choose leaders who highly oppose these endless, awful wars."

Morgan remained quiet. Solemn.

"I'm sorry, Morgan. I know it's heart-wrenching and..."

"No. It's all right. It's certainly painful. But necessary."

"Thank you for understanding why I need to do this."

"The best we can do in life is to speak about the truth we know, no matter how much it hurts."

Lorna hugged Morgan tightly.

"Thank you so much for stopping by."

"It's been so good to see you again, Morgan. We'll stop back again sometime if that's okay?"

"I'm counting on it."

"Thank you." Lorna stood. "Well, we're heading to Rehoboth Beach this morning. Better get going so we don't hit too much bridge traffic. It'll be Win's first time seeing the ocean."

"How fun! Make sure she knows to dig for diggers—those fast little sand crabs always enthralled my boys."

"We will be sure to dig for diggers."

"Have a blast. I know you will."

Lorna watched Winnie's eyes expand as they crossed the Chesapeake Bay Bridge, her tiny fingers spread wide against the windowpane.

Flocks of birds dashed across the choppy water before swooping up into a cloudless sapphire sky.

"I can't wait to see the ocean, Lolo!"

"It's incredible. You'll love it! You just have to be careful, okay? The bay is calmer and more predictable."

"Grandpa Kevin told me that in the sea, the waves can get taller than *he* is."

"Yes, and sometimes you don't realize how big they are until they're right there in front of you."

"What do I do if I get hit by one?"

"Well, the more you start flailing around, the harder it is to find your way. Wait for the wave to ride over, for the ocean to calm again, then rise up to the surface."

"What if another one smashes me, then? Don't they sometimes come one after another?"

"Yes, sometimes. You have to be patient. A break will come."

Winnie thought for a minute. "Okay. You'll hold my hand, though, right?"

"I will not let go of you, Winter."

"Do you promise?"

"I promise."

After a few hours of butchering the lyrics to songs on the radio and playing a few dozen games of "I Spy," the *Welcome to Rehoboth Beach* sign magically appeared.

"We made it!" Lorna yelled.

"We made it!" Winnie echoed.

They miraculously found a parking spot along crowded Rehoboth Avenue. Lorna lugged two colorful beach chairs, a giant umbrella, a bucket of sand toys, and a bag with towels, while Winnie sprinted straight toward the ocean with her short little shovel.

When Lorna finally caught up, the first thing Win wanted her to do was cover her entire body with sand.

"Let's start with your legs and see how you like it. And if you want, I can even make them into a mermaid tail like Aunt Kate and I used to do."

"Really?"

"Really."

Lorna trickled the gritty grains of sand onto Winnie's skinny legs as she giggled wildly. Was it possible that Lorna enjoyed watching her sister experience the newness of life even more than she did discovering it herself?

Winnie waited as Lorna packed a mound of sand all the way down to her toes, then watched carefully as her big sister etched miniature scales all over her "tail."

"It's perfect!" Winnie screamed as Lorna stepped back to view her creation. She only had a few seconds before the girl's legs popped out of the mound and went darting toward the water. Lorna turned and yelled, "Wait!" running after her at full tilt.

But Winnie didn't stop. She went straight into the sea, flailing and squealing as the water's frigid touch smacked itself against her skin.

Lorna stopped just shy of the shoreline, her nerves catching, but Winnie's smile, complete with chattering teeth, revealed she was cold but safe. Shaking her head, Lorna watched Winnie frolic, sea foam encircling her, the waves breaking just before her, as if bowing to her intrepid spirit.

It was for her, wasn't it? It was all for her.

Gratitude gathered inside Lorna, leaving a gentle calmness in its wake.

But her momentary peace was overcome by an inkling of apprehension the moment Winnie sprung from the ocean and scampered back toward her. Just as she'd suspected, Win's ice-cold fingers suddenly clutched Lorna's forearm, sending goosebumps across every inch of her body.

"Come in with me!" Winnie cried.

"But it's freezing!" Lorna yelled, peering down at her exhilarated little face.

"Please. You're missing out on so much fun if you just stare from here."

Lorna sighed as she peeked up at the thrashing tide, its motion never ceasing. What lay below its surface, she knew not. *It's time, though.* She inhaled a final breath of salted air, squeezed her eyes shut, saw his face, and stepped back in.

Chapter 39

Annapolis
August 2023

Five years later

"I still can't believe they found it," ten-year-old Winnie whispered across the table to Lorna, whose chest tightened—the reminder, as thrilling as it was piercing.

Weathered fieldstone walls surrounded them, its lime mortar holding strong for centuries. It felt like a lifetime since Lorna had last been in the basement of the Brooks Inn—the endless cobwebs and Arthur's scattered antiques now replaced by round, polished wooden tables and plush modern chairs. The entrance to the tunnel had been bolted shut but adorned with an oversized, framed sketch of *her* staring out at the restaurant, that massive necklace dangling audaciously from her neck.

"Welcome to Caroline's," came a voice. Lorna knew it well. She looked up to see Conor.

"What can I get you ladies to drink? Winnie, I know you're the Shirley Temple Queen."

"Yes, sir. You guessed right."

"Perfect. And Lorna, double Jack with a splash of Coke?"

"How about just a Coke? I work tonight. No need to pass out halfway through my shift."

"I could see that being a problem. Thanks for making it over for our opening day. It means a lot to Allie. Especially *this week.*"

"How's she holding up?"

"She's doing okay. Of course, some days are harder than others. The irony of it all, right?"

Lorna shook her head. "I still can't believe it."

Nana appeared behind Conor and tapped his shoulder. "Hello, dear."

"Oh, hi, Aunt Bea," Conor hugged her.

She continued, "Congratulations, on your vision come to life, Conor! It looks lovely in here!"

"Thank you. That means a lot. Allie mostly did the décor—with Lorna and Winnie's help."

Nana looked to them. "Wow, well done, ladies." Her eyes then drifted back to Conor. "Where is your wife? I want to congratulate her, too, on the Brooks Inn's first ever restaurant!"

"She's upstairs taking care of the inn. She'll be down soon, I'm sure."

"I'll catch her in a bit then." Nana looked back down at Lorna and Winnie. "First, I need to catch up with these two beauties. Oh, and decaf coffee for me, please."

"You got it." Conor disappeared to get their drinks. Winnie jumped up and wrapped her arms tightly around Nana whose face lit up like a Christmas tree. "Oh, my sweet, Winnie, so good to see you. Will you come over soon for some more ribs?"

"You know I will! They're *so* yummy!"

A vast grin spread across Nana's face, and Lorna suddenly felt an immense sense of pride for Will's grandma. It may have taken nearly a century, but Nana had finally found something she could cook that other people genuinely enjoyed—crock-pot ribs smothered in barbeque sauce which overcooking, for once, didn't ruin, but actually made more tender and delicious.

Nana sat down in the chair next to Winnie. As they spoke,

Lorna's gaze once again met the enlarged drawing of Caroline on the wall. She felt beyond grateful to have finally found the sketch, made by an eighteenth-century British officer at Cornwallis's dinner party in Wilmington. Her eyes moved from Caroline to Conor as she stole a quick glance at him behind the bar. While they'd certainly had their ups and downs, she found herself genuinely happy for him. He'd always wanted his own restaurant and creating a pub in the basement of the Brooks Inn was the perfect opportunity. Ever since he and Allison had gotten back together and were eventually married two years ago, he had seemed on top of the world—ecstatic to be at every one of Charlie's high school baseball games, seemingly more in love with Allison than ever, and finally able to kick the bottle.

"Did you see the *Capital Gazette* article?" Nana's voice brought Lorna back.

"No, I haven't."

Nana pulled a newspaper from her purse and slid it across the table to Lorna. "Even made the front page."

The headline reached out and grabbed her:

Legendary Missing 600-Year-Old Necklace Recovered as Local Man is Laid to Rest

Her stomach caught. Seeing the words formally written out completely overwhelmed her; yet she couldn't help but read on.

Annapolis, Md. – On Friday, an area resident unearthed the famous Three Brothers jewel in the St. Margaret's Church graveyard in Annapolis. The necklace had been missing for two hundred years.

The family of Annapolis bed and breakfast owner, Arthur C. Brooks, was having his burial plot dug up following his death this past week when a metal box was located by Edward Schuyler, the St. Margaret's Cemetery groundskeeper.

Schuyler, a longtime member of St. Margaret's Church and friend of the Brooks family, notified Arthur's daughter, Allison Brooks, also of Annapolis, when he discovered it.

Ms. Brooks, a New York Times Bestselling Author, told the Capital Gazette, "We are just so grateful Ed came to us. He knew the necklace was something our family had been trying to locate for a very long time."

A full glass of Coke slid in beside the newspaper, pulling Lorna from the page. She looked up to see Allison standing beside her, handing Winnie her Shirley Temple and Nana her coffee. Lorna felt awkward reading about Arthur's death in front of Allison and pushed the paper aside.

"I heard the article was pretty good," Allison said, pulling out the only chair left at the table and sitting down.

Nana thankfully jumped in. "They did a really nice job, Allie."

"I'm not ready to read it yet, but someday," Allison said.

"How are you holding up, hun?" Nana asked.

"Having all our customers around is a helpful distraction, but it's still hard. How I wanted my dad to be here to see this." Her eyes welled slightly, but when she blinked, the tears vanished just as quickly as they'd come. Allison continued on, "And I even want to feel guilty for having our grand opening so shortly after the funeral, but then I know he wouldn't have wanted us to sit around and mope."

Lorna finally found her words. "Allison, this was his happy place. You and Conor taking over the inn and adding a pub, Charlie always stopping in to see him...it meant everything to your dad. Don't you think this is exactly where he'd want you to be?"

The tears formed in Allison's eyes again, and nodding, she squeezed Lorna's hand. "Thank you. And thank all three of you for coming. Seeing your faces helps more than I can say." She stood and wiped her eyes. "Well, I need to get back up to the inn. We have several guests arriving this afternoon. Lunch is on the house."

"Oh, stop it, Allie. I am here to support this fine new establishment and don't even try to stop me from paying for us," Nana announced.

"Don't even try to stop her," Winnie repeated, making Allison chuckle. It felt good to see her laugh. Lorna had been there in Arthur's hospital room, standing next to Allison, just before he passed. He'd been at Anne Arundel Medical Center for a few weeks prior, his heart gradually fading. On multiple occasions during Lorna's breaks from the NICU, she'd make her way to the Cardiology Department and slide quietly into a chair next to Allison. Sometimes they talked—sharing old memories or catching up on life; other times they barely said a word.

Suddenly a green napkin wrapper turned origami frog leapt toward Lorna from across the table. Winnie was already showing Nana how to make her own by the time Lorna looked up. "Hey, thanks for the cute little hopper, Win. Don't forget to choose something from the menu," she told her.

It still seemed too good to be true that the adoption was finalized—Win was finally hers. Lorna's mom, Maggie, with her years of nonprofit child services work, had helped make it happen. It didn't come easy. Hailey was constantly in and out of jail and on and off of pills. And while she desperately wanted to raise Winnie, she eventually realized Winnie didn't want to be raised by her. Lorna and her sister still saw their biological mother every so often. They continued to show they cared. Yet, it was painful to see her slowly slipping away.

Later that night, Lorna tucked Winnie into bed, found the newspaper Nana had given her inside her purse, curled up in her blue chair, and continued where she'd left off:

The Three Brothers disappeared in 1820 following the death of its owner, Gabriel Brooks, an Annapolitan and ancestor of Arthur Brooks. Their burial plots are located directly beside one another.

"We believe Gabriel had the Three Brothers buried by his grave so his daughter, Penelope, could find it when she returned from England. Sadly, she never made it back to America, so the necklace remained a secret, hidden in St. Margaret's Cemetery for two centuries," Ms. Brooks explained.

She said her father, Arthur, and his brother, Colonel William "Bill" Brooks, also of Annapolis, had been searching for the necklace for as long as she could remember. "It was part of our family's history, a legendary mystery that my dad and uncle deeply believed would be solved one day."

Colonel Brooks, who passed away in 2010, is buried just a few feet from his brother under three large magnolia trees in the center of the cemetery.

For a more detailed background of the Brooks family's connection to the Three Brothers and the necklace's fascinating 600-year-old history, available for purchase is Where the Foxgloves Bloom, *a historical fiction by Allison Brooks. She dedicated the novel to her father and included a special thanks to her relative, William "Will" Brooks, and his wife, Lorna. Will, the late grandson of Colonel Brooks, passed away on April 8, 2011, while serving his country in Afghanistan. Lorna is a nurse at Anne Arundel Medical Center in the Neonatal Intensive Care Unit.*

"Will and Lorna are the reason I was able to finally publish my book. If it wasn't for them, it wouldn't have been possible," Ms. Brooks said.

Lorna's heart swelled just a little as she glanced up at her bookshelf. The revised and newly released version of *Where the Foxgloves Bloom* was peeking down at her. A deep red foxglove coiled around the book's spine, with a pale-yellow butterfly resting on its petal. A profound gratitude filled her. She marveled at the way a story had transformed her life. But it was more than that, wasn't it? *Our lives,* she thought, *with their thrilling highs, devastating lows, and everything in between, are the most remarkable stories of all.* Slipping from her chair, she padded to the nearby doorway of Winnie's bedroom and stood in awe; her beauty was breathtaking. Lorna had known many forms of love—each one she was endlessly thankful for—but she had never known a love quite like this. Apparently, prayers were rarely answered in the way you expected them to be. She supposed God was far too creative for that.

She returned to her chair to finish the article:

Lorna Brooks and her sisters, Katherine and Winter, attended Arthur Brooks's funeral on Saturday at St. Margaret's Church. She told the Capital Gazette: "Arthur and Bill may never have found the jewel in life, but they certainly did in death. I have a feeling they're finally together again, laughing at the irony of it all."

While her family doesn't plan on keeping the necklace, Allison Brooks was grateful to finally hold it in her hands. "It's heavier than I imagined and even more stunning than in the drawings. But most importantly, it's remarkable to think of all the people who carried it on down the line." For this reason, Ms. Brooks is determined to ensure it never gets lost again. "Like my father always wished, I too believe the piece belongs in the Smithsonian National Museum of Natural History in Washington, D.C. It'll have a safe and worthy home in the museum's collection of minerals and gems, a place where it can share its story. We want museum visitors to know the unbelievable journey this necklace took to get to them and the power it's had to both deliver and devour. I've seen the ruin it can bring, but it's also been known to win wars, save lives, and rescue families. There's a reason Queen Elizabeth the First has this thing wrapped around her neck on her tomb effigy at Westminster Abbey—for better or worse, it leaves its mark on you."

Chapter 40
Annapolis
December 19, 2030

Seven years later

In the dark hours just after midnight, bright overhead lights illuminated a deserted hospital hallway. The sound of an infant's thin, shrill wail pierced the air in a nearby room.

Lorna, not yet halfway through a twelve-hour shift in the NICU, was already hitting a wall.

"Surprise!" boomed from behind her.

Lorna instinctively said, "Shhhhh." No need to wake any babies on her watch. She turned, and much to her shock, her two sisters were standing before her.

Holding three blue balloons and the first to reach Lorna was eighteen-year-old Winnie. She was just back from her semester abroad and immediately flung her arms around her big sister. "Happy 40th Birthday, Lolo," she whispered.

"Win, I thought you couldn't make it until Sunday?" Lorna gasped, holding her close as she savored her fresh, familiar scent. Despite being taller than her older sister, Winnie would in some ways always be two years old, curled up in the same bed as Lorna so they could both sleep through the night.

"I found another flight," Winnie said, grinning. "I couldn't miss your big 4-0! Besides, I missed you terribly."

"How I've missed you too," Lorna returned, noticing how long Winnie's own "mousy" brown hair had gotten.

Kate stepped toward the birthday girl next. "Hey, old lady, we had to be the first to welcome you to a new decade." She handed Lorna a small bag. "We'll do gifts later today, but for now, here are some chocolate-covered espresso beans. Even on your birthday, I know there's always a tiny one to watch through the night."

Lorna leaned in and squeezed Kate tightly, appreciating how thoughtful and selfless she'd grown to be.

"Thanks, guys. Talk about a late-night pick-me-up."

The pitter-patter of footsteps echoing off hallway walls reached Lorna's ears. She looked up to see someone running toward them. As the figure floundered, large items in both hands, and eventually drew closer, a cascade of red hair came into view—Emma.

"I'm late, I'm late, but happy fortieth birthday, beautiful baby saver!" She lifted a bottle with a shiny gold top. "I brought champagne!"

Shaking her head and smiling, Lorna spoke softly, "Great, just what we need, something to make you louder." She winked.

Emma clenched her teeth and lowered her voice slightly. "Oh, sorry, I'm being too loud, as always. I'll save it for tonight when we hit the town."

Lorna hugged her, imagining how Emma would be pressing her to "hit the town" until they were at least ninety. "I love you, Em. Thank you."

Stepping back with flushed cheeks and a broad smile, Lorna glanced at each of them. "You ladies are the best, truly. If you wouldn't mind taking this stuff to our break room, I'll be right in. I just have one more room to check on."

They shuffled back down the hall, whispering jovially.

Lorna stood alone again, checking her clipboard, when a

young mother rushed up to her with a fussy infant, wrapped haphazardly in a blanket. Bags hung beneath the woman's eyes; her face marked with exhaustion. "I don't know if I can do this. She won't stop crying, and when she finally sleeps, I'm horrified she'll stop breathing again."

Reaching out and gently taking the baby, Lorna cocooned the half-swaddled newborn in her arms, rocking her gently. She looked into the mother's weary eyes. "You *will* be able to do this. I promise, there's no limit to what we'll overcome for the ones we love. I'll reconnect her to the heart monitor and check on her constantly tonight. Get some rest."

"Thank you. I could use some sleep. I just didn't expect her to start life out like this."

"She'll get stronger by the day. And so will you."

Historical Notes

While many of the main characters in this book are fictitious, some are based on actual people, and many of the objects and locations in *Because of Winter* are real as well. I wanted to take a few moments to share with you some of the historical context that shaped this story.

Three Brothers jewel – It truly was one of the most coveted jewels in Renaissance Europe. The Brothers was created in 1389, commissioned by Duke John the Fearless of Burgundy (which covered part of modern-day France, Belgium, Luxembourg, the Netherlands, and Germany). It became one of the most precious treasures in the House of Burgundy for nearly a century. The jewel was carried into battle by Charles the Bold, the last Duke of Burgundy, and stolen by the Swiss during his catastrophic loss at the Battle of Grandson in 1476.

The piece was eventually purchased by the uber-wealthy German banker Jakob Fugger and remained in his family until it was sold to England's Edward VI. From 1551 to 1643, it was part of the Crown Jewels of England. The Three Brothers appeared in several portraits, worn as a necklace by Queen Elizabeth I, and as a hat ornament by King James VI and I. Renowned English art historian, Sir Roy Strong, described it as "the most famous and romantic" of the Tudor and Stuart Crown Jewels.

In the 1640s, when the British monarchy faced financial collapse, Henrietta Maria, the wife of Charles I, traveled to The Netherlands with the Crown Jewels, later taking them to Paris to raise funds for the English Civil War. While the Three Brothers was reportedly among the items she carried, it remains unclear whether she succeeded in selling it. The jewel's whereabouts after 1645 are unknown, leaving us with a captivating mystery.

I began imagining what could have happened to the Three Brothers after it disappeared. Since I knew Henrietta Maria traveled to both The Netherlands and France, I searched for historical figures from those areas who might have ended up with the piece.

But as I thought more about it, I wanted to believe that despite all the turmoil in Henrietta Maria's life, she chose to keep the precious relic to pass onto future generations, who simply decided to keep the jewel a secret. Around this time, I somehow came upon the three Howe brothers and realized they were not only descendants of British royalty, but that two of the three came into close contact with Annapolis when they sailed up the Chesapeake Bay together during the American Revolution. This was when my imagined theory connecting the Howe brothers to the Three Brothers began to take shape.

Charity Folks – Born into slavery, Charity was owned by Maryland Governor Samuel Ogle and lived at Belair Plantation in Bowie, Maryland, with her mother, Rachel Burke, and brother James until around the age of twelve. Just as in the story, her father is believed to have been Colonel Benjamin Tasker, the plantation manager and Molly Ridout's uncle. Charity was later transferred to John Ridout, who described her in his will as having repeatedly cared for his family during times of illness. He stipulated that she be freed in 1807 with an annual stipend. However, upon his death in 1797, Molly granted her immediate freedom.

Charity went on to become one of the first African American women to own property in Annapolis. She purchased land and homes on Church Circle, South Street, and Franklin Street, generating income and leaving a legacy for her descendants—many of whom still reside in Annapolis today.

Mary "Molly" Ridout – Another real-life figure, Molly was the daughter of Maryland Governor Samuel Ogle and Anne Tasker Ogle. She and her husband, John Ridout, first lived on Duke of Gloucester Street in Annapolis, where George Washington once noted dining in his diary. When Governor Horatio Sharpe—believed to have been in love with Molly, as mentioned in the story—returned to England before the American Revolution, he allowed the Ridouts to live at Whitehall. After Sharpe decided not to return to America, the estate passed to the Ridout family, where they remained for the rest of their lives. Though John and Molly respected the American cause, their strong attachment to England led them to remain neutral during the war. The Ridouts are buried in the cemetery on Whitehall's grounds, and some of their descendants still live in Annapolis.

George Washington's Resignation – Just as in the story, Washington resigned as commander-in-chief of the Continental Army in the Old Senate Chamber of the Maryland State House on December 23, 1783, a few months after the Treaty of Paris officially ended the Revolution.

In 1784, thirty-eight-year-old Molly Ridout wrote to her mother in England, describing the resignation, which she observed from the visitors' gallery—the one area in the Chamber where women were permitted. In her letter, the only known female account of the event, she wrote: "The General seemed so much affected himself that everybody felt for him. He addressed Congress in a short speech, but very affecting. Many tears were shed...I think the world never produced a greater man and very few so good."

The Annapolis State House served as the U.S. capital during Washington's resignation, functioning as the head of government from November 26, 1783, to August 13, 1784.

The Brooks Inn – This fictional inn, located on State Circle, is inspired by the Governor Calvert House, which also sits across from the Maryland State House. Now a historic inn, the Calvert House experienced a devastating fire in 1764. In the story, the Brooks Inn is situated just around State Circle, closer to the Maryland Inn, to account for its shared tunnel. I also want to mention that the Brooks Inn and the Collins-Brooks House are the only fictional locations on the map of Annapolis at the beginning of this book.

Tunnel from the Maryland Inn – An intriguing Annapolis legend holds that a tunnel once connected the Maryland Inn's tavern to the Maryland State House. Some say it was constructed as an escape route for officials in case Annapolis came under attack during the Revolutionary War. Others believe it was built to allow influential politicians easy, discreet access to the inn's basement tavern.

Though the supposed tunnel entrance is now sealed off with iron bars, it remains in the basement lounge, and its rumored existence continues to spark the imagination of visitors. In my story, Lorna and her mom have coffee there, as there was, at one point, the most charming, historic Starbucks located under the inn.

The alleged Maryland Inn tunnel, along with another that currently runs below the Maryland State House and other historic tunnels in Wilmington, NC, inspired the fictional underground passage that connects the Brooks Inn to the Maryland Inn in *Because of Winter*.

Burning of the *Peggy Stewart* — Just as depicted in *Because of Winter*, Annapolis witnessed its own version of the Boston Tea Party on October 19, 1774. Pressured by outspoken Patriots, Anthony Stewart set fire to his brig, the *Peggy Stewart*, in the bay near the present-day site of Luce Hall on the U.S. Naval Academy grounds. The burning took place within sight of the Peggy Stewart House on Hanover Street.

During colonial times, the land now occupied by the Naval Academy (established in 1845) was partially underwater and formed part of the bay's shoreline. Over time, this area was expanded and filled in to accommodate the academy.

Selima – Although Caroline Brooks and the chestnut mare she rides in the beginning of *Where the Foxgloves Bloom* are both fictional, the horse's ancestor is very real. Selima, a legendary English Thoroughbred mare, played a pivotal role in American horse racing. Purchased by Colonel Benjamin Tasker Jr. (Molly Ridout's uncle) in England, Selima was brought to Belair, the Maryland estate owned by Samuel Ogle, Molly's father.

Tasker entered Selima in a high-stakes four-mile race in Gloucester, Virginia, in 1752. She beat four competitors, igniting a lasting rivalry between Maryland and Virginia horse breeders. After her racing career, Selima became a broodmare, producing ten foals who greatly influenced the lineage of Thoroughbreds in the U.S.

Acknowledgments

I'd like to start by thanking God. Through the darkest seasons of my life, Jesus has remained my safe place to rest.

To my grandma—how terribly I miss you. I was inspired to write this story shortly after your passing. I still crave our long talks and the warmest hugs that only you could give. I like to picture you reading a book in heaven, always on a porch with Pap.

Adam, my love, you're the toughest early reader a writer could ask for. While it may have caused a few minor battles, this story is endlessly better because of you. Thank you for all the time you dedicated to it and for holding down the fort during the many hours I spent in my chair, tapping away at the keyboard.

To my girls, the four chambers of my heart—your love and creativity inspire me daily. Thank you for your patience and encouragement throughout the writing of this book. I still can't believe I get to be your mom.

To my little fur guy, not a word was written without you by my side—or warming my lap. Of course, the tiny spaniel heroically saved Caroline.

Mom, you've always been my selfless supporter, and this endeavor was no different. You've nurtured in me a love for history and a deep connection with stories that resonate through time. I appreciate your thoughtful feedback on the manuscript—and Bob's advice and encouragement too!

Dad, your unwavering support, along with the research you did to help me navigate self-publishing, gave me the courage to pursue my dreams. I'm also deeply thankful for the financial generosity you and Sally have shown. And Sally, to you and Susan—my diligent early readers/editors—thank you for the time and care you put into polishing the manuscript so beautifully!

To my sister, Mandi—your passion for guiding others back to health inspired me while writing that part of Lorna's story. You were also the very first person to read this book, and I'm incredibly grateful for your advice and encouragement.

To my brother, Mike—please know I appreciate your support more than I can express and that you inspired a scene in this story.

To my editor, Janet—your positive energy, keen eye, and gift for finding what truly matters have added so much depth and polish to this story. Thank you for the many, many hours you poured into our book and for cheering me on throughout the editing process.

To my insightful beta readers/marketing team, Lauren Burleigh and Megan Crabtree—I'm forever grateful that you helped bring this story to the Annapolis community and beyond. Lauren, so appreciative of the time you spent reaching out to publications. Megan, to you and Jordan, both so gifted with design, I can't thank you enough for all your help with the cover.

Andrew Brochetti, my artistically talented brother-in-law, I so appreciate your input on the cover design as well.

To the rest of my incredible early readers—this novel wouldn't be what it is without you! Thank you so much to Megan Pomputius, Laurie Gregory, Emily Kruse, Alissa Merritt, Cindy Merritt, Kristyn Brochetti, Kathy Rautenbach, Desiree Monsilovich, Mia

Monsilovich, Elena Boone, Jessica Goodman, Lauren Mueller, Shannon Grossman, and Nicki Wagner. Your selfless time, thoughtful advice, and wonderful feedback have truly made a difference, and I am forever grateful.

To my father-in-law, John—thank you for your love and support, as well as the stories you've shared over the years about your brother, Frank. Though he passed far too soon in a place far too distant, he certainly lives on in the hearts of so many. I'm so grateful he's finally with Bubba and Nonno.

To my mother-in-law, Lisa, I genuinely appreciate your encouragement throughout this process and your help spreading the word about the book.

Ashley Brooks Causey—our chilly night at Reynolds Tavern and the 1747 pub, tucked by the fire with Jeff and Adam, inspired me to use the fireplace as one of the places the necklace might have been hidden.

I'm beyond grateful to The Brandywine Foundation for allowing me to visit Whitehall, and to my wonderful tour guide, Susie Swindell, for showing me around the grounds. It truly was a magical day.

A special thanks to Christine Lamberton, Museum Director of the Burgwin-Wright House, for her assistance during my visit and for answering my questions afterward—you are a wealth of knowledge. A special thanks to Chuck, our gracious tour guide, as well.

To all my family and friends who encouraged me along the way—I appreciate you more than words can say.

And to you, dear reader, thank you from the bottom of my heart for joining me on this journey.

Book Club Questions

1. Dual Timeline Dynamics: How do the past and present timelines mirror or contrast with each other? What impact do these timelines have on the characters' development? Did you connect with one timeline more than the other?

2. Sisters/Mother-Child Themes: How does Lorna's relationship with her sister, Winnie, evolve throughout the story? Why do you think she becomes so attached to Winnie despite her initial negative feelings toward her?

3. Parenthood: In what ways do the characters grow or change after becoming parents? How does parenthood influence their decisions and relationships?

4. Secrets: What role do secrets play in the story? How does uncovering the past change the characters' perspectives on their present lives?

5. Setting as a Character: How does the setting enhance the story's mood and themes?

6. Character Growth: Which character did you connect with the most, and why? How did they change by the story's conclusion?

7. Relationships: Which relationship resonated with you the most, and why? How did it change throughout the story?

8. Forgiveness and Redemption: Do you believe the characters were able to forgive themselves and each other? How important is forgiveness to the narrative?

9. Title Reflection: What do you think "Because of Winter" symbolizes in the context of the story? Did you discover multiple meanings?

10. Book Club Favorites: Which moments or themes stood out to you the most? Were there any scenes that surprised or challenged your expectations?

11. Friendship: How does the theme of friendship manifest in this story, and what impact does it have on the characters' lives and decisions? In what ways do the friendships explored influence their development and the overall narrative?

12. The Ending: How did you feel about the conclusion of the story? Were you satisfied with how it wrapped up? If not, what alternative ending would you have preferred?

A Final Note

If you enjoyed this story, it would mean the world to me if you shared it with friends and family.

A quick review on Amazon or Goodreads would also go a long way in helping more people discover *Because of Winter*.

As an independent author, your support truly makes a difference. Every share, recommendation, and review helps inspire others to experience this story too.

Thank you so much for being part of this journey.

xo, nikki

Made in the USA
Columbia, SC
19 November 2024